W9-ANQ-999

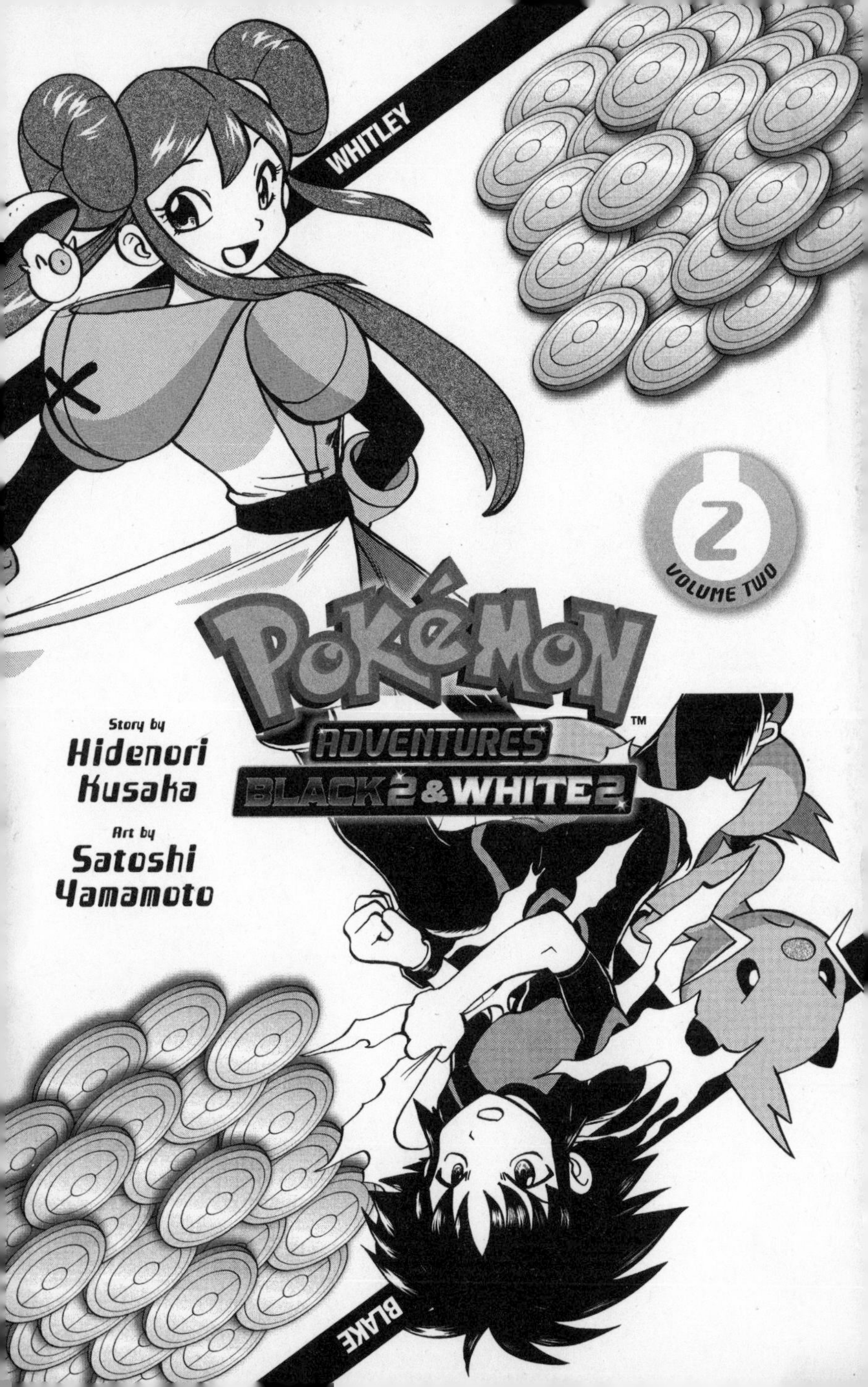
WHITLEY
2
VOLUME TWO
BLAKE

Pokémon™ Adventures Black 2 & White 2

Story by
Hidenori Kusaka

Art by
Satoshi Yamamoto

The Story Thus Far, Tenth Chapter

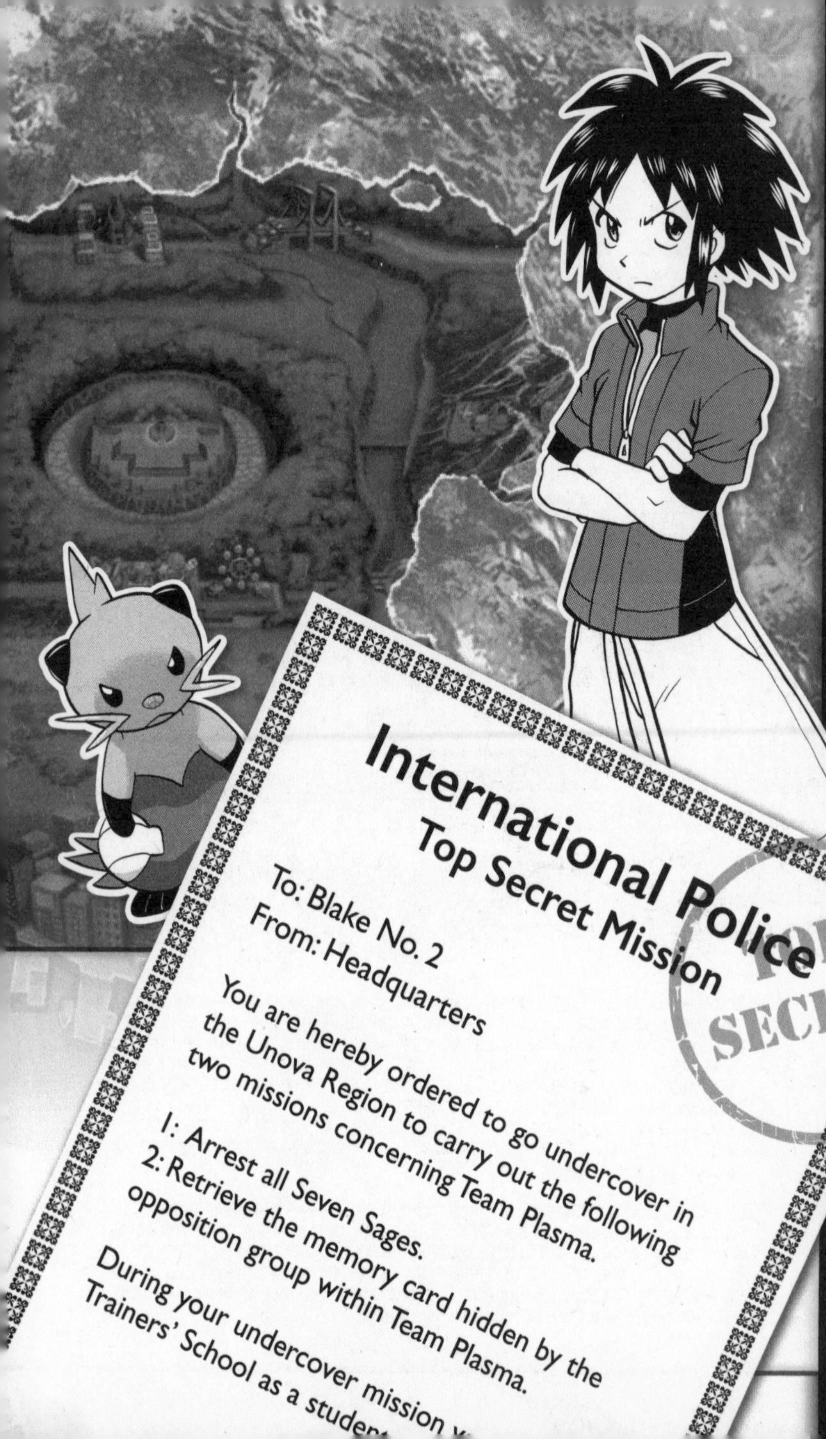
International Police
Top Secret Mission
To: Blake No. 2
From: Headquarters
You are hereby ordered to go undercover in the Unova Region to carry out the following two missions concerning Team Plasma.
1: Arrest all Seven Sages.
2: Retrieve the memory card hidden by the opposition group within Team Plasma.
During your undercover mission
Trainers' School as a studen
TOP SECRET

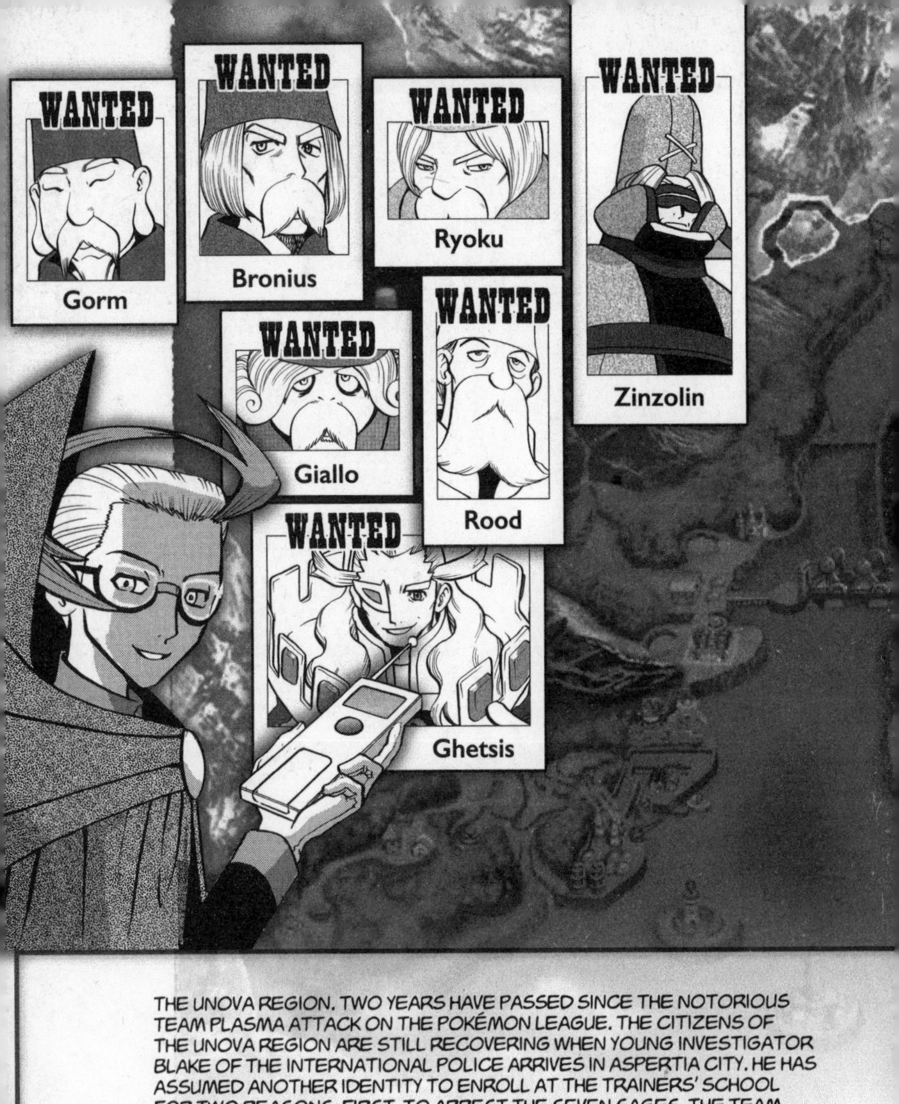
WANTED
Gorm
WANTED
Bronius
WANTED
Ryoku
WANTED
Zinzolin
WANTED
Giallo
WANTED
Rood
WANTED
Ghetsis

THE UNOVA REGION. TWO YEARS HAVE PASSED SINCE THE NOTORIOUS TEAM PLASMA ATTACK ON THE POKÉMON LEAGUE. THE CITIZENS OF THE UNOVA REGION ARE STILL RECOVERING WHEN YOUNG INVESTIGATOR BLAKE OF THE INTERNATIONAL POLICE ARRIVES IN ASPERTIA CITY. HE HAS ASSUMED ANOTHER IDENTITY TO ENROLL AT THE TRAINERS' SCHOOL FOR TWO REASONS: FIRST, TO ARREST THE SEVEN SAGES, THE TEAM PLASMA EXECUTIVES WHO HAVE SCATTERED ALL OVER THE REGION; SECOND, TO RETRIEVE THE MEMORY CARD HIDDEN BY THE OPPOSITION GROUP WITHIN TEAM PLASMA.

BLAKE DEDUCES THAT A NEW TRANSFER STUDENT, WHITLEY, MIGHT POSSESS THE MEMORY CARD IN QUESTION, SO HE APPROACHES HER WHENEVER AN OPPORTUNITY PRESENTS ITSELF AT SCHOOL EVENTS. MEANWHILE, THE LEADER OF THE NEW TEAM PLASMA, COLRESS, SEARCHES FOR ZINZOLIN IN ORDER TO CAPTURE THE DRAGON- AND ICE-TYPE LEGENDARY POKÉMON KYUREM...

The Characters...

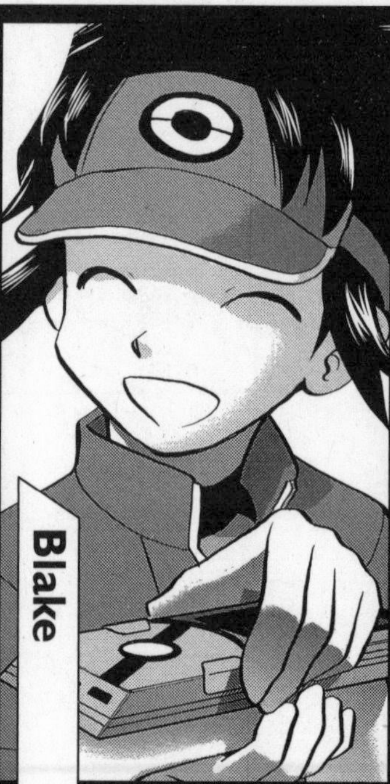

Blake

A young International Police investigator and inspector. A perfectionist who excels in Pokémon battles and capturing everything—Pokémon and criminals alike. Currently working undercover in the Unova Region.

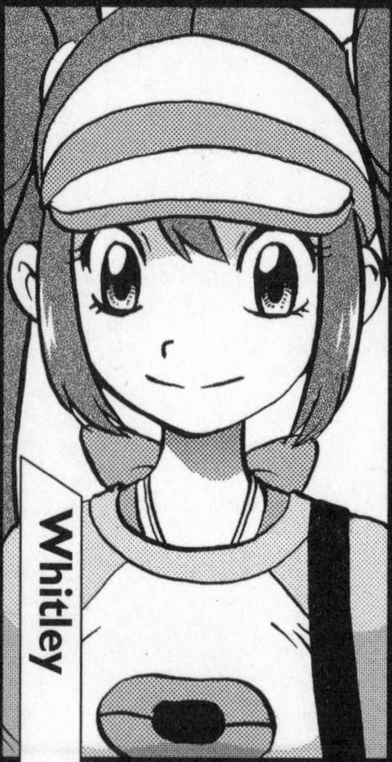

Whitley

A girl who recently transferred to the Trainers' School. She is a former member of Team Plasma and wears a locket with N's photo inside it...

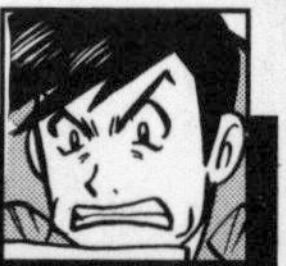

Looker

A veteran International Police investigator. Currently serving under Blake to help apprehend the Seven Sages.

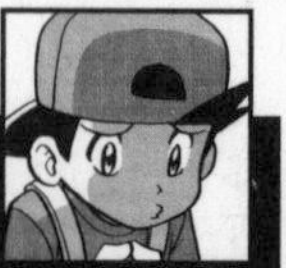

Leo

Blake's classmate. A skilled Trainer who made it into the top eight at the Pokémon League. Awkward and nervous around girls.

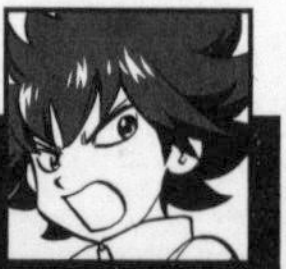

Hugh

Blake's classmate. Harbors a deep-seated hatred of Team Plasma ever since they kidnapped his little sister's Purrloin.

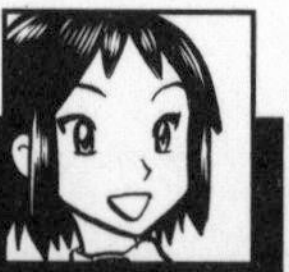

Cheren

Blake's childhood friend who has taken a post as a rookie teacher at Aspertia City's Trainers' School. Currently missing.

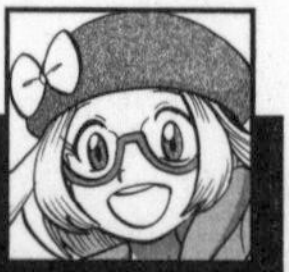

Bianca

Blake's childhood friend who is currently working as an assistant at Professor Juniper's laboratory in Nuvema Town. Also currently missing.

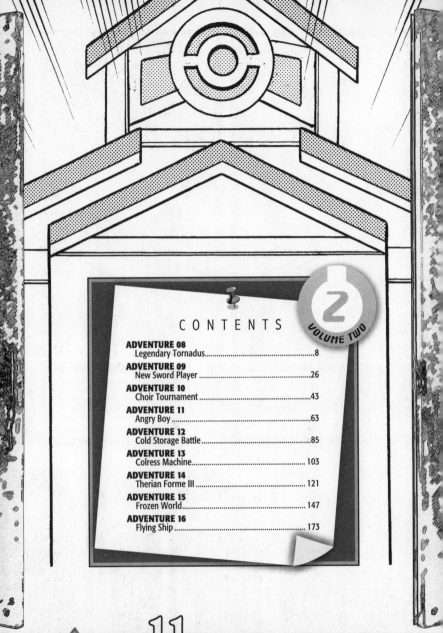

CONTENTS

VOLUME TWO

POKÉMON ADVENTURES the 11th Chapter B2-W2
eleventh

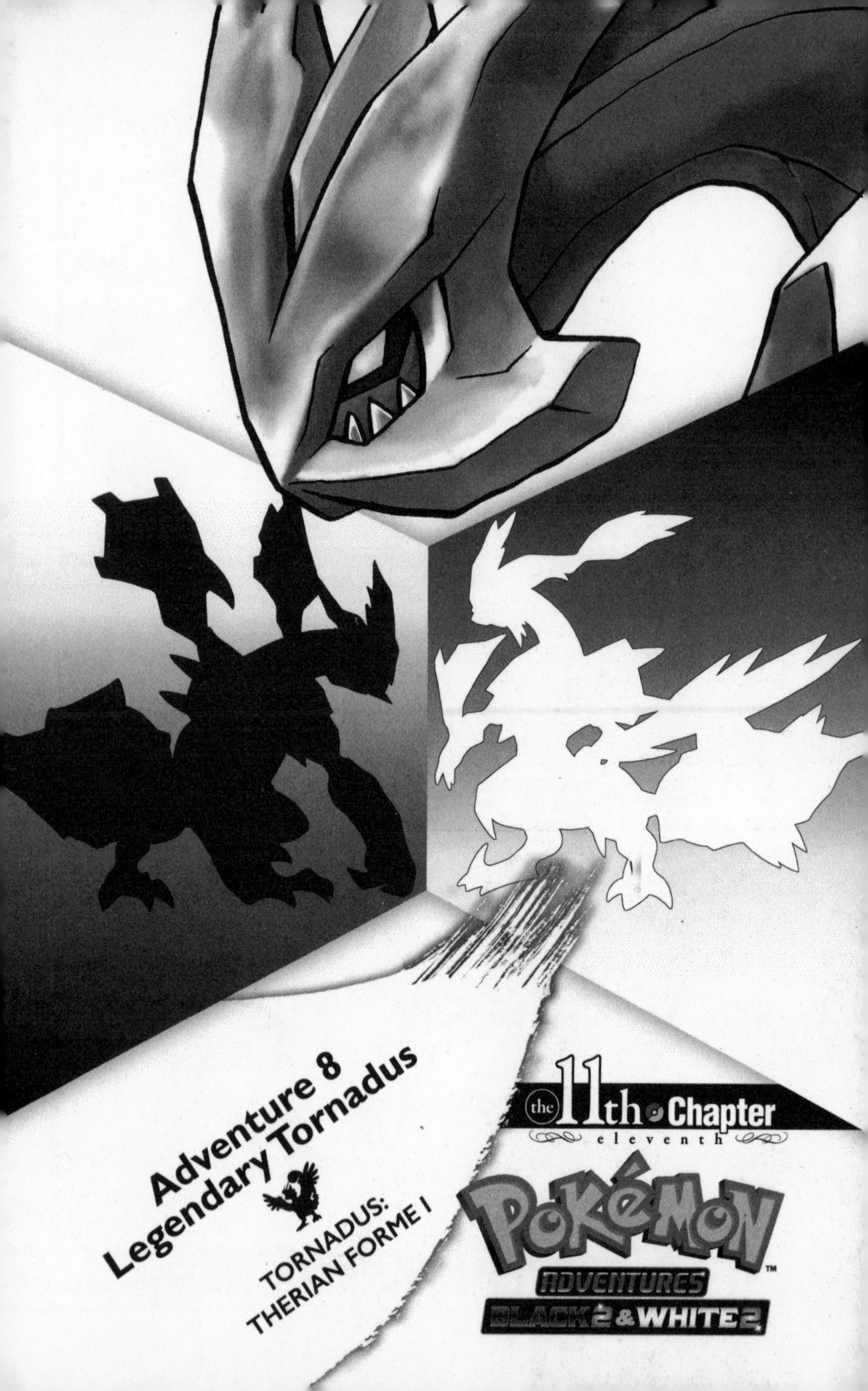
the 11th Chapter
eleventh
Adventure 8
Legendary Tornadus
TORNADUS:
THERIAN FORME I
POKÉMON
ADVENTURES
BLACK 2 & WHITE 2

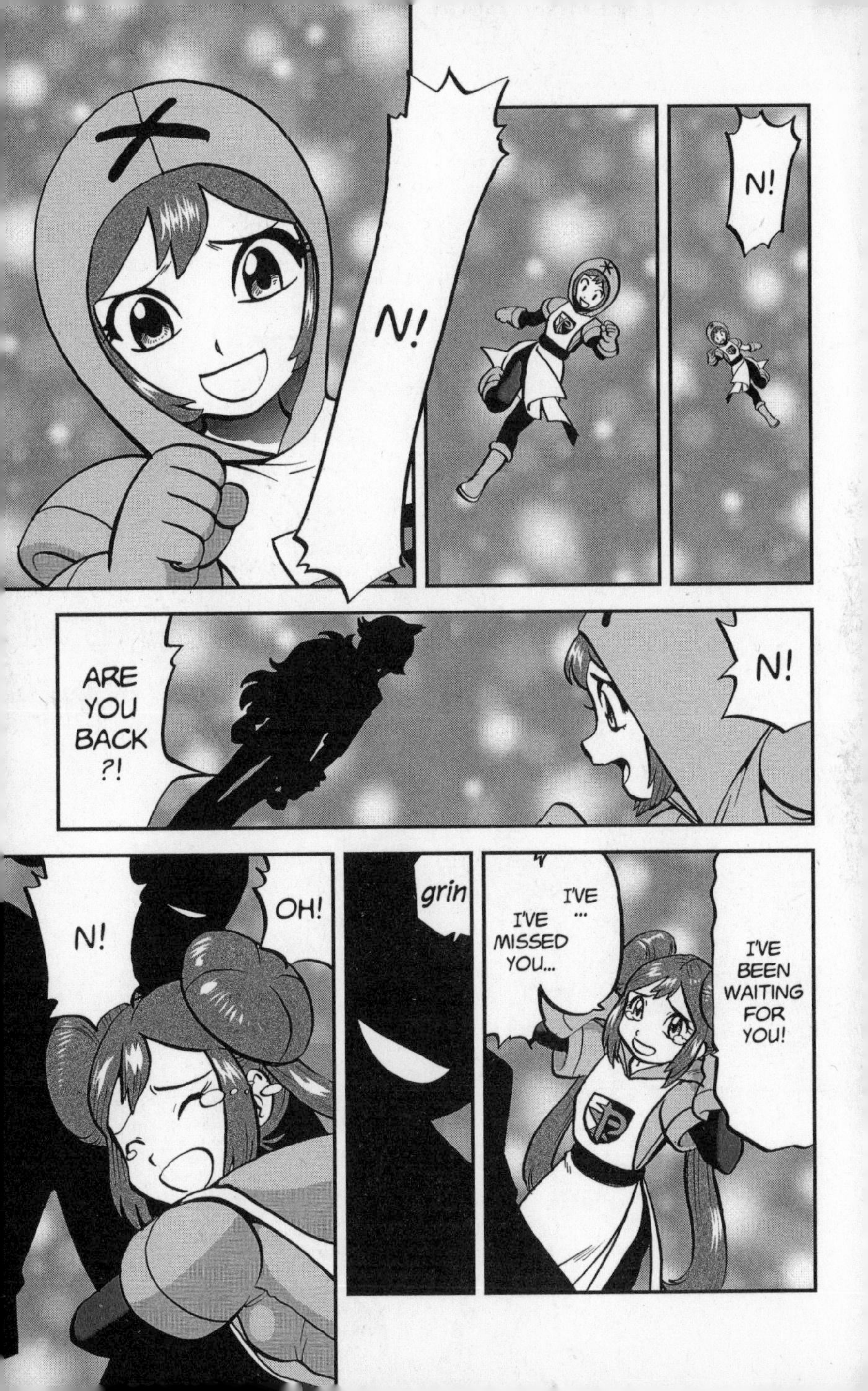
N!
N!
N!
ARE YOU BACK ?!
I'VE BEEN WAITING FOR YOU!
I'VE ...
I'VE MISSED YOU...
grin
OH!
N!

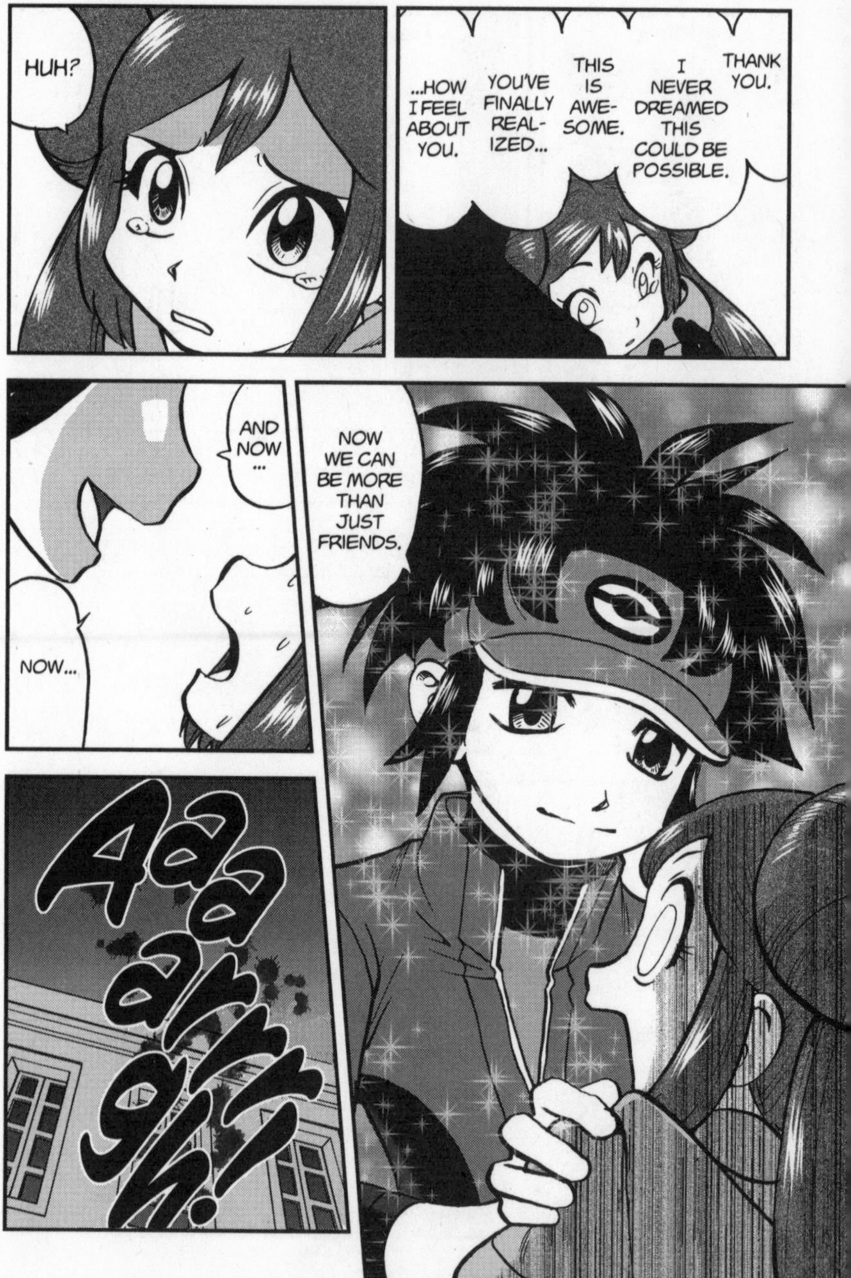
THANK YOU.
I NEVER DREAMED THIS COULD BE POSSIBLE.
THIS IS AWE-SOME.
YOU'VE FINALLY REAL-IZED...
...HOW I FEEL ABOUT YOU.
HUH?
NOW WE CAN BE MORE THAN JUST FRIENDS.
AND NOW ...
NOW...
Aaaarrrgh!

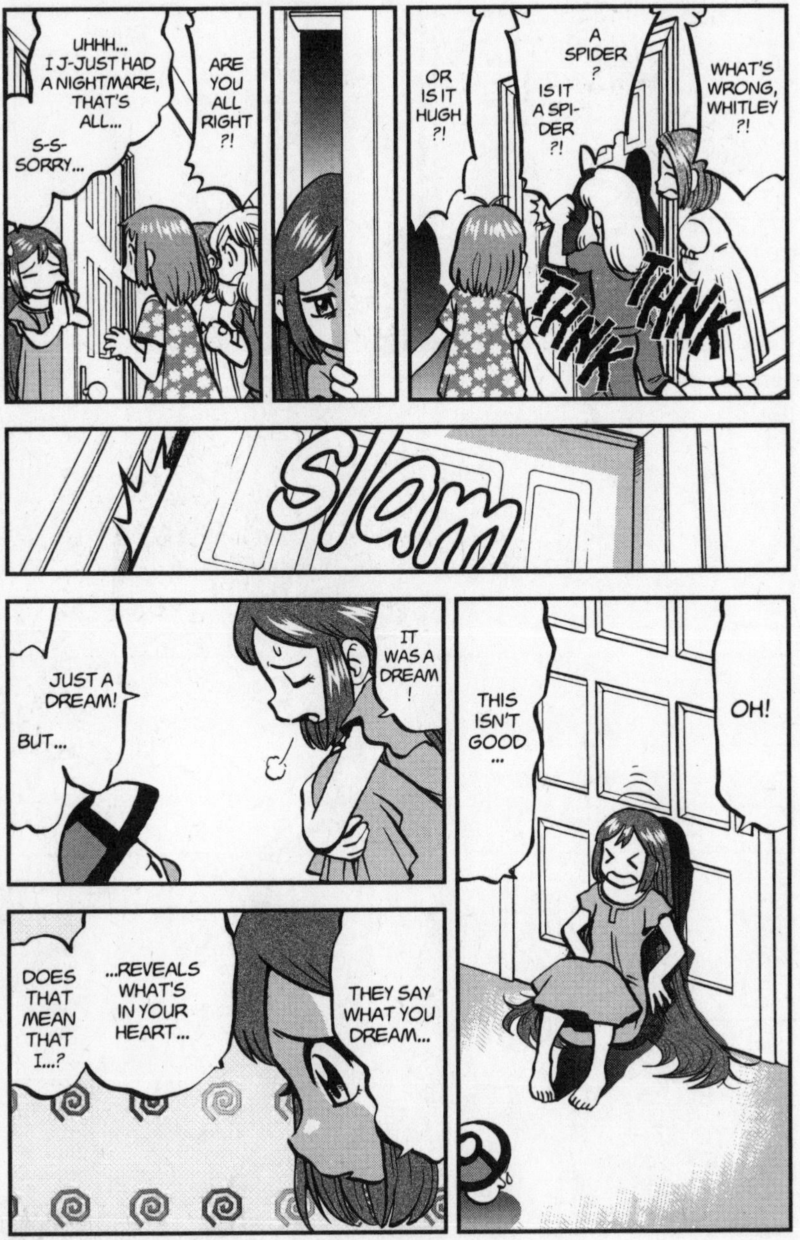
WHAT'S WRONG, WHITLEY?!
A SPIDER?
IS IT A SPI-DER?!
OR IS IT HUGH?!
THNK
THNK
ARE YOU ALL RIGHT?!
UHHH... I J-JUST HAD A NIGHTMARE, THAT'S ALL...
S-S-SORRY...
slam
OH!
THIS ISN'T GOOD...
IT WAS A DREAM!
JUST A DREAM!
BUT...
THEY SAY WHAT YOU DREAM...
...REVEALS WHAT'S IN YOUR HEART...
DOES THAT MEAN THAT I...?

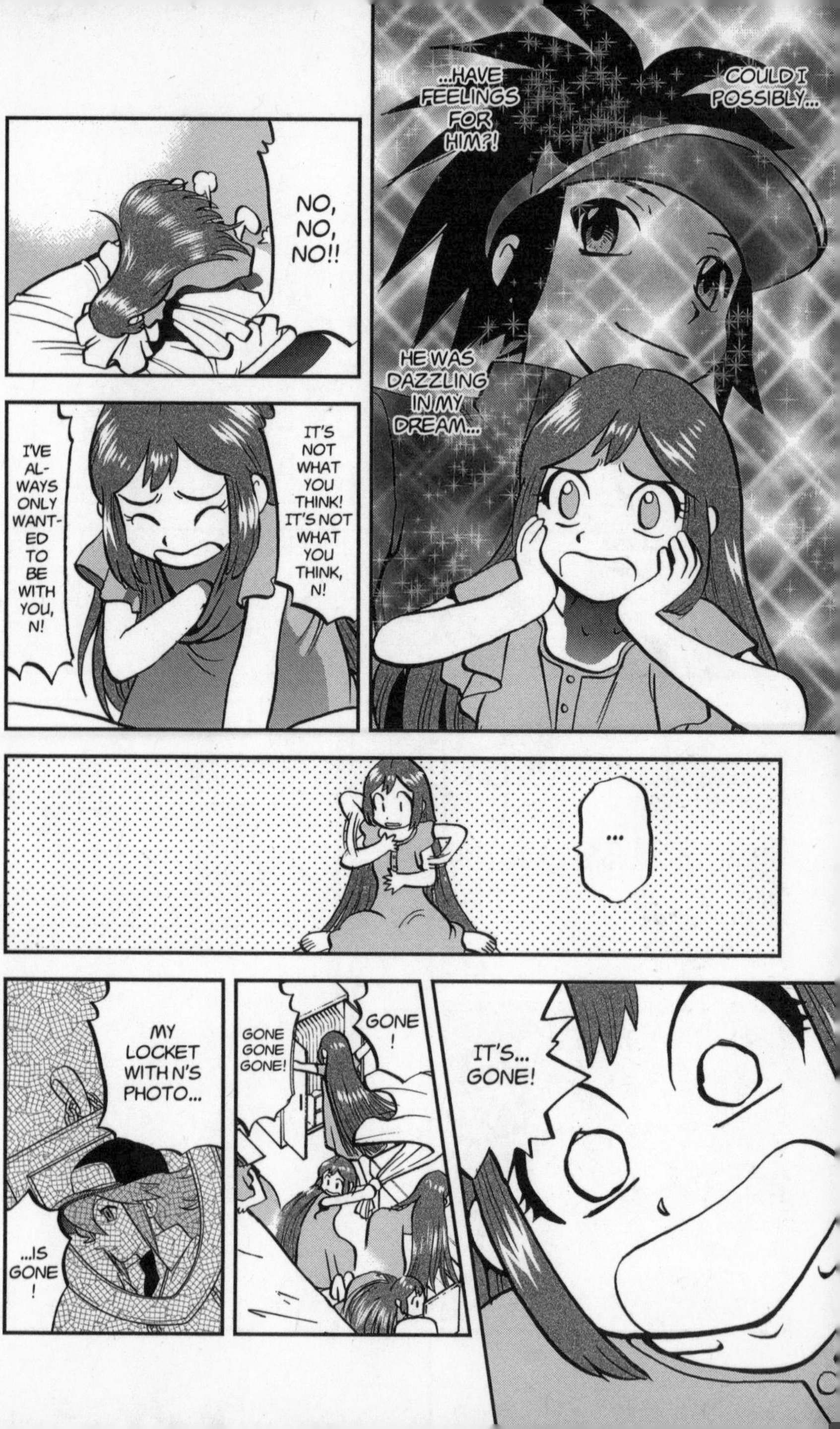
COULD I POSSIBLY...
...HAVE FEELINGS FOR HIM?!
HE WAS DAZZLING IN MY DREAM...
NO, NO, NO!!
IT'S NOT WHAT YOU THINK! IT'S NOT WHAT YOU THINK, N!
I'VE AL-WAYS ONLY WANT-ED TO BE WITH YOU, N!
...
IT'S... GONE!
GONE!
GONE GONE GONE!
MY LOCKET WITH N'S PHOTO...
...IS GONE!

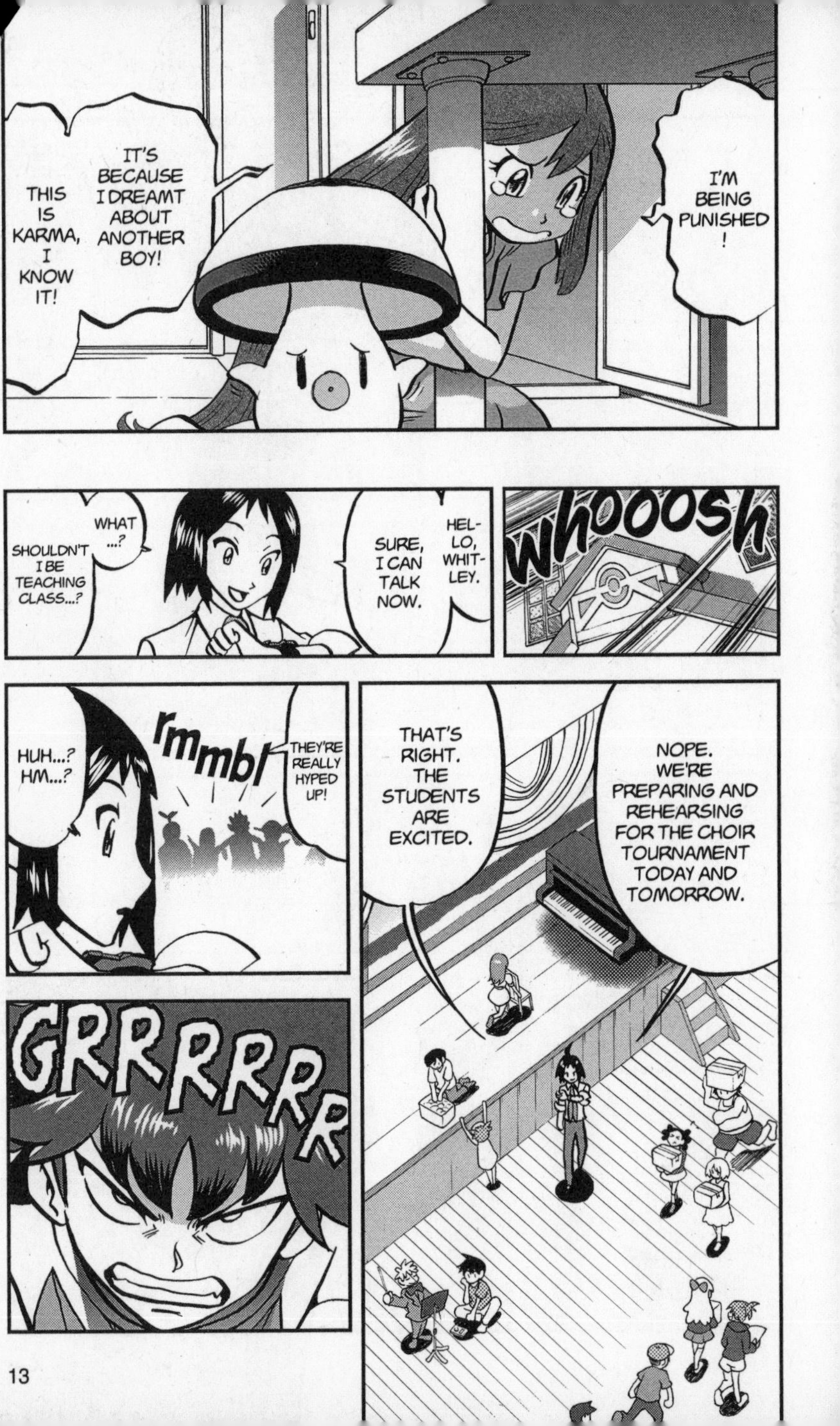
I'M BEING PUNISHED!
IT'S BECAUSE I DREAMT ABOUT ANOTHER BOY!
THIS IS KARMA, I KNOW IT!
whoooosh
HEL-LO, WHIT-LEY.
SURE, I CAN TALK NOW.
WHAT ...?
SHOULDN'T I BE TEACHING CLASS...?
NOPE. WE'RE PREPARING AND REHEARSING FOR THE CHOIR TOURNAMENT TODAY AND TOMORROW.
THAT'S RIGHT. THE STUDENTS ARE EXCITED.
rmmbl
THEY'RE REALLY HYPED UP!
HUH...? HM...?
GRRRRRR

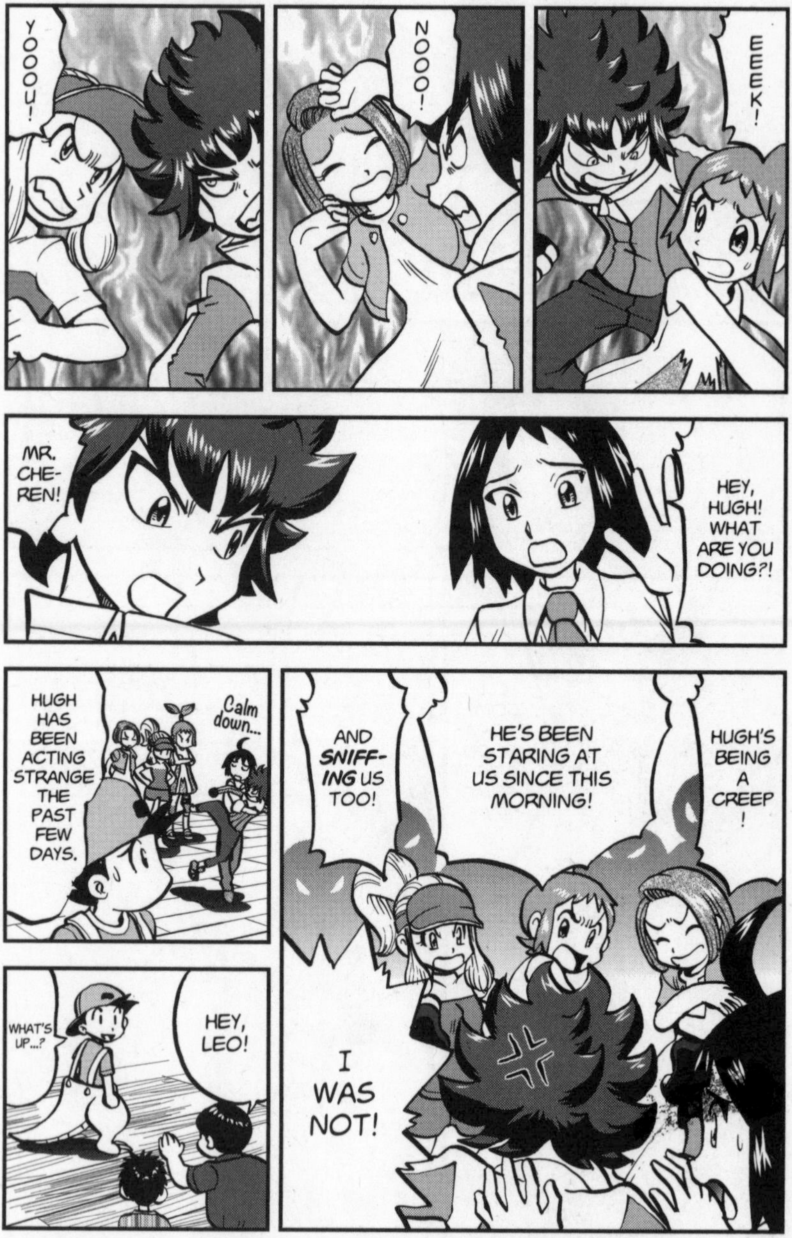
EEEK!
NOOOO!
YOOOU!
HEY, HUGH! WHAT ARE YOU DOING?!
MR. CHEREN!
HUGH'S BEING A CREEP!
HE'S BEEN STARING AT US SINCE THIS MORNING!
AND ***SNIFFING*** US TOO!
I WAS NOT!
Calm down...
HUGH HAS BEEN ACTING STRANGE THE PAST FEW DAYS.
HEY, LEO!
WHAT'S UP...?

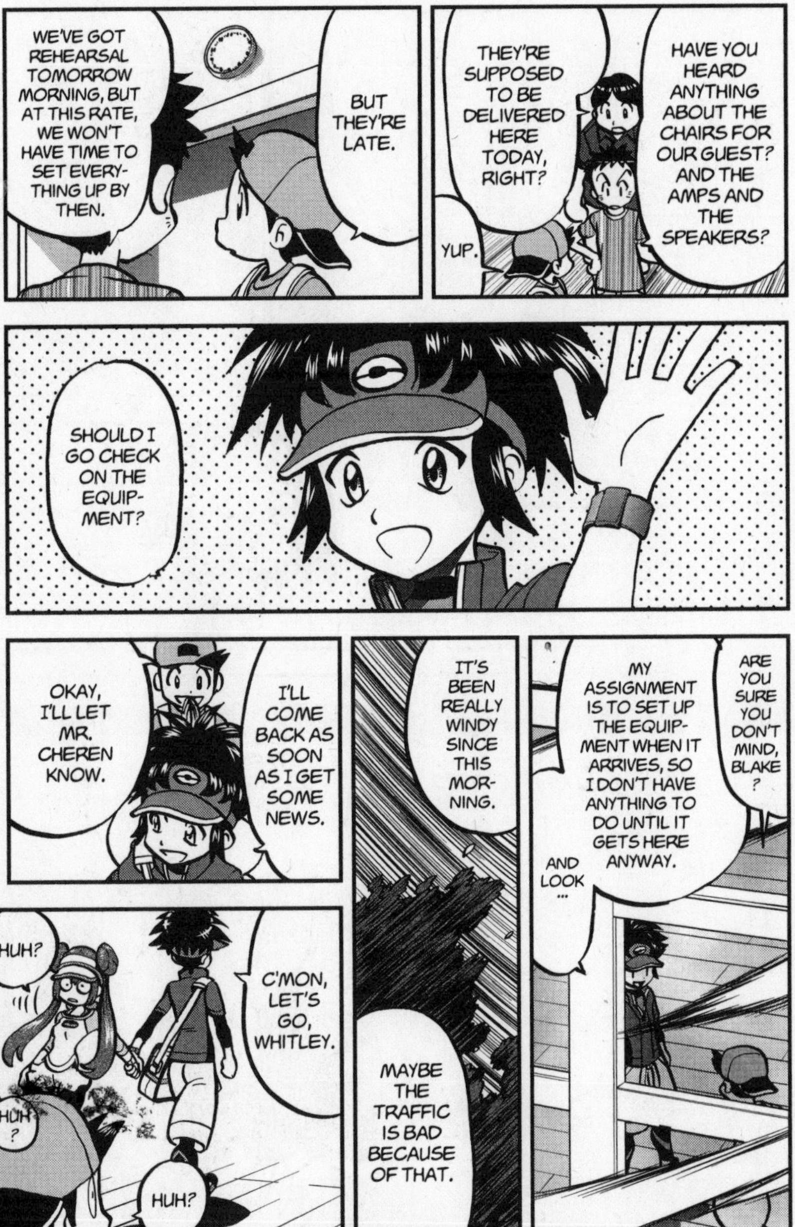
HAVE YOU HEARD ANYTHING ABOUT THE CHAIRS FOR OUR GUEST? AND THE AMPS AND THE SPEAKERS?
THEY'RE SUPPOSED TO BE DELIVERED HERE TODAY, RIGHT?
YUP.
BUT THEY'RE LATE.
WE'VE GOT REHEARSAL TOMORROW MORNING, BUT AT THIS RATE, WE WON'T HAVE TIME TO SET EVERYTHING UP BY THEN.
SHOULD I GO CHECK ON THE EQUIPMENT?
ARE YOU SURE YOU DON'T MIND, BLAKE?
MY ASSIGNMENT IS TO SET UP THE EQUIPMENT WHEN IT ARRIVES, SO I DON'T HAVE ANYTHING TO DO UNTIL IT GETS HERE ANYWAY.
AND LOOK...
IT'S BEEN REALLY WINDY SINCE THIS MORNING.
MAYBE THE TRAFFIC IS BAD BECAUSE OF THAT.
I'LL COME BACK AS SOON AS I GET SOME NEWS.
OKAY, I'LL LET MR. CHEREN KNOW.
C'MON, LET'S GO, WHITLEY.
HUH?
HUH?
HUH?

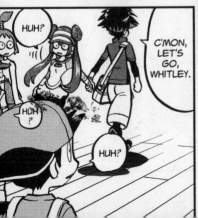

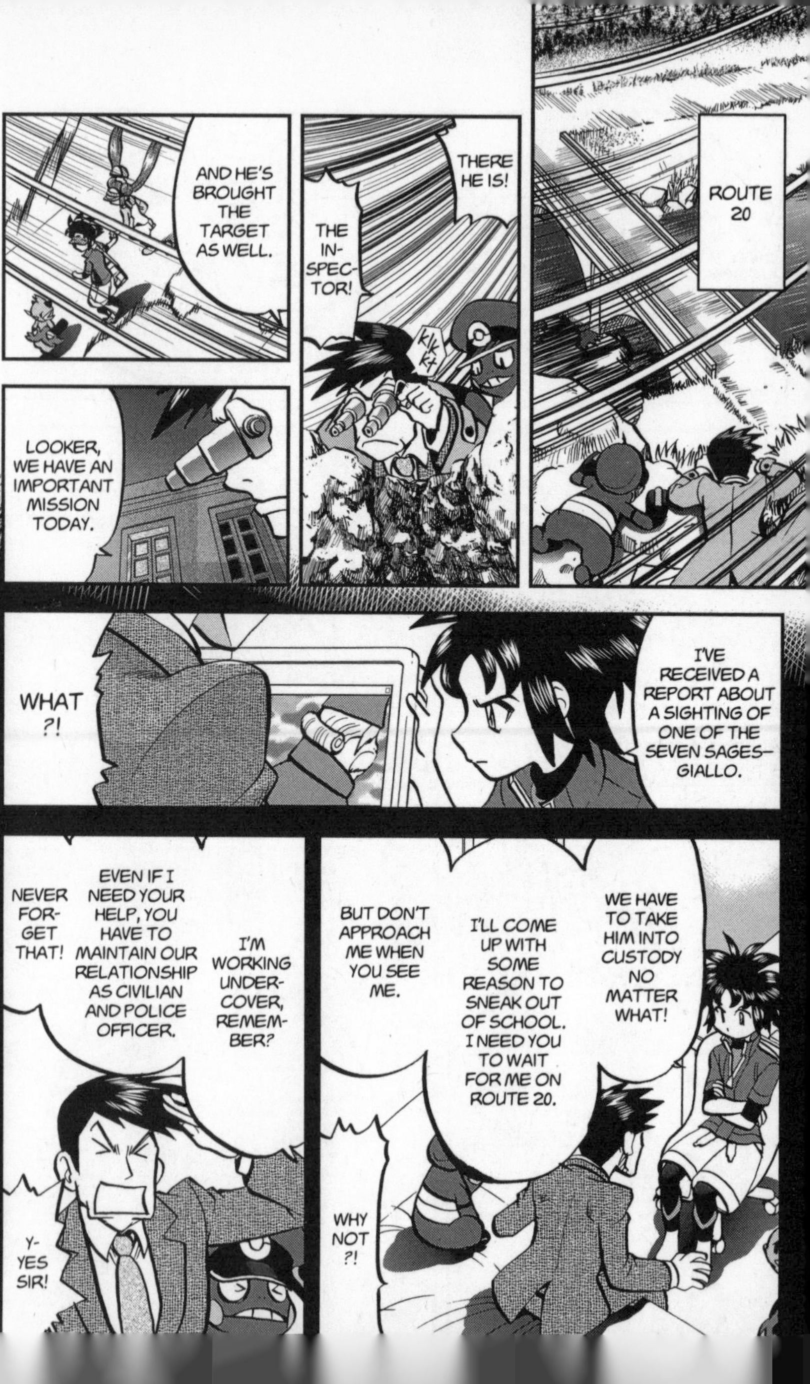
ROUTE 20
THERE HE IS!
THE IN-SPECTOR!
AND HE'S BROUGHT THE TARGET AS WELL.
LOOKER, WE HAVE AN IMPORTANT MISSION TODAY.
I'VE RECEIVED A REPORT ABOUT A SIGHTING OF ONE OF THE SEVEN SAGES—GIALLO.
WHAT ?!
WE HAVE TO TAKE HIM INTO CUSTODY NO MATTER WHAT!
I'LL COME UP WITH SOME REASON TO SNEAK OUT OF SCHOOL. I NEED YOU TO WAIT FOR ME ON ROUTE 20.
BUT DON'T APPROACH ME WHEN YOU SEE ME.
WHY NOT ?!
I'M WORKING UNDER-COVER, REMEM-BER?
EVEN IF I NEED YOUR HELP, YOU HAVE TO MAINTAIN OUR RELATIONSHIP AS CIVILIAN AND POLICE OFFICER.
NEVER FOR-GET THAT!
Y-YES SIR!

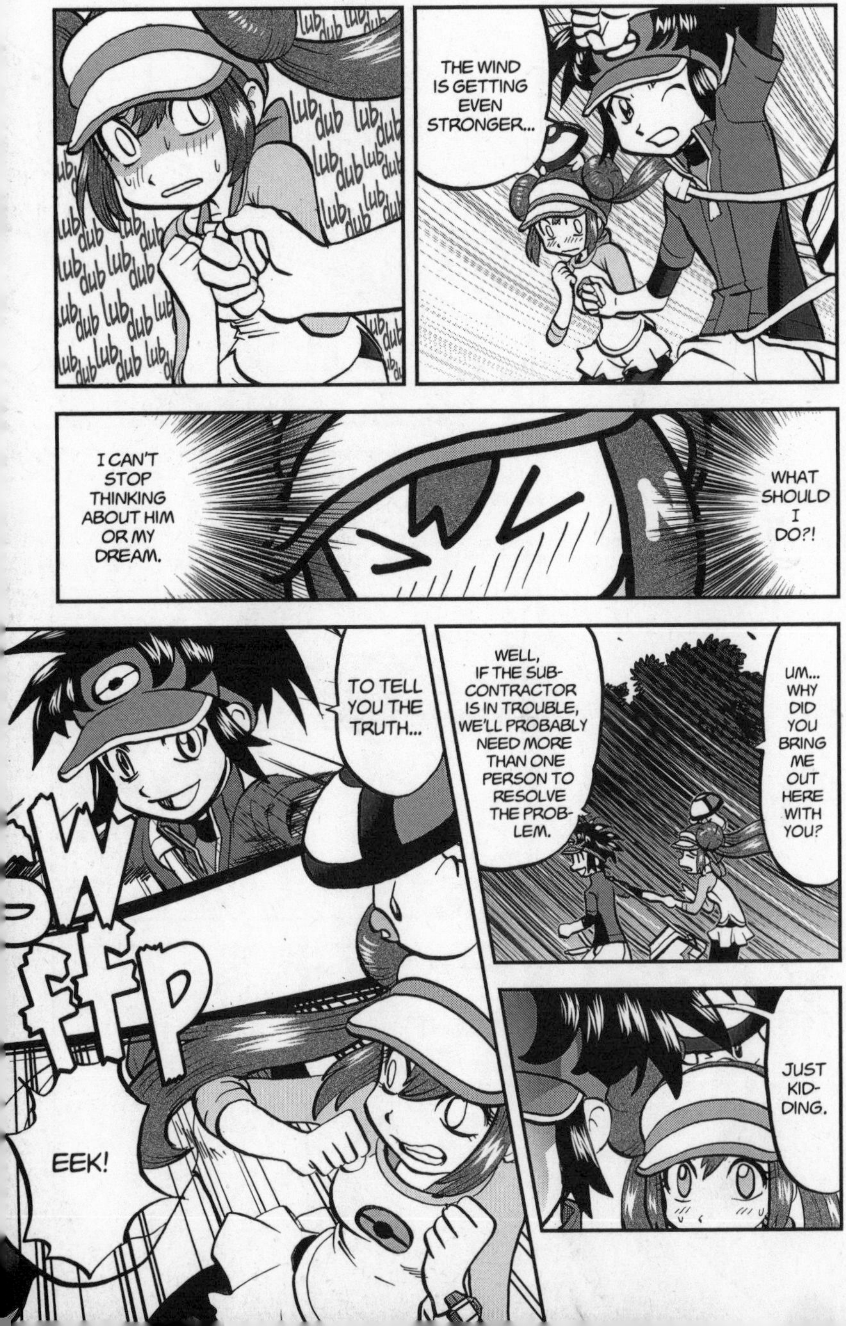
THE WIND IS GETTING EVEN STRONGER...
lub dub lub dub lub dub lub dub lub dub lub dub lub dub lub dub lub dub lub dub
WHAT SHOULD I DO?!
I CAN'T STOP THINKING ABOUT HIM OR MY DREAM.
UM... WHY DID YOU BRING ME OUT HERE WITH YOU?
WELL, IF THE SUB-CONTRACTOR IS IN TROUBLE, WE'LL PROBABLY NEED MORE THAN ONE PERSON TO RESOLVE THE PROB-LEM.
JUST KID-DING.
TO TELL YOU THE TRUTH...
SWFFP
EEK!

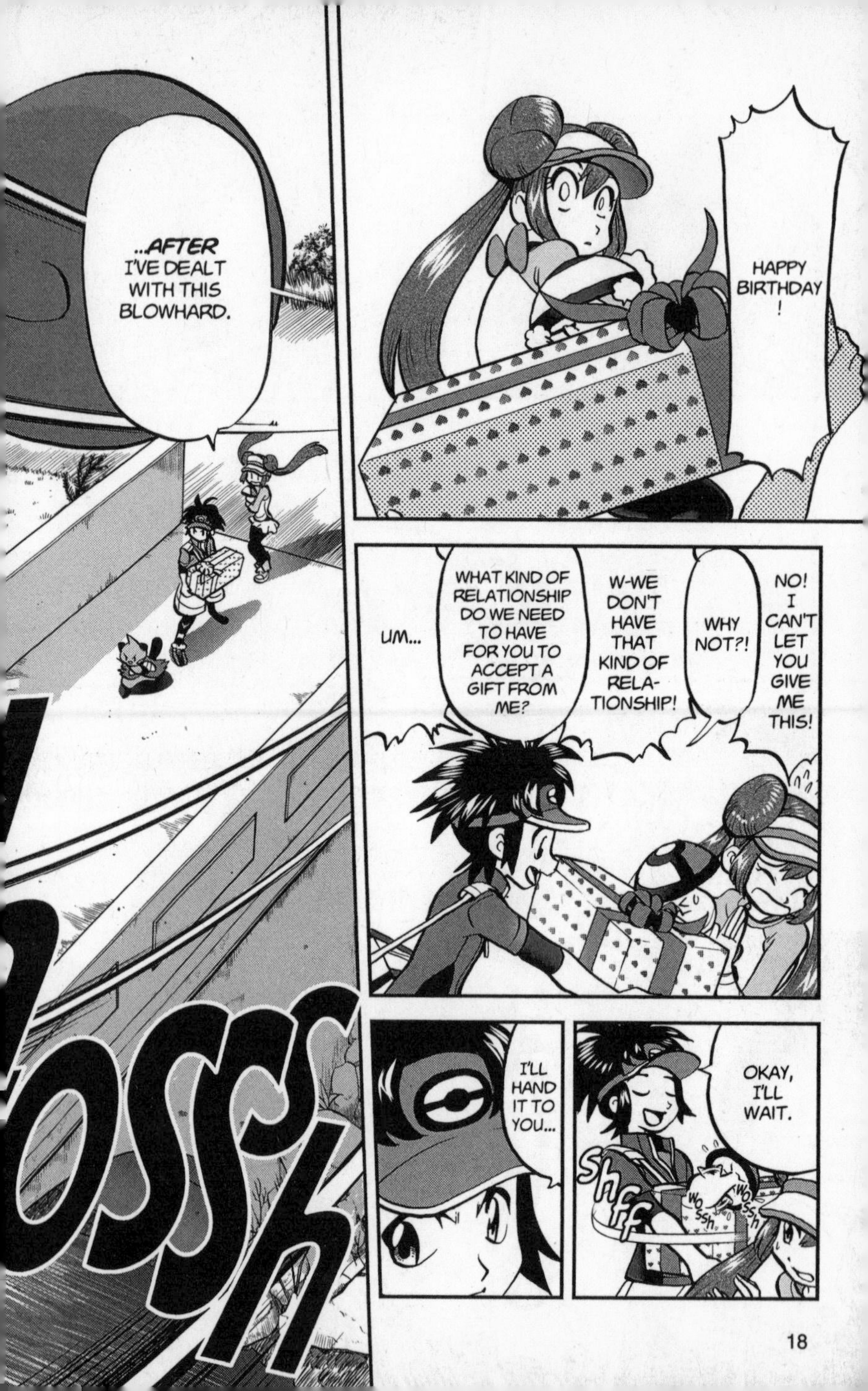
HAPPY BIRTHDAY!
NO! I CAN'T LET YOU GIVE ME THIS!
WHY NOT?!
W-WE DON'T HAVE THAT KIND OF RELA-TIONSHIP!
WHAT KIND OF RELATIONSHIP DO WE NEED TO HAVE FOR YOU TO ACCEPT A GIFT FROM ME?
UM...
OKAY, I'LL WAIT.
shff
WOSSH
WOSSH
I'LL HAND IT TO YOU...
...AFTER I'VE DEALT WITH THIS BLOWHARD.

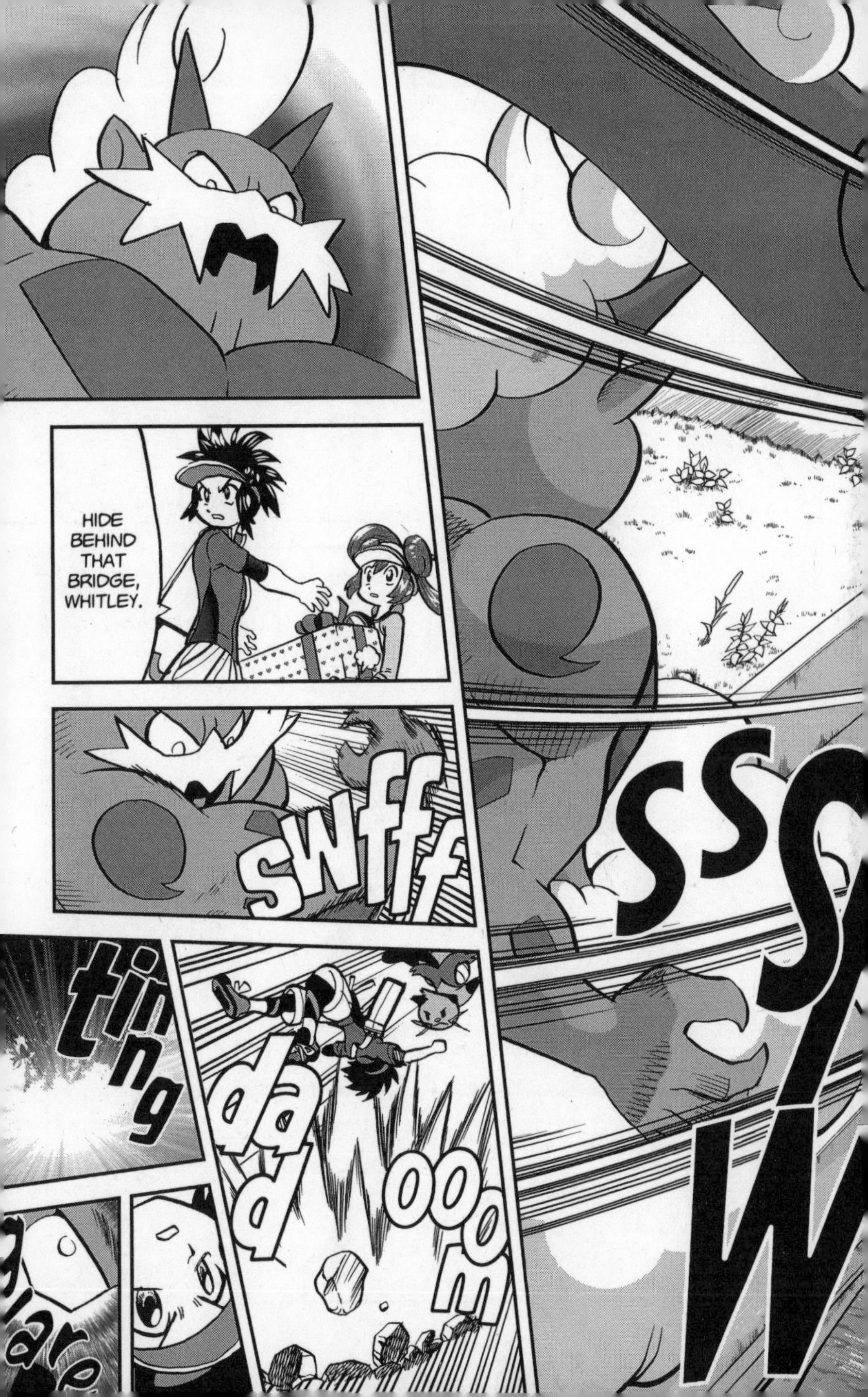
HIDE BEHIND THAT BRIDGE, WHITLEY.
swfff

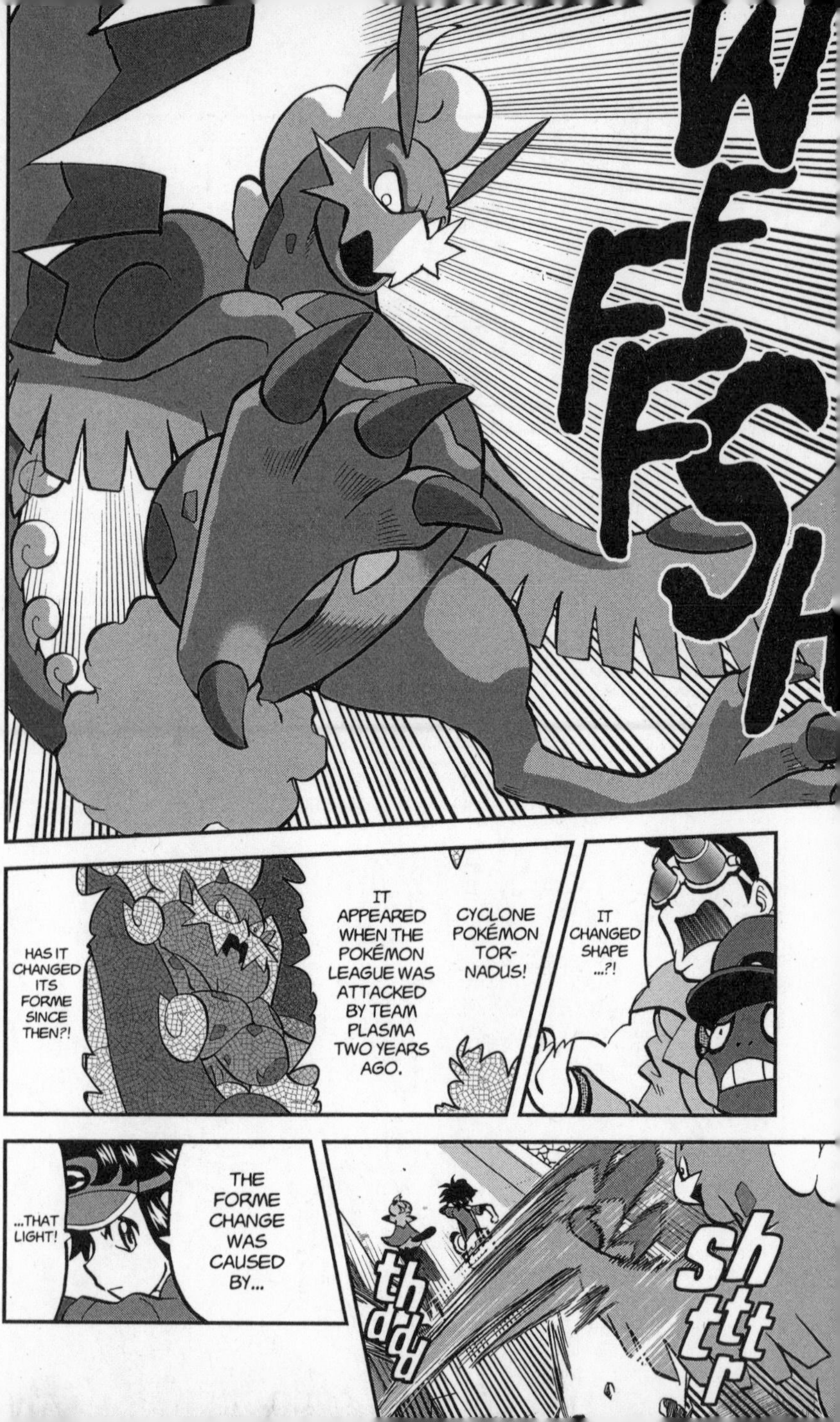
WFFFSH
IT CHANGED SHAPE ...?!
CYCLONE POKÉMON TOR-NADUS!
IT APPEARED WHEN THE POKÉMON LEAGUE WAS ATTACKED BY TEAM PLASMA TWO YEARS AGO.
HAS IT CHANGED ITS FORME SINCE THEN?!
shtttr
thddd
THE FORME CHANGE WAS CAUSED BY...
...THAT LIGHT!

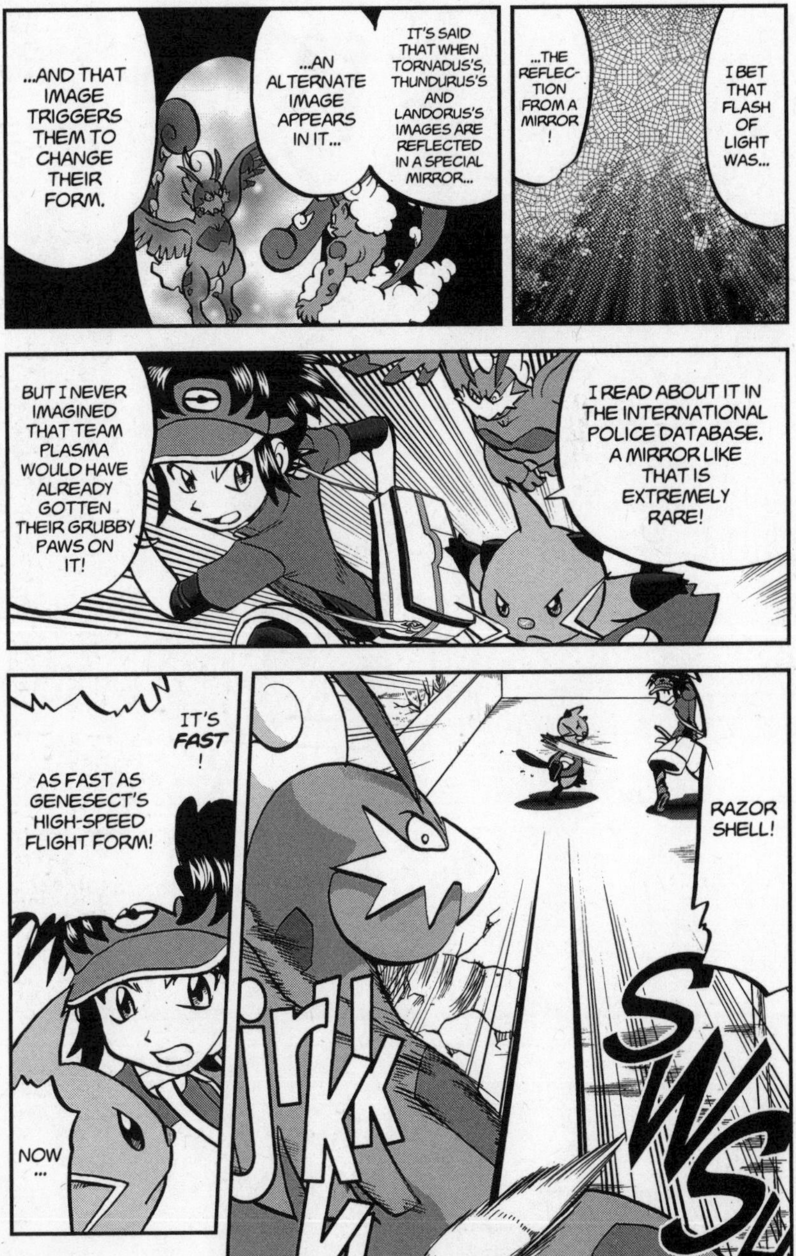
I BET THAT FLASH OF LIGHT WAS...
...THE REFLECTION FROM A MIRROR!
IT'S SAID THAT WHEN TORNADUS'S, THUNDURUS'S AND LANDORUS'S IMAGES ARE REFLECTED IN A SPECIAL MIRROR...
...AN ALTERNATE IMAGE APPEARS IN IT...
...AND THAT IMAGE TRIGGERS THEM TO CHANGE THEIR FORM.
I READ ABOUT IT IN THE INTERNATIONAL POLICE DATABASE. A MIRROR LIKE THAT IS EXTREMELY RARE!
BUT I NEVER IMAGINED THAT TEAM PLASMA WOULD HAVE ALREADY GOTTEN THEIR GRUBBY PAWS ON IT!
RAZOR SHELL!
SWSH
JIRKKKK
IT'S *FAST*!
AS FAST AS GENESECT'S HIGH-SPEED FLIGHT FORM!
NOW...

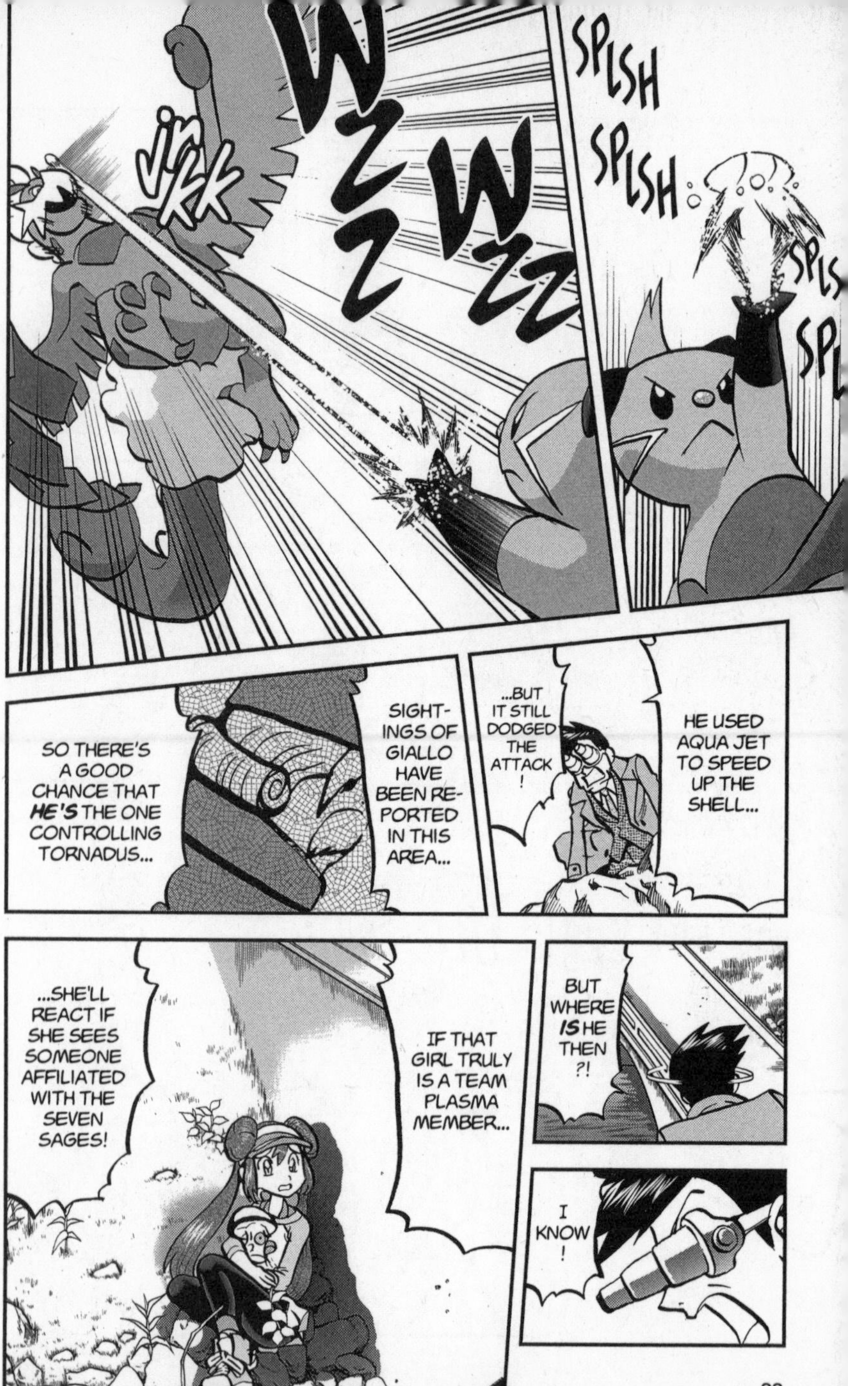
SPLSH
SPLSH
WZZ
WZZ
HE USED AQUA JET TO SPEED UP THE SHELL...
...BUT IT STILL DODGED THE ATTACK!
SIGHT-INGS OF GIALLO HAVE BEEN RE-PORTED IN THIS AREA...
SO THERE'S A GOOD CHANCE THAT **HE'S** THE ONE CONTROLLING TORNADUS...
BUT WHERE **IS** HE THEN?!
I KNOW!
IF THAT GIRL TRULY IS A TEAM PLASMA MEMBER...
...SHE'LL REACT IF SHE SEES SOMEONE AFFILIATED WITH THE SEVEN SAGES!

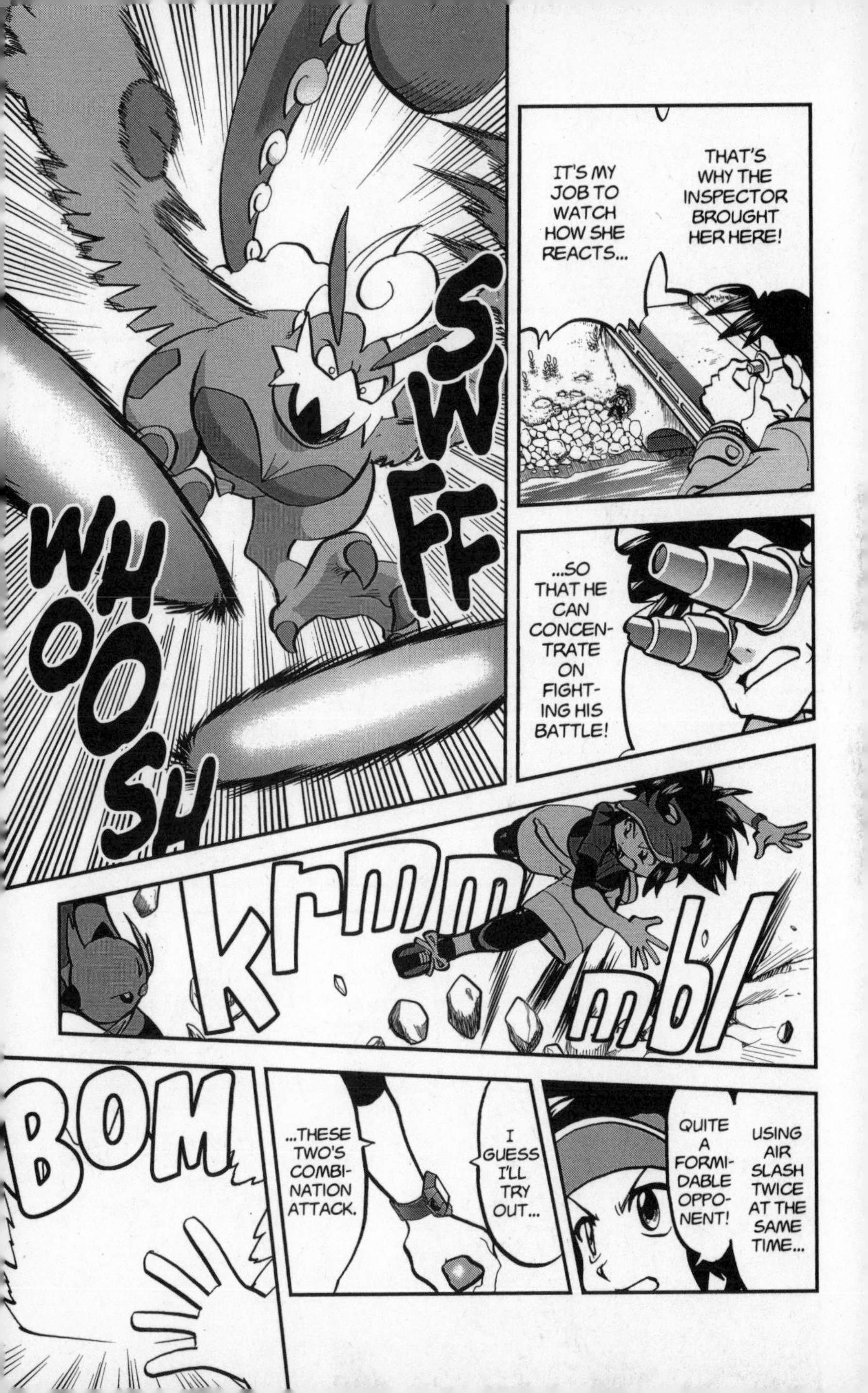
THAT'S WHY THE INSPECTOR BROUGHT HER HERE!
IT'S MY JOB TO WATCH HOW SHE REACTS...
...SO THAT HE CAN CONCENTRATE ON FIGHTING HIS BATTLE!
SWFF
WHOOSH
krmmmbl
USING AIR SLASH TWICE AT THE SAME TIME...
QUITE A FORMIDABLE OPPONENT!
I GUESS I'LL TRY OUT...
...THESE TWO'S COMBINATION ATTACK.
BOM

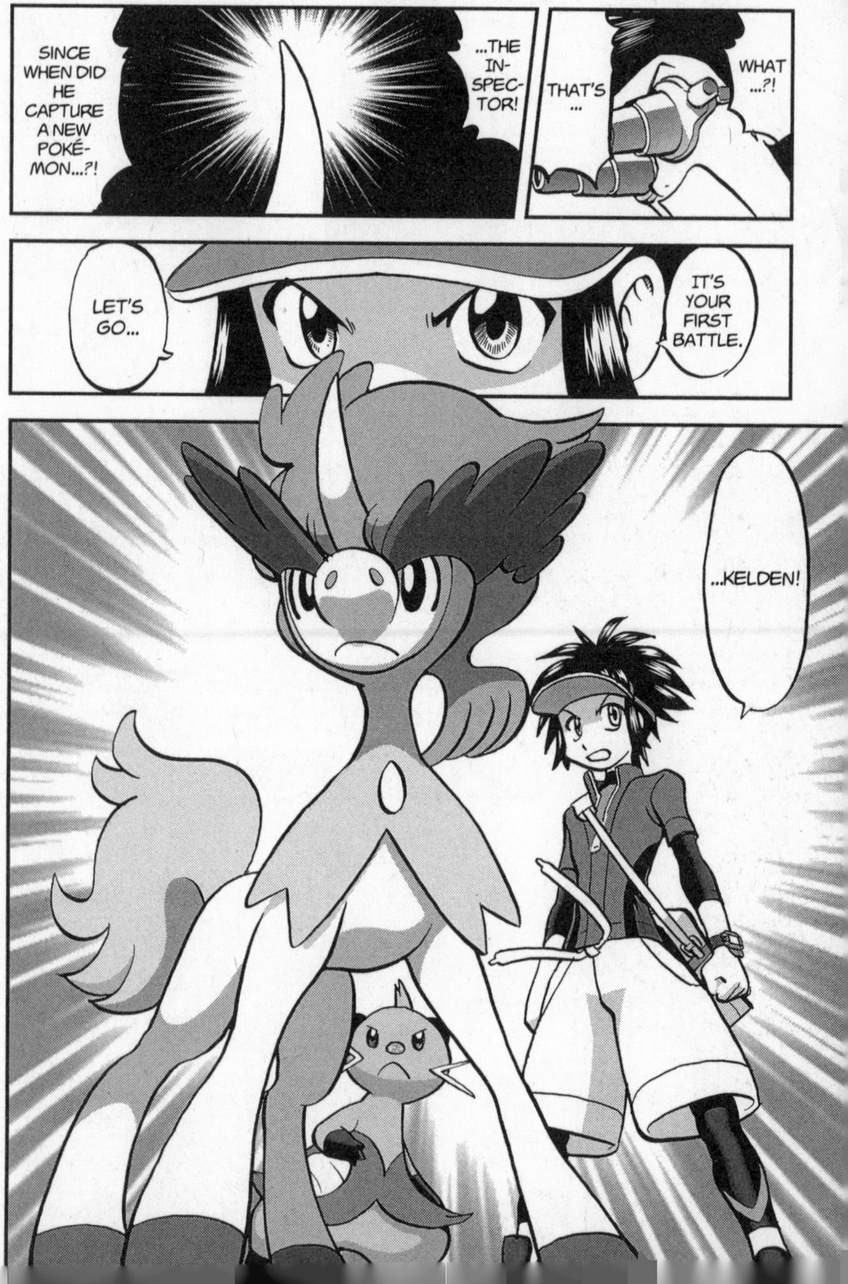
WHAT ...?!
THAT'S ...
...THE IN-SPECTOR!
SINCE WHEN DID HE CAPTURE A NEW POKÉMON...?!
IT'S YOUR FIRST BATTLE.
LET'S GO...
...KELDEN!

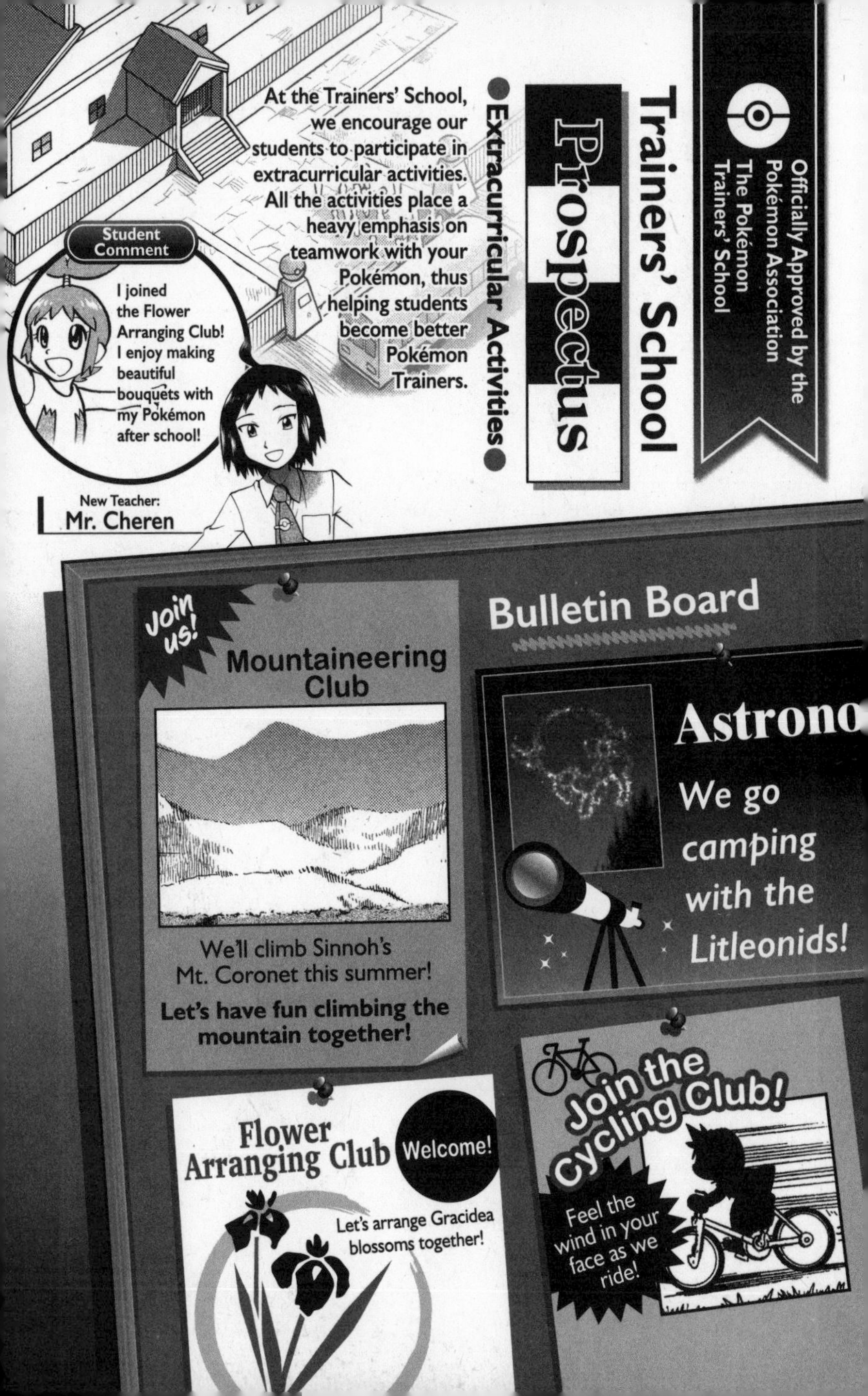

Officially Approved by the Pokémon Association
The Pokémon Trainers' School
Trainers' School
Prospectus
●Extracurricular Activities●
At the Trainers' School, we encourage our students to participate in extracurricular activities. All the activities place a heavy emphasis on teamwork with your Pokémon, thus helping students become better Pokémon Trainers.
Student Comment
I joined the Flower Arranging Club! I enjoy making beautiful bouquets with my Pokémon after school!
New Teacher:
Mr. Cheren
Bulletin Board
Astrono
We go camping with the Litleonids!
Join us!
Mountaineering Club
We'll climb Sinnoh's Mt. Coronet this summer!
Let's have fun climbing the mountain together!
Join the Cycling Club!
Feel the wind in your face as we ride!
Flower Arranging Club
Welcome!
Let's arrange Gracidea blossoms together!

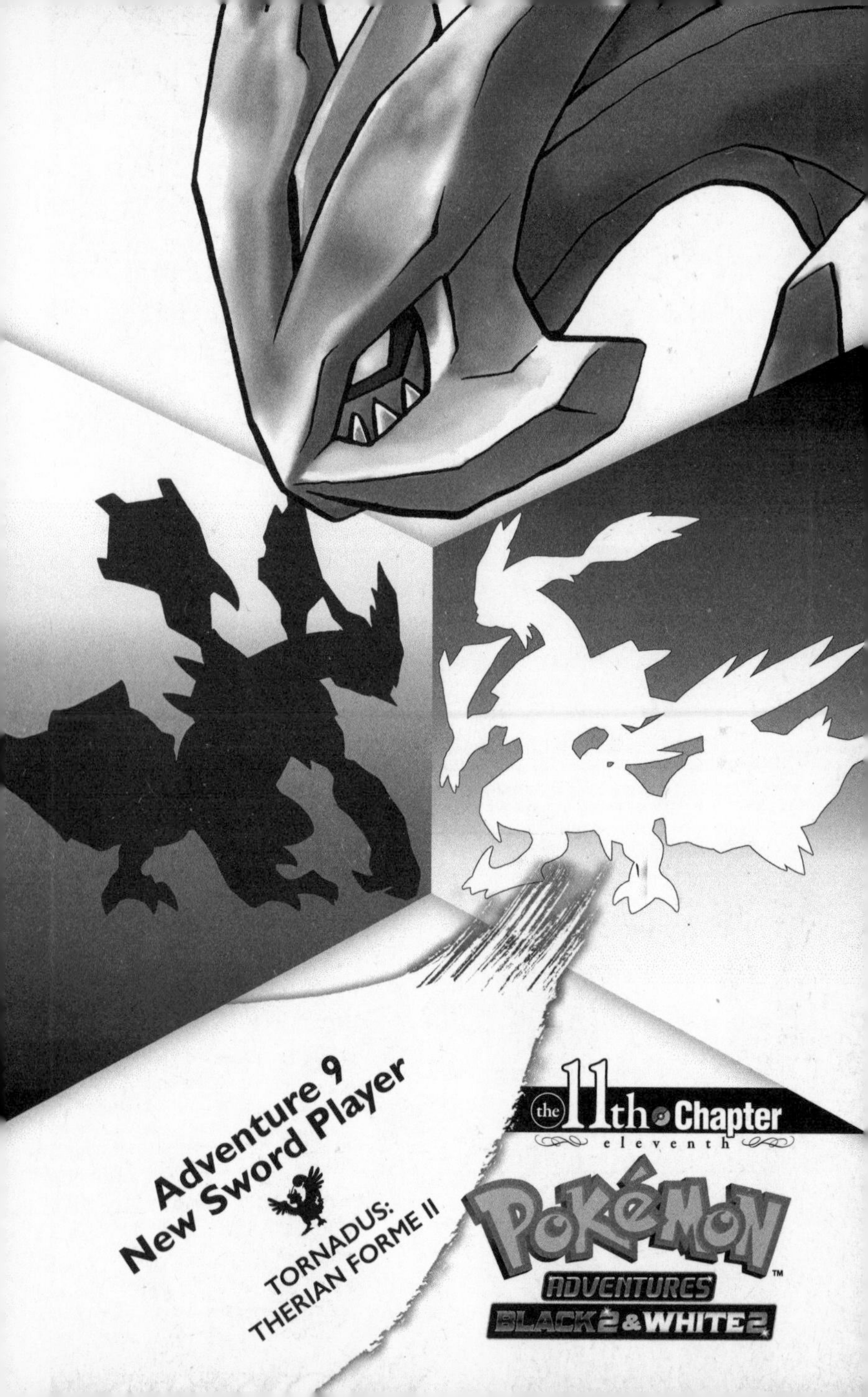
Adventure 9
New Sword Player
TORNADUS:
THERIAN FORME II
the 11th Chapter
eleventh
POKÉMON™
ADVENTURES
BLACK 2 & WHITE 2

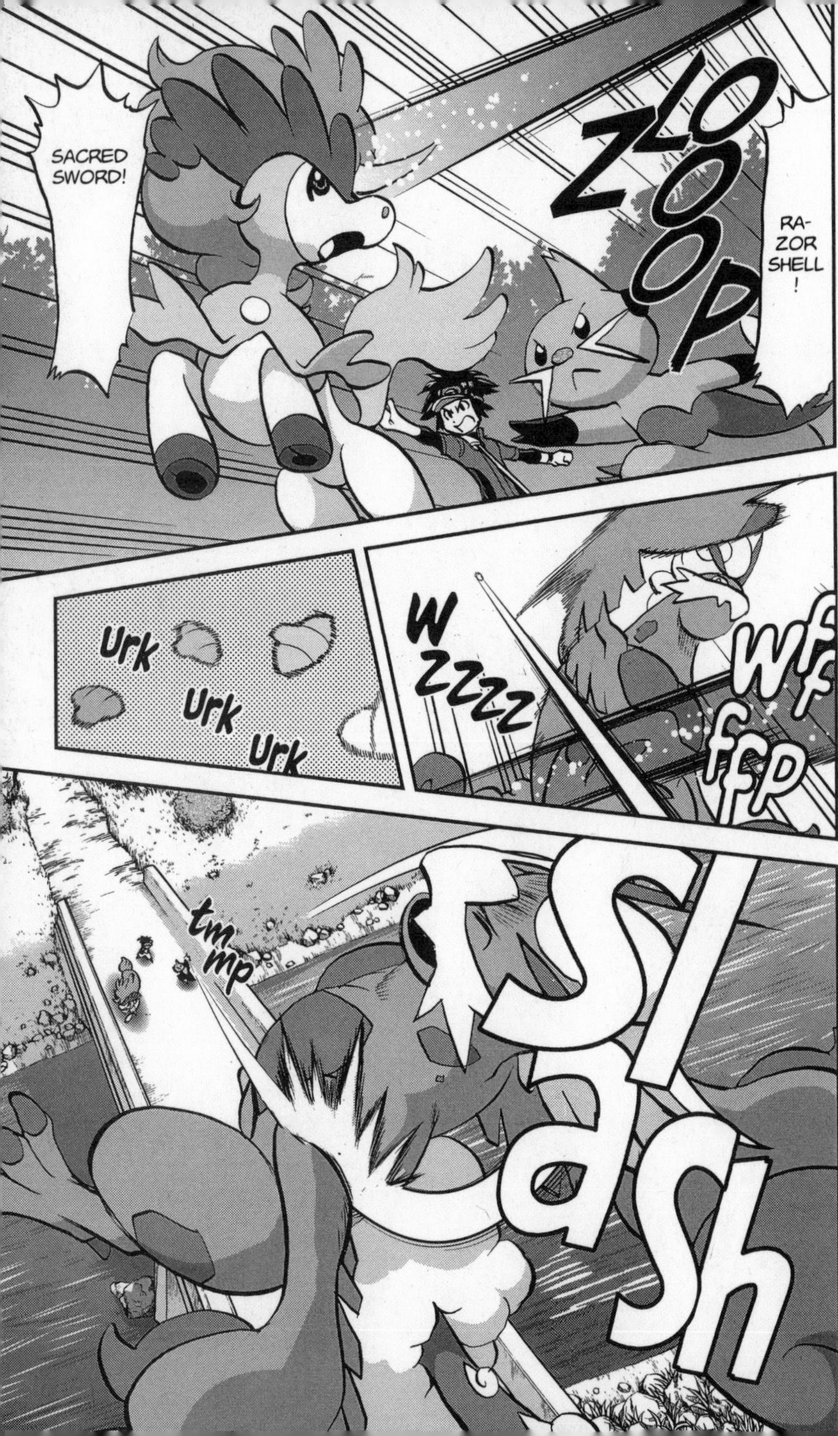
ZOOOP
RA-
ZOR
SHELL
!
SACRED
SWORD!
wf
f
ffp
Wzzzzz
Urk
Urk
Urk
Slash
tm
mp

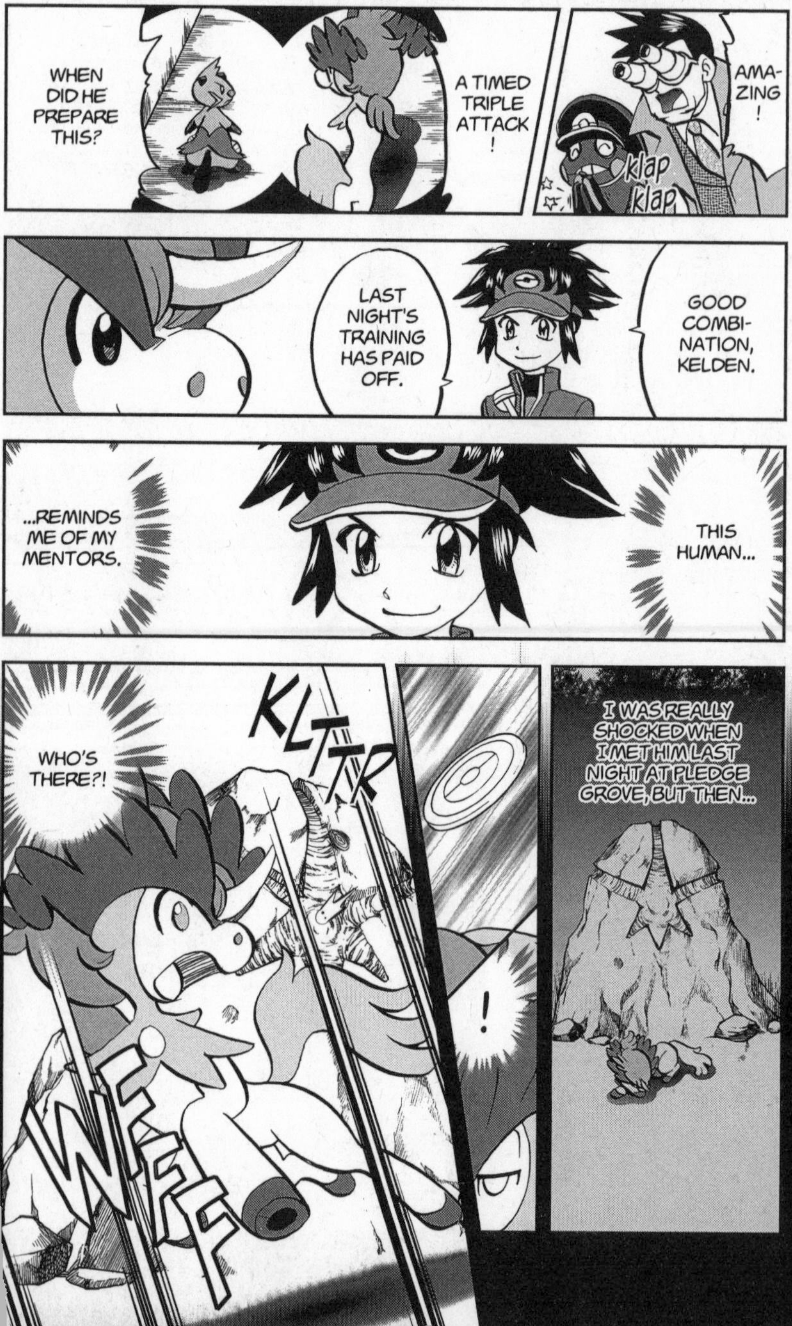
AMA-ZING!
klap klap
A TIMED TRIPLE ATTACK!
WHEN DID HE PREPARE THIS?
GOOD COMBI-NATION, KELDEN.
LAST NIGHT'S TRAINING HAS PAID OFF.
THIS HUMAN...
...REMINDS ME OF MY MENTORS.
I WAS REALLY SHOCKED WHEN I MET HIM LAST NIGHT AT PLEDGE GROVE, BUT THEN...
KLTTTR
!
WHO'S THERE?!
WFFF

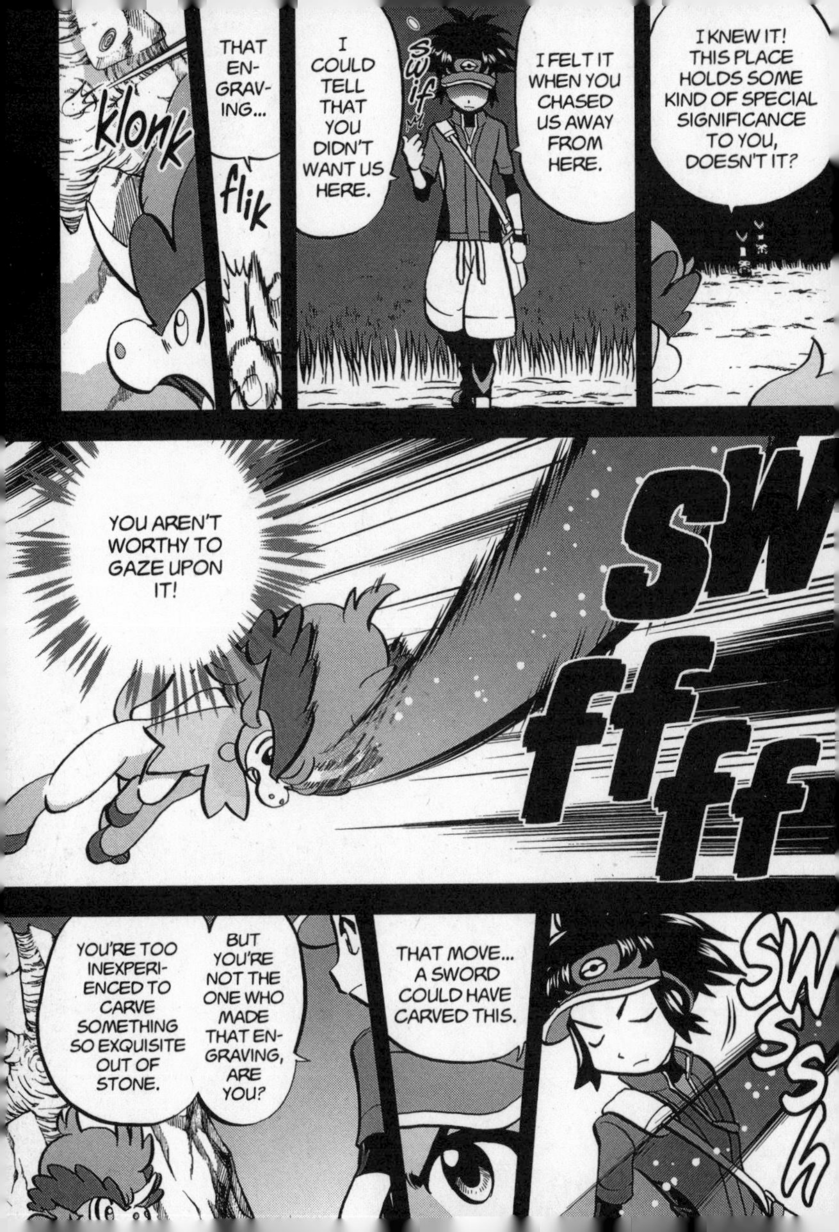
I KNEW IT! THIS PLACE HOLDS SOME KIND OF SPECIAL SIGNIFICANCE TO YOU, DOESN'T IT?
I FELT IT WHEN YOU CHASED US AWAY FROM HERE.
swif
I COULD TELL THAT YOU DIDN'T WANT US HERE.
THAT EN-GRAVING...
flik
klonk
SWffff
YOU AREN'T WORTHY TO GAZE UPON IT!
SWSSSh
THAT MOVE... A SWORD COULD HAVE CARVED THIS.
BUT YOU'RE NOT THE ONE WHO MADE THAT EN-GRAVING, ARE YOU?
YOU'RE TOO INEXPERI-ENCED TO CARVE SOMETHING SO EXQUISITE OUT OF STONE.

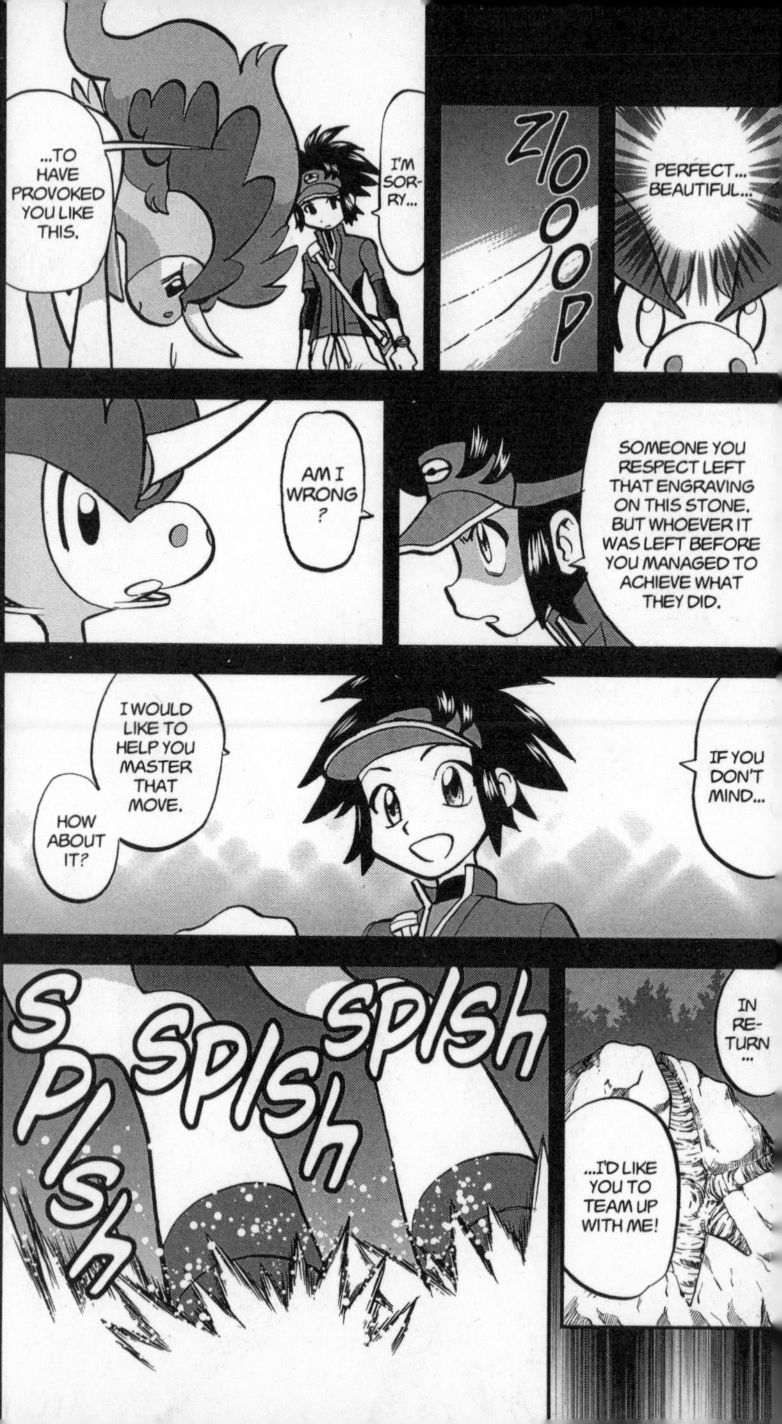
PERFECT... BEAUTIFUL...
ZOOOOP
I'M SORRY...
...TO HAVE PROVOKED YOU LIKE THIS.
SOMEONE YOU RESPECT LEFT THAT ENGRAVING ON THIS STONE. BUT WHOEVER IT WAS LEFT BEFORE YOU MANAGED TO ACHIEVE WHAT THEY DID.
AM I WRONG?
IF YOU DON'T MIND...
I WOULD LIKE TO HELP YOU MASTER THAT MOVE.
HOW ABOUT IT?
IN RETURN...
...I'D LIKE YOU TO TEAM UP WITH ME!
SPLSH SPLSH SPLSH SPLSH

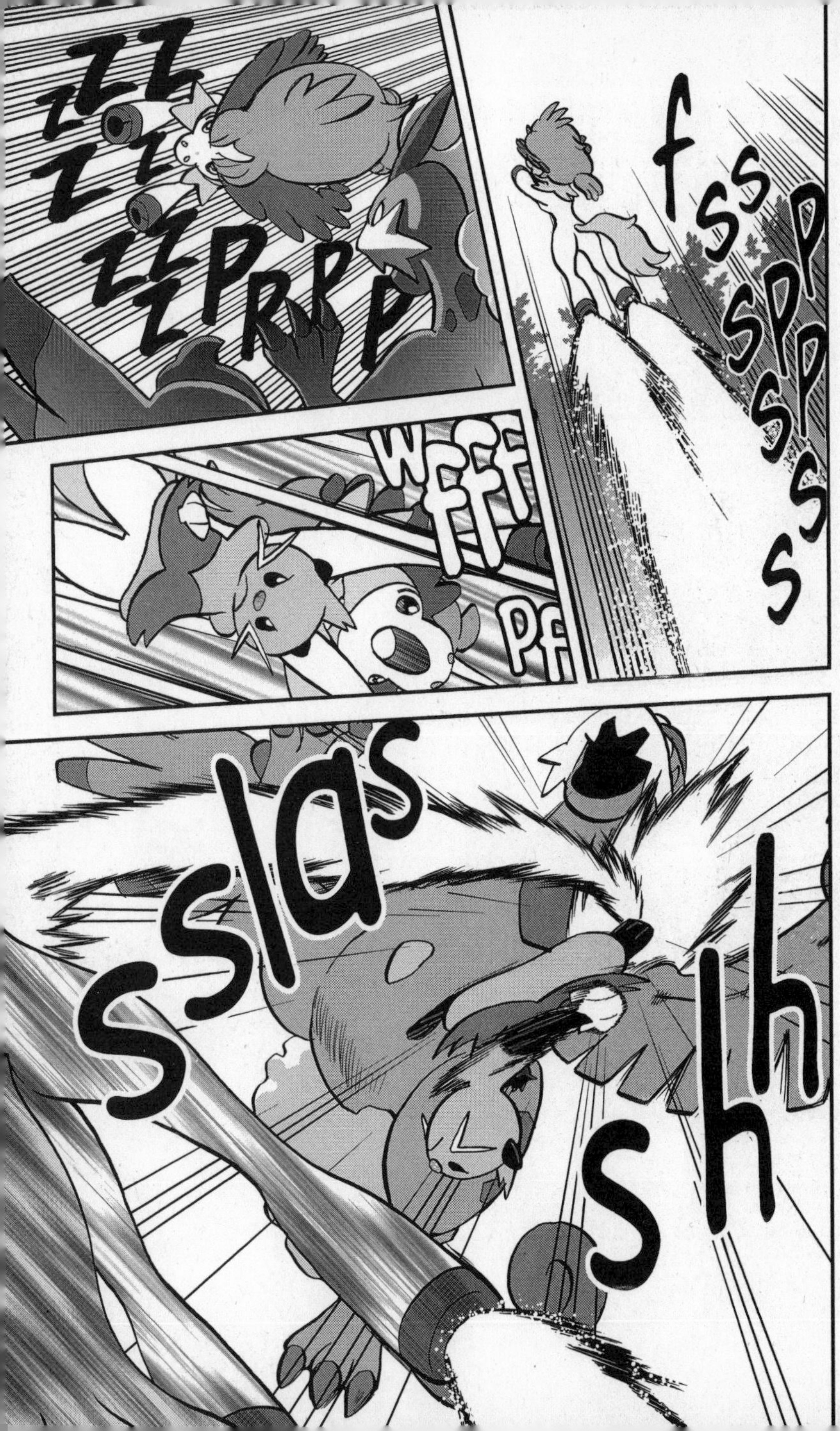
fss
PSPSPSSS
ZZZZZZZZ
PRPP
WFFF
PF
SSLAS
SHH

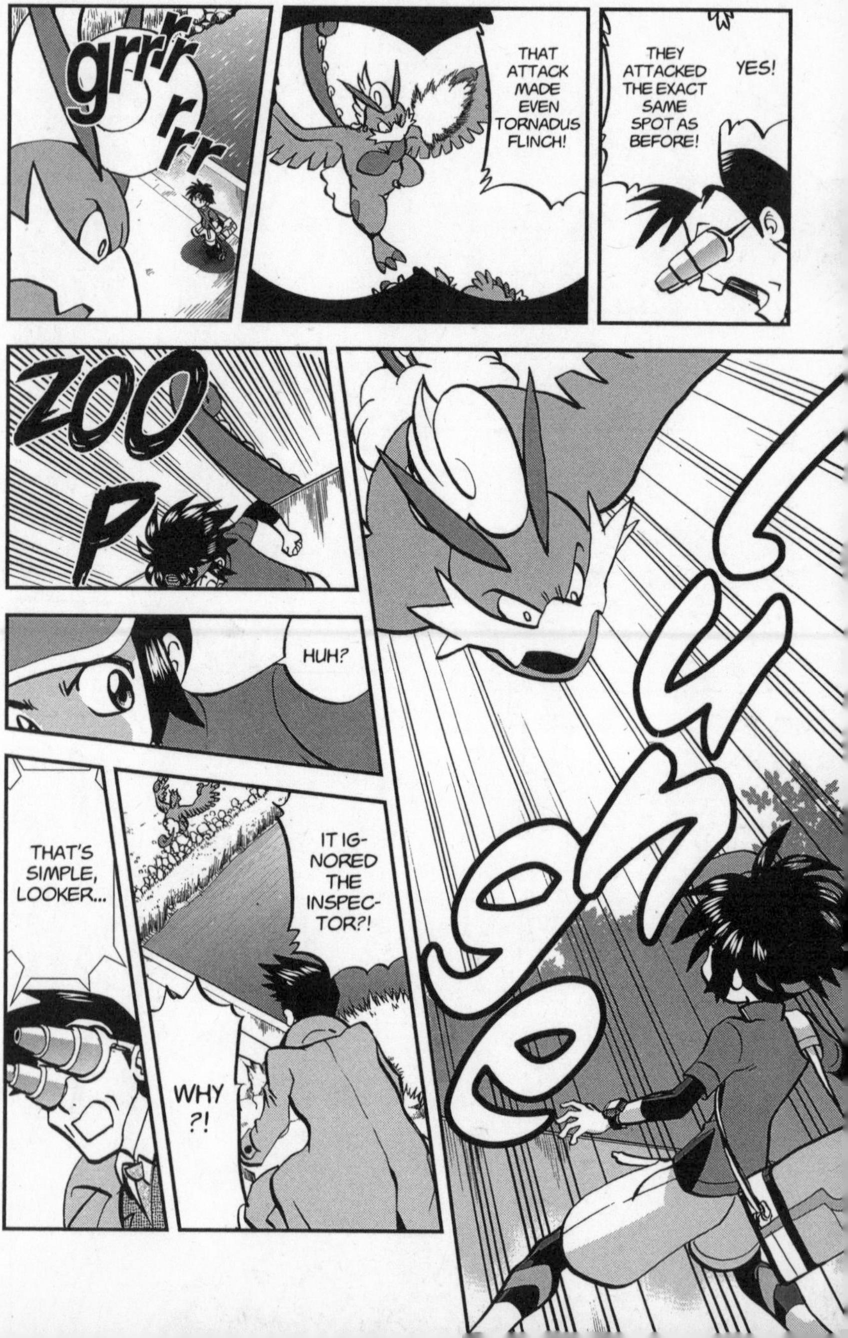
YES!
THEY ATTACKED THE EXACT SAME SPOT AS BEFORE!
THAT ATTACK MADE EVEN TORNADUS FLINCH!
grrrrrr
ZOOP
HUH?
IT IG-NORED THE INSPEC-TOR?!
WHY?!
THAT'S SIMPLE, LOOKER...

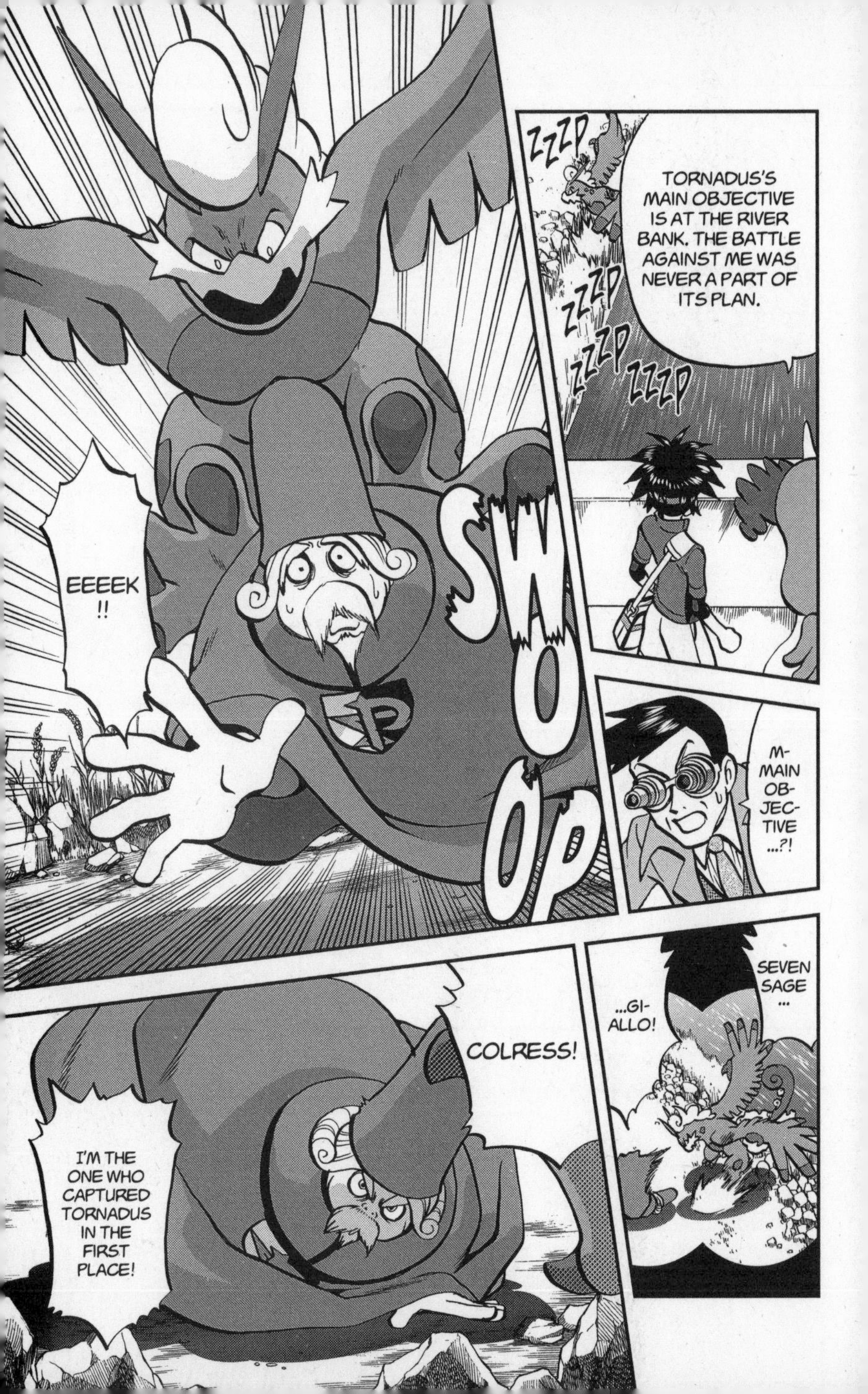
TORNADUS'S MAIN OBJECTIVE IS AT THE RIVER BANK. THE BATTLE AGAINST ME WAS NEVER A PART OF ITS PLAN.
ZZZP
ZZZP
ZZZP
ZZZP
M-MAIN OBJEC-TIVE ...?!
SWOOP
EEEEK !!
SEVEN SAGE ...
...GI-ALLO!
COLRESS!
I'M THE ONE WHO CAPTURED TORNADUS IN THE FIRST PLACE!

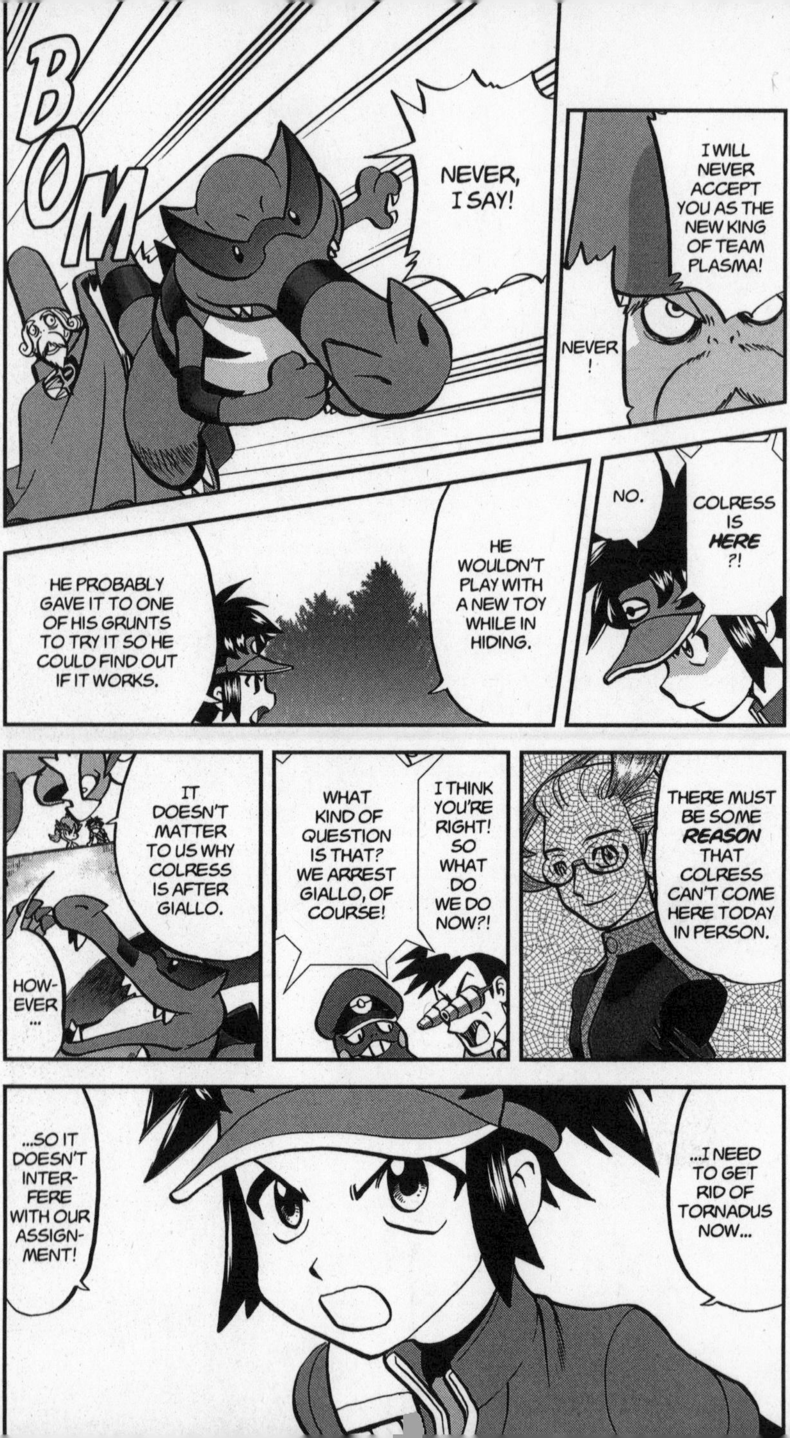
I WILL NEVER ACCEPT YOU AS THE NEW KING OF TEAM PLASMA!
NEVER!
NEVER, I SAY!
BOM
COLRESS IS HERE?!
NO.
HE WOULDN'T PLAY WITH A NEW TOY WHILE IN HIDING.
HE PROBABLY GAVE IT TO ONE OF HIS GRUNTS TO TRY IT SO HE COULD FIND OUT IF IT WORKS.
THERE MUST BE SOME REASON THAT COLRESS CAN'T COME HERE TODAY IN PERSON.
I THINK YOU'RE RIGHT! SO WHAT DO WE DO NOW?!
WHAT KIND OF QUESTION IS THAT? WE ARREST GIALLO, OF COURSE!
IT DOESN'T MATTER TO US WHY COLRESS IS AFTER GIALLO.
HOW-EVER...
...I NEED TO GET RID OF TORNADUS NOW...
...SO IT DOESN'T INTERFERE WITH OUR ASSIGNMENT!

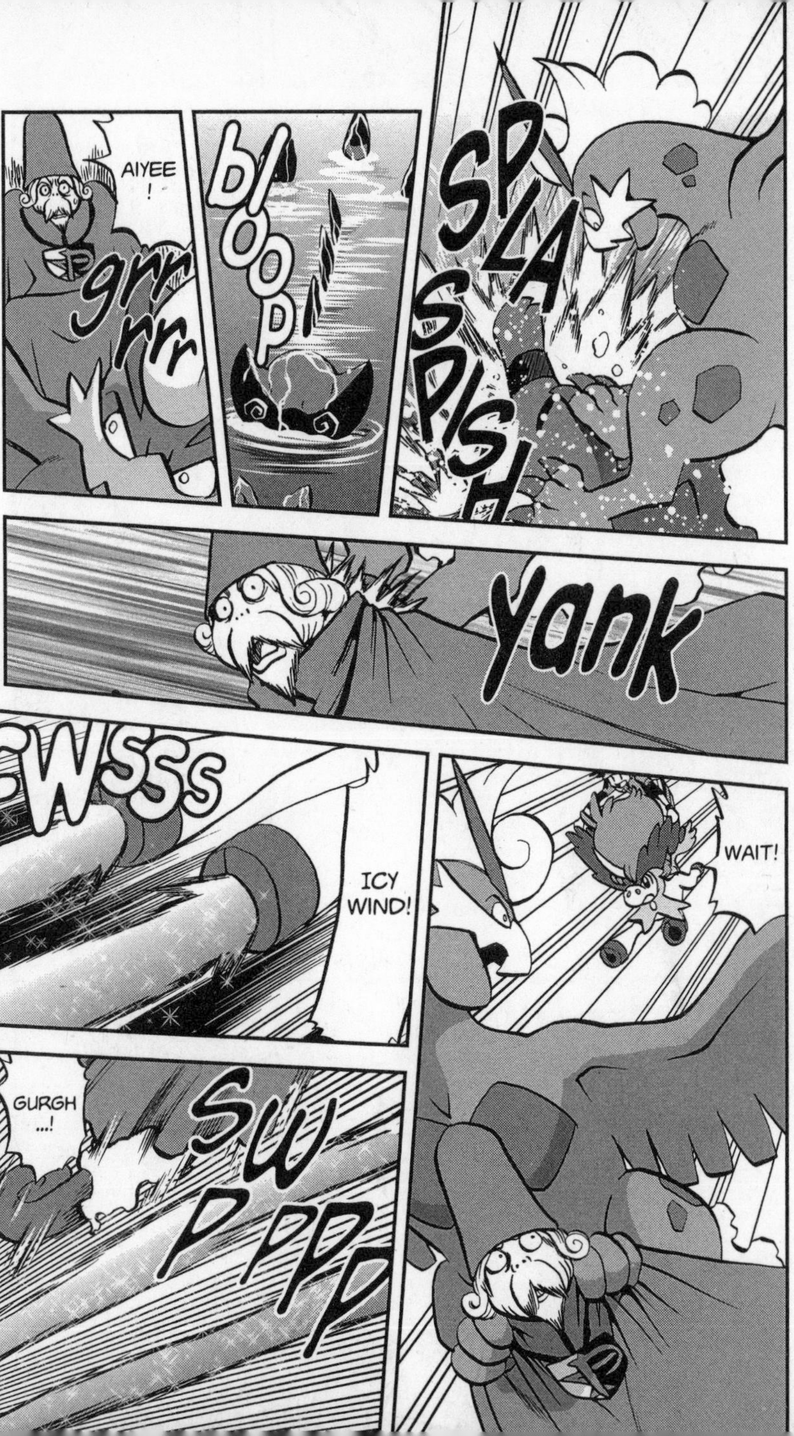
SPLASH
SPLISH
bloop...
AIYEE!
grrr rrr
yank
WAIT!
fwsss
ICY WIND!
GURGH ...!
SWPPPP

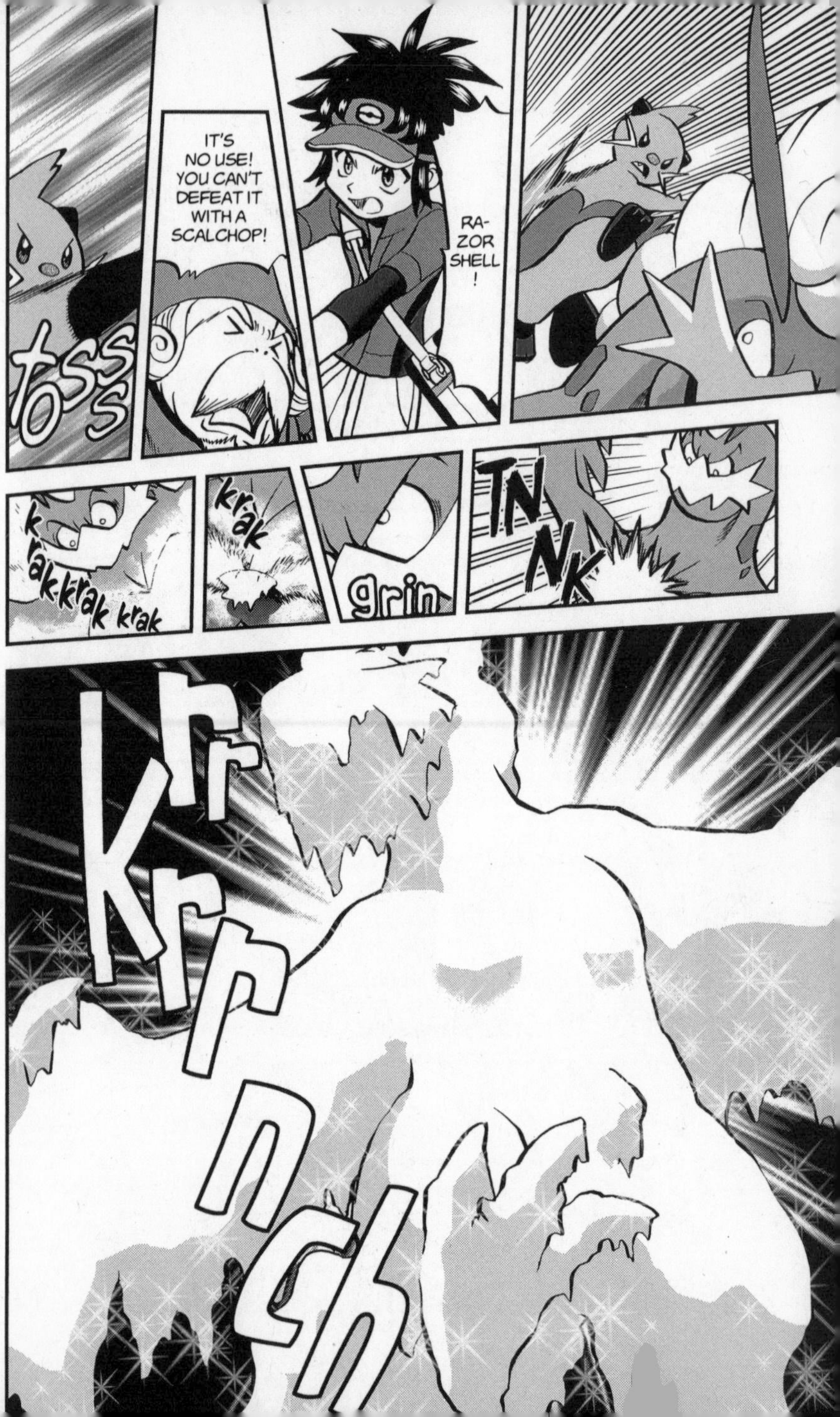
RAZOR SHELL!
IT'S NO USE! YOU CAN'T DEFEAT IT WITH A SCALCHOP!
toss
TNNK
grin
krak
krak krak krak krak
Krrrrnnch

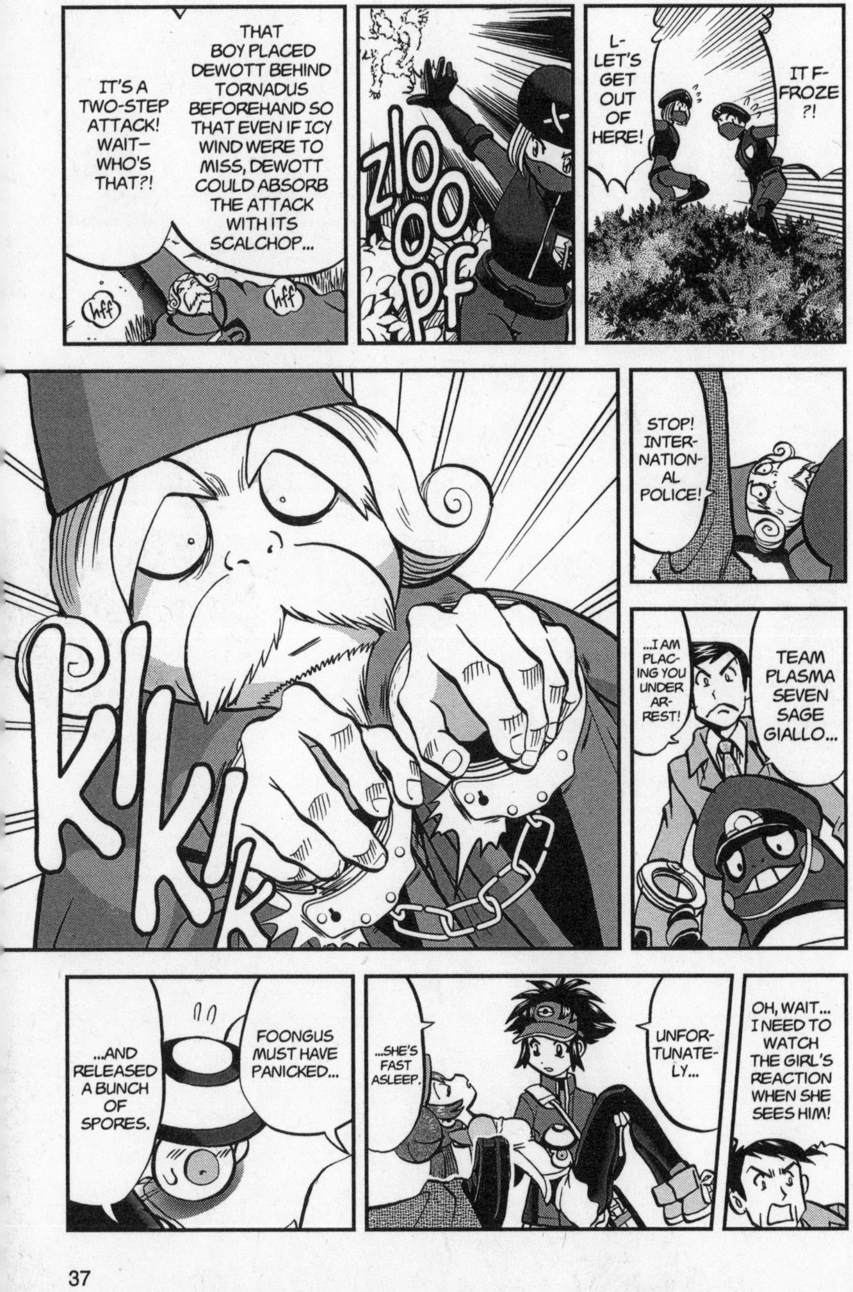
IT F-FROZE?!
L-LET'S GET OUT OF HERE!
ZIOOOOPF
THAT BOY PLACED DEWOTT BEHIND TORNADUS BEFOREHAND SO THAT EVEN IF ICY WIND WERE TO MISS, DEWOTT COULD ABSORB THE ATTACK WITH ITS SCALCHOP...
IT'S A TWO-STEP ATTACK! WAIT—WHO'S THAT?!
hff
hff
STOP! INTERNATIONAL POLICE!
TEAM PLASMA SEVEN SAGE GIALLO...
...I AM PLACING YOU UNDER ARREST!
KLKKK
OH, WAIT... I NEED TO WATCH THE GIRL'S REACTION WHEN SHE SEES HIM!
UNFORTUNATELY...
...SHE'S FAST ASLEEP.
FOONGUS MUST HAVE PANICKED...
...AND RELEASED A BUNCH OF SPORES.

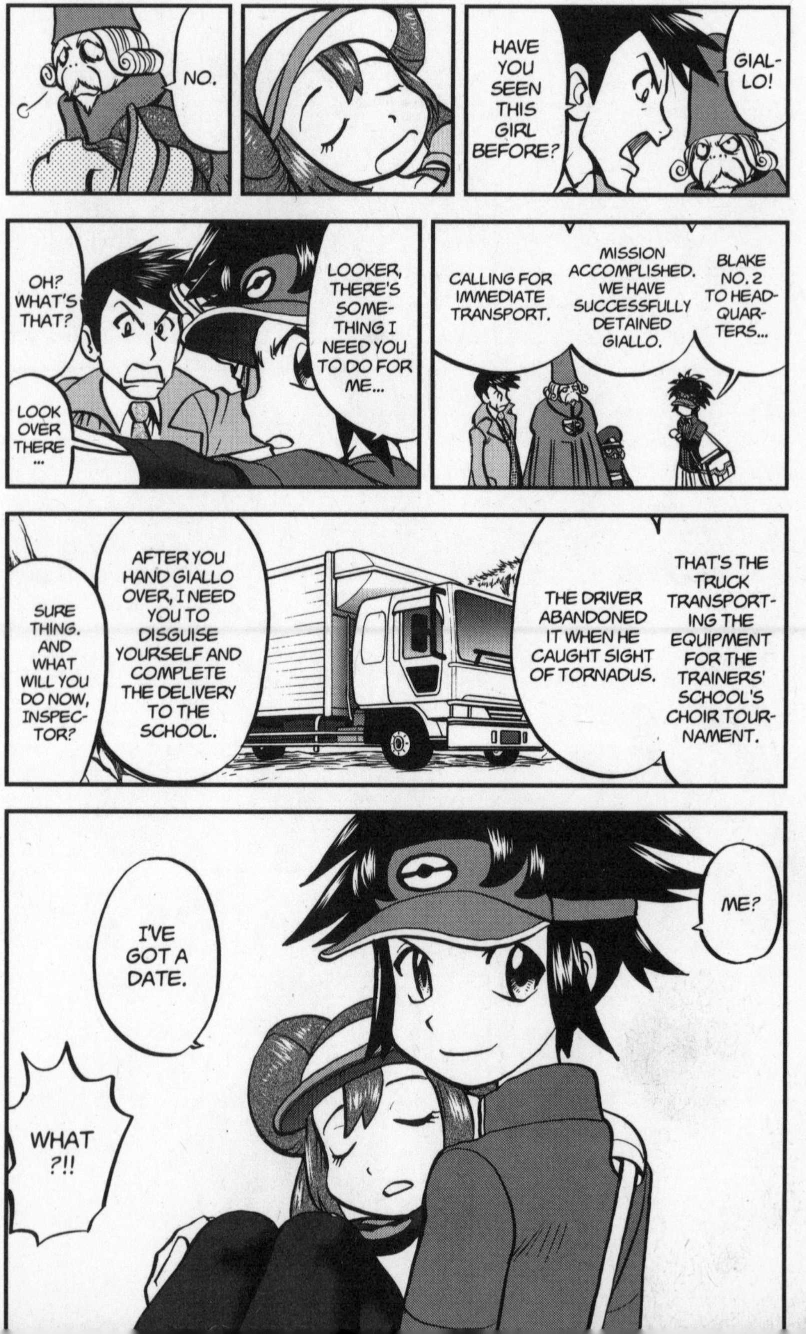
GIALLO!
HAVE YOU SEEN THIS GIRL BEFORE?
NO.
BLAKE NO. 2 TO HEADQUARTERS...
MISSION ACCOMPLISHED. WE HAVE SUCCESSFULLY DETAINED GIALLO.
CALLING FOR IMMEDIATE TRANSPORT.
LOOKER, THERE'S SOMETHING I NEED YOU TO DO FOR ME...
OH? WHAT'S THAT?
LOOK OVER THERE...
THAT'S THE TRUCK TRANSPORTING THE EQUIPMENT FOR THE TRAINERS' SCHOOL'S CHOIR TOURNAMENT.
THE DRIVER ABANDONED IT WHEN HE CAUGHT SIGHT OF TORNADUS.
AFTER YOU HAND GIALLO OVER, I NEED YOU TO DISGUISE YOURSELF AND COMPLETE THE DELIVERY TO THE SCHOOL.
SURE THING. AND WHAT WILL YOU DO NOW, INSPECTOR?
ME?
I'VE GOT A DATE.
WHAT?!!

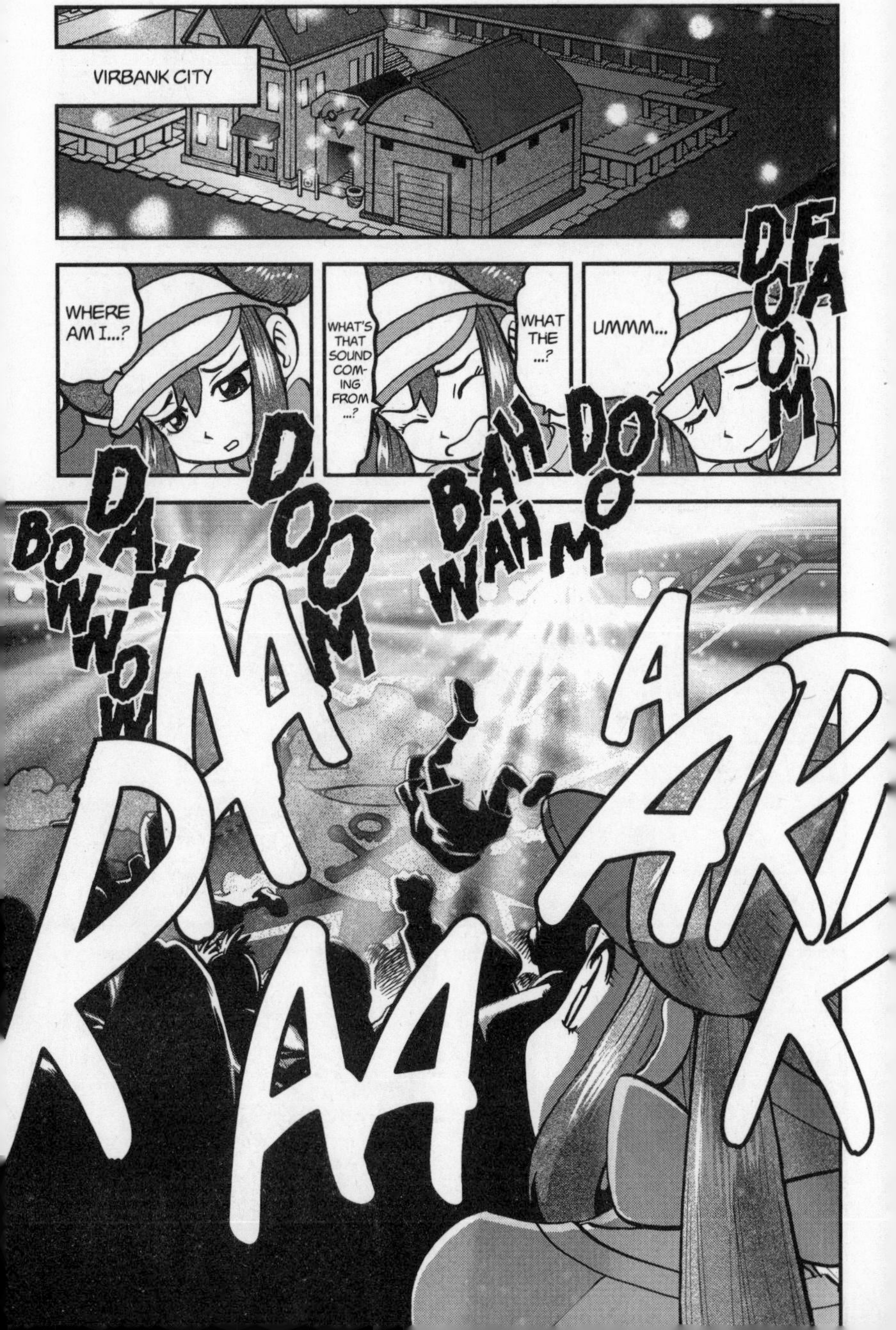
VIRBANK CITY
UMMM...
WHAT THE ...?
WHAT'S THAT SOUND COMING FROM ...?
WHERE AM I...?

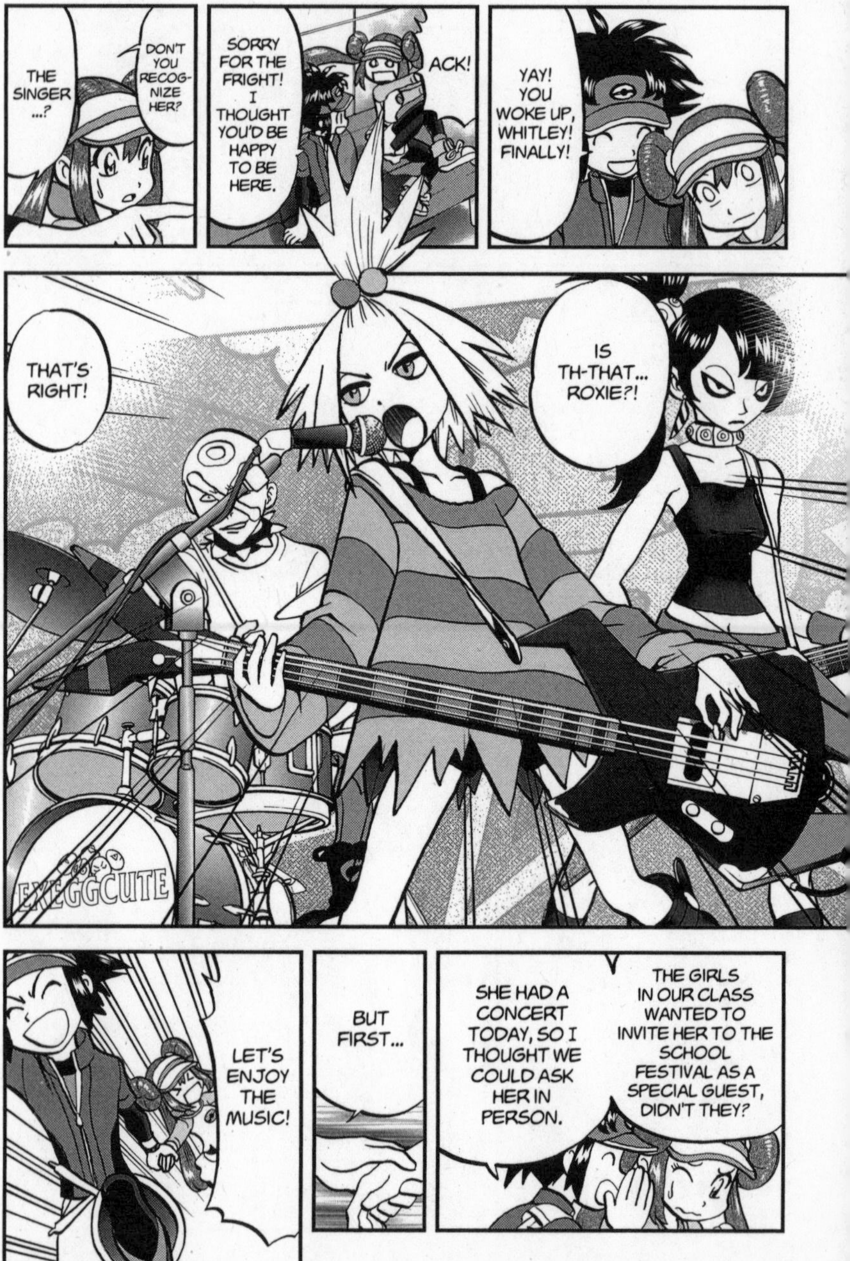
YAY! YOU WOKE UP, WHITLEY! FINALLY!
ACK!
SORRY FOR THE FRIGHT! I THOUGHT YOU'D BE HAPPY TO BE HERE.
DON'T YOU RECOGNIZE HER?
THE SINGER ...?
IS TH-THAT... ROXIE?!
THAT'S RIGHT!
EXEGGCUTE
THE GIRLS IN OUR CLASS WANTED TO INVITE HER TO THE SCHOOL FESTIVAL AS A SPECIAL GUEST, DIDN'T THEY?
SHE HAD A CONCERT TODAY, SO I THOUGHT WE COULD ASK HER IN PERSON.
BUT FIRST...
LET'S ENJOY THE MUSIC!

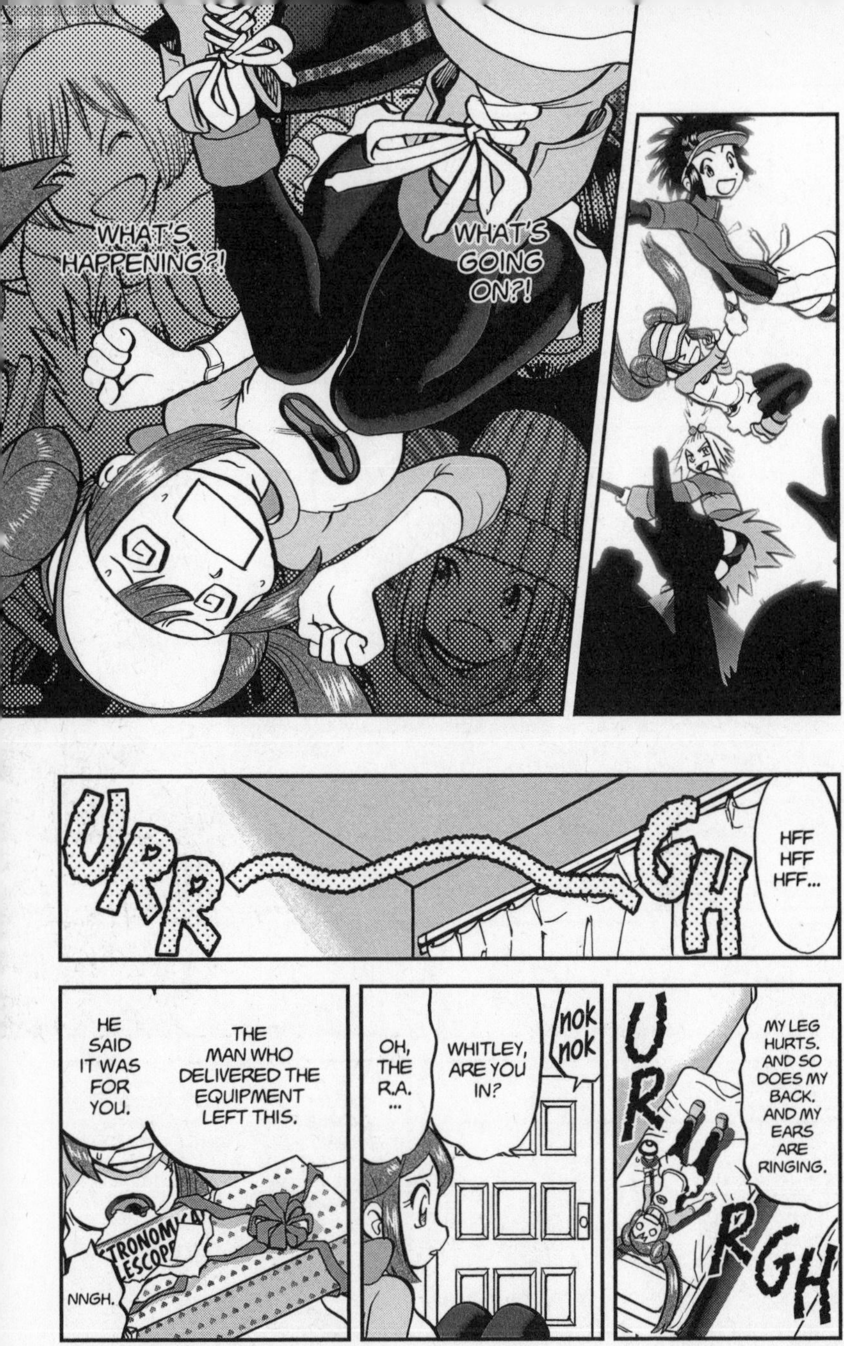
WHAT'S GOING ON?!
WHAT'S HAPPENING?!
HFF HFF HFF...
URR~GH
MY LEG HURTS. AND SO DOES MY BACK. AND MY EARS ARE RINGING.
URRGH
nok nok
WHITLEY, ARE YOU IN?
OH, THE R.A. ...
THE MAN WHO DELIVERED THE EQUIPMENT LEFT THIS.
HE SAID IT WAS FOR YOU.
NNGH.

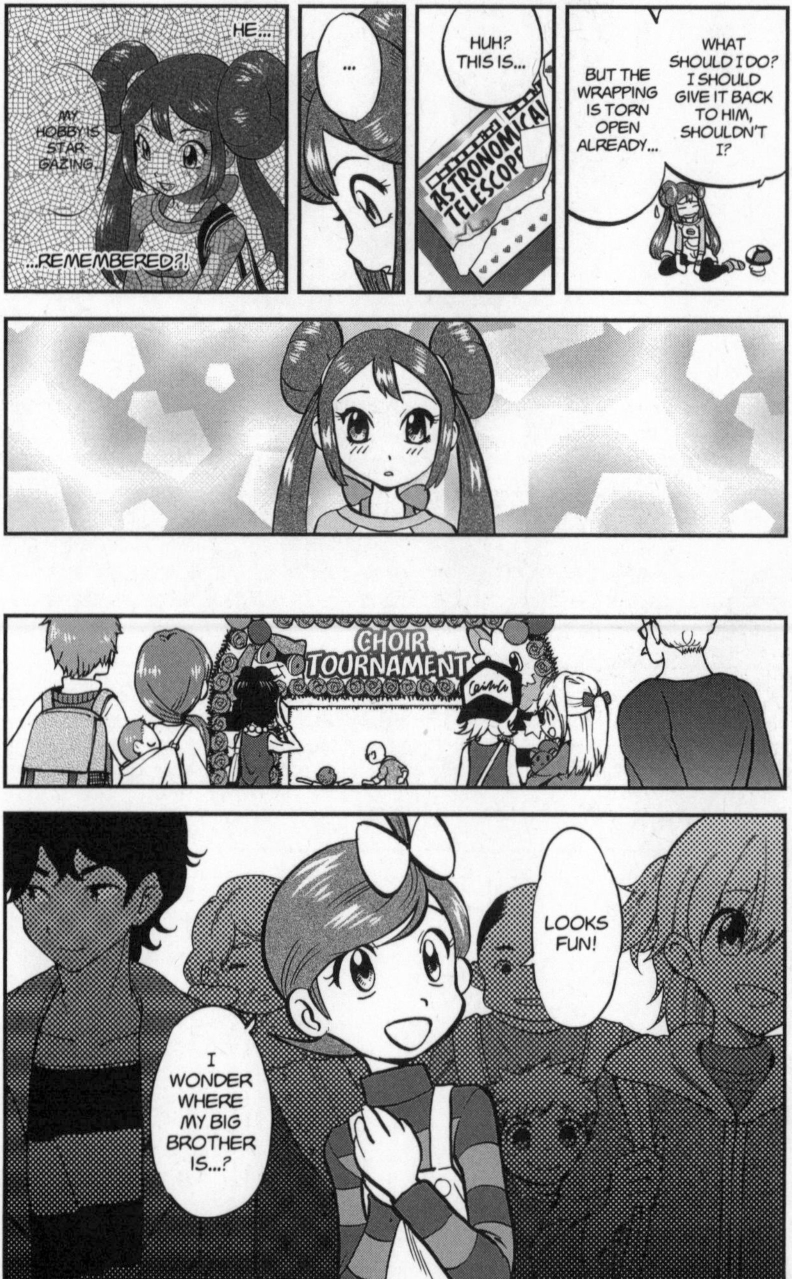
WHAT SHOULD I DO? I SHOULD GIVE IT BACK TO HIM, SHOULDN'T I?
BUT THE WRAPPING IS TORN OPEN ALREADY...
HUH? THIS IS...
ASTRONOMICAL TELESCOPE
...
HE...
MY HOBBY IS STAR-GAZING...
...REMEMBERED?!
CHOIR TOURNAMENT
LOOKS FUN!
I WONDER WHERE MY BIG BROTHER IS...?

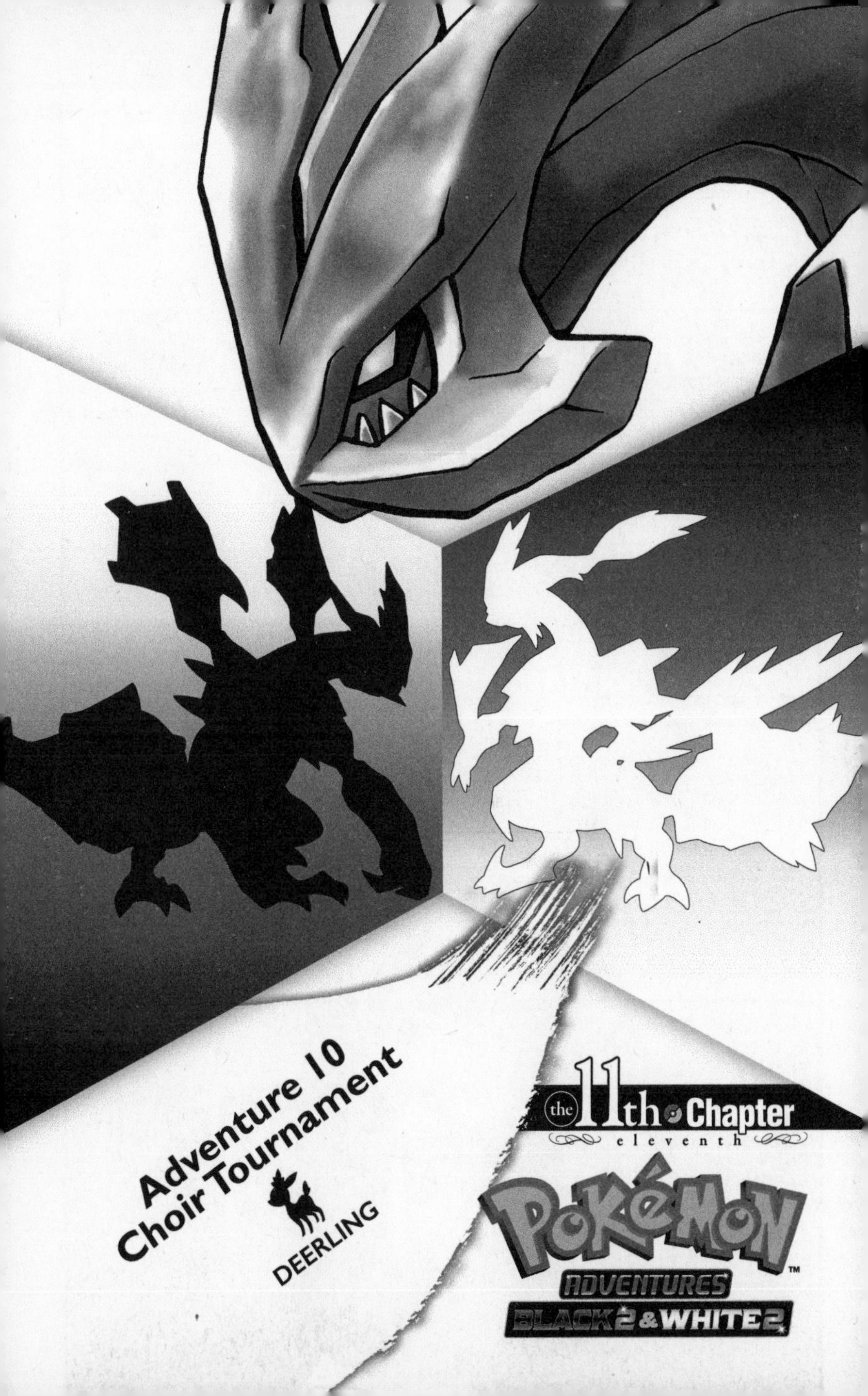
Adventure 10
Choir Tournament
DEERLING
the 11th Chapter
eleventh
POKÉMON
ADVENTURES
BLACK 2 & WHITE 2

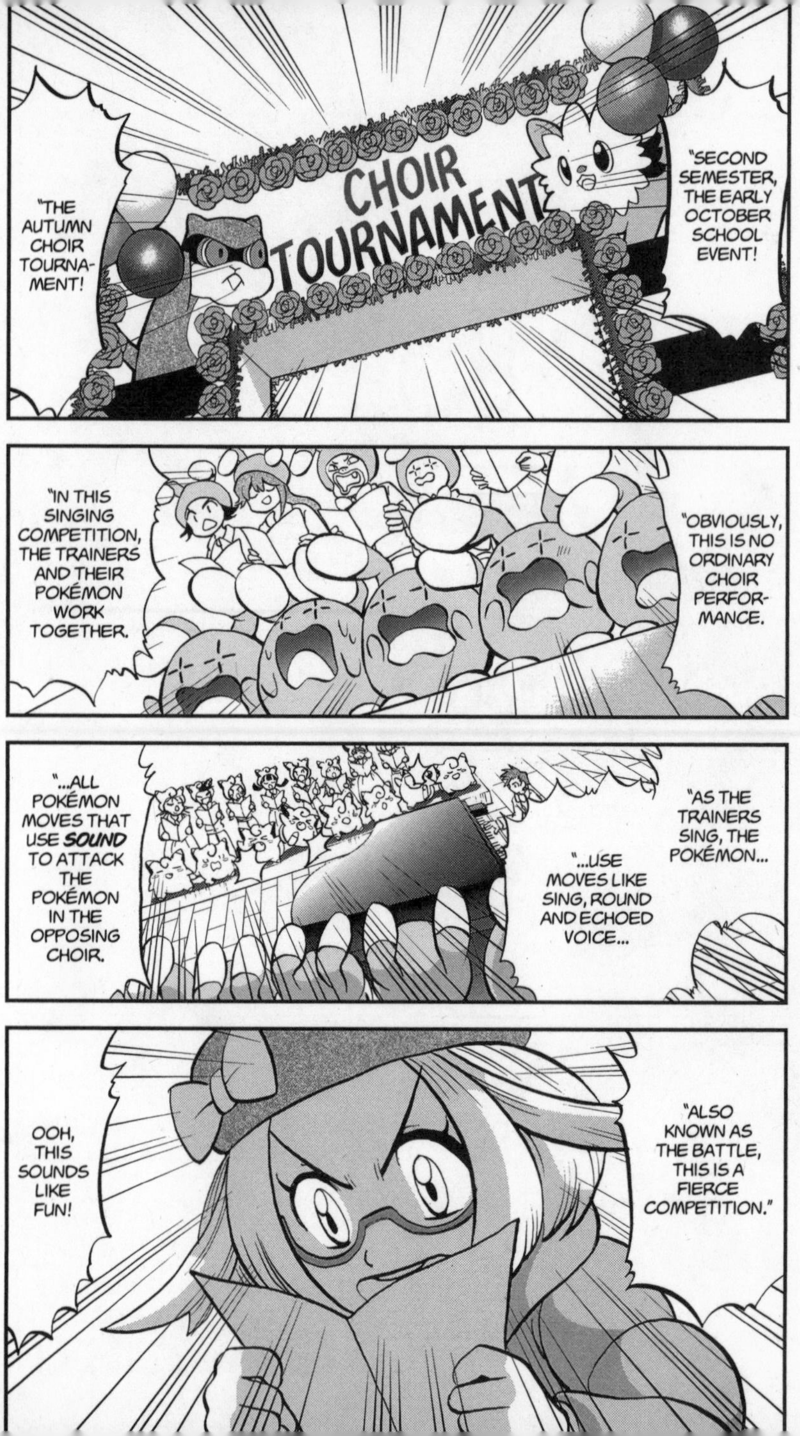
"SECOND SEMESTER, THE EARLY OCTOBER SCHOOL EVENT!
CHOIR TOURNAMENT
"THE AUTUMN CHOIR TOURNA-MENT!
"OBVIOUSLY, THIS IS NO ORDINARY CHOIR PERFOR-MANCE.
"IN THIS SINGING COMPETITION, THE TRAINERS AND THEIR POKÉMON WORK TOGETHER.
"AS THE TRAINERS SING, THE POKÉMON...
"...USE MOVES LIKE SING, ROUND AND ECHOED VOICE...
"...ALL POKÉMON MOVES THAT USE **SOUND** TO ATTACK THE POKÉMON IN THE OPPOSING CHOIR.
"ALSO KNOWN AS THE BATTLE, THIS IS A FIERCE COMPETITION."
OOH, THIS SOUNDS LIKE FUN!

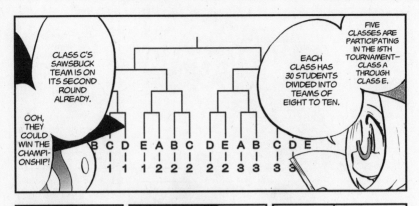

FIVE CLASSES ARE PARTICIPATING IN THE 15TH TOURNAMENT—CLASS A THROUGH CLASS E.
EACH CLASS HAS 30 STUDENTS DIVIDED INTO TEAMS OF EIGHT TO TEN.
CLASS C'S SAWSBUCK TEAM IS ON ITS SECOND ROUND ALREADY.
OOH, THEY COULD WIN THE CHAMPIONSHIP!
B C D E A B C D E A B C D E
1 1 1 2 2 2 2 2 3 3 3 3
I HOPE THE WINNING TEAM COMES FROM CHEREN'S CLASS E!
CLASS B TEAM CHATOT! WE'RE GONNA WIN!
WE'RE SO TOTALLY, ABSOLUTELY GONNA WIN THIS TOURNAMENT!
twitch
I'M SO TOTALLY, ABSOLUTELY GONNA...
...WIN THAT TOURNAMENT!

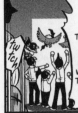

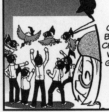

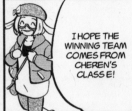

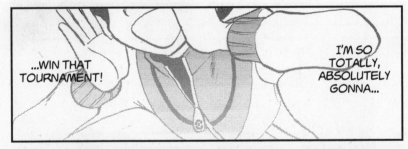

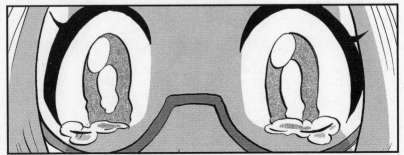

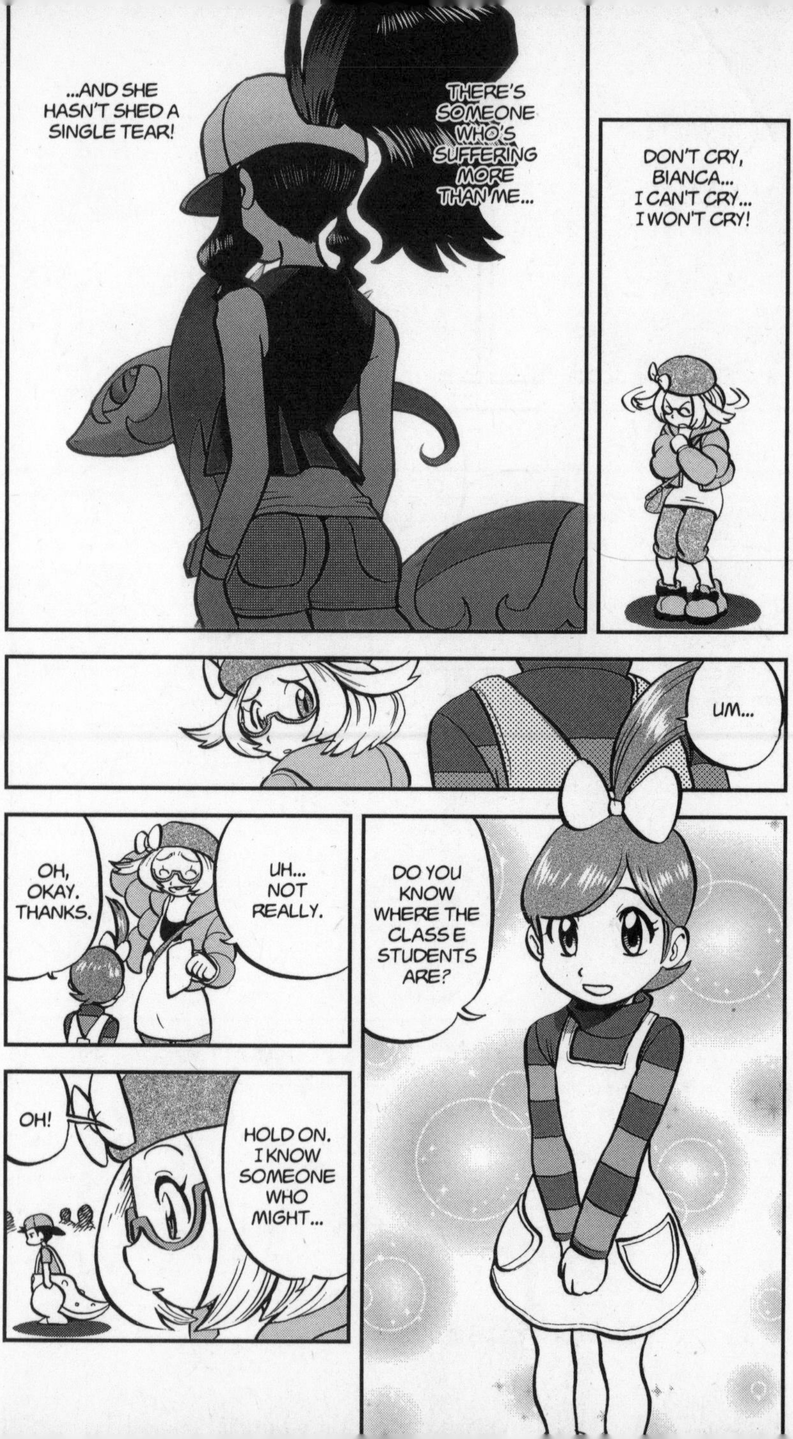
DON'T CRY, BIANCA... I CAN'T CRY... I WON'T CRY!
THERE'S SOMEONE WHO'S SUFFERING MORE THAN ME...
...AND SHE HASN'T SHED A SINGLE TEAR!
UM...
DO YOU KNOW WHERE THE CLASS E STUDENTS ARE?
UH... NOT REALLY.
OH, OKAY. THANKS.
OH!
HOLD ON. I KNOW SOMEONE WHO MIGHT...

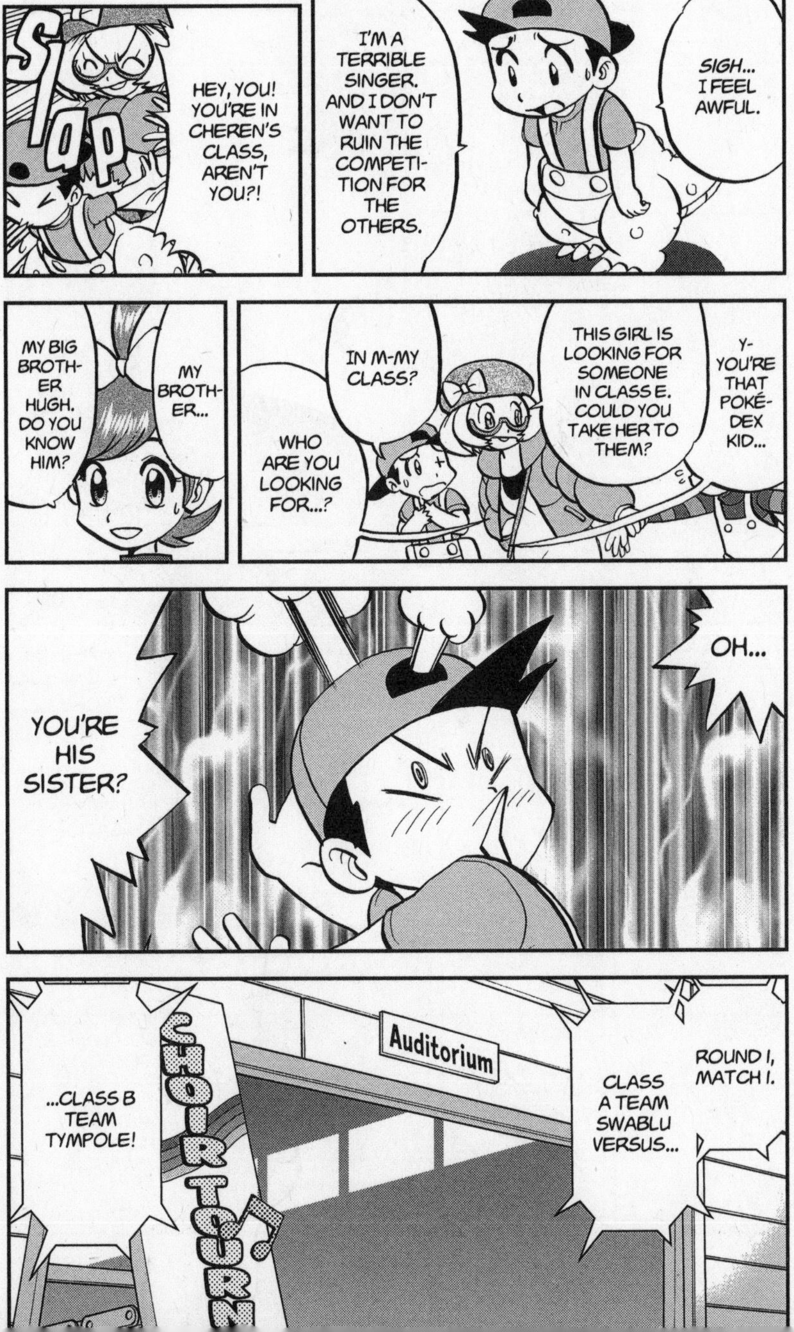
SIGH... I FEEL AWFUL.
I'M A TERRIBLE SINGER. AND I DON'T WANT TO RUIN THE COMPETITION FOR THE OTHERS.
SLAP
HEY, YOU! YOU'RE IN CHEREN'S CLASS, AREN'T YOU?!
Y-YOU'RE THAT POKÉDEX KID...
THIS GIRL IS LOOKING FOR SOMEONE IN CLASS E. COULD YOU TAKE HER TO THEM?
IN M-MY CLASS?
WHO ARE YOU LOOKING FOR...?
MY BROTHER...
MY BIG BROTHER HUGH. DO YOU KNOW HIM?
OH...
YOU'RE HIS SISTER?
ROUND 1, MATCH 1.
CLASS A TEAM SWABLU VERSUS...
Auditorium
CHOIR TOURN
...CLASS B TEAM TYMPOLE!

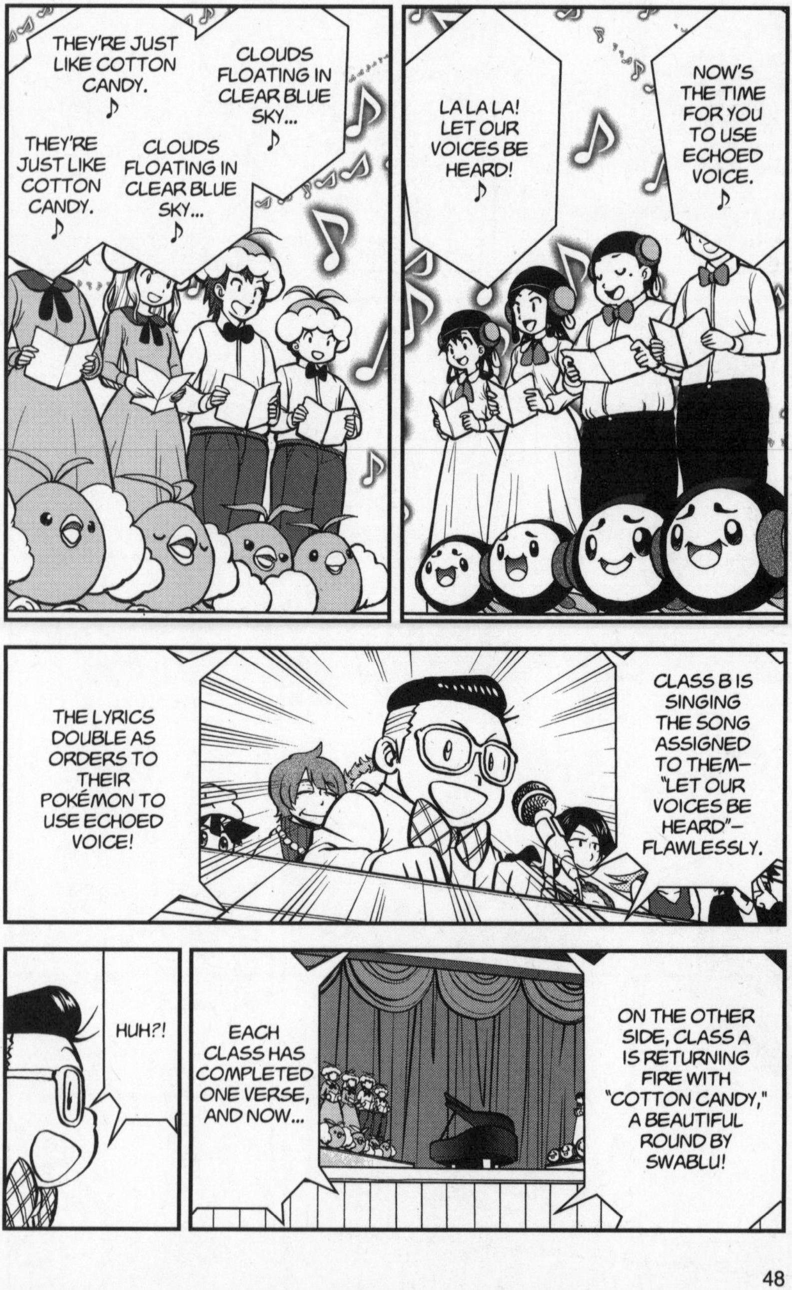
NOW'S THE TIME FOR YOU TO USE ECHOED VOICE. ♪
LA LA LA! LET OUR VOICES BE HEARD! ♪
CLOUDS FLOATING IN CLEAR BLUE SKY... ♪
THEY'RE JUST LIKE COTTON CANDY. ♪
CLOUDS FLOATING IN CLEAR BLUE SKY... ♪
THEY'RE JUST LIKE COTTON CANDY. ♪
CLASS B IS SINGING THE SONG ASSIGNED TO THEM—"LET OUR VOICES BE HEARD"—FLAWLESSLY.
THE LYRICS DOUBLE AS ORDERS TO THEIR POKÉMON TO USE ECHOED VOICE!
ON THE OTHER SIDE, CLASS A IS RETURNING FIRE WITH "COTTON CANDY," A BEAUTIFUL ROUND BY SWABLU!
EACH CLASS HAS COMPLETED ONE VERSE, AND NOW...
HUH?!

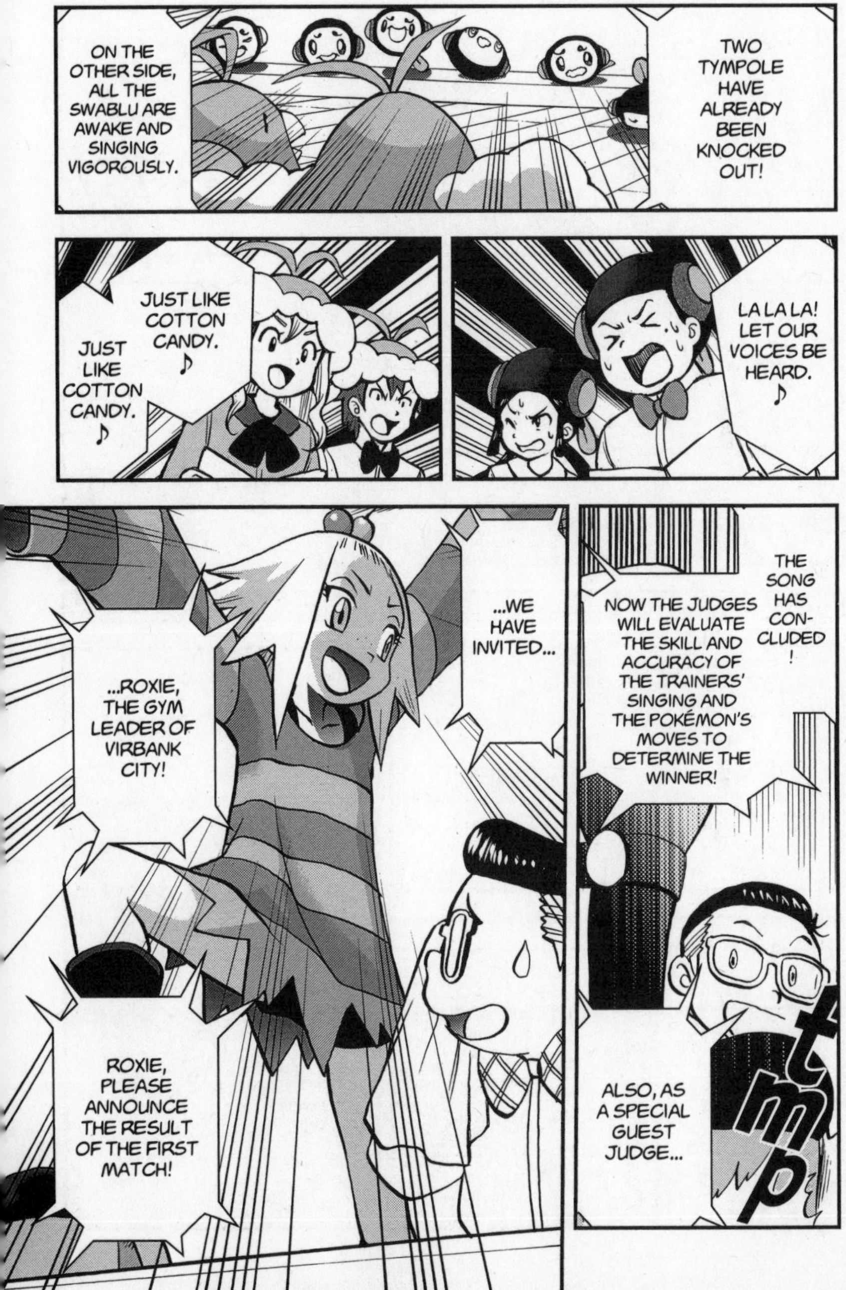
TWO TYMPOLE HAVE ALREADY BEEN KNOCKED OUT!
ON THE OTHER SIDE, ALL THE SWABLU ARE AWAKE AND SINGING VIGOROUSLY.
LA LA LA! LET OUR VOICES BE HEARD. ♪
JUST LIKE COTTON CANDY. ♪
JUST LIKE COTTON CANDY. ♪
THE SONG HAS CON-CLUDED!
NOW THE JUDGES WILL EVALUATE THE SKILL AND ACCURACY OF THE TRAINERS' SINGING AND THE POKÉMON'S MOVES TO DETERMINE THE WINNER!
ALSO, AS A SPECIAL GUEST JUDGE...
tmp
...WE HAVE INVITED...
...ROXIE, THE GYM LEADER OF VIRBANK CITY!
ROXIE, PLEASE ANNOUNCE THE RESULT OF THE FIRST MATCH!

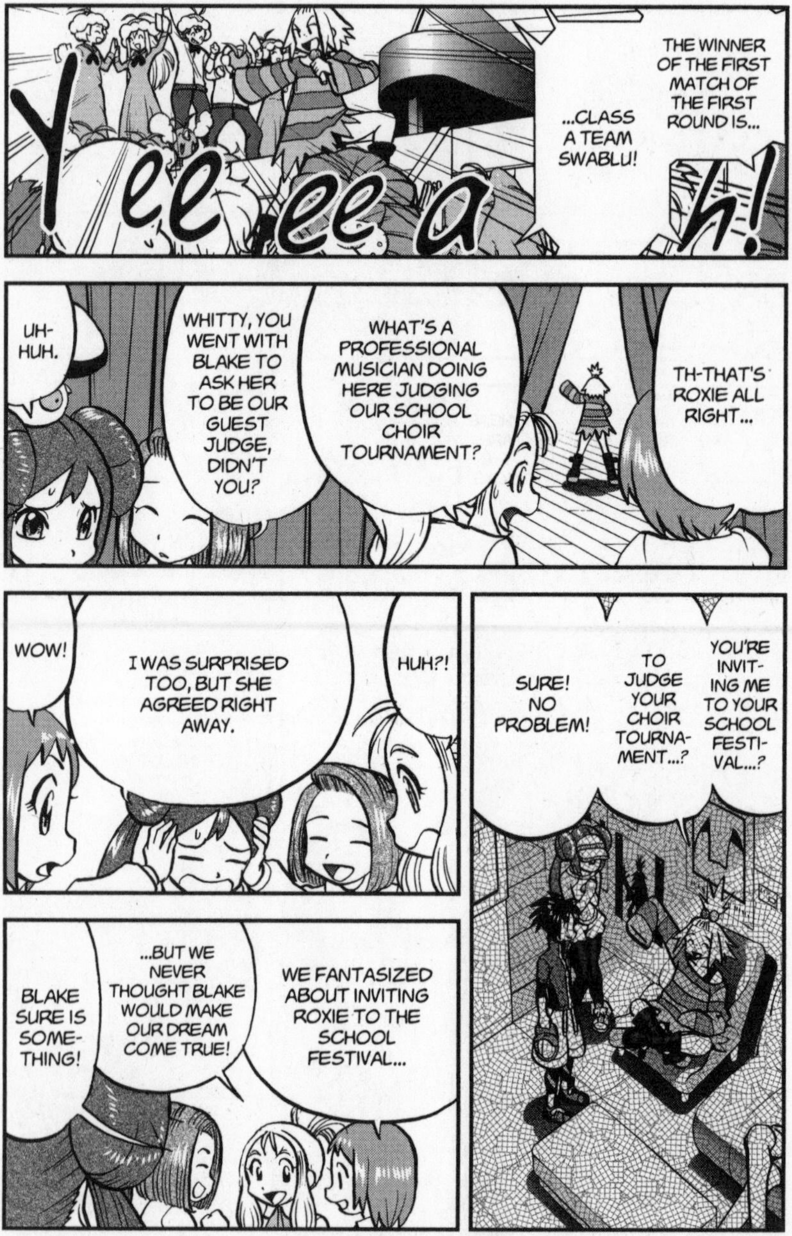
THE WINNER OF THE FIRST MATCH OF THE FIRST ROUND IS...
...CLASS A TEAM SWABLU!
Yeeeeah!
TH-THAT'S ROXIE ALL RIGHT...
WHAT'S A PROFESSIONAL MUSICIAN DOING HERE JUDGING OUR SCHOOL CHOIR TOURNAMENT?
WHITTY, YOU WENT WITH BLAKE TO ASK HER TO BE OUR GUEST JUDGE, DIDN'T YOU?
UH-HUH.
YOU'RE INVITING ME TO YOUR SCHOOL FESTIVAL...?
TO JUDGE YOUR CHOIR TOURNAMENT...?
SURE! NO PROBLEM!
HUH?!
I WAS SURPRISED TOO, BUT SHE AGREED RIGHT AWAY.
WOW!
WE FANTASIZED ABOUT INVITING ROXIE TO THE SCHOOL FESTIVAL...
...BUT WE NEVER THOUGHT BLAKE WOULD MAKE OUR DREAM COME TRUE!
BLAKE SURE IS SOMETHING!

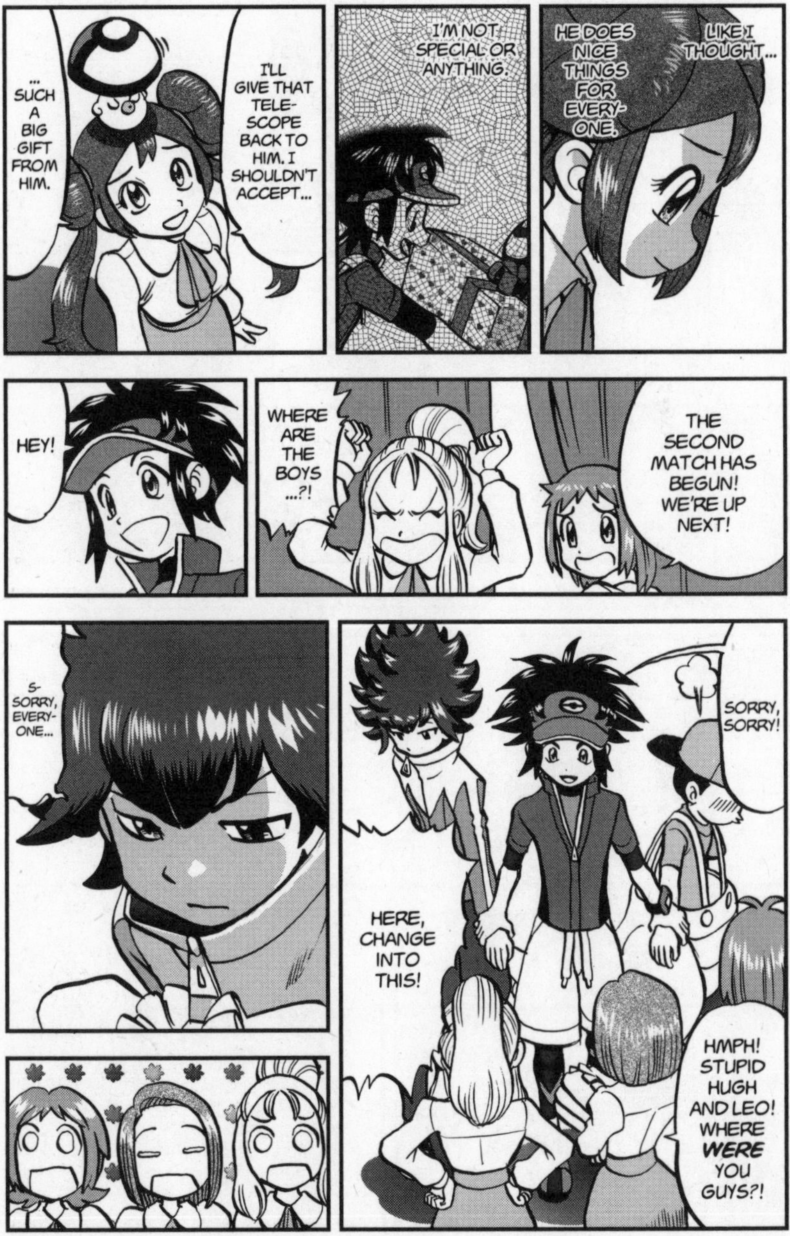
LIKE I THOUGHT...
HE DOES NICE THINGS FOR EVERY-ONE.
I'M NOT SPECIAL OR ANYTHING.
I'LL GIVE THAT TELE-SCOPE BACK TO HIM. I SHOULDN'T ACCEPT...
...SUCH A BIG GIFT FROM HIM.
THE SECOND MATCH HAS BEGUN! WE'RE UP NEXT!
WHERE ARE THE BOYS ...?!
HEY!
SORRY, SORRY!
HERE, CHANGE INTO THIS!
HMPH! STUPID HUGH AND LEO! WHERE **WERE** YOU GUYS?!
S-SORRY, EVERY-ONE...

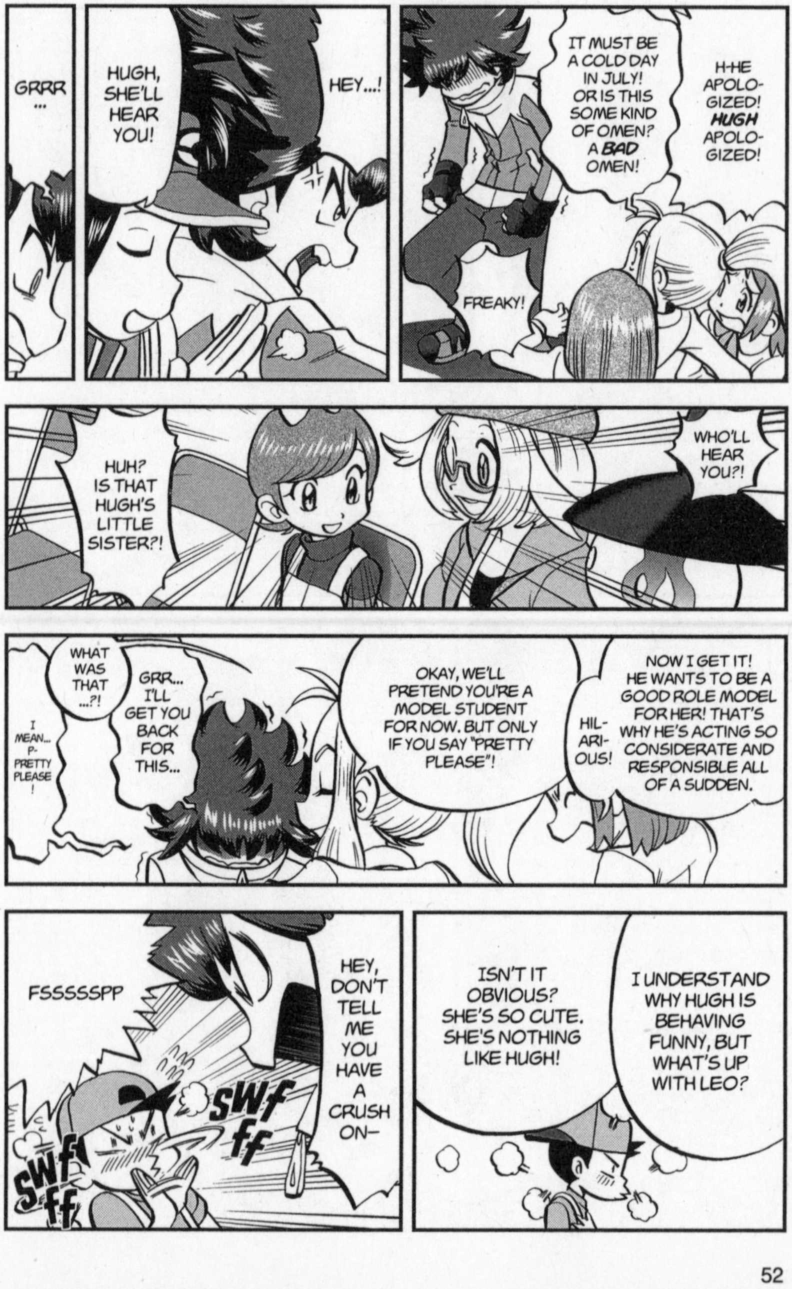
H-HE APOLOGIZED! HUGH APOLOGIZED!
IT MUST BE A COLD DAY IN JULY! OR IS THIS SOME KIND OF OMEN? A BAD OMEN!
FREAKY!
HEY...!
HUGH, SHE'LL HEAR YOU!
GRRR ...
WHO'LL HEAR YOU?!
HUH? IS THAT HUGH'S LITTLE SISTER?!
NOW I GET IT! HE WANTS TO BE A GOOD ROLE MODEL FOR HER! THAT'S WHY HE'S ACTING SO CONSIDERATE AND RESPONSIBLE ALL OF A SUDDEN.
HIL-ARI-OUS!
OKAY, WE'LL PRETEND YOU'RE A MODEL STUDENT FOR NOW. BUT ONLY IF YOU SAY "PRETTY PLEASE"!
GRR... I'LL GET YOU BACK FOR THIS...
WHAT WAS THAT ...?!
I MEAN... P-PRETTY PLEASE!
I UNDERSTAND WHY HUGH IS BEHAVING FUNNY, BUT WHAT'S UP WITH LEO?
ISN'T IT OBVIOUS? SHE'S SO CUTE. SHE'S NOTHING LIKE HUGH!
HEY, DON'T TELL ME YOU HAVE A CRUSH ON-
FSSSSSPP
SWF FF
SWF FF

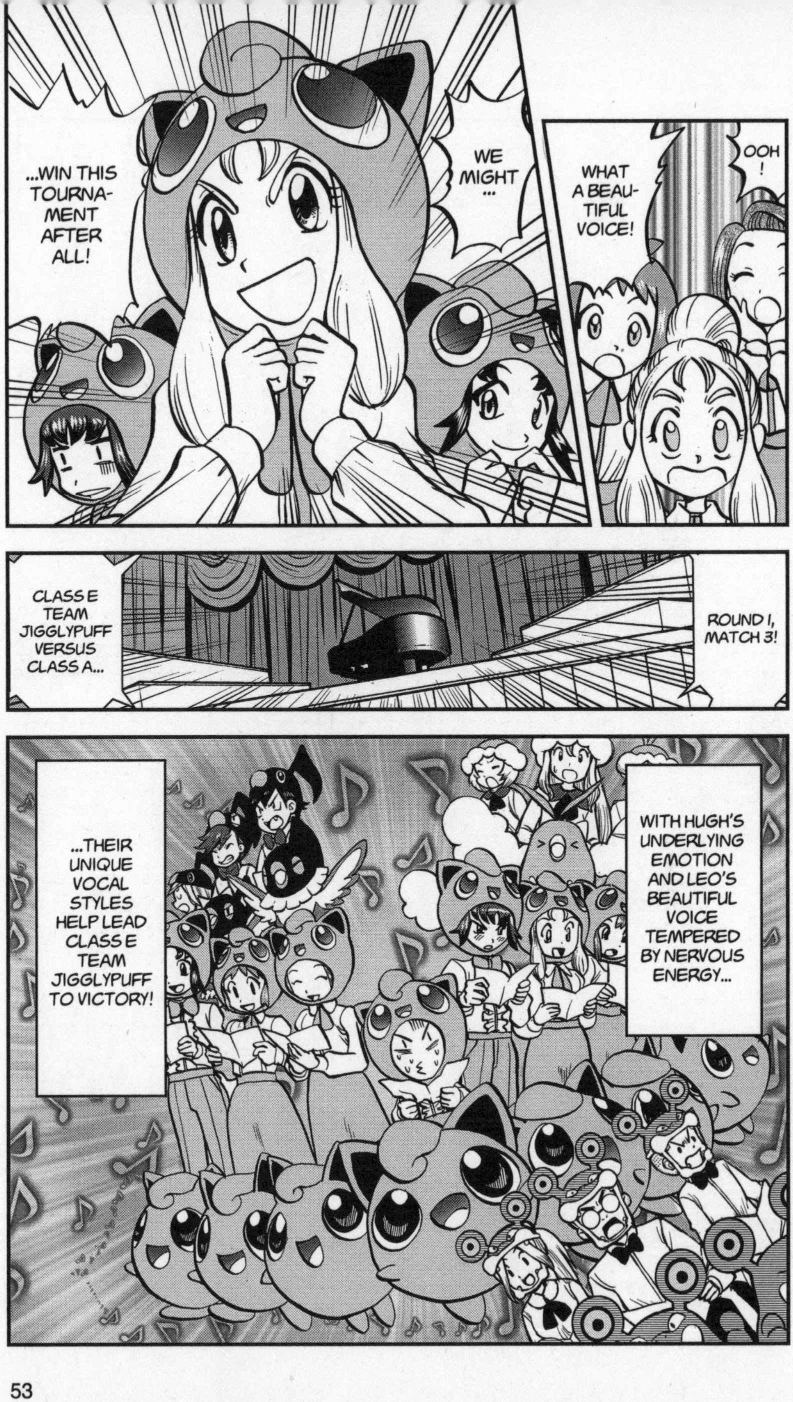
OOH!
WHAT A BEAUTIFUL VOICE!
WE MIGHT...
...WIN THIS TOURNAMENT AFTER ALL!
ROUND 1, MATCH 3!
CLASS E TEAM JIGGLYPUFF VERSUS CLASS A...
WITH HUGH'S UNDERLYING EMOTION AND LEO'S BEAUTIFUL VOICE TEMPERED BY NERVOUS ENERGY...
...THEIR UNIQUE VOCAL STYLES HELP LEAD CLASS E TEAM JIGGLYPUFF TO VICTORY!

THE FRONT RUNNER, CLASS C TEAM SAWSBUCK, VERSUS CLASS E TEAM JIGGLYPUFF!

A	B	C	D		E	A	B	C	D	E
1	1	1	1		2	3	3	3	3	3

...THE FINAL MATCH!

AND NOW FOR...

ON THE OTHER SIDE, TEAM JIGGLYPUFF WAS NEVER CONSIDERED TO BE A SERIOUS CONTENDER, BUT TO THE SURPRISE OF EVEN THEIR TEACHER MR. CHEREN, THEY HAVE BECOME UNSTOPPABLE!

TEAM SAWSBUCK'S MAGNIFICENT HARMONIES AND GRASS WHISTLE NOT ONLY PUT THEIR OPPONENTS TO SLEEP BUT SEND THE AUDIENCE AND JUDGES INTO A STATE OF SLUMBER AS WELL!

EXCUSE ME... TEAM JIGGLYPUFF WOULD LIKE TO ADD A RHYTHM INSTRUMENT FOR ACCOMPANIMENT.

...BUT I DON'T THINK WE'LL BE ABLE TO USE THE SAME TACTIC ON THEM AGAIN!

WE'VE MANAGED TO GET THIS FAR WITH JUST SING...

OH! BUT THEY AREN'T HOLDING ANYTHING IN THEIR HANDS. HOW WILL THEY...?

IN ADDITION TO PIANO AND GUITAR, RHYTHM INSTRUMENTS SUCH AS TRIANGLES, CASTANETS AND TAMBOURINES ARE ALLOWED.

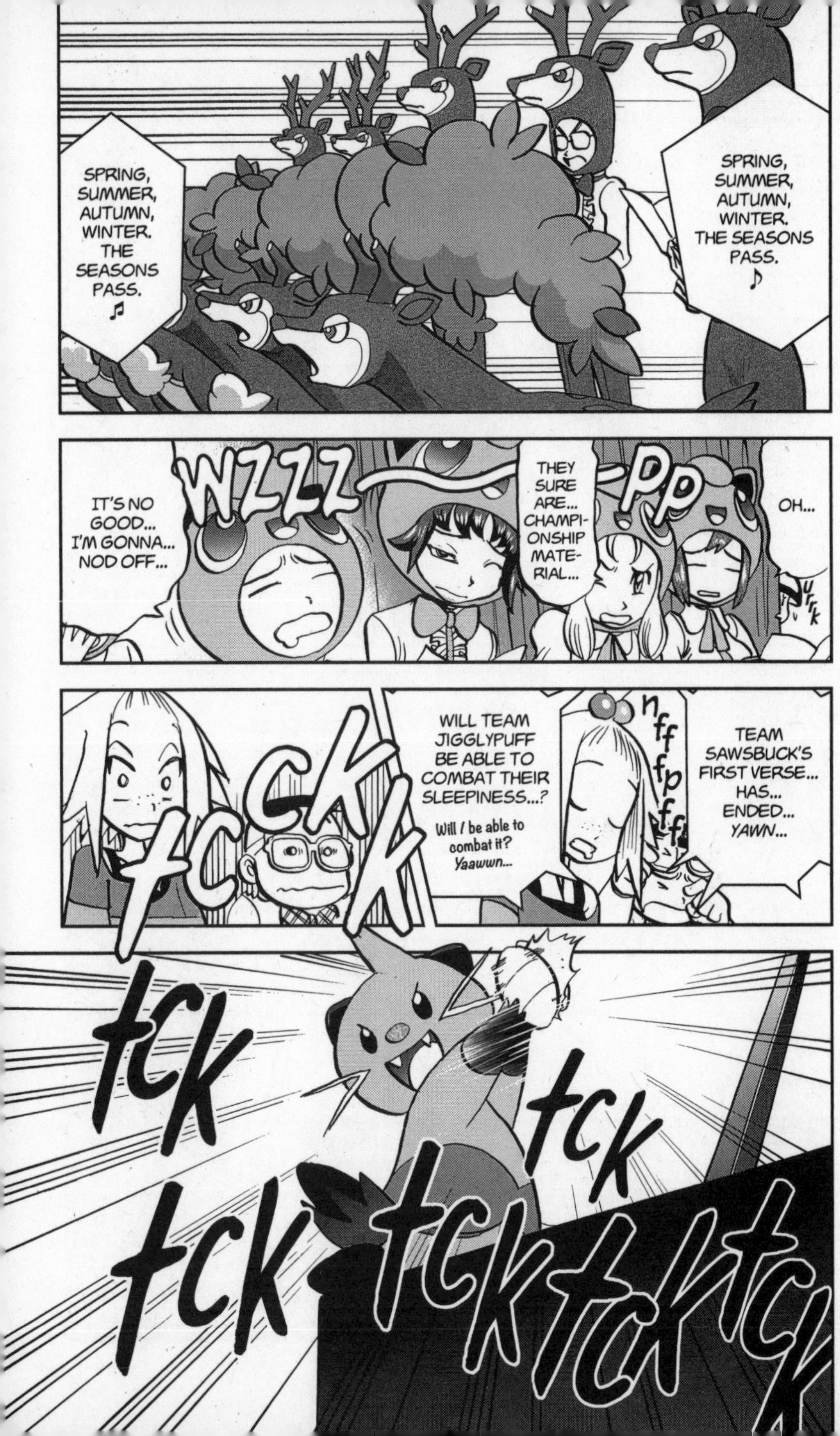
SPRING, SUMMER, AUTUMN, WINTER. THE SEASONS PASS. ♪
SPRING, SUMMER, AUTUMN, WINTER. THE SEASONS PASS. ♪
OH...
urrk
THEY SURE ARE... CHAMPIONSHIP MATERIAL...
WZZZ—Pp
IT'S NO GOOD... I'M GONNA... NOD OFF...
TEAM SAWSBUCK'S FIRST VERSE... HAS... ENDED... YAWN...
nffpff
WILL TEAM JIGGLYPUFF BE ABLE TO COMBAT THEIR SLEEPINESS...?
Will I be able to combat it? Yaawwn...
tcck
tck
tck
tck
tck
tck tck tck

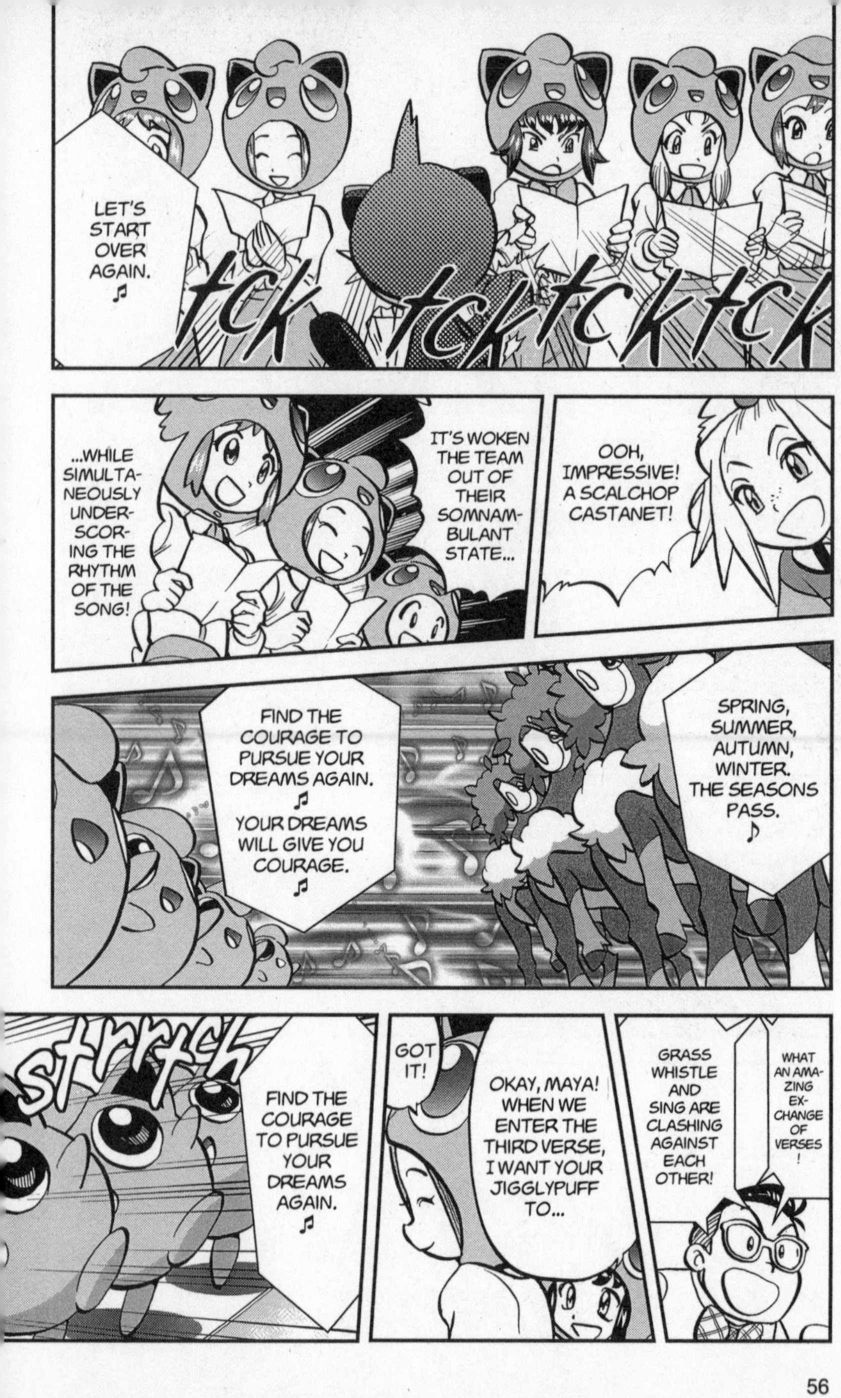
LET'S START OVER AGAIN. ♪
tck tcktcktck
OOH, IMPRESSIVE! A SCALCHOP CASTANET!
IT'S WOKEN THE TEAM OUT OF THEIR SOMNAMBULANT STATE...
...WHILE SIMULTANEOUSLY UNDERSCORING THE RHYTHM OF THE SONG!
SPRING, SUMMER, AUTUMN, WINTER. THE SEASONS PASS. ♪
FIND THE COURAGE TO PURSUE YOUR DREAMS AGAIN. ♪ YOUR DREAMS WILL GIVE YOU COURAGE. ♪
WHAT AN AMAZING EXCHANGE OF VERSES!
GRASS WHISTLE AND SING ARE CLASHING AGAINST EACH OTHER!
OKAY, MAYA! WHEN WE ENTER THE THIRD VERSE, I WANT YOUR JIGGLYPUFF TO...
GOT IT!
strrtch
FIND THE COURAGE TO PURSUE YOUR DREAMS AGAIN. ♪

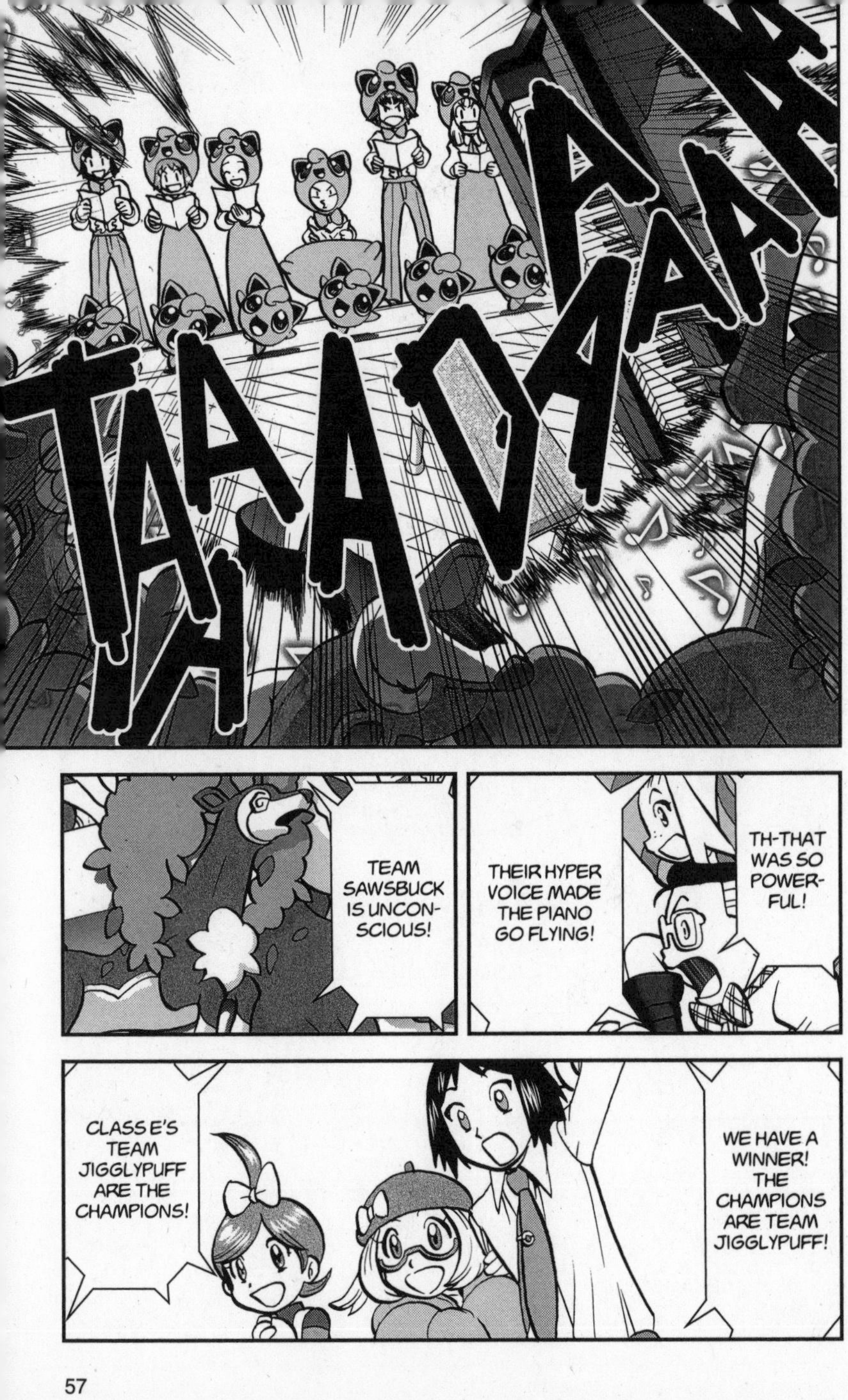
TAAADAAAAH!
TH-THAT WAS SO POWER-FUL!
THEIR HYPER VOICE MADE THE PIANO GO FLYING!
TEAM SAWSBUCK IS UNCONSCIOUS!
WE HAVE A WINNER! THE CHAMPIONS ARE TEAM JIGGLYPUFF!
CLASS E'S TEAM JIGGLYPUFF ARE THE CHAMPIONS!

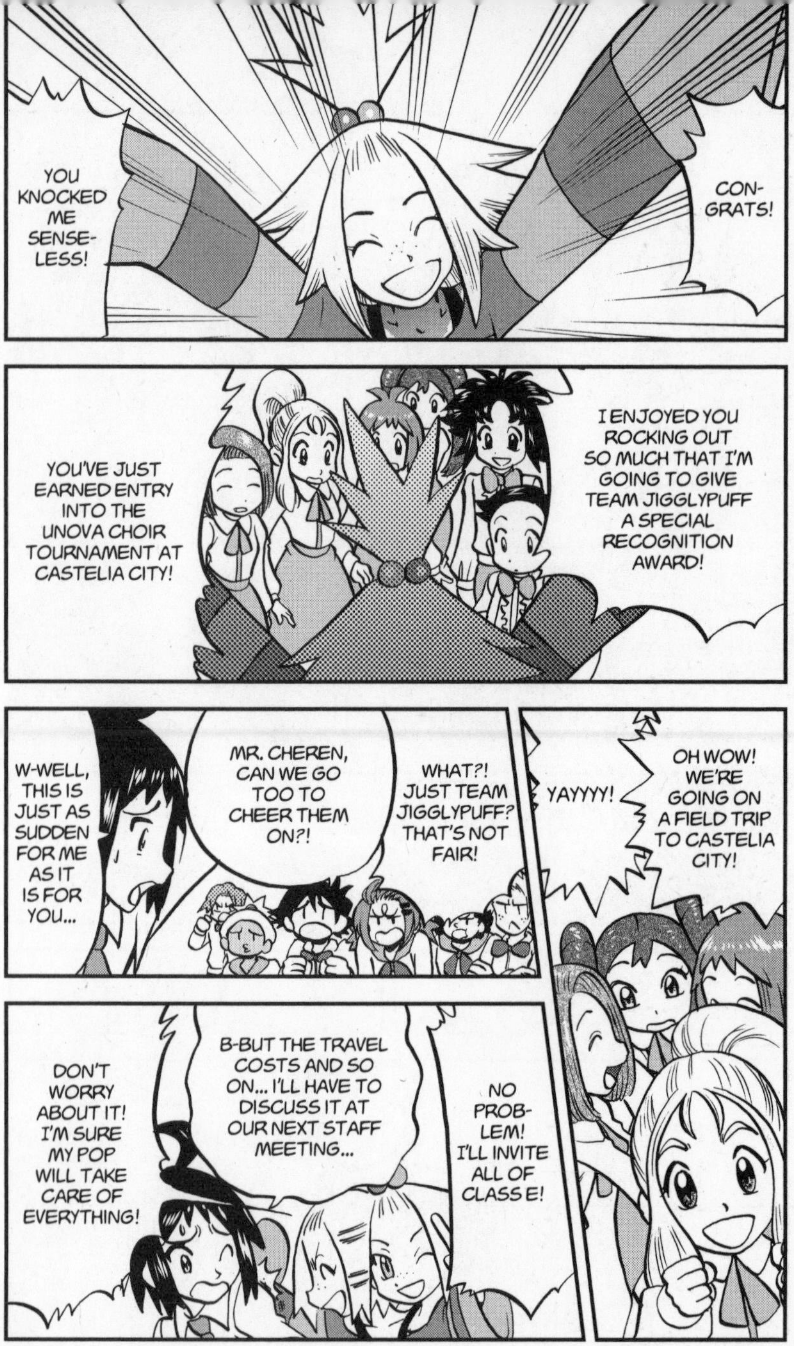
CON-GRATS!
YOU KNOCKED ME SENSE-LESS!
I ENJOYED YOU ROCKING OUT SO MUCH THAT I'M GOING TO GIVE TEAM JIGGLYPUFF A SPECIAL RECOGNITION AWARD!
YOU'VE JUST EARNED ENTRY INTO THE UNOVA CHOIR TOURNAMENT AT CASTELIA CITY!
OH WOW! WE'RE GOING ON A FIELD TRIP TO CASTELIA CITY!
YAYYYY!
WHAT?! JUST TEAM JIGGLYPUFF? THAT'S NOT FAIR!
MR. CHEREN, CAN WE GO TOO TO CHEER THEM ON?!
W-WELL, THIS IS JUST AS SUDDEN FOR ME AS IT IS FOR YOU...
NO PROB-LEM! I'LL INVITE ALL OF CLASS E!
B-BUT THE TRAVEL COSTS AND SO ON... I'LL HAVE TO DISCUSS IT AT OUR NEXT STAFF MEETING...
DON'T WORRY ABOUT IT! I'M SURE MY POP WILL TAKE CARE OF EVERYTHING!

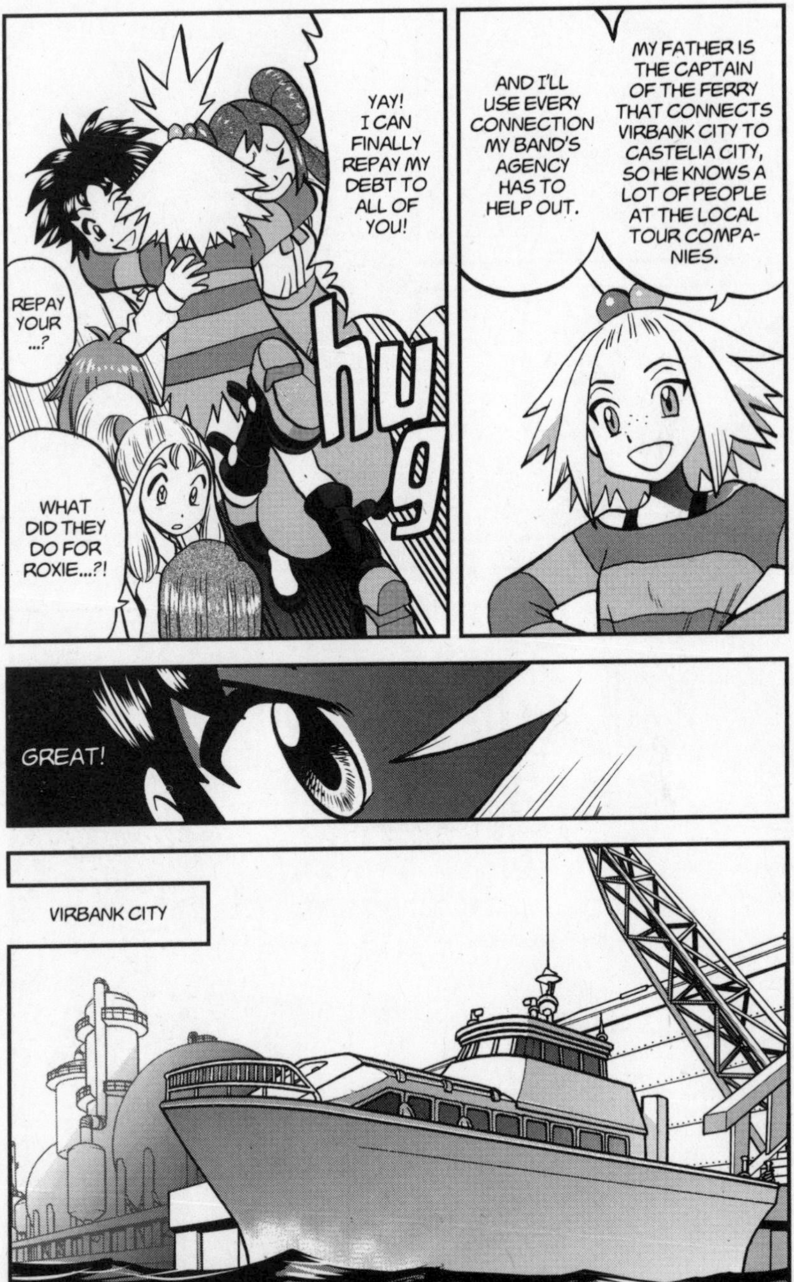
MY FATHER IS THE CAPTAIN OF THE FERRY THAT CONNECTS VIRBANK CITY TO CASTELIA CITY, SO HE KNOWS A LOT OF PEOPLE AT THE LOCAL TOUR COMPA-NIES.
AND I'LL USE EVERY CONNECTION MY BAND'S AGENCY HAS TO HELP OUT.
YAY! I CAN FINALLY REPAY MY DEBT TO ALL OF YOU!
hug
REPAY YOUR ...?
WHAT DID THEY DO FOR ROXIE...?!
GREAT!
VIRBANK CITY

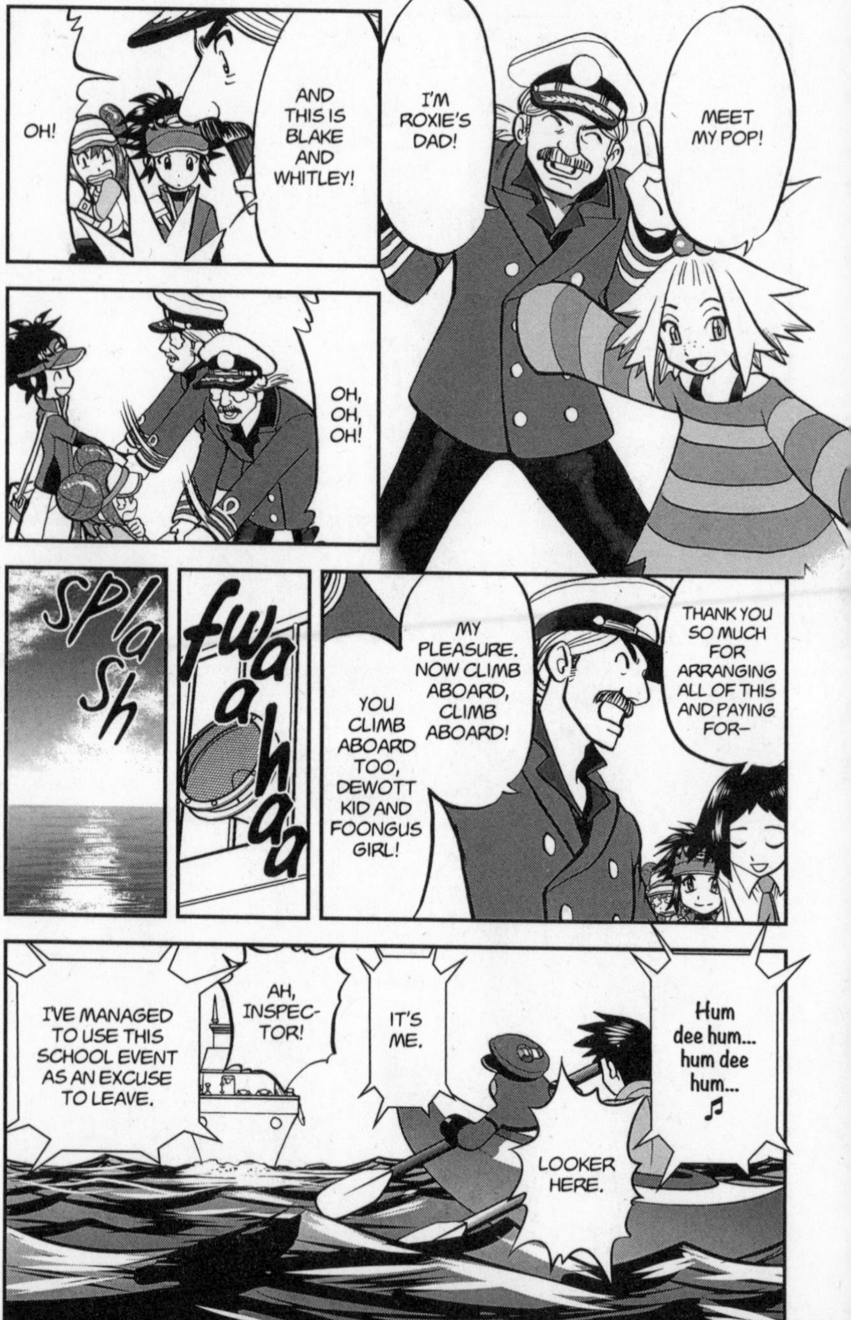
MEET MY POP!
I'M ROXIE'S DAD!
AND THIS IS BLAKE AND WHITLEY!
OH!
OH, OH, OH!
THANK YOU SO MUCH FOR ARRANGING ALL OF THIS AND PAYING FOR–
MY PLEASURE. NOW CLIMB ABOARD, CLIMB ABOARD!
YOU CLIMB ABOARD TOO, DEWOTT KID AND FOONGUS GIRL!
fwaahaa
SPLaSh
Hum dee hum... hum dee hum... ♪
LOOKER HERE.
IT'S ME.
AH, INSPECTOR!
I'VE MANAGED TO USE THIS SCHOOL EVENT AS AN EXCUSE TO LEAVE.

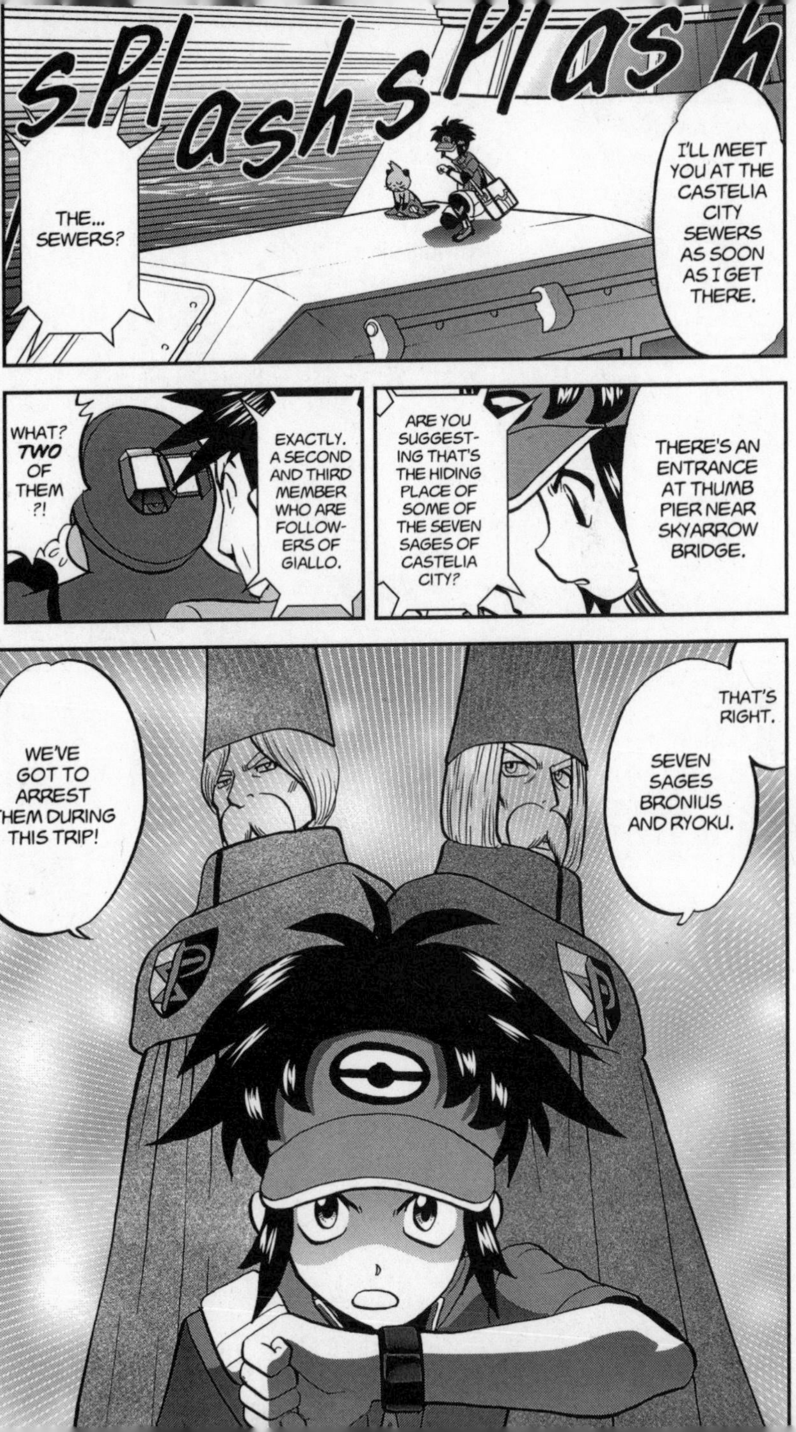
SPLASHSPLASH
I'LL MEET YOU AT THE CASTELIA CITY SEWERS AS SOON AS I GET THERE.
THE... SEWERS?
THERE'S AN ENTRANCE AT THUMB PIER NEAR SKYARROW BRIDGE.
ARE YOU SUGGESTING THAT'S THE HIDING PLACE OF SOME OF THE SEVEN SAGES OF CASTELIA CITY?
EXACTLY. A SECOND AND THIRD MEMBER WHO ARE FOLLOWERS OF GIALLO.
WHAT? *TWO* OF THEM?!
THAT'S RIGHT.
SEVEN SAGES BRONIUS AND RYOKU.
WE'VE GOT TO ARREST THEM DURING THIS TRIP!

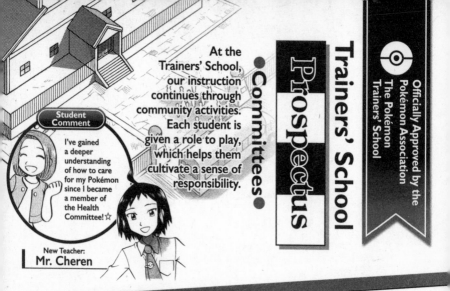

Officially Approved by the Pokémon Association
The Pokémon Trainers' School

Trainers' School Prospectus

●Committees●

Student Comment
I've gained a deeper understanding of how to care for my Pokémon since I became a member of the Health Committee!☆
New Teacher:
Mr. Cheren

At the Trainers' School, our instruction continues through community activities. Each student is given a role to play, which helps them cultivate a sense of responsibility.

■ Major Activities of the Various Committees ■

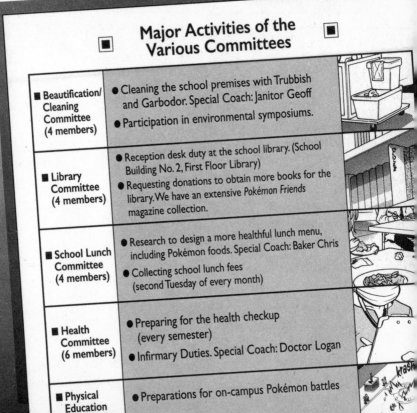

■ Beautification/ Cleaning Committee (4 members)	● Cleaning the school premises with Trubbish and Garbodor. Special Coach: Janitor Geoff ● Participation in environmental symposiums.
■ Library Committee (4 members)	● Reception desk duty at the school library. (School Building No. 2, First Floor Library) ● Requesting donations to obtain more books for the library. We have an extensive *Pokémon Friends* magazine collection.
■ School Lunch Committee (4 members)	● Research to design a more healthful lunch menu, including Pokémon foods. Special Coach: Baker Chris ● Collecting school lunch fees (second Tuesday of every month)
■ Health Committee (6 members)	● Preparing for the health checkup (every semester) ● Infirmary Duties. Special Coach: Doctor Logan
■ Physical Education	● Preparations for on-campus Pokémon battles

krash

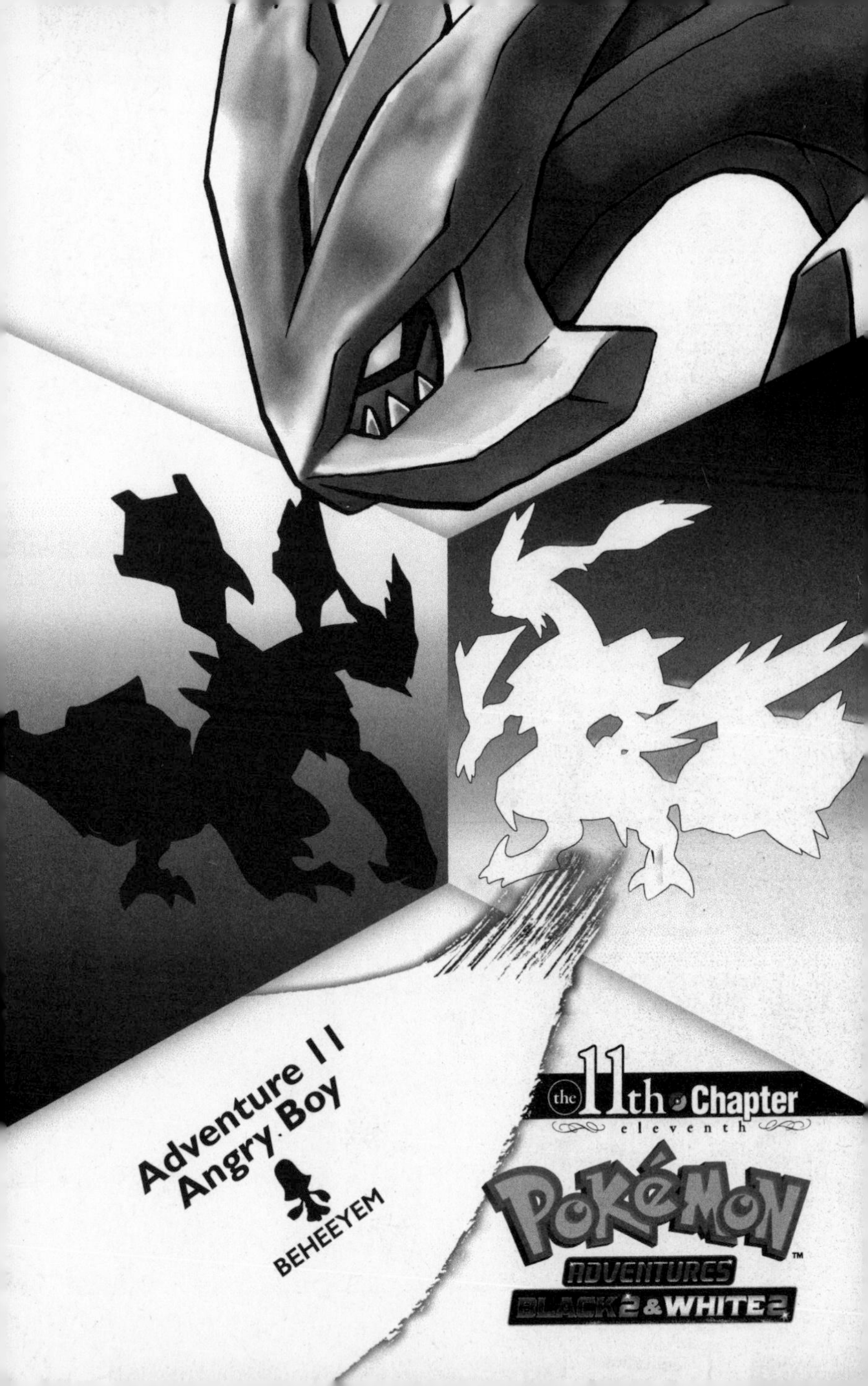

Adventure 11
Angry Boy
BEHEEYEM
the 11th Chapter
eleventh
POKÉMON™
ADVENTURES
BLACK 2 & WHITE 2

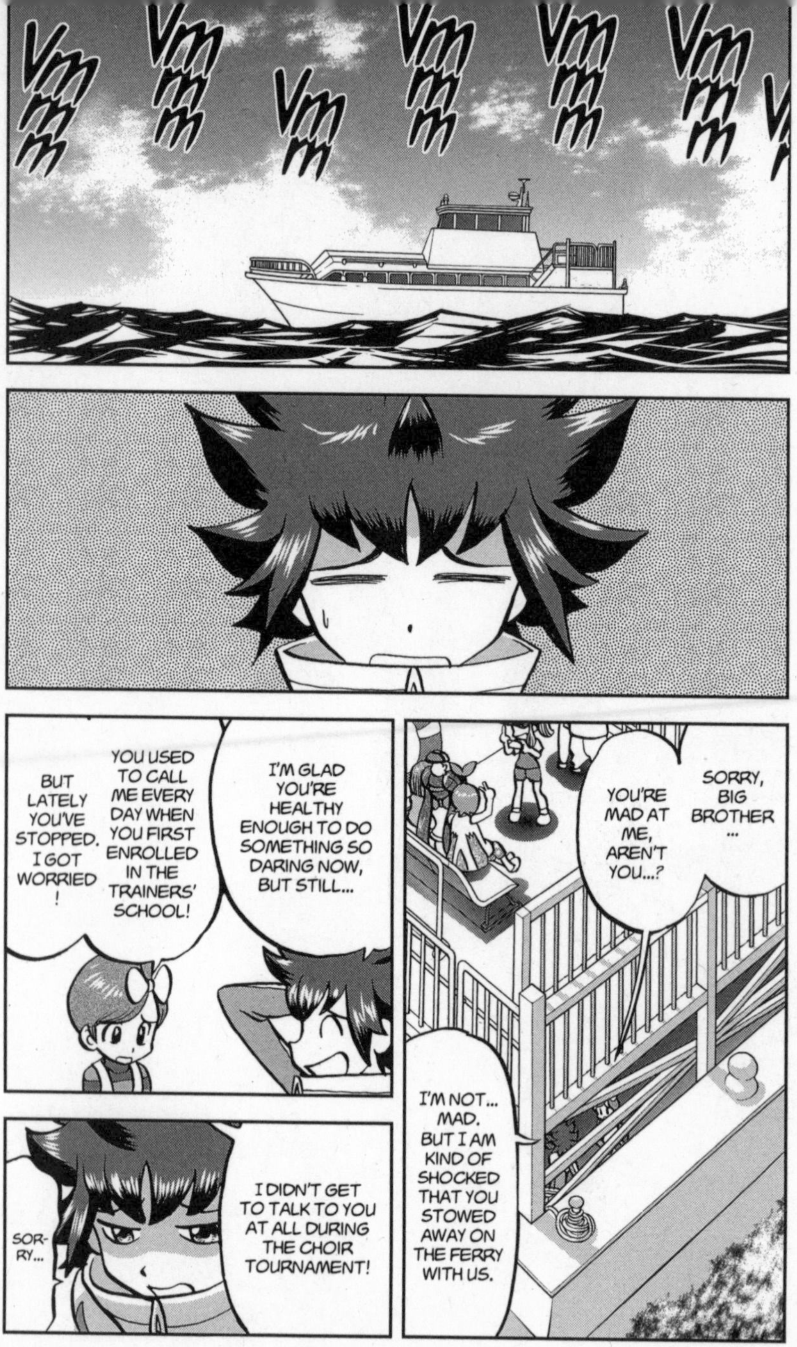
Vmmm
Vmmm
Vmmm
Vmmm
Vmmm
Vmmm
SORRY, BIG BROTHER...
YOU'RE MAD AT ME, AREN'T YOU...?
I'M NOT... MAD. BUT I AM KIND OF SHOCKED THAT YOU STOWED AWAY ON THE FERRY WITH US.
I'M GLAD YOU'RE HEALTHY ENOUGH TO DO SOMETHING SO DARING NOW, BUT STILL...
YOU USED TO CALL ME EVERY DAY WHEN YOU FIRST ENROLLED IN THE TRAINERS' SCHOOL!
BUT LATELY YOU'VE STOPPED. I GOT WORRIED!
I DIDN'T GET TO TALK TO YOU AT ALL DURING THE CHOIR TOURNAMENT!
SOR-RY...

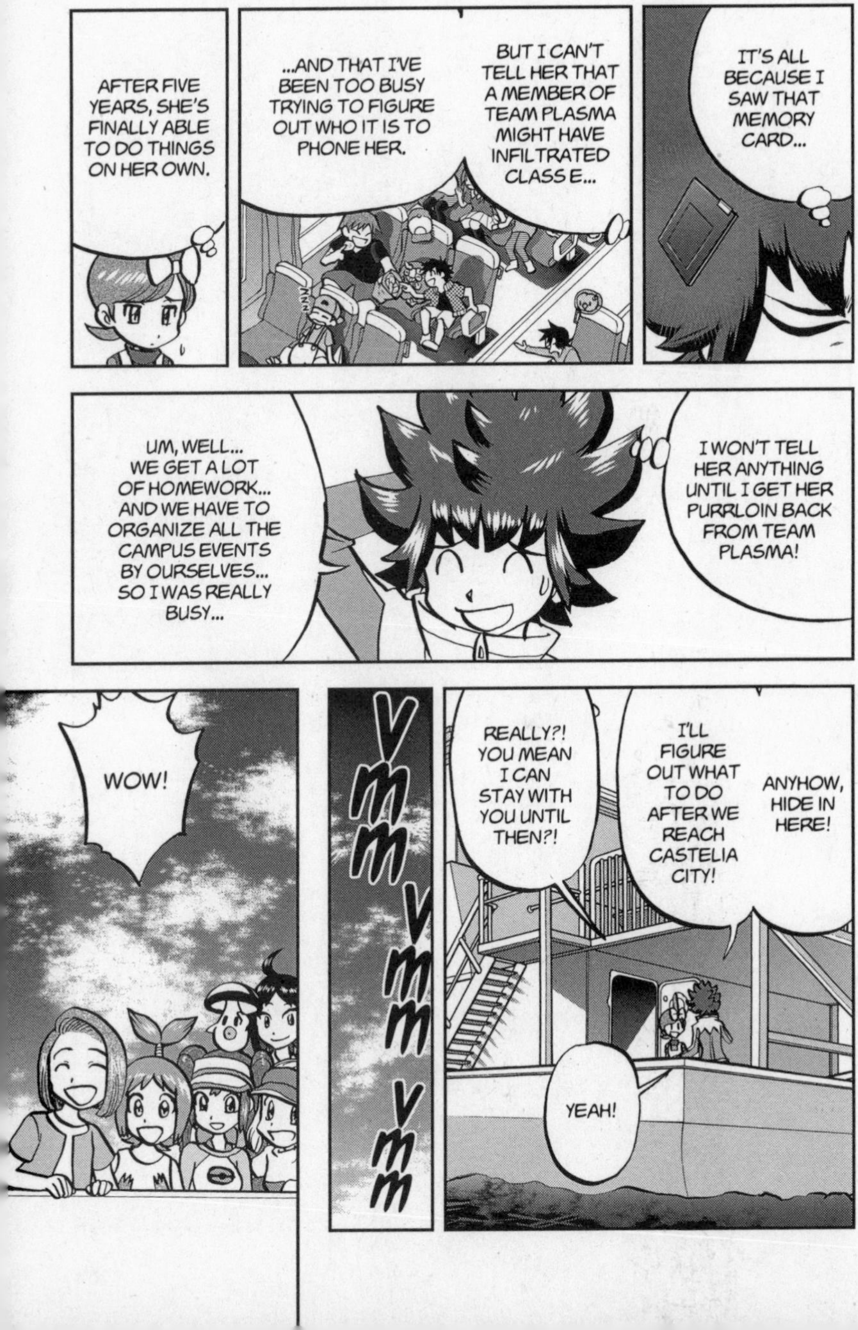
IT'S ALL BECAUSE I SAW THAT MEMORY CARD...
BUT I CAN'T TELL HER THAT A MEMBER OF TEAM PLASMA MIGHT HAVE INFILTRATED CLASS E...
...AND THAT I'VE BEEN TOO BUSY TRYING TO FIGURE OUT WHO IT IS TO PHONE HER.
AFTER FIVE YEARS, SHE'S FINALLY ABLE TO DO THINGS ON HER OWN.
I WON'T TELL HER ANYTHING UNTIL I GET HER PURRLOIN BACK FROM TEAM PLASMA!
UM, WELL... WE GET A LOT OF HOMEWORK... AND WE HAVE TO ORGANIZE ALL THE CAMPUS EVENTS BY OURSELVES... SO I WAS REALLY BUSY...
ANYHOW, HIDE IN HERE!
I'LL FIGURE OUT WHAT TO DO AFTER WE REACH CASTELIA CITY!
REALLY?! YOU MEAN I CAN STAY WITH YOU UNTIL THEN?!
YEAH!
VMM VMM VMM
WOW!

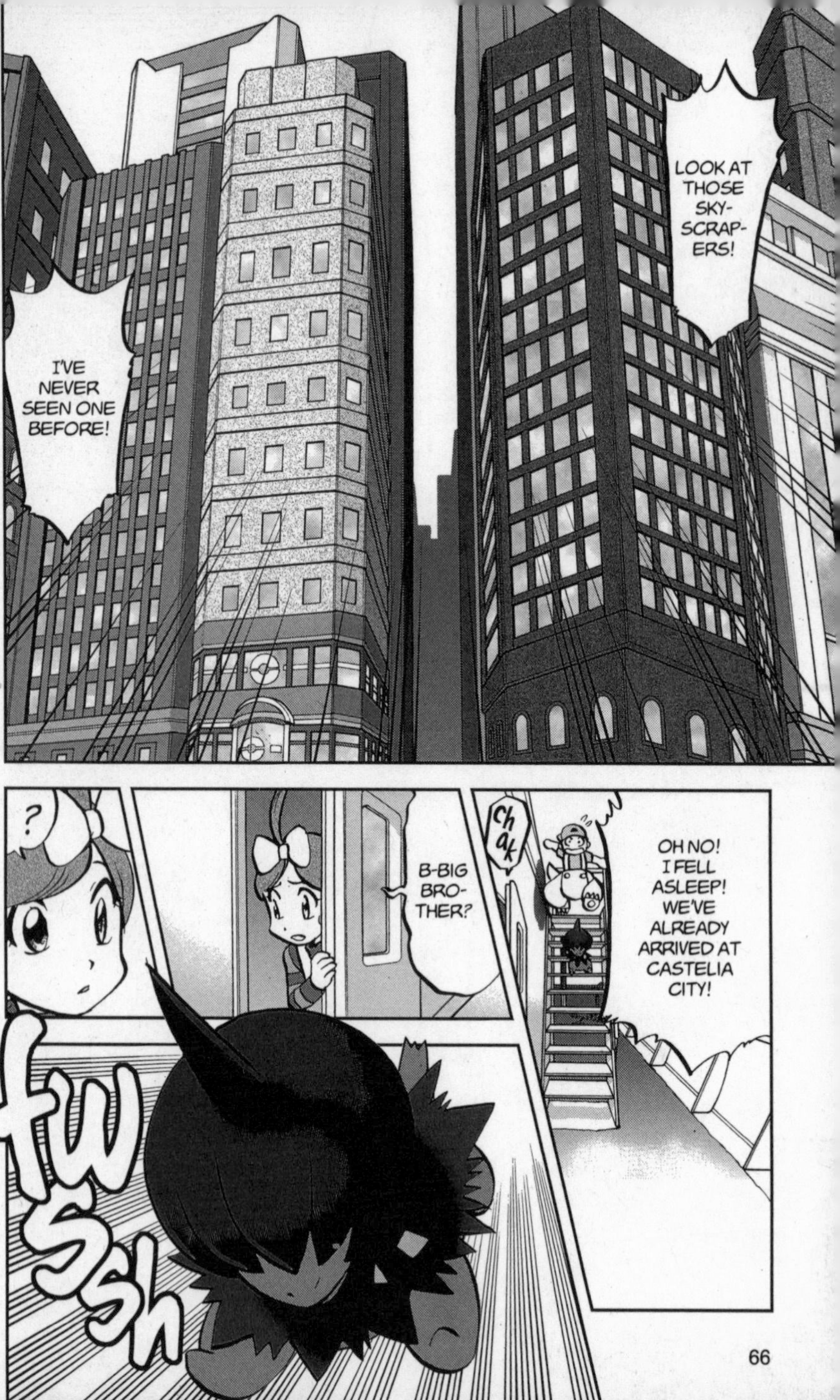
LOOK AT THOSE SKY-SCRAPERS!
I'VE NEVER SEEN ONE BEFORE!
Chak
OH NO! I FELL ASLEEP! WE'VE ALREADY ARRIVED AT CASTELIA CITY!
B-BIG BRO-THER?
?
fwssh

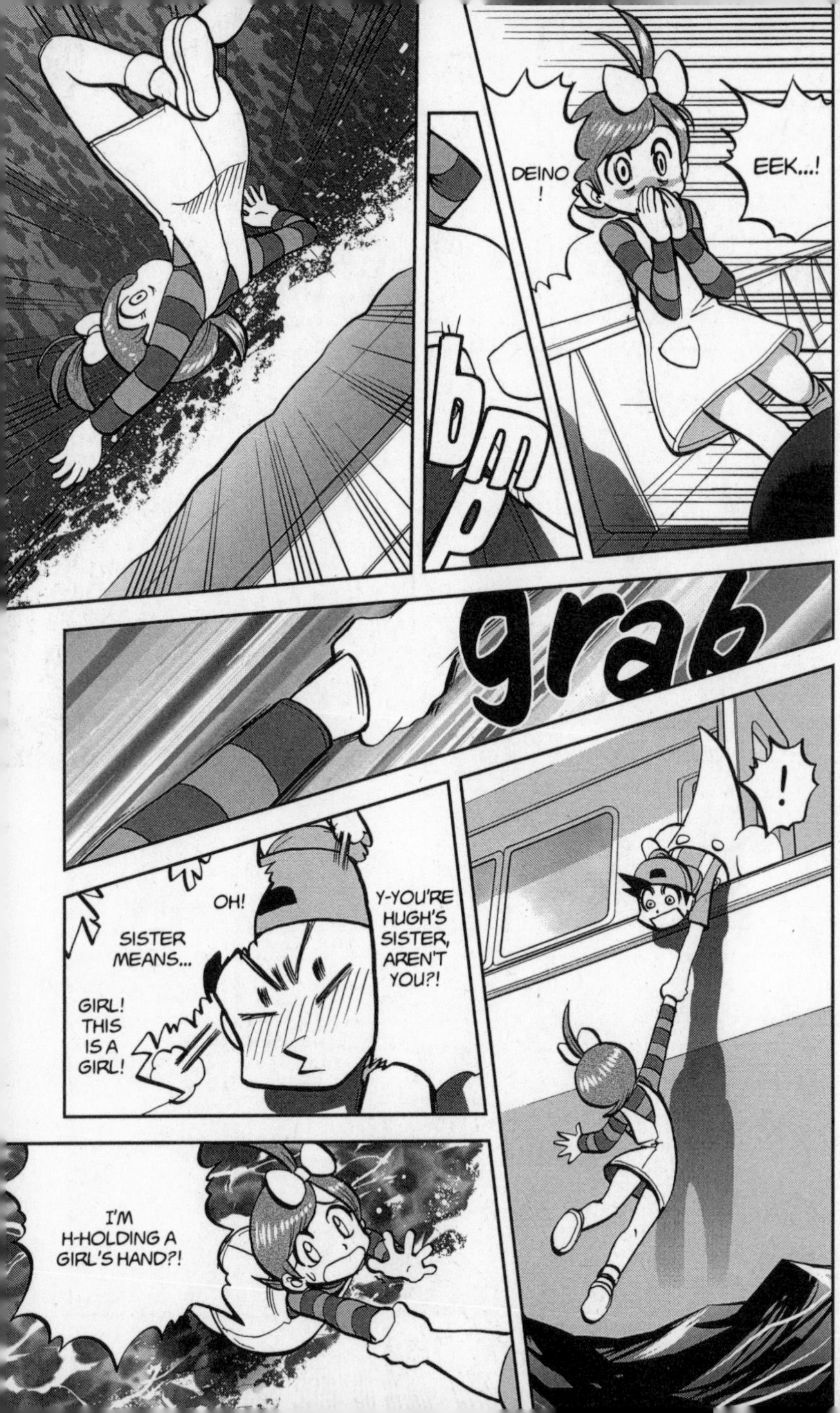
EEK...!
DEINO!
bmp
grab
!
Y-YOU'RE HUGH'S SISTER, AREN'T YOU?!
OH!
SISTER MEANS...
GIRL! THIS IS A GIRL!
I'M H-HOLDING A GIRL'S HAND?!

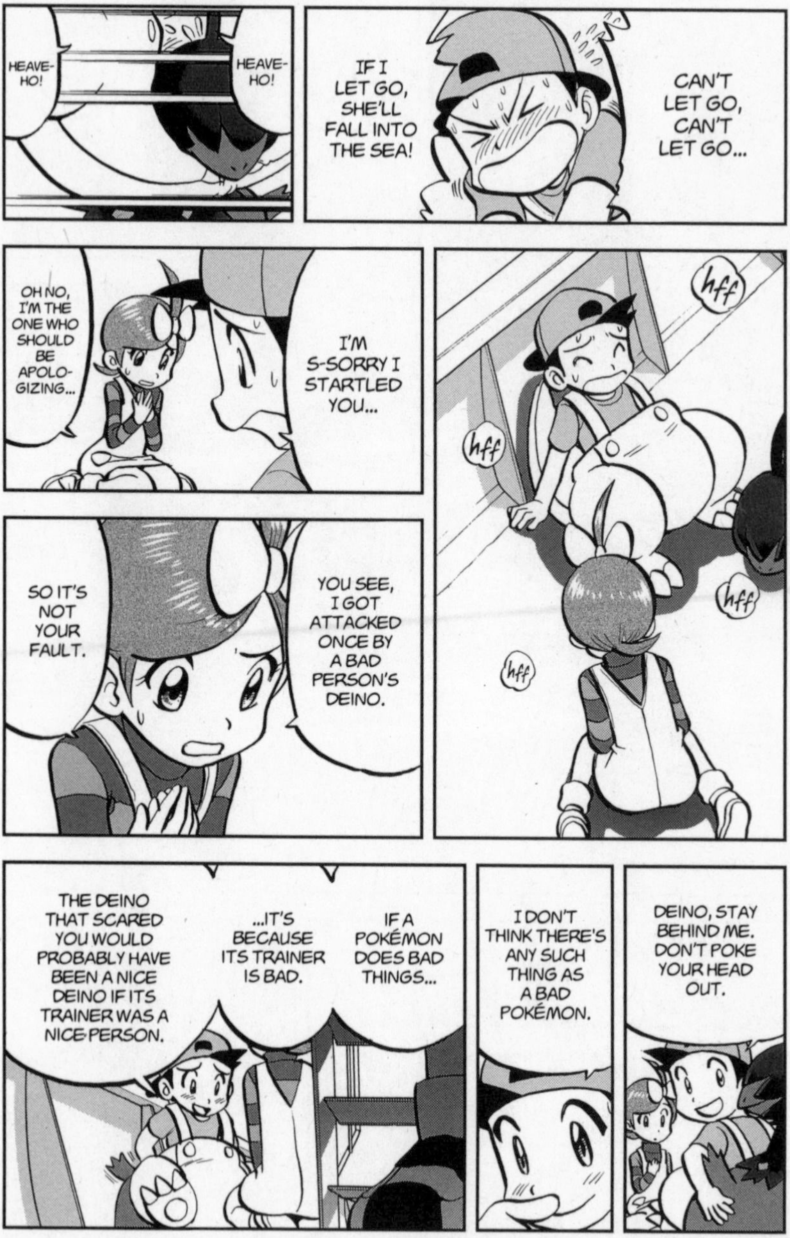
CAN'T LET GO, CAN'T LET GO...
IF I LET GO, SHE'LL FALL INTO THE SEA!
HEAVE-HO!
HEAVE-HO!
hff
hff
hff
hff
I'M S-SORRY I STARTLED YOU...
OH NO, I'M THE ONE WHO SHOULD BE APOLOGIZING...
YOU SEE, I GOT ATTACKED ONCE BY A BAD PERSON'S DEINO.
SO IT'S NOT YOUR FAULT.
DEINO, STAY BEHIND ME. DON'T POKE YOUR HEAD OUT.
I DON'T THINK THERE'S ANY SUCH THING AS A BAD POKÉMON.
IF A POKÉMON DOES BAD THINGS...
...IT'S BECAUSE ITS TRAINER IS BAD.
THE DEINO THAT SCARED YOU WOULD PROBABLY HAVE BEEN A NICE DEINO IF ITS TRAINER WAS A NICE PERSON.

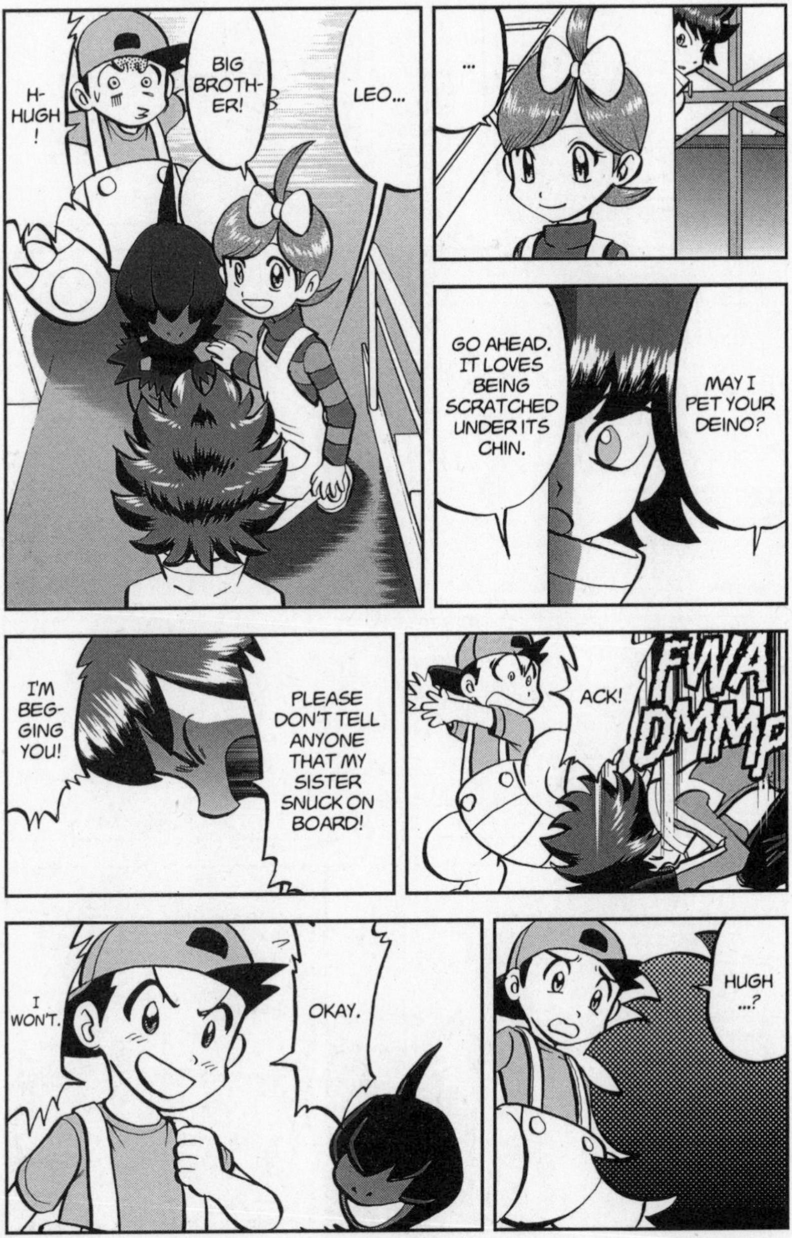
...
MAY I PET YOUR DEINO?
GO AHEAD. IT LOVES BEING SCRATCHED UNDER ITS CHIN.
LEO...
BIG BROTHER!
H-HUGH!
FWADMMP
ACK!
PLEASE DON'T TELL ANYONE THAT MY SISTER SNUCK ON BOARD!
I'M BEGGING YOU!
HUGH...?
OKAY.
I WON'T.

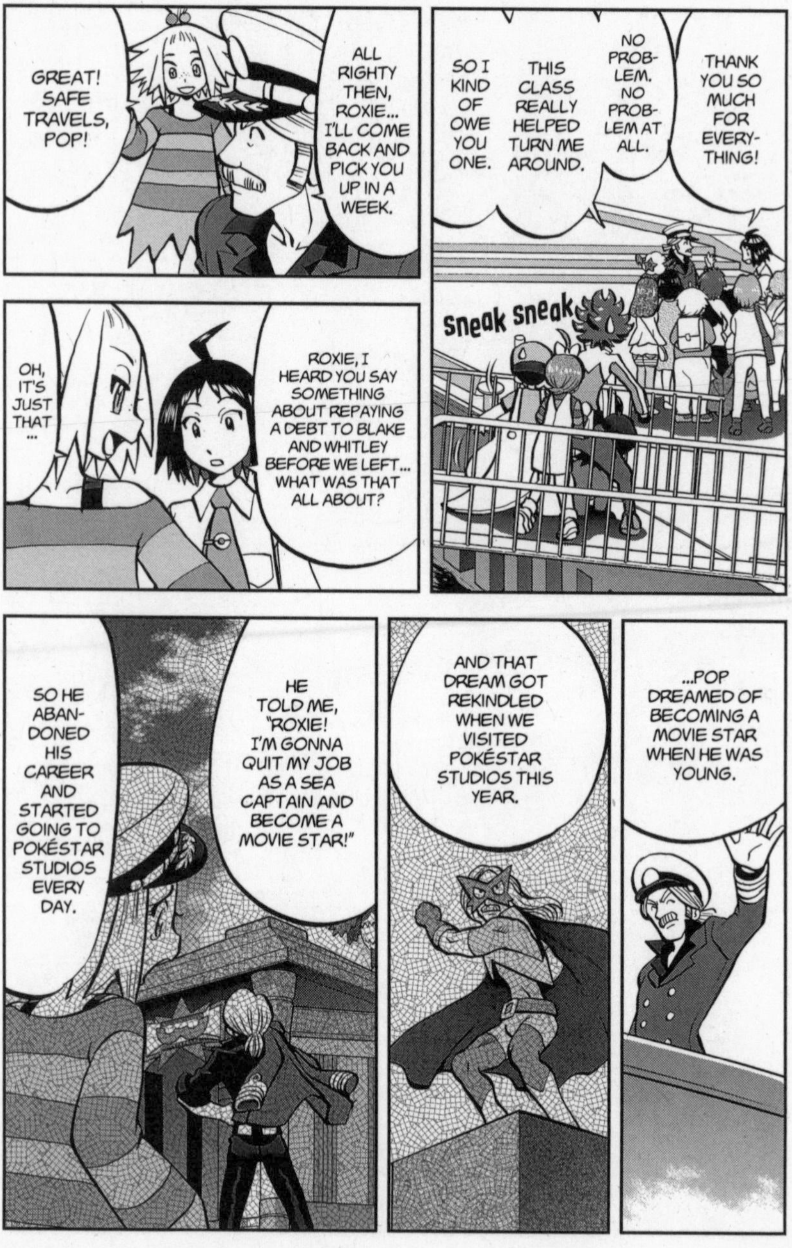
THANK YOU SO MUCH FOR EVERYTHING!
NO PROBLEM. NO PROBLEM AT ALL.
THIS CLASS REALLY HELPED TURN ME AROUND.
SO I KIND OF OWE YOU ONE.
Sneak Sneak
ALL RIGHTY THEN, ROXIE... I'LL COME BACK AND PICK YOU UP IN A WEEK.
GREAT! SAFE TRAVELS, POP!
ROXIE, I HEARD YOU SAY SOMETHING ABOUT REPAYING A DEBT TO BLAKE AND WHITLEY BEFORE WE LEFT... WHAT WAS THAT ALL ABOUT?
OH, IT'S JUST THAT ...
...POP DREAMED OF BECOMING A MOVIE STAR WHEN HE WAS YOUNG.
AND THAT DREAM GOT REKINDLED WHEN WE VISITED POKÉSTAR STUDIOS THIS YEAR.
HE TOLD ME, "ROXIE! I'M GONNA QUIT MY JOB AS A SEA CAPTAIN AND BECOME A MOVIE STAR!"
SO HE ABANDONED HIS CAREER AND STARTED GOING TO POKÉSTAR STUDIOS EVERY DAY.

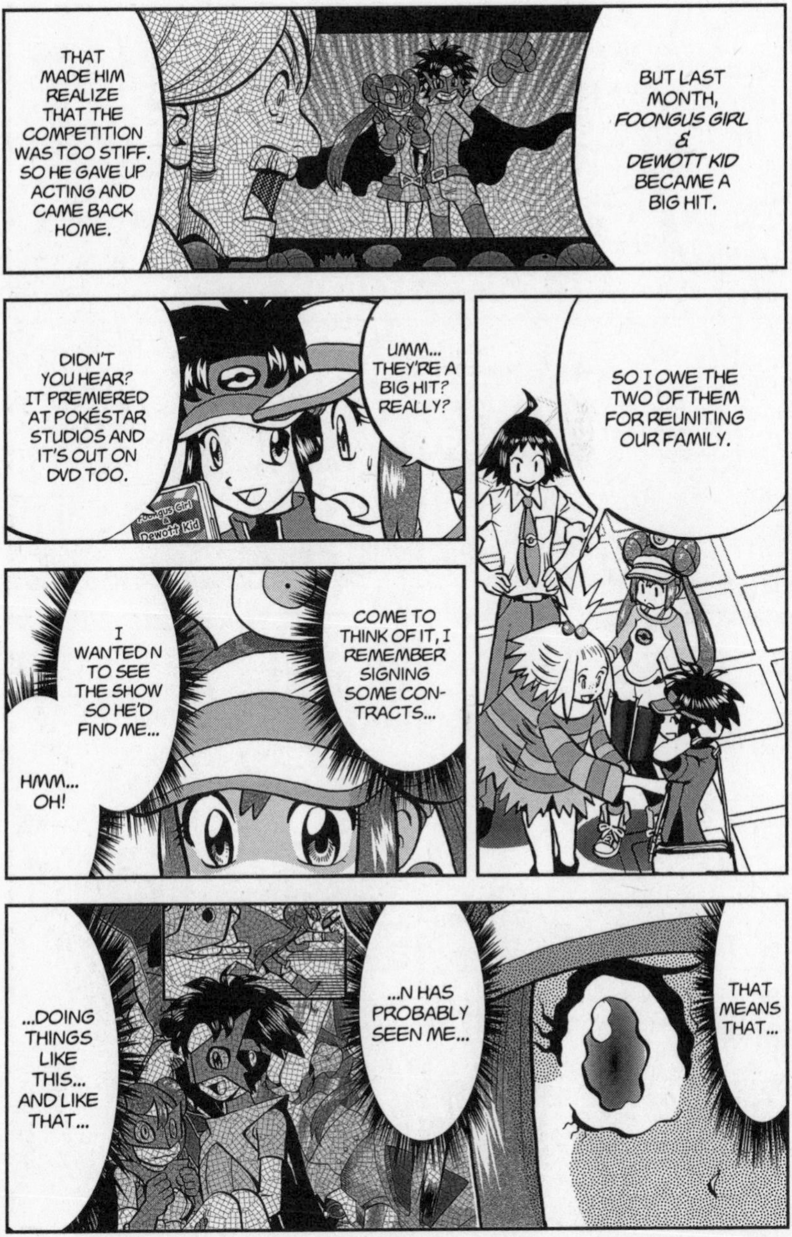
BUT LAST MONTH, FOONGUS GIRL & DEWOTT KID BECAME A BIG HIT.
THAT MADE HIM REALIZE THAT THE COMPETITION WAS TOO STIFF. SO HE GAVE UP ACTING AND CAME BACK HOME.
SO I OWE THE TWO OF THEM FOR REUNITING OUR FAMILY.
UMM... THEY'RE A BIG HIT? REALLY?
DIDN'T YOU HEAR? IT PREMIERED AT POKÉSTAR STUDIOS AND IT'S OUT ON DVD TOO.
Foongus Girl & Dewott Kid
COME TO THINK OF IT, I REMEMBER SIGNING SOME CON-TRACTS...
I WANTED N TO SEE THE SHOW SO HE'D FIND ME...
HMM... OH!
THAT MEANS THAT...
...N HAS PROBABLY SEEN ME...
...DOING THINGS LIKE THIS... AND LIKE THAT...

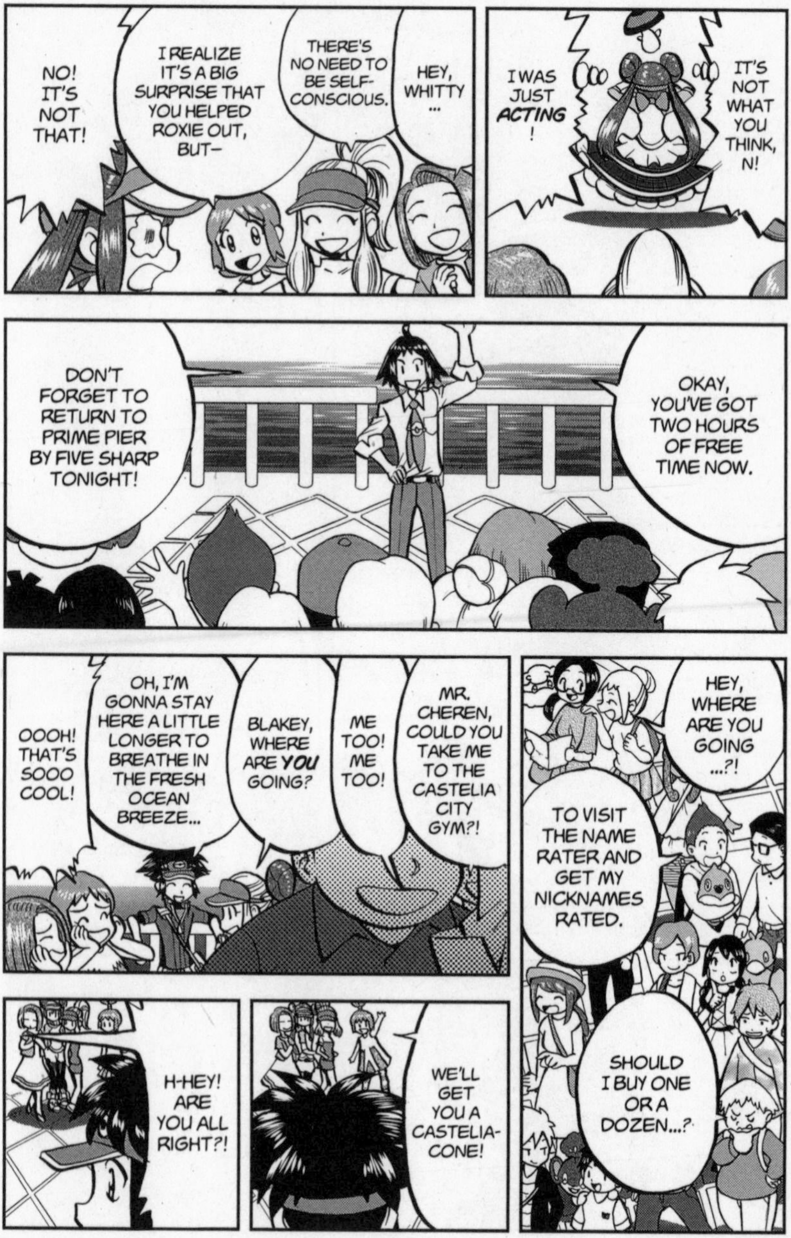
IT'S NOT WHAT YOU THINK, N!
I WAS JUST *ACTING*!
HEY, WHITTY...
THERE'S NO NEED TO BE SELF-CONSCIOUS.
I REALIZE IT'S A BIG SURPRISE THAT YOU HELPED ROXIE OUT, BUT–
NO! IT'S NOT THAT!
OKAY, YOU'VE GOT TWO HOURS OF FREE TIME NOW.
DON'T FORGET TO RETURN TO PRIME PIER BY FIVE SHARP TONIGHT!
HEY, WHERE ARE YOU GOING...?!
TO VISIT THE NAME RATER AND GET MY NICKNAMES RATED.
SHOULD I BUY ONE OR A DOZEN...?
MR. CHEREN, COULD YOU TAKE ME TO THE CASTELIA CITY GYM?!
ME TOO! ME TOO!
BLAKEY, WHERE ARE *YOU* GOING?
OH, I'M GONNA STAY HERE A LITTLE LONGER TO BREATHE IN THE FRESH OCEAN BREEZE...
OOOH! THAT'S SOOO COOL!
WE'LL GET YOU A CASTELIA-CONE!
H-HEY! ARE YOU ALL RIGHT?!

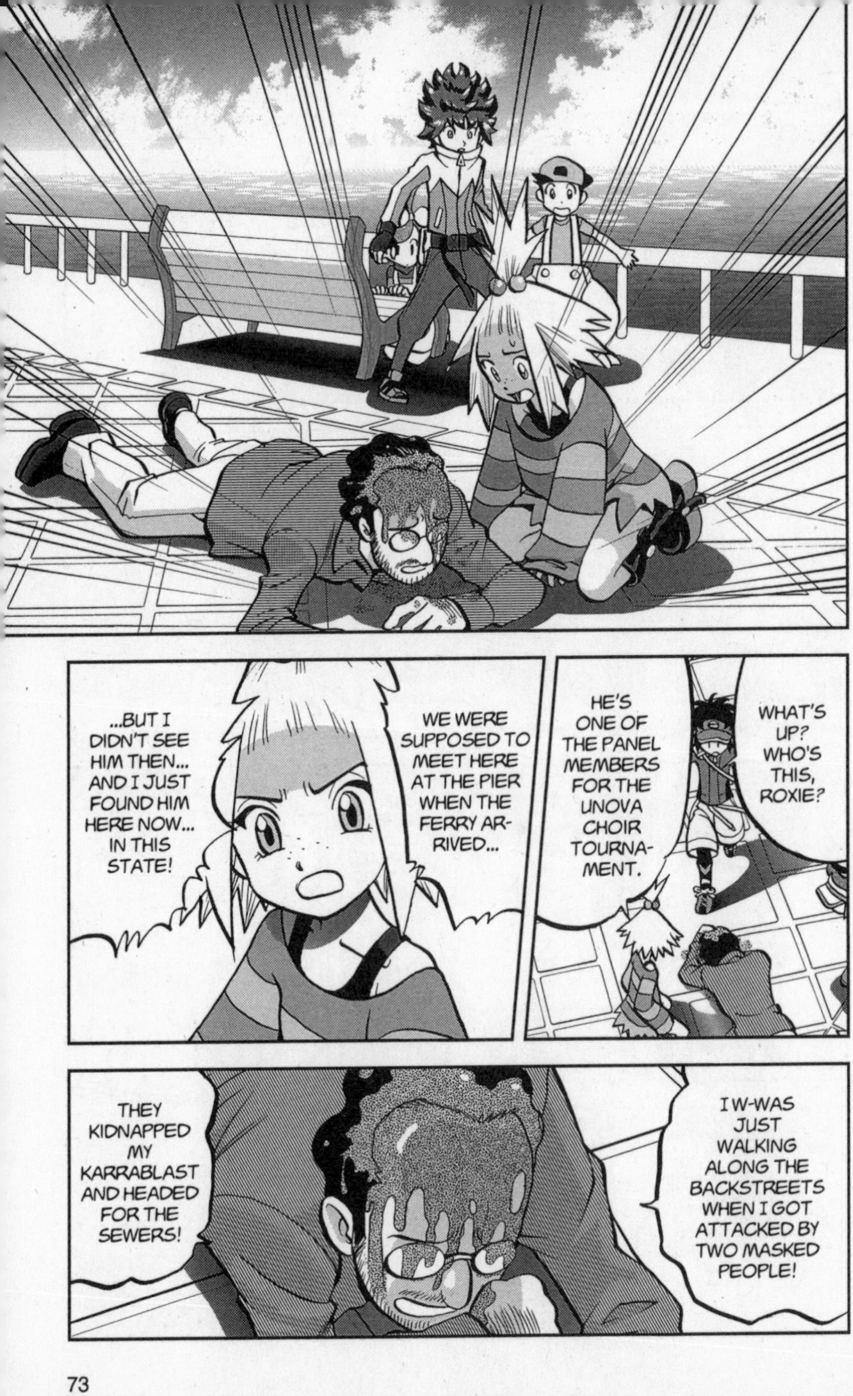
WHAT'S UP? WHO'S THIS, ROXIE?
HE'S ONE OF THE PANEL MEMBERS FOR THE UNOVA CHOIR TOURNAMENT.
WE WERE SUPPOSED TO MEET HERE AT THE PIER WHEN THE FERRY ARRIVED...
...BUT I DIDN'T SEE HIM THEN... AND I JUST FOUND HIM HERE NOW... IN THIS STATE!
I W-WAS JUST WALKING ALONG THE BACKSTREETS WHEN I GOT ATTACKED BY TWO MASKED PEOPLE!
THEY KIDNAPPED MY KARRABLAST AND HEADED FOR THE SEWERS!

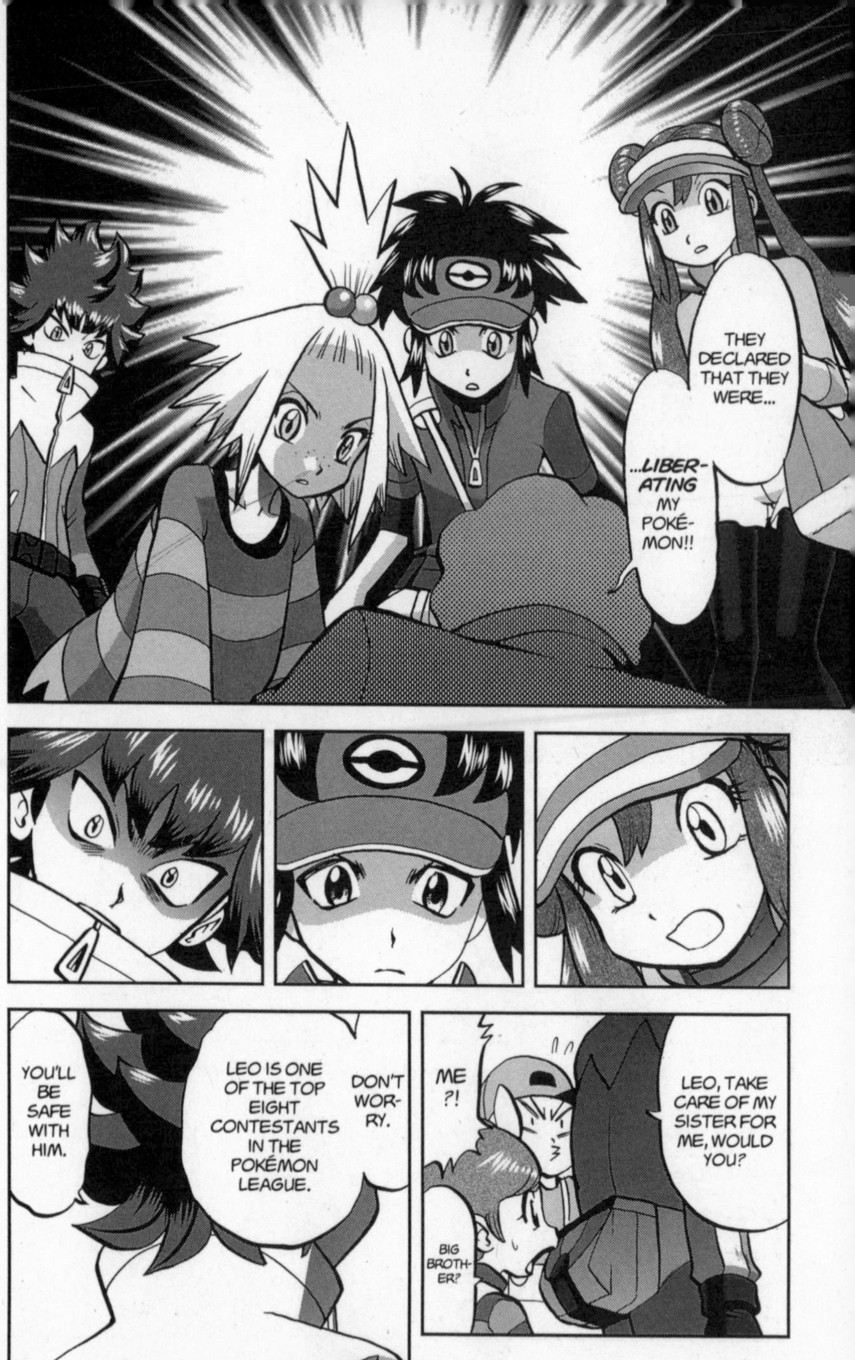
THEY DECLARED THAT THEY WERE...
...LIBERATING MY POKÉMON!!
LEO, TAKE CARE OF MY SISTER FOR ME, WOULD YOU?
ME ?!
BIG BROTHER?
DON'T WORRY.
LEO IS ONE OF THE TOP EIGHT CONTESTANTS IN THE POKÉMON LEAGUE.
YOU'LL BE SAFE WITH HIM.

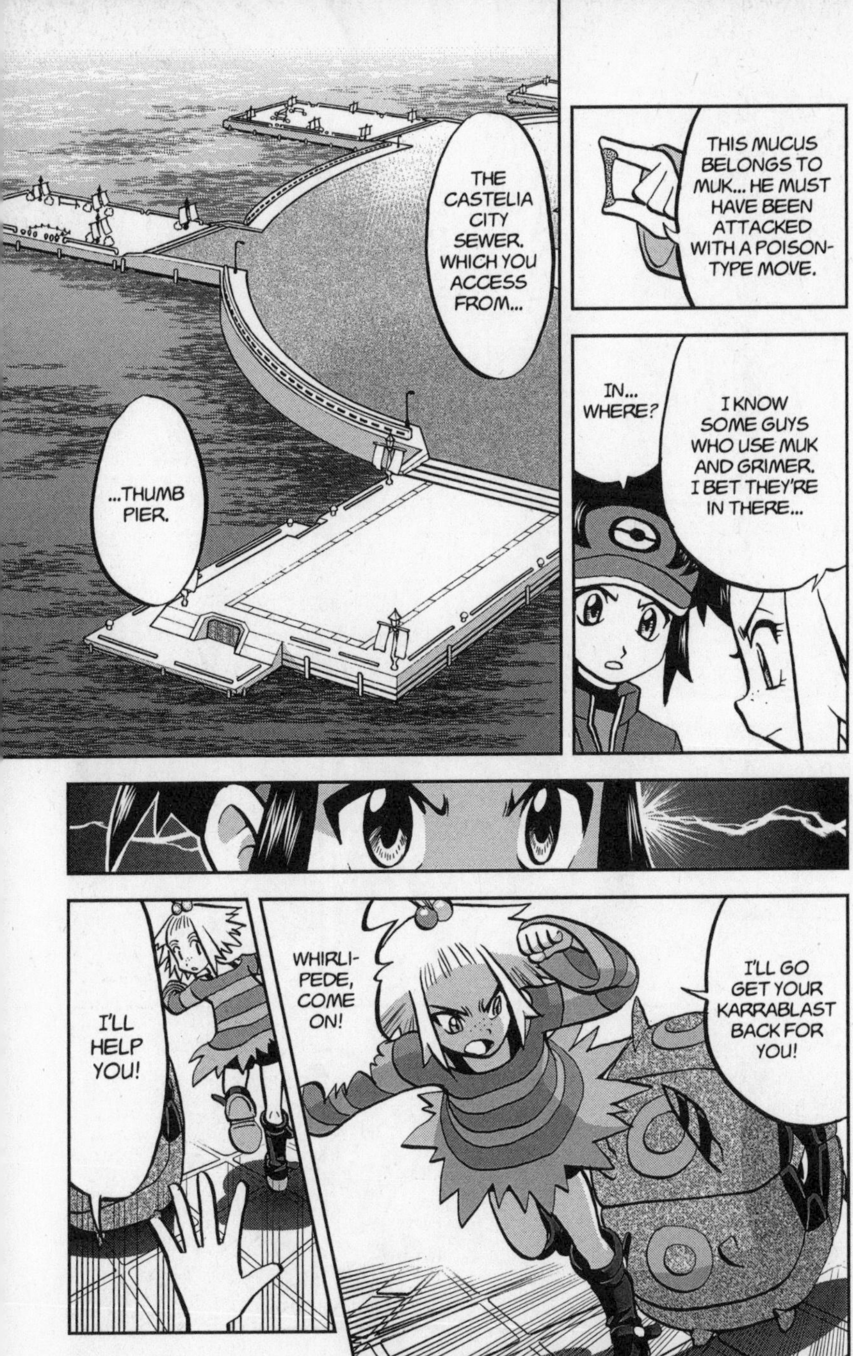
THIS MUCUS BELONGS TO MUK... HE MUST HAVE BEEN ATTACKED WITH A POISON-TYPE MOVE.
I KNOW SOME GUYS WHO USE MUK AND GRIMER. I BET THEY'RE IN THERE...
IN... WHERE?
THE CASTELIA CITY SEWER. WHICH YOU ACCESS FROM...
...THUMB PIER.
I'LL GO GET YOUR KARRABLAST BACK FOR YOU!
WHIRLI-PEDE, COME ON!
I'LL HELP YOU!

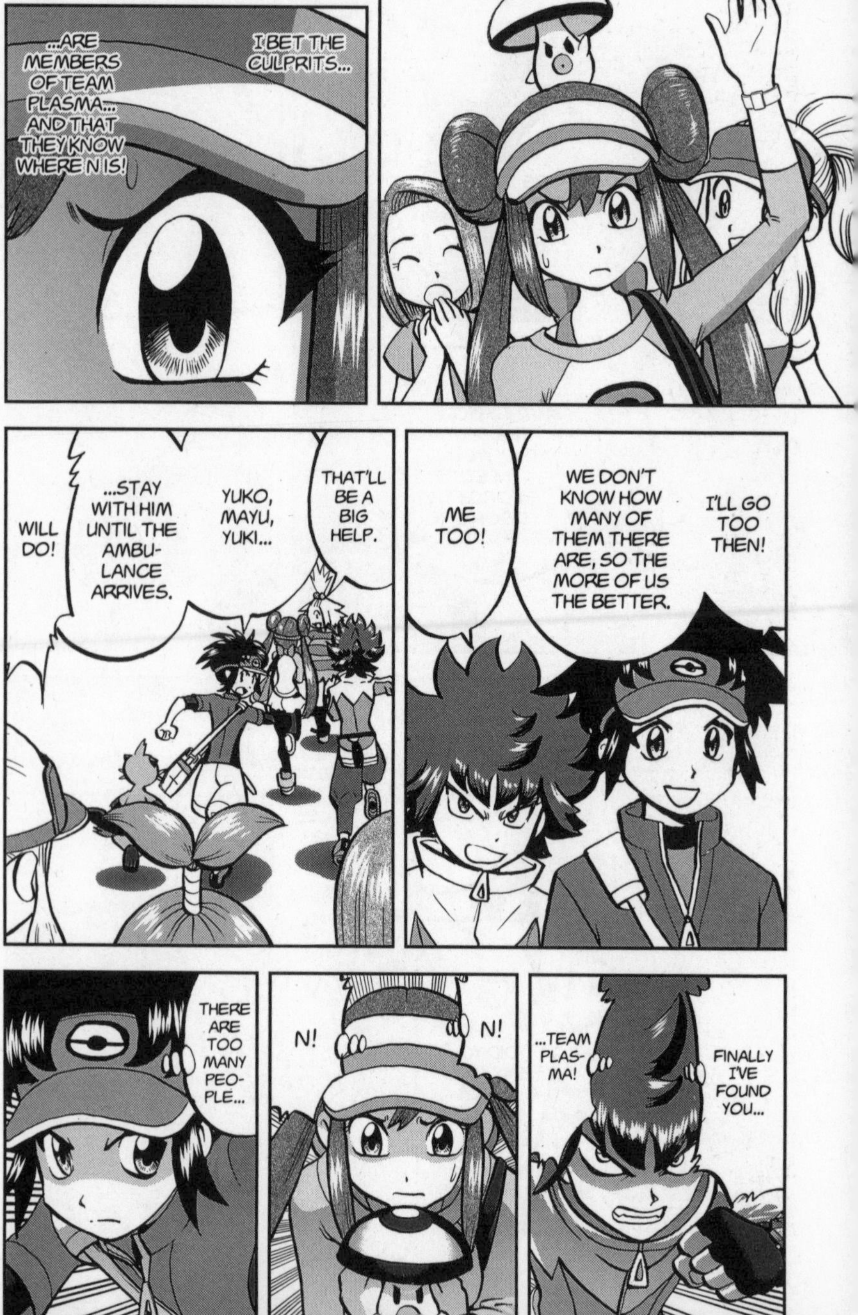
I BET THE CULPRITS...
...ARE MEMBERS OF TEAM PLASMA... AND THAT THEY KNOW WHERE N IS!
I'LL GO TOO THEN!
WE DON'T KNOW HOW MANY OF THEM THERE ARE, SO THE MORE OF US THE BETTER.
ME TOO!
THAT'LL BE A BIG HELP.
YUKO, MAYU, YUKI...
...STAY WITH HIM UNTIL THE AMBU-LANCE ARRIVES.
WILL DO!
FINALLY I'VE FOUND YOU...
...TEAM PLAS-MA!
N!
N!
THERE ARE TOO MANY PEO-PLE...

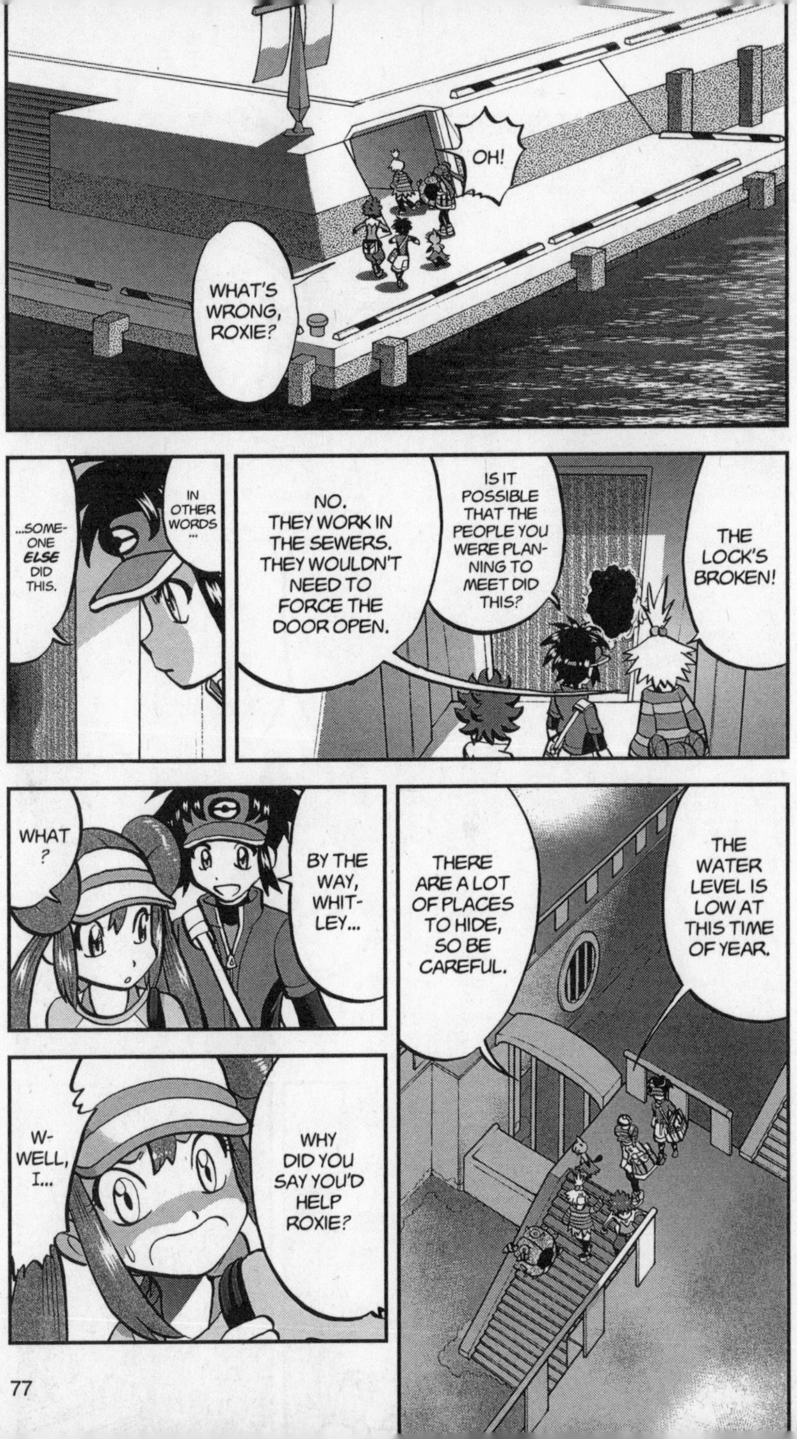
OH!
WHAT'S WRONG, ROXIE?
THE LOCK'S BROKEN!
IS IT POSSIBLE THAT THE PEOPLE YOU WERE PLAN-NING TO MEET DID THIS?
NO. THEY WORK IN THE SEWERS. THEY WOULDN'T NEED TO FORCE THE DOOR OPEN.
IN OTHER WORDS...
...SOME-ONE ELSE DID THIS.
THE WATER LEVEL IS LOW AT THIS TIME OF YEAR.
THERE ARE A LOT OF PLACES TO HIDE, SO BE CAREFUL.
BY THE WAY, WHIT-LEY...
WHAT?
WHY DID YOU SAY YOU'D HELP ROXIE?
W-WELL, I...

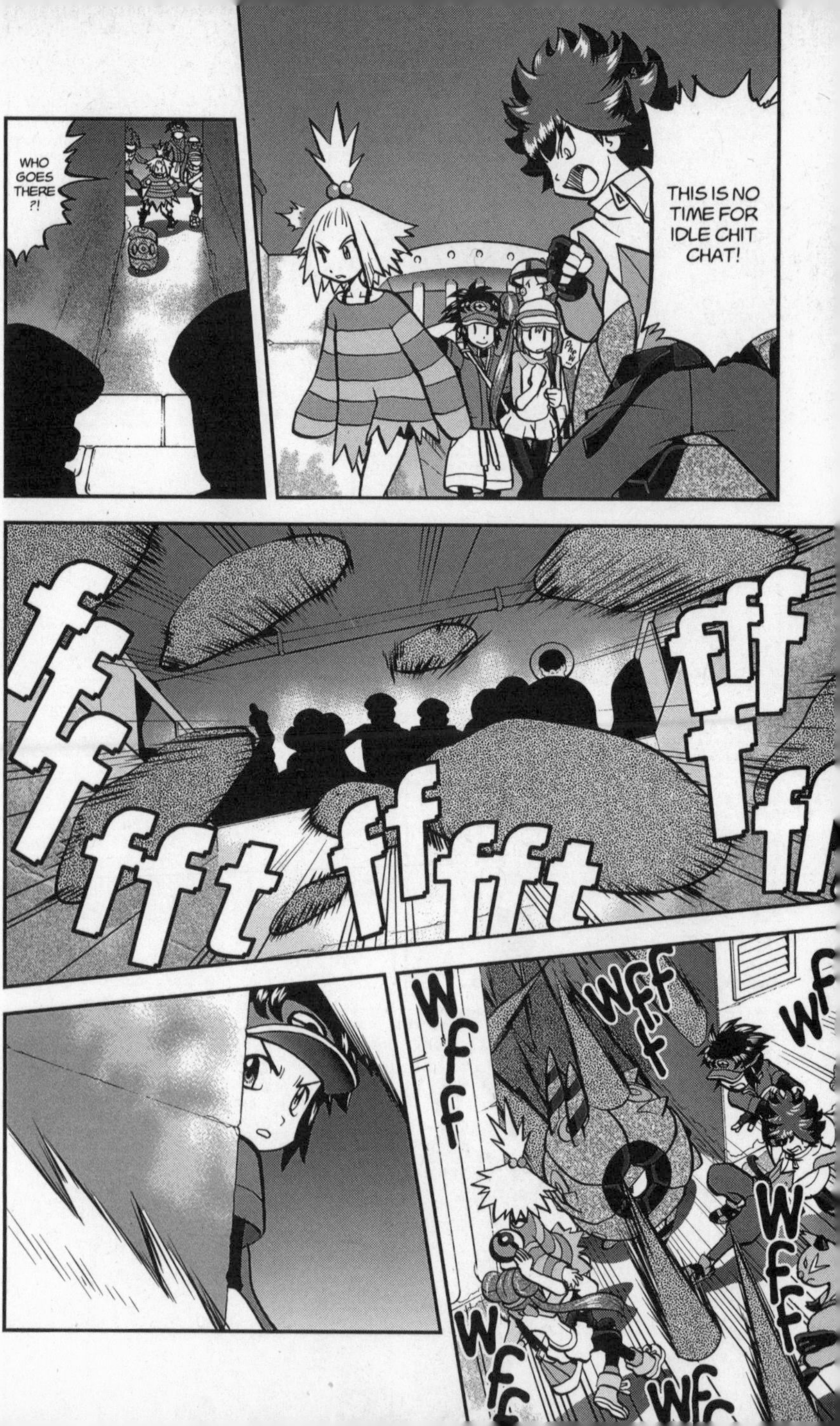
THIS IS NO TIME FOR IDLE CHIT CHAT!
PHEW
WHO GOES THERE?!
fff
fff
fft
ffft
WFF
WFF
WFF
WFF
WFF
WFF

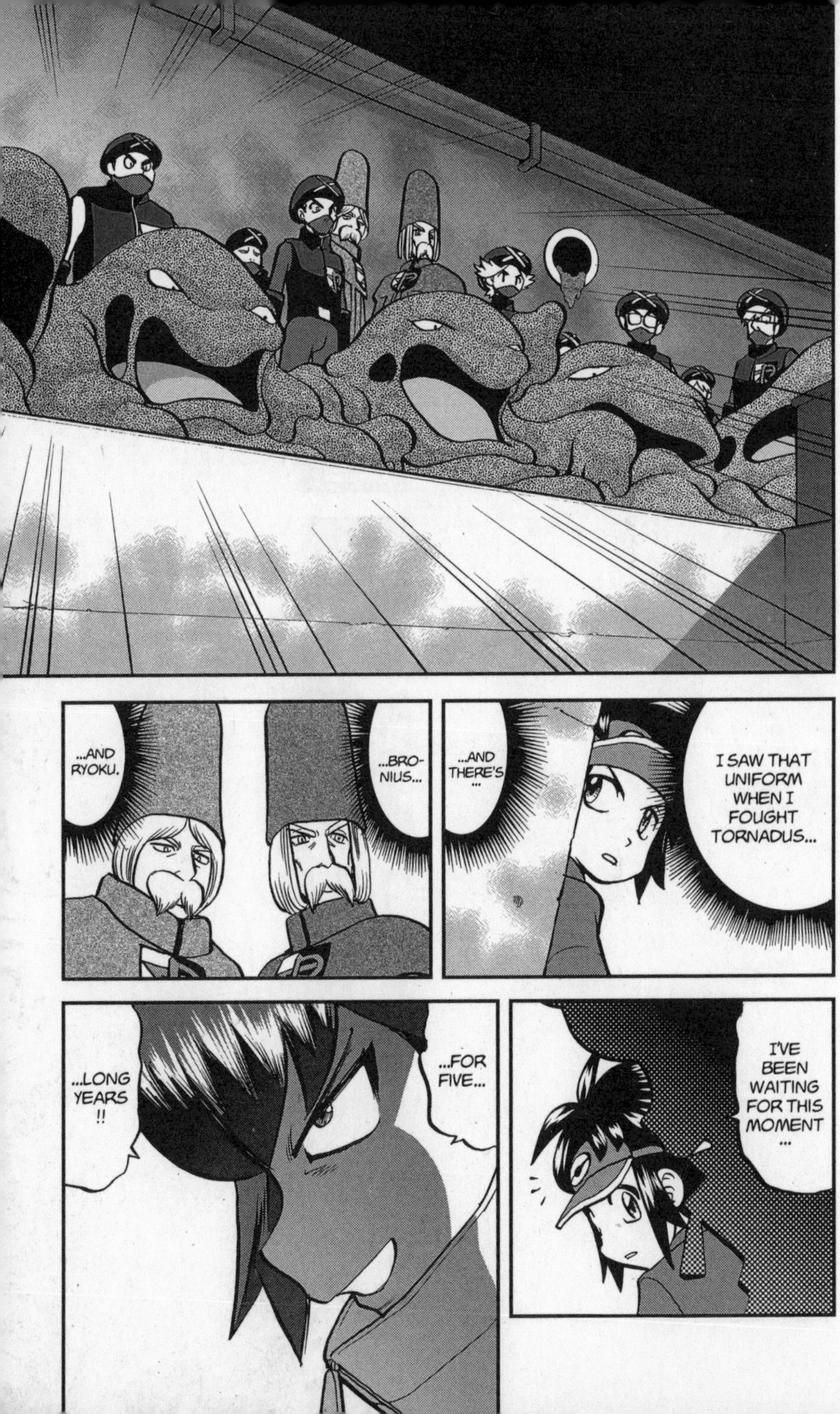
I SAW THAT UNIFORM WHEN I FOUGHT TORNADUS...
...AND THERE'S ...
...BRONIUS...
...AND RYOKU.
I'VE BEEN WAITING FOR THIS MOMENT ...
...FOR FIVE...
...LONG YEARS !!

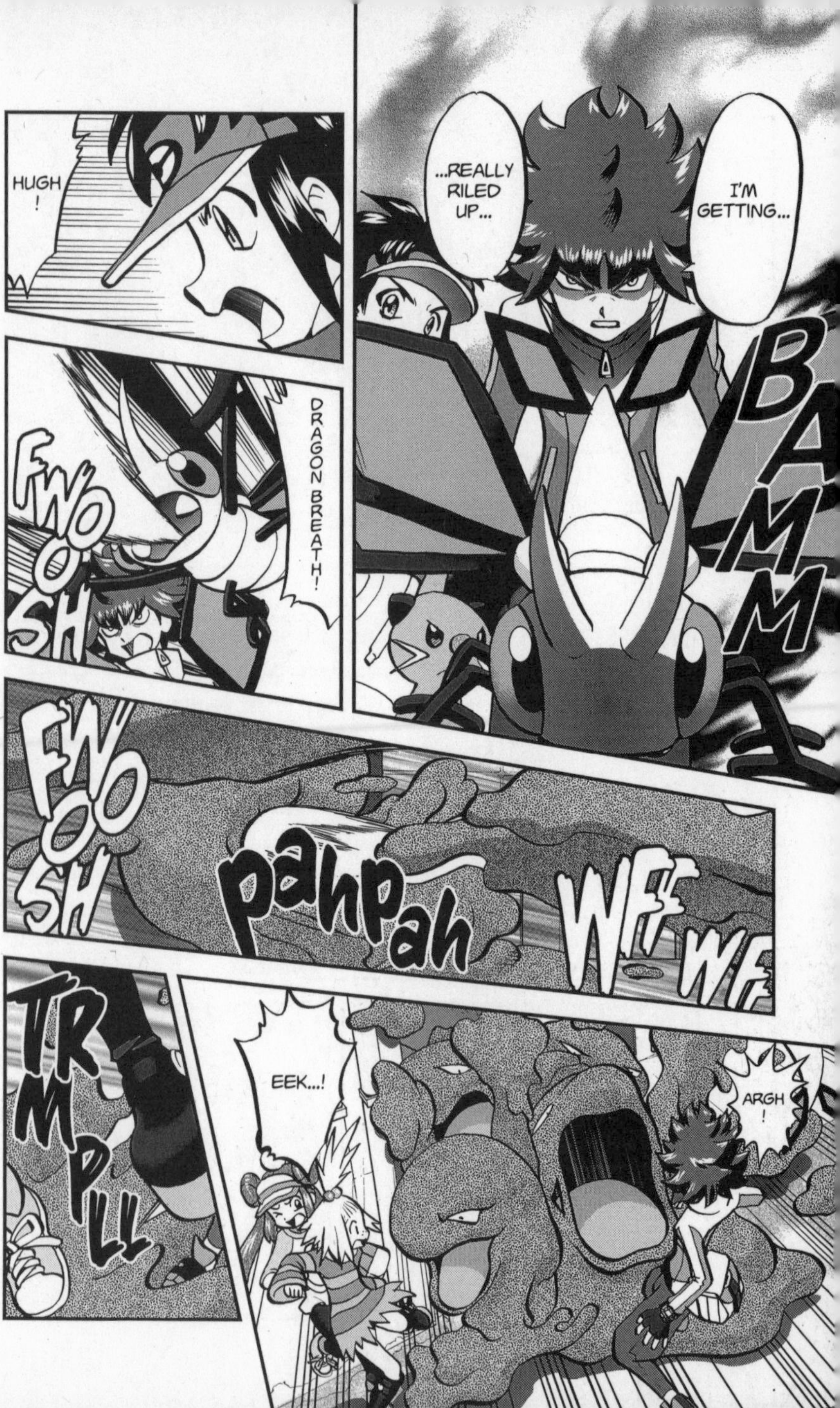
I'M GETTING...
...REALLY RILED UP...
BAMMM
HUGH!
DRAGON BREATH!
FWOOSH
WFF WFF
panpah
FWOOSH
ARGH!
EEK...!
TRMPLL

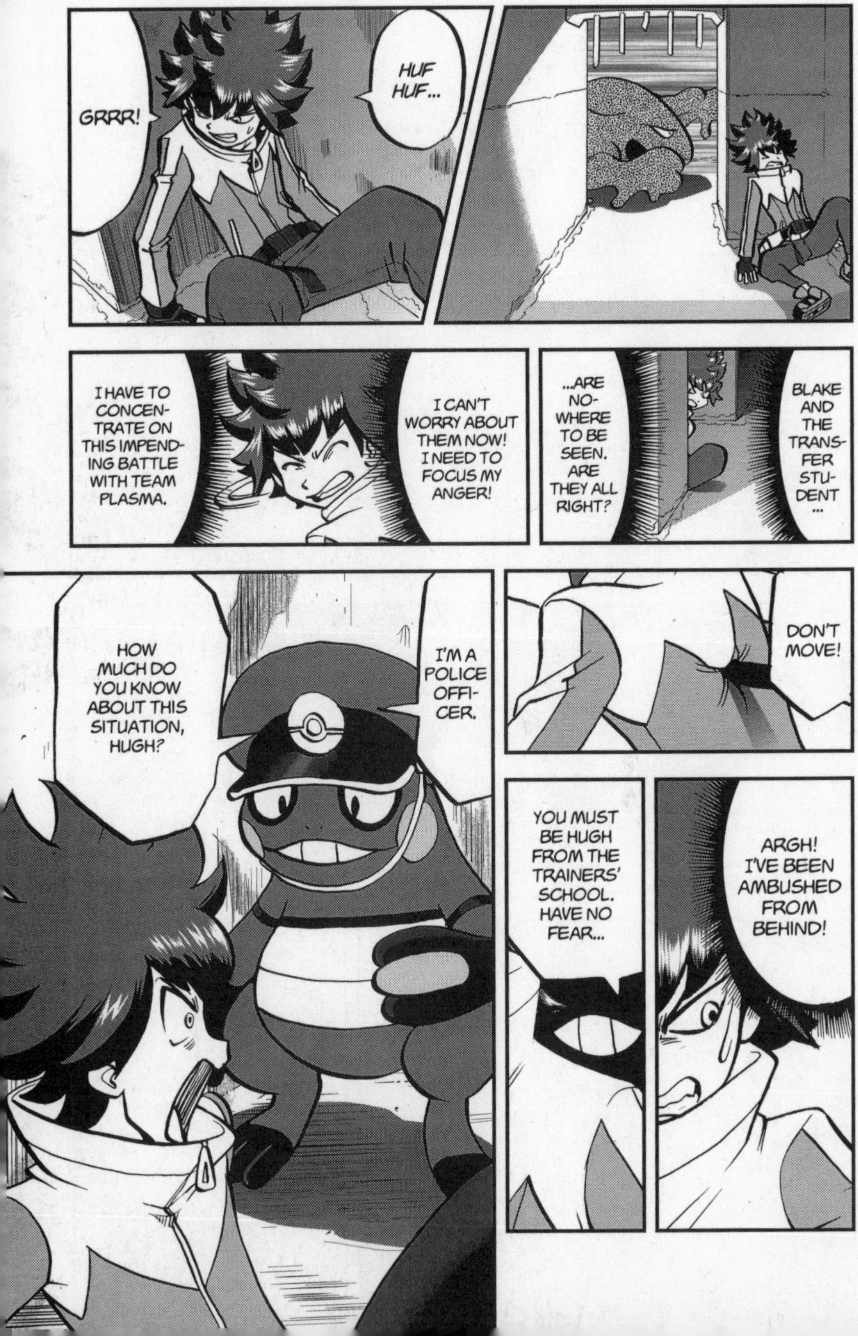
HUF HUF...
GRRR!
BLAKE AND THE TRANSFER STUDENT ...
...ARE NOWHERE TO BE SEEN. ARE THEY ALL RIGHT?
I CAN'T WORRY ABOUT THEM NOW! I NEED TO FOCUS MY ANGER!
I HAVE TO CONCENTRATE ON THIS IMPENDING BATTLE WITH TEAM PLASMA.
DON'T MOVE!
ARGH! I'VE BEEN AMBUSHED FROM BEHIND!
YOU MUST BE HUGH FROM THE TRAINERS' SCHOOL. HAVE NO FEAR...
I'M A POLICE OFFICER.
HOW MUCH DO YOU KNOW ABOUT THIS SITUATION, HUGH?

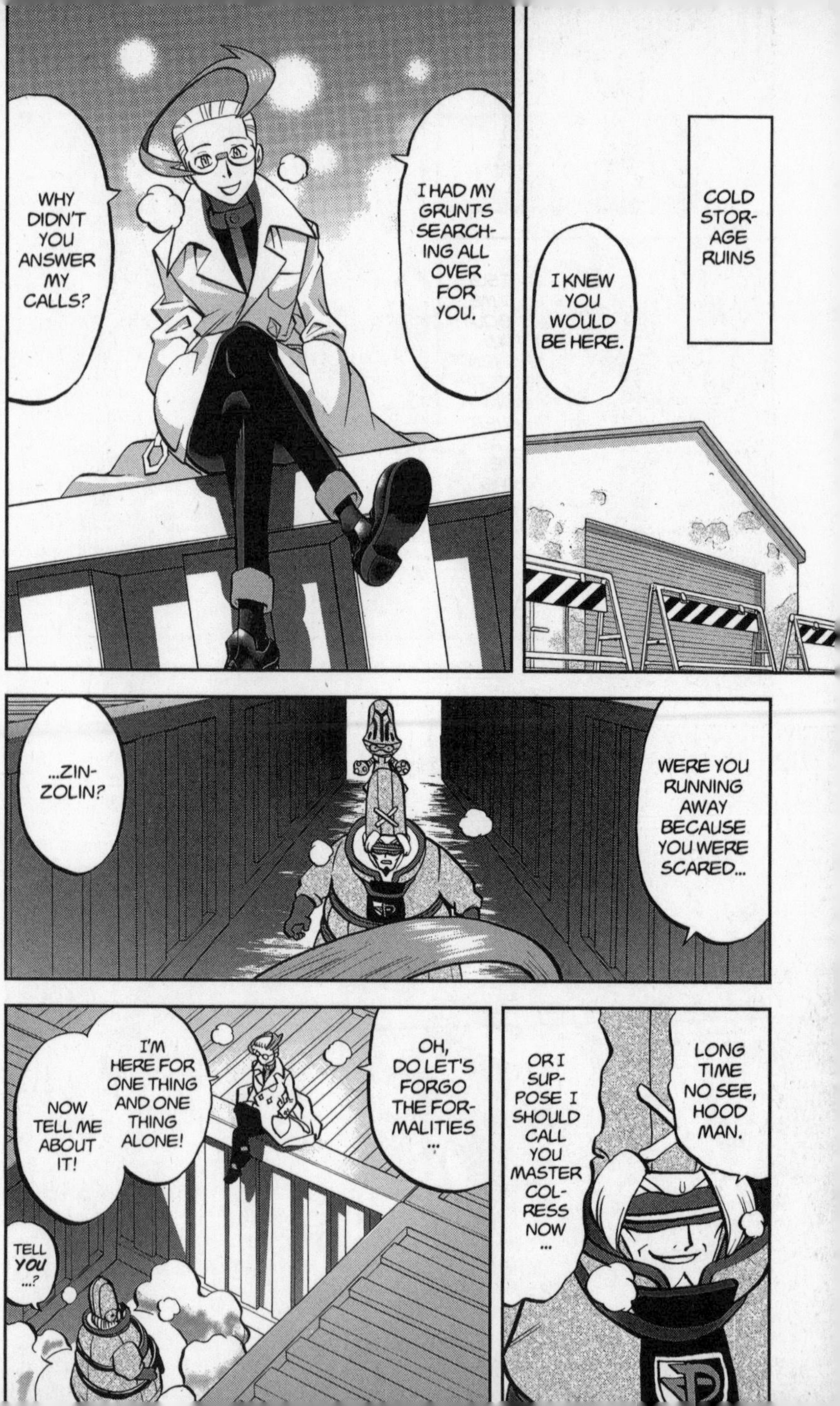
COLD STORAGE RUINS
I KNEW YOU WOULD BE HERE.
I HAD MY GRUNTS SEARCHING ALL OVER FOR YOU.
WHY DIDN'T YOU ANSWER MY CALLS?
WERE YOU RUNNING AWAY BECAUSE YOU WERE SCARED...
...ZINZOLIN?
LONG TIME NO SEE, HOOD MAN.
OR I SUPPOSE I SHOULD CALL YOU MASTER COLRESS NOW...
OH, DO LET'S FORGO THE FORMALITIES...
I'M HERE FOR ONE THING AND ONE THING ALONE!
NOW TELL ME ABOUT IT!
TELL *YOU*...?

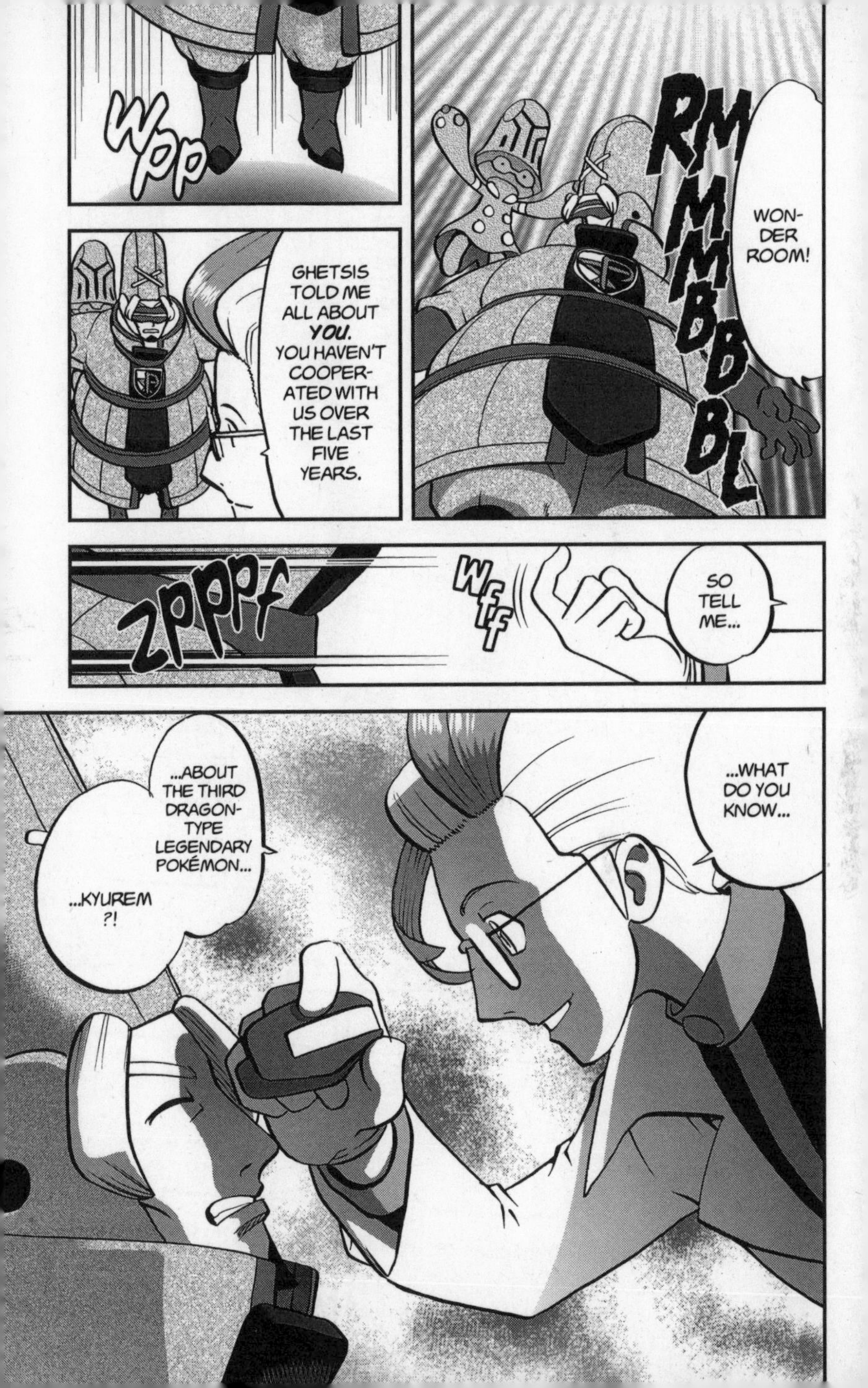
RMMMBBBL
WON-DER ROOM!
Wpp
GHETSIS TOLD ME ALL ABOUT ***YOU.*** YOU HAVEN'T COOPER-ATED WITH US OVER THE LAST FIVE YEARS.
SO TELL ME...
Wfff
ZPPPF
...WHAT DO YOU KNOW...
...ABOUT THE THIRD DRAGON-TYPE LEGENDARY POKÉMON...
...KYUREM ?!

Officially Approved by the Pokémon Trainers' Association
The Pokémon Trainers' School

Trainers' School

Prospectus

● Student Council ●

Each May, the members of the Student Council are chosen by a vote of the entire student body. After much consideration, the student who has the strongest relationship with their Pokémon is elected Student Council President.

Student Comment

I think the reason our campus is so safe is thanks to the efforts of the Student Council.

New Teacher:
Mr. Cheren

■ **Student Council Election** ■

☐ The Student Council President, Vice-President, Accountant and Clerk are chosen through a democratic voting process. The students who are elected remain in their positions for one year.

Nominations	May 1–7	
Election Campaign	May 7–14	
Election Day	May 15	

＊Only a designated number of flyers may be posted on the designated bulletin boards.

＊Nominees must deliver a speech outlining their policies before election da

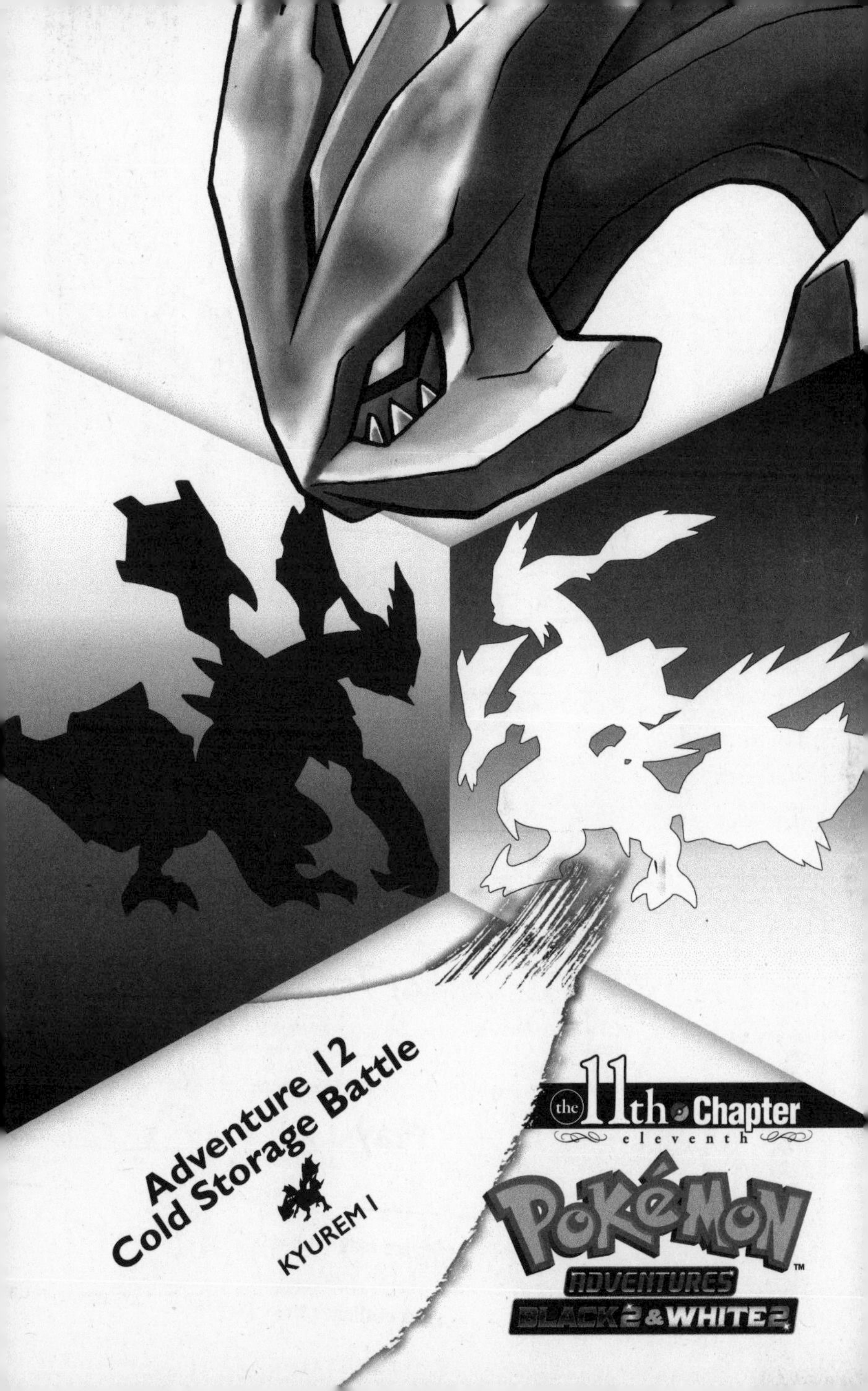
Adventure 12
Cold Storage Battle
KYUREM I
the 11th Chapter
eleventh
POKéMON™
ADVENTURES
BLACK 2 & WHITE 2

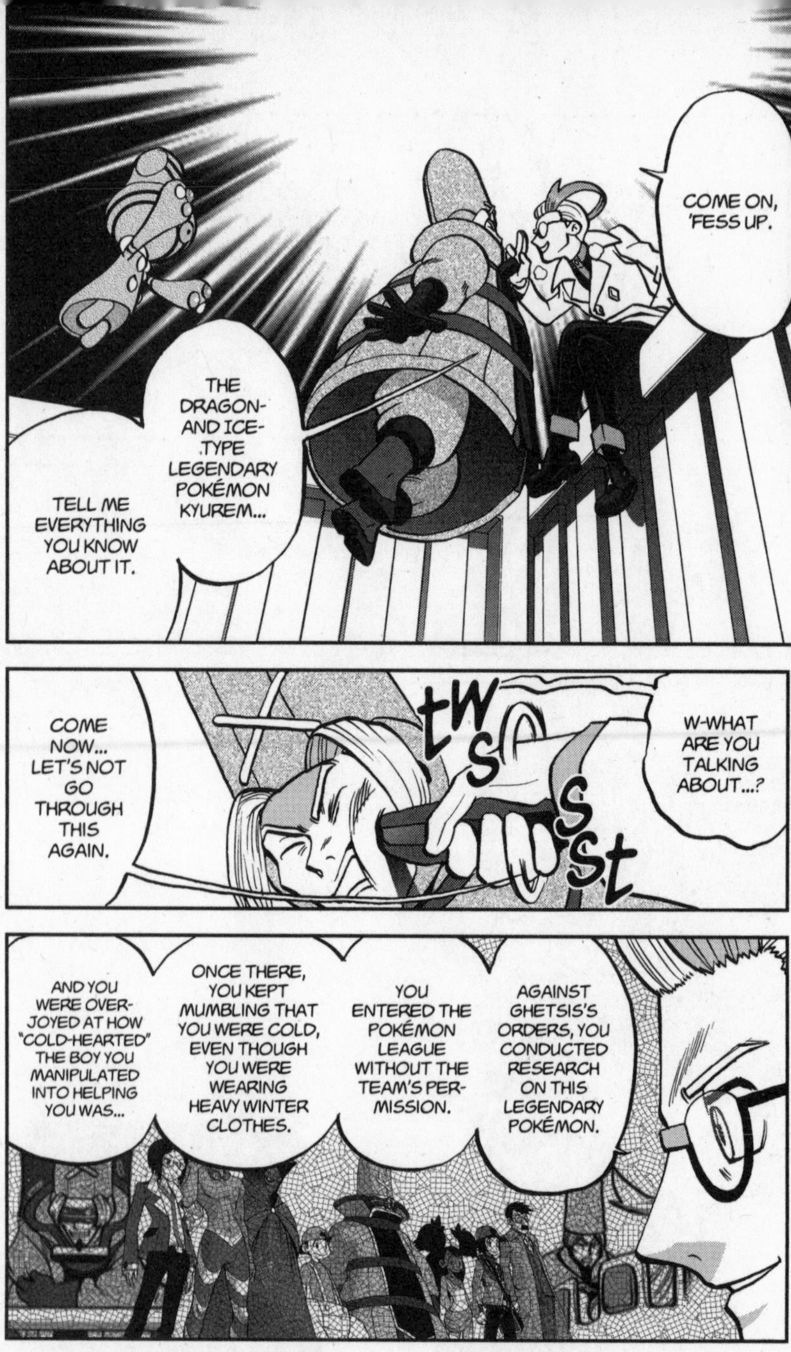
COME ON, 'FESS UP.
THE DRAGON- AND ICE-TYPE LEGENDARY POKÉMON KYUREM...
TELL ME EVERYTHING YOU KNOW ABOUT IT.
W-WHAT ARE YOU TALKING ABOUT...?
tWSSSt
COME NOW... LET'S NOT GO THROUGH THIS AGAIN.
AGAINST GHETSIS'S ORDERS, YOU CONDUCTED RESEARCH ON THIS LEGENDARY POKÉMON.
YOU ENTERED THE POKÉMON LEAGUE WITHOUT THE TEAM'S PER-MISSION.
ONCE THERE, YOU KEPT MUMBLING THAT YOU WERE COLD, EVEN THOUGH YOU WERE WEARING HEAVY WINTER CLOTHES.
AND YOU WERE OVER-JOYED AT HOW "COLD-HEARTED" THE BOY YOU MANIPULATED INTO HELPING YOU WAS...

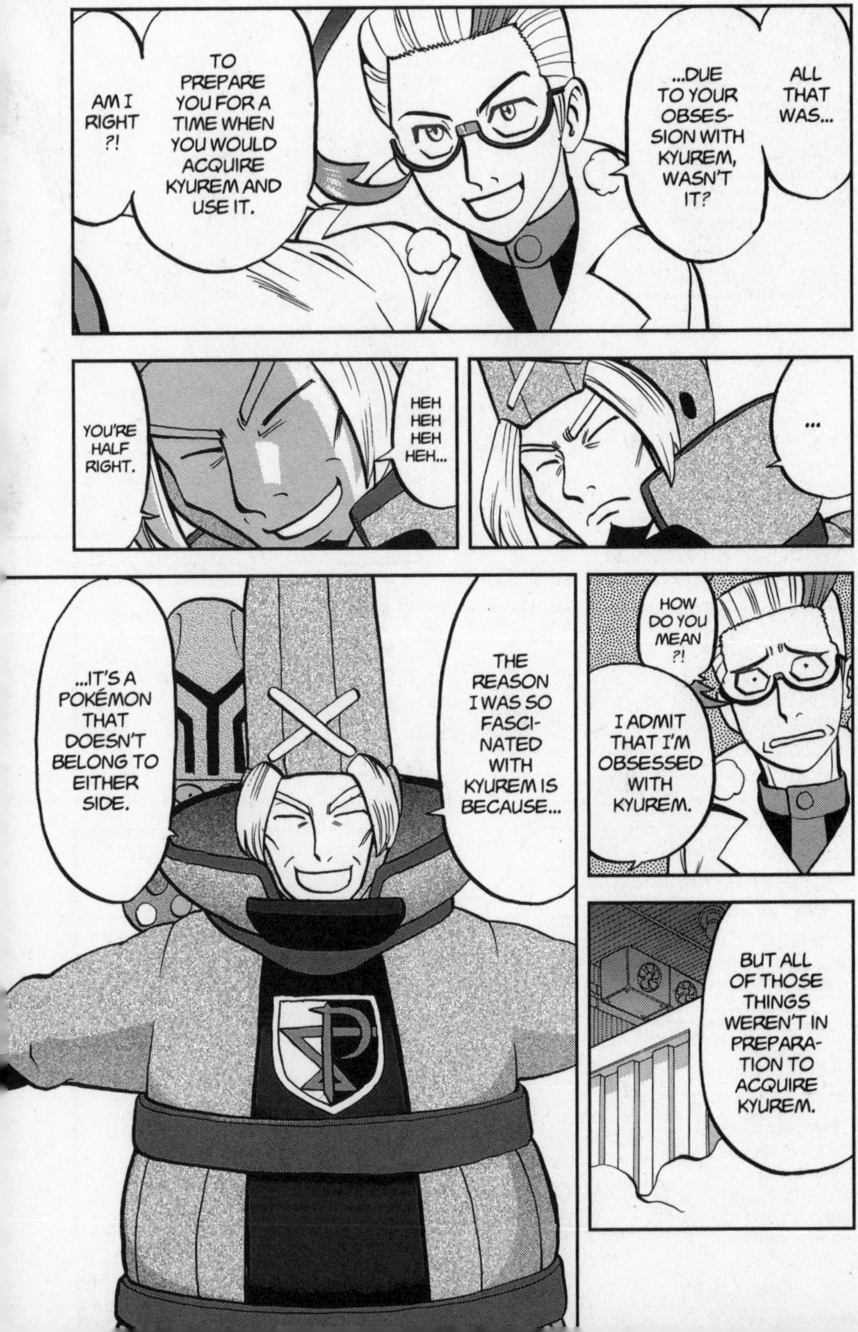
ALL THAT WAS...
...DUE TO YOUR OBSESSION WITH KYUREM, WASN'T IT?
TO PREPARE YOU FOR A TIME WHEN YOU WOULD ACQUIRE KYUREM AND USE IT.
AM I RIGHT ?!
...
HEH HEH HEH HEH...
YOU'RE HALF RIGHT.
HOW DO YOU MEAN ?!
I ADMIT THAT I'M OBSESSED WITH KYUREM.
BUT ALL OF THOSE THINGS WEREN'T IN PREPARATION TO ACQUIRE KYUREM.
THE REASON I WAS SO FASCINATED WITH KYUREM IS BECAUSE...
...IT'S A POKÉMON THAT DOESN'T BELONG TO EITHER SIDE.

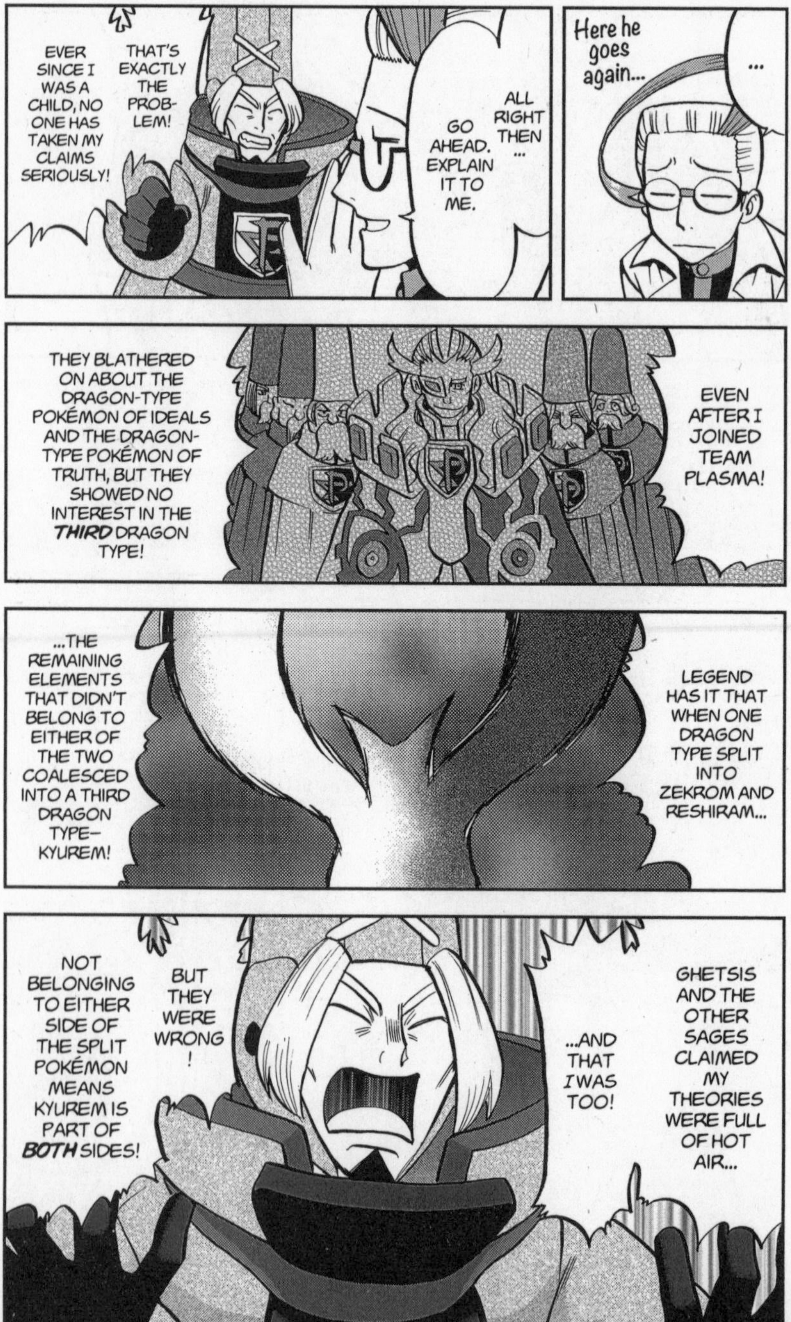
Here he goes again...
...
ALL RIGHT THEN ...
GO AHEAD. EXPLAIN IT TO ME.
THAT'S EXACTLY THE PROBLEM!
EVER SINCE I WAS A CHILD, NO ONE HAS TAKEN MY CLAIMS SERIOUSLY!
EVEN AFTER I JOINED TEAM PLASMA!
THEY BLATHERED ON ABOUT THE DRAGON-TYPE POKÉMON OF IDEALS AND THE DRAGON-TYPE POKÉMON OF TRUTH, BUT THEY SHOWED NO INTEREST IN THE ***THIRD*** DRAGON TYPE!
LEGEND HAS IT THAT WHEN ONE DRAGON TYPE SPLIT INTO ZEKROM AND RESHIRAM...
...THE REMAINING ELEMENTS THAT DIDN'T BELONG TO EITHER OF THE TWO COALESCED INTO A THIRD DRAGON TYPE—KYUREM!
GHETSIS AND THE OTHER SAGES CLAIMED MY THEORIES WERE FULL OF HOT AIR...
...AND THAT *I* WAS TOO!
BUT THEY WERE WRONG!
NOT BELONGING TO EITHER SIDE OF THE SPLIT POKÉMON MEANS KYUREM IS PART OF ***BOTH*** SIDES!

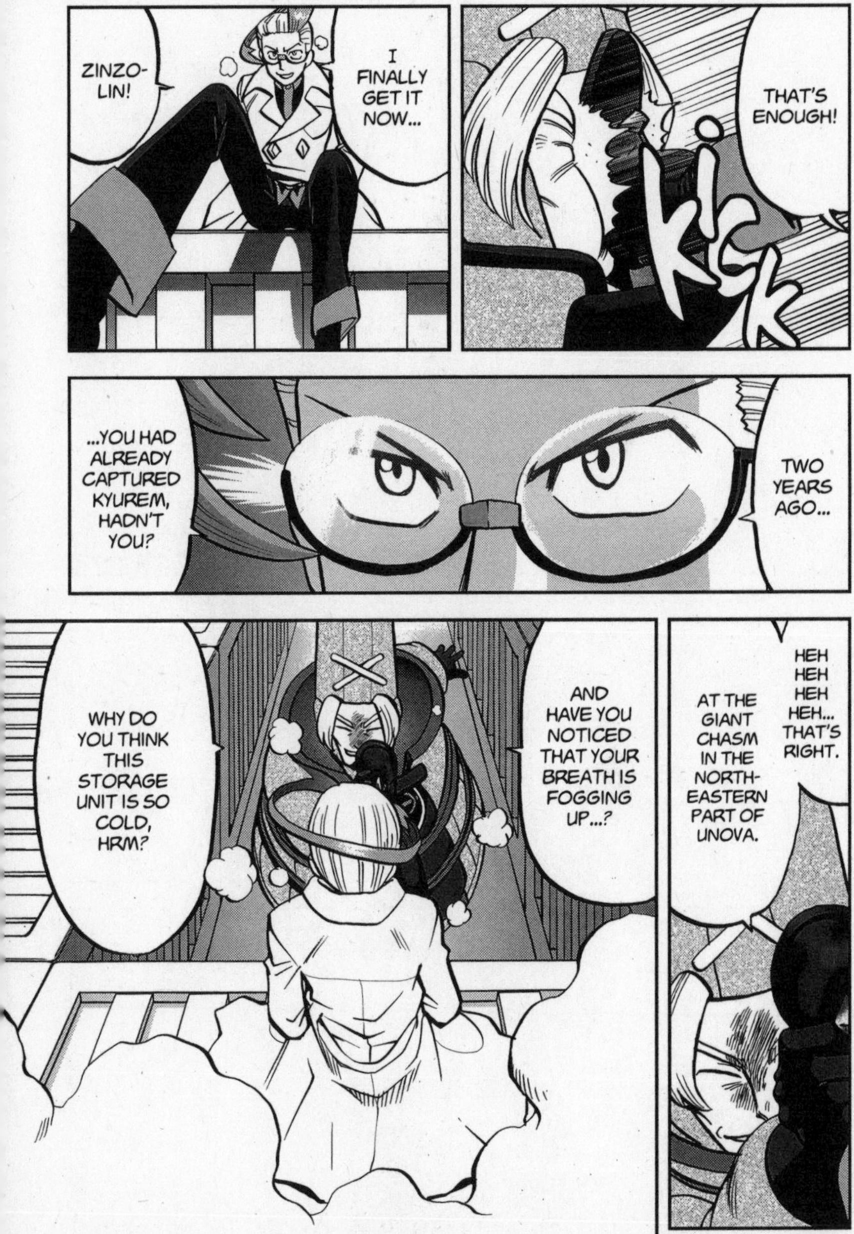
THAT'S ENOUGH!
KICK
I FINALLY GET IT NOW...
ZINZO-LIN!
TWO YEARS AGO...
...YOU HAD ALREADY CAPTURED KYUREM, HADN'T YOU?
HEH HEH HEH HEH... THAT'S RIGHT.
AT THE GIANT CHASM IN THE NORTH-EASTERN PART OF UNOVA.
AND HAVE YOU NOTICED THAT YOUR BREATH IS FOGGING UP...?
WHY DO YOU THINK THIS STORAGE UNIT IS SO COLD, HRM?

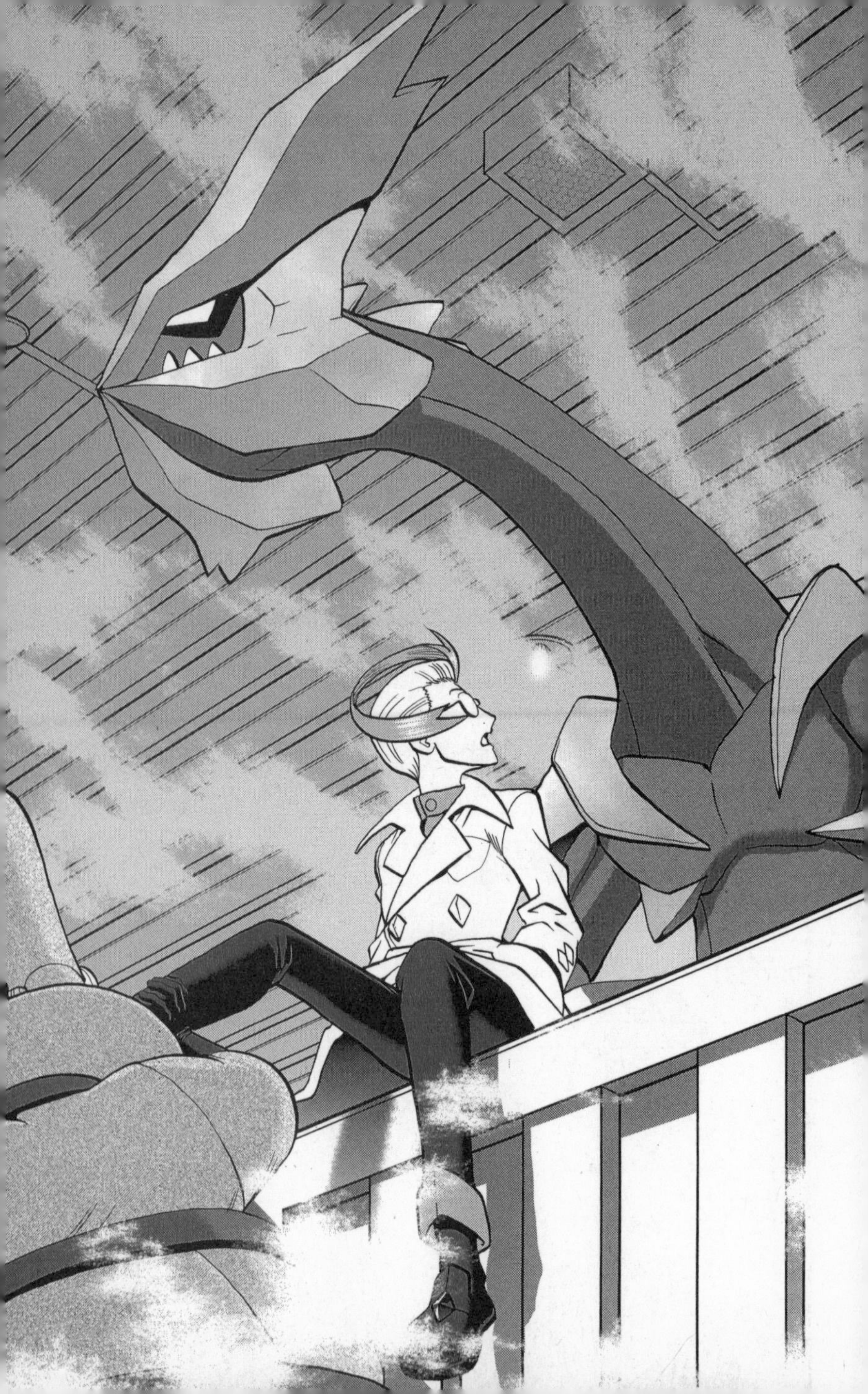

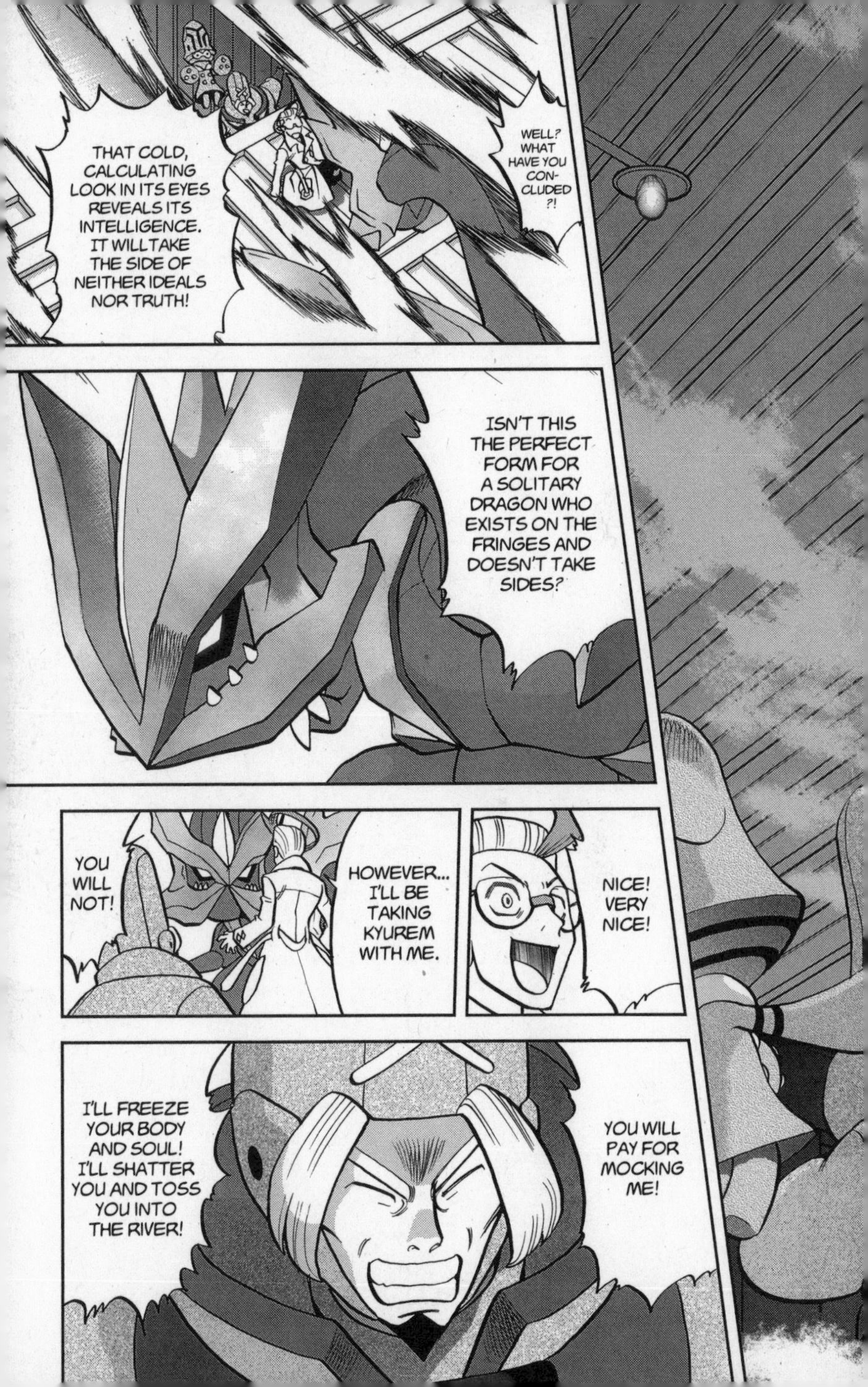
WELL? WHAT HAVE YOU CON-CLUDED?!
THAT COLD, CALCULATING LOOK IN ITS EYES REVEALS ITS INTELLIGENCE. IT WILL TAKE THE SIDE OF NEITHER IDEALS NOR TRUTH!
ISN'T THIS THE PERFECT FORM FOR A SOLITARY DRAGON WHO EXISTS ON THE FRINGES AND DOESN'T TAKE SIDES?
NICE! VERY NICE!
HOWEVER... I'LL BE TAKING KYUREM WITH ME.
YOU WILL NOT!
YOU WILL PAY FOR MOCKING ME!
I'LL FREEZE YOUR BODY AND SOUL! I'LL SHATTER YOU AND TOSS YOU INTO THE RIVER!

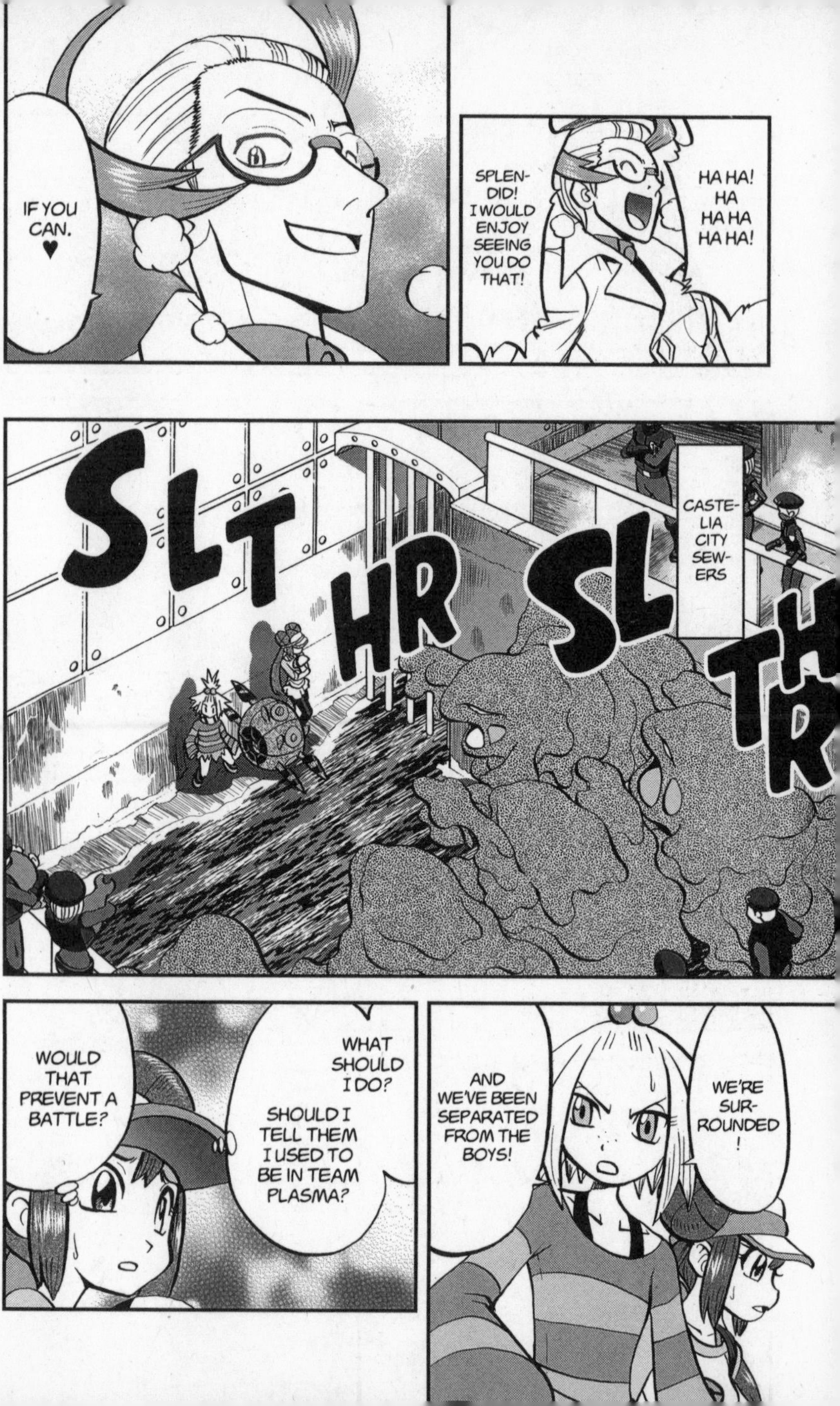
HA HA! HA HA HA HA HA!
SPLEN-DID! I WOULD ENJOY SEEING YOU DO THAT!
IF YOU CAN. ♥
CASTE-LIA CITY SEW-ERS
SLT HR SL TH TR
WE'RE SUR-ROUNDED!
AND WE'VE BEEN SEPARATED FROM THE BOYS!
WHAT SHOULD I DO?
SHOULD I TELL THEM I USED TO BE IN TEAM PLASMA?
WOULD THAT PREVENT A BATTLE?

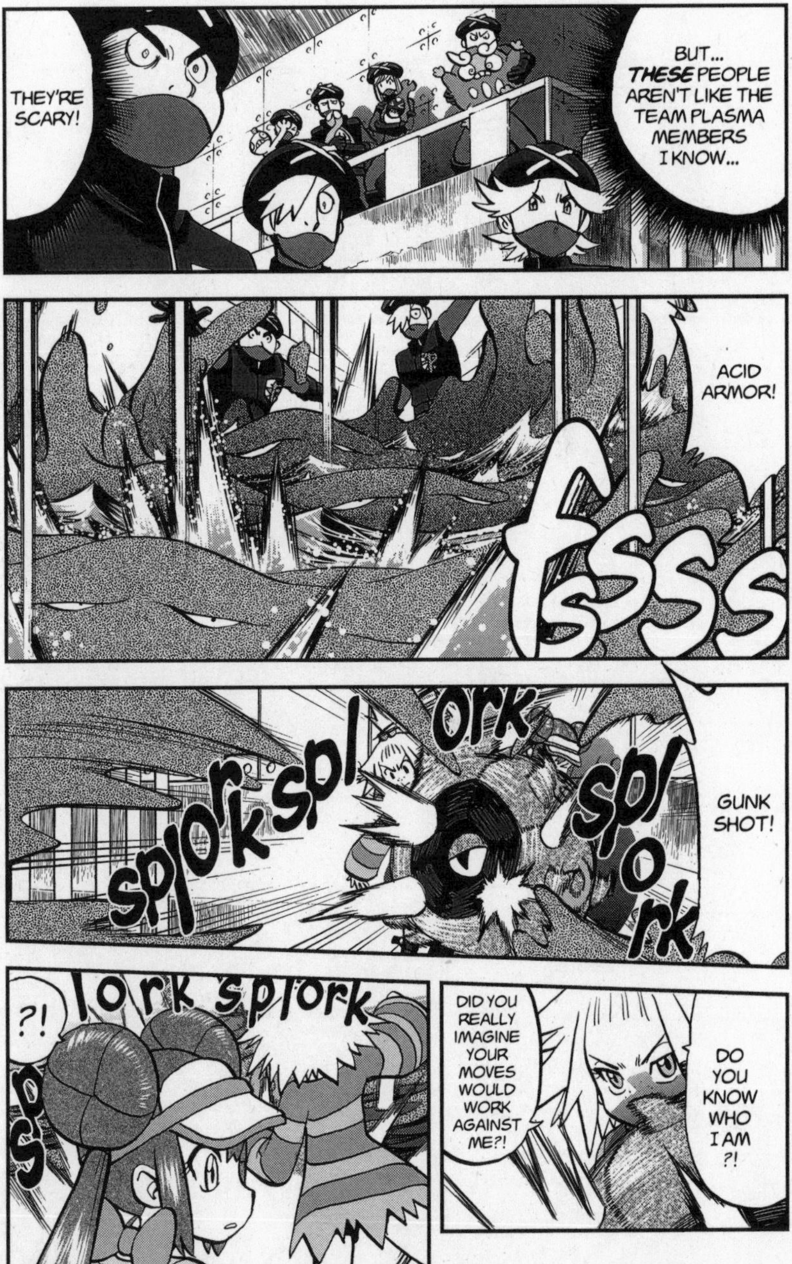
BUT... THESE PEOPLE AREN'T LIKE THE TEAM PLASMA MEMBERS I KNOW...
THEY'RE SCARY!
ACID ARMOR!
fSSSSS
GUNK SHOT!
splork
splorksplork
DO YOU KNOW WHO I AM ?!
DID YOU REALLY IMAGINE YOUR MOVES WOULD WORK AGAINST ME?!
lork splork
?!

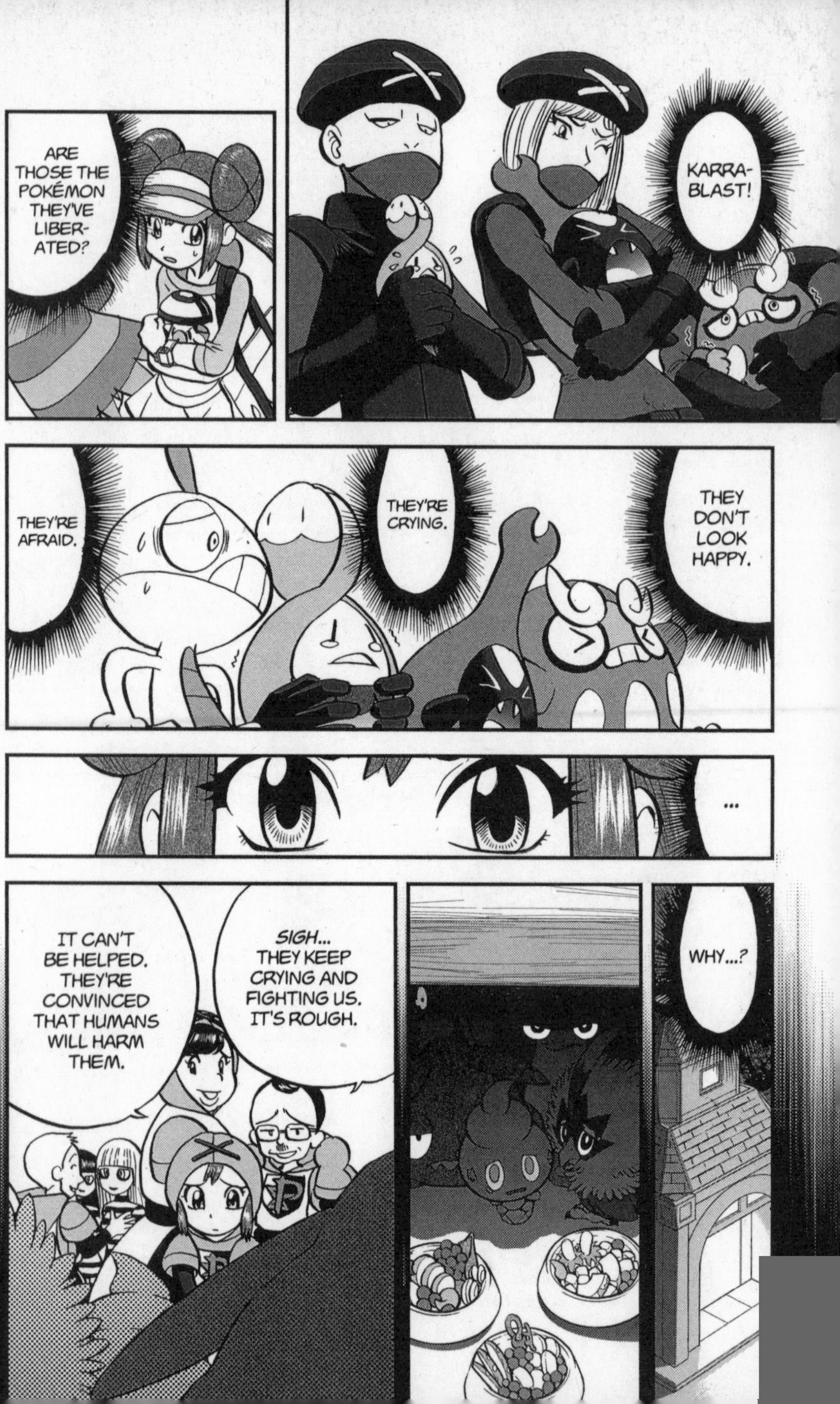
KARRA-BLAST!
ARE THOSE THE POKÉMON THEY'VE LIBER-ATED?
THEY DON'T LOOK HAPPY.
THEY'RE CRYING.
THEY'RE AFRAID.
...
WHY...?
SIGH... THEY KEEP CRYING AND FIGHTING US. IT'S ROUGH.
IT CAN'T BE HELPED. THEY'RE CONVINCED THAT HUMANS WILL HARM THEM.

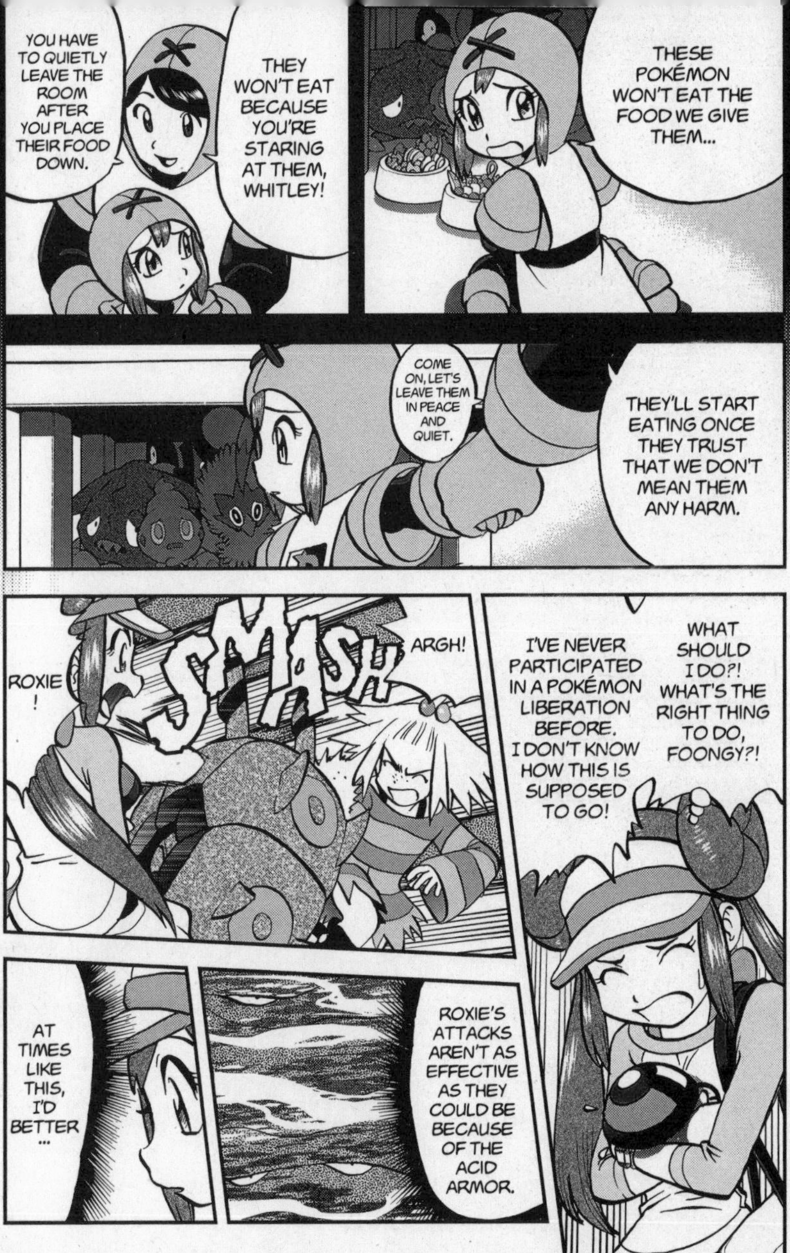
THESE POKÉMON WON'T EAT THE FOOD WE GIVE THEM...
THEY WON'T EAT BECAUSE YOU'RE STARING AT THEM, WHITLEY!
YOU HAVE TO QUIETLY LEAVE THE ROOM AFTER YOU PLACE THEIR FOOD DOWN.
THEY'LL START EATING ONCE THEY TRUST THAT WE DON'T MEAN THEM ANY HARM.
COME ON, LET'S LEAVE THEM IN PEACE AND QUIET.
WHAT SHOULD I DO?! WHAT'S THE RIGHT THING TO DO, FOONGY?!
I'VE NEVER PARTICIPATED IN A POKÉMON LIBERATION BEFORE. I DON'T KNOW HOW THIS IS SUPPOSED TO GO!
ARGH!
SMASH
ROXIE!
ROXIE'S ATTACKS AREN'T AS EFFECTIVE AS THEY COULD BE BECAUSE OF THE ACID ARMOR.
AT TIMES LIKE THIS, I'D BETTER...

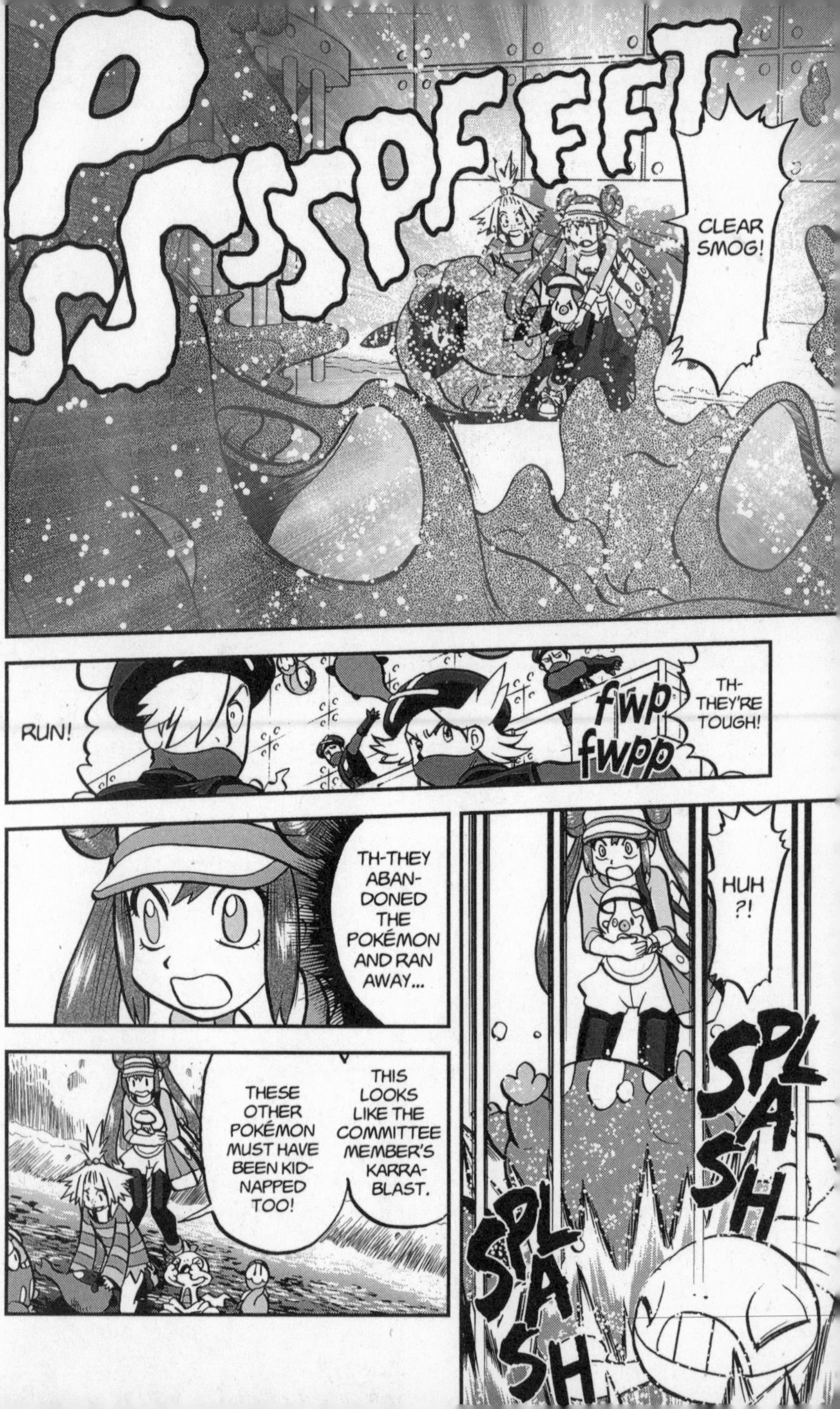
PSSSPFFFT
CLEAR SMOG!
TH-THEY'RE TOUGH!
fwp fwpp
RUN!
HUH?!
SPLASH
SPLASH
TH-THEY ABANDONED THE POKÉMON AND RAN AWAY...
THIS LOOKS LIKE THE COMMITTEE MEMBER'S KARRABLAST.
THESE OTHER POKÉMON MUST HAVE BEEN KIDNAPPED TOO!

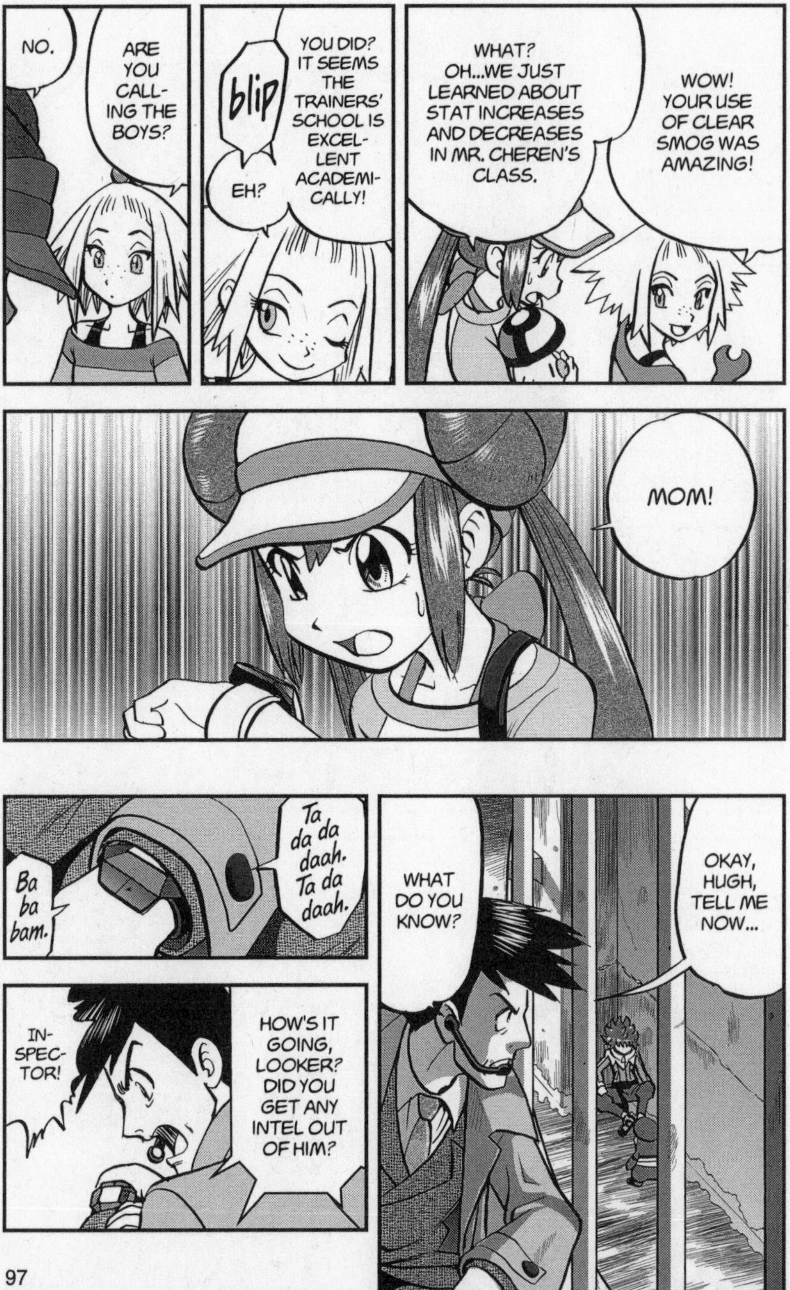
WOW! YOUR USE OF CLEAR SMOG WAS AMAZING!
WHAT? OH...WE JUST LEARNED ABOUT STAT INCREASES AND DECREASES IN MR. CHEREN'S CLASS.
YOU DID? IT SEEMS THE TRAINERS' SCHOOL IS EXCEL-LENT ACADEMI-CALLY!
blip
EH?
ARE YOU CALL-ING THE BOYS?
NO.
MOM!
OKAY, HUGH, TELL ME NOW...
WHAT DO YOU KNOW?
Ta da da daah. Ta da daah.
Ba ba bam.
HOW'S IT GOING, LOOKER? DID YOU GET ANY INTEL OUT OF HIM?
IN-SPEC-TOR!

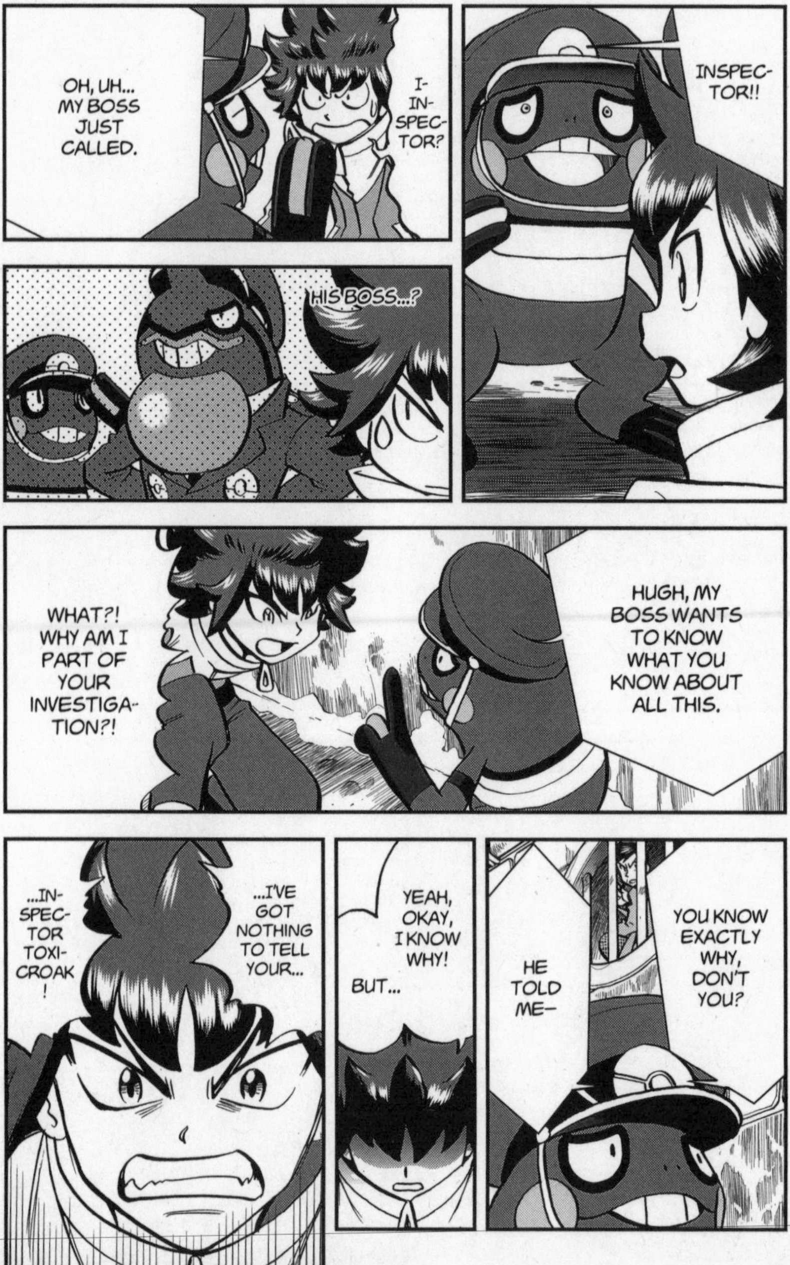
INSPECTOR!!
I-INSPECTOR?
OH, UH... MY BOSS JUST CALLED.
HIS BOSS...?
HUGH, MY BOSS WANTS TO KNOW WHAT YOU KNOW ABOUT ALL THIS.
WHAT?! WHY AM I PART OF YOUR INVESTIGATION?!
YOU KNOW EXACTLY WHY, DON'T YOU?
HE TOLD ME—
YEAH, OKAY, I KNOW WHY!
BUT...
...I'VE GOT NOTHING TO TELL YOUR...
...INSPECTOR TOXICROAK!

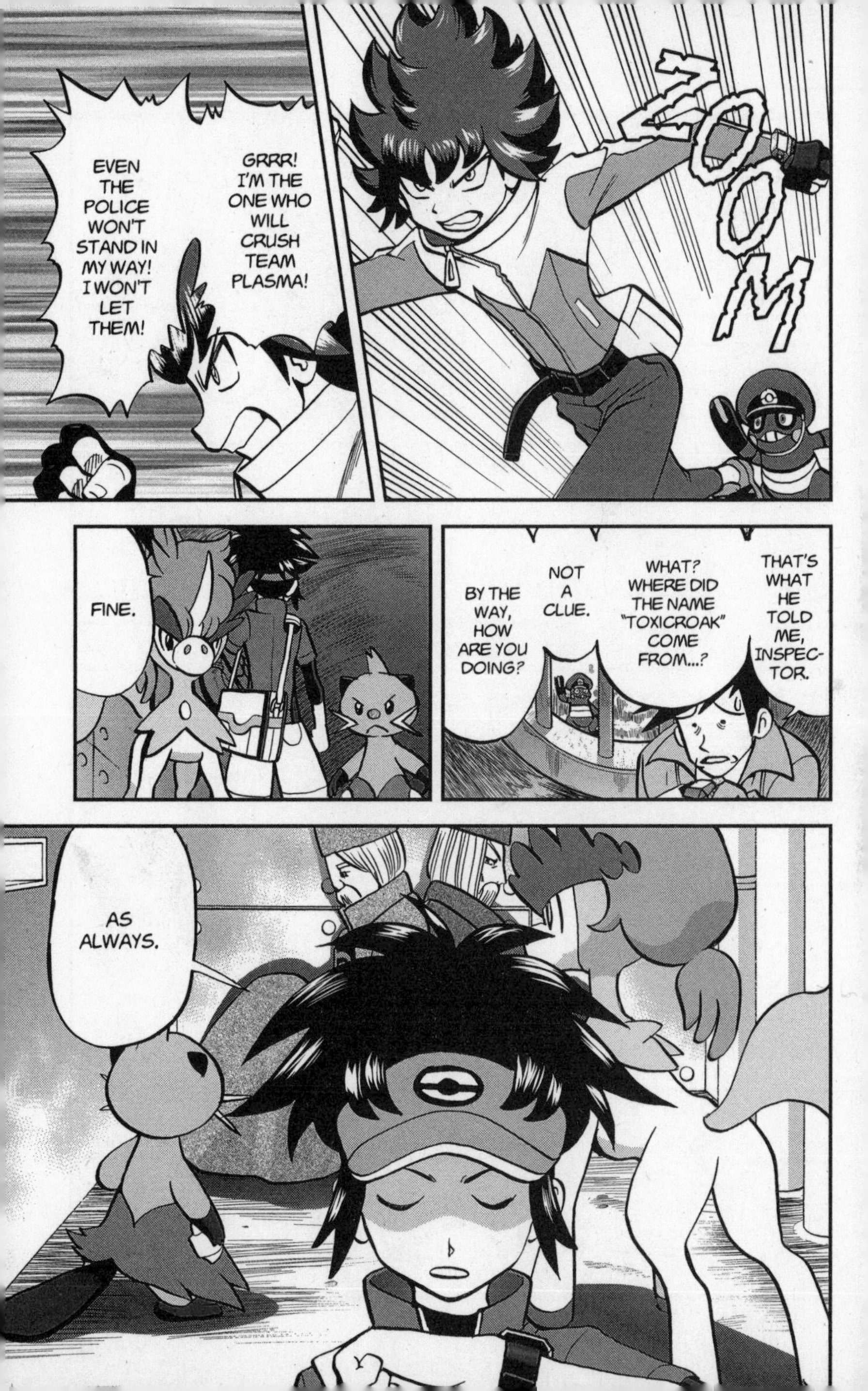
ZOOM
GRRR! I'M THE ONE WHO WILL CRUSH TEAM PLASMA!
EVEN THE POLICE WON'T STAND IN MY WAY! I WON'T LET THEM!
THAT'S WHAT HE TOLD ME, INSPECTOR.
WHAT? WHERE DID THE NAME "TOXICROAK" COME FROM...?
NOT A CLUE.
BY THE WAY, HOW ARE YOU DOING?
FINE.
AS ALWAYS.

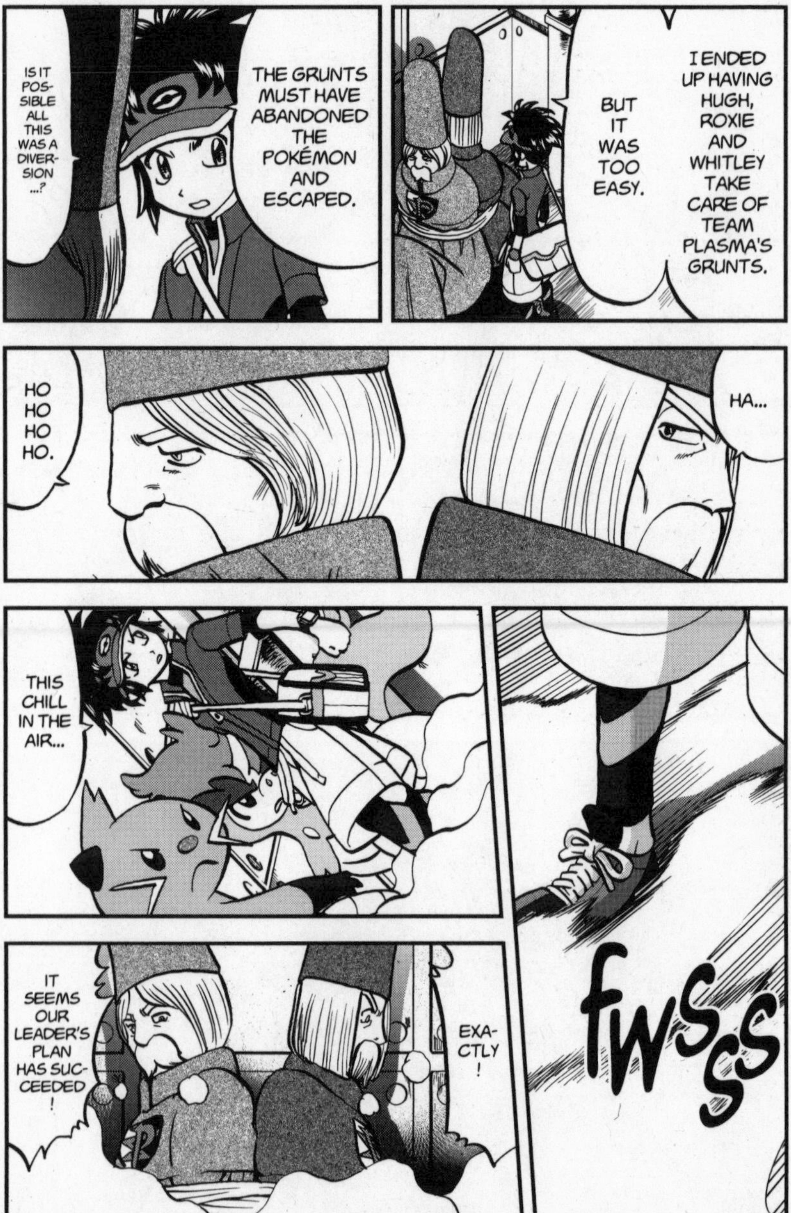
I ENDED UP HAVING HUGH, ROXIE AND WHITLEY TAKE CARE OF TEAM PLASMA'S GRUNTS.
BUT IT WAS TOO EASY.
THE GRUNTS MUST HAVE ABANDONED THE POKéMON AND ESCAPED.
IS IT POSSIBLE ALL THIS WAS A DIVERSION...?
HA...
HO HO HO HO.
fwSSS
THIS CHILL IN THE AIR...
IT SEEMS OUR LEADER'S PLAN HAS SUCCEEDED!
EXACTLY!

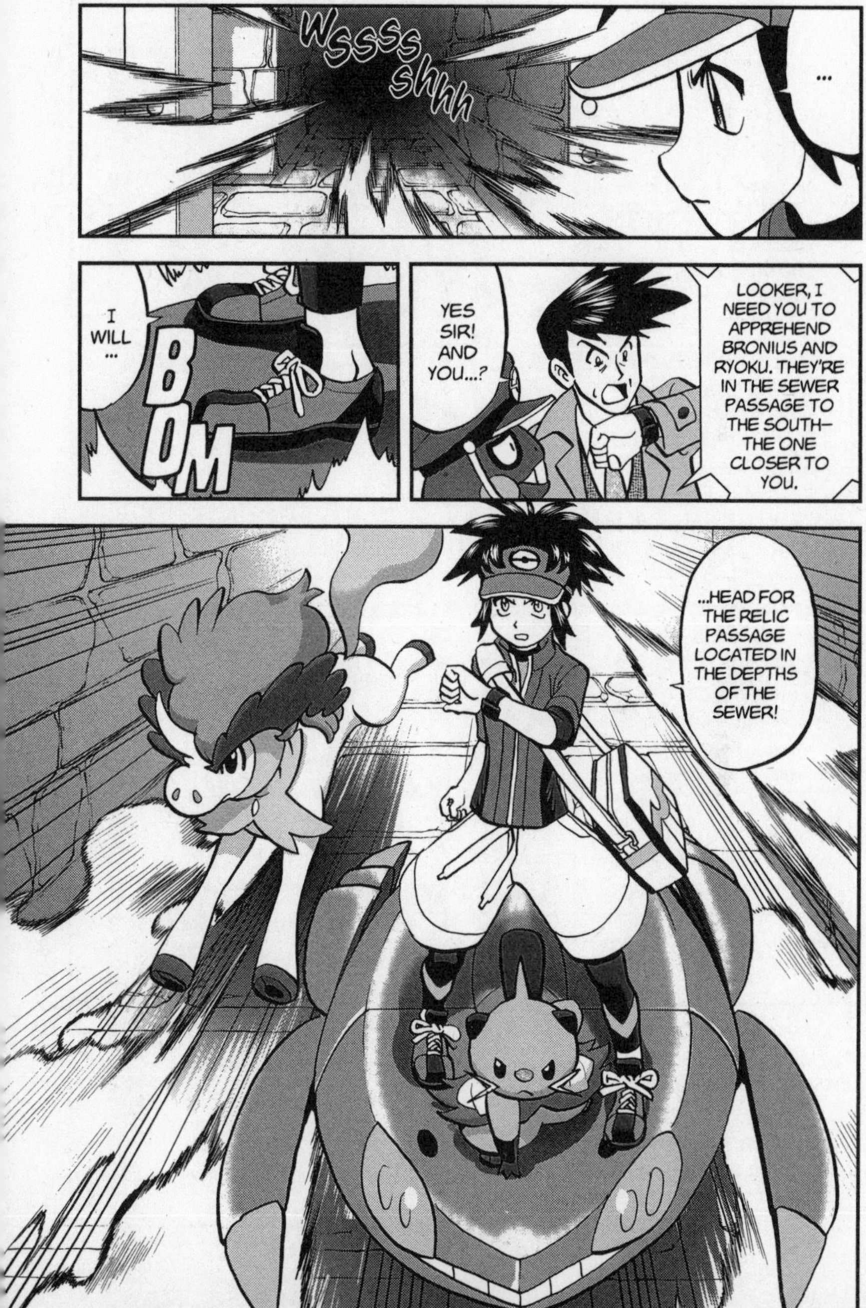
...
WSSSSSHHHH
LOOKER, I NEED YOU TO APPREHEND BRONIUS AND RYOKU. THEY'RE IN THE SEWER PASSAGE TO THE SOUTH—THE ONE CLOSER TO YOU.
YES SIR! AND YOU...?
I WILL ...
BOOM
...HEAD FOR THE RELIC PASSAGE LOCATED IN THE DEPTHS OF THE SEWER!

CHARACTER PROFILE

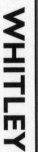

WHITLEY

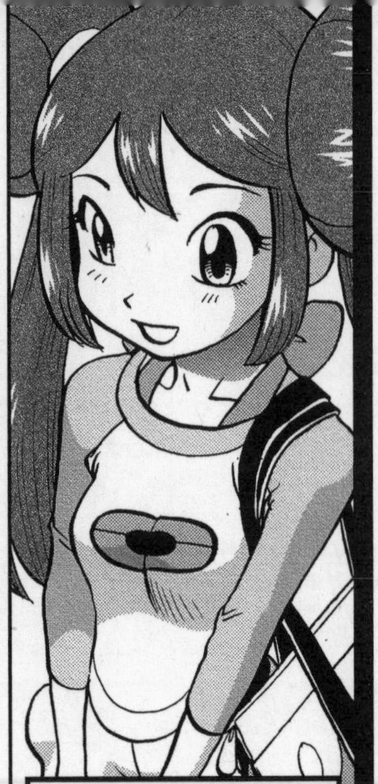

- Affiliated with: Trainers' School 75th Graduating Class, Class E (a boarding student who transferred for the second semester)
- Age: 12 years old (as of Adventure 12)
- Birthday: September16
- Zodiac: Gothorita
- Place of Birth: White Forest
- Family Member: Mother
- Hobby: Stargazing
- Favorite Food: Parfait
- Favorite Flower: Gracidea
- Favorite Color: Blue
- Favorite Subject: Status Condition Studies

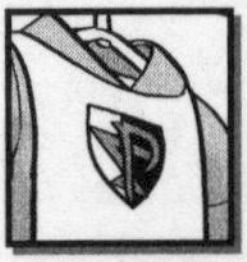

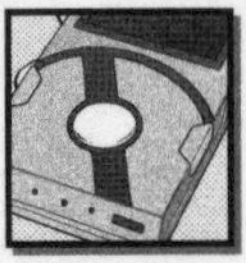

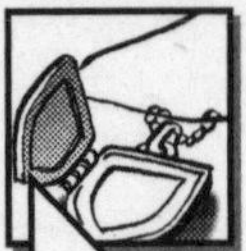

WHITLEY

A girl who transferred to the Trainers' School in Aspertia City for the second semester. She is skilled at Pokémon battles and has been using a Foongus, which she has grown very fond of, for a very long time. She is a former member of Team Plasma. She used to live with her mother in a village governed by Seven Sage Rood. She enrolled in the Trainers' School at her mother's suggestion and has been trying hard not to draw undue attention there. The opposition group within Team Plasma—which includes Rood and Gorm—undertook secret research, and the data has been discreetly hidden in Whitley's locket, now lost to her. Whitley has very strong feelings for N. As the winner of the practical Pokémon battle (girls' division) on the first day she transferred to the school, she was awarded a Pokédex. However, she has been hesitant to use it because N doesn't approve of them.

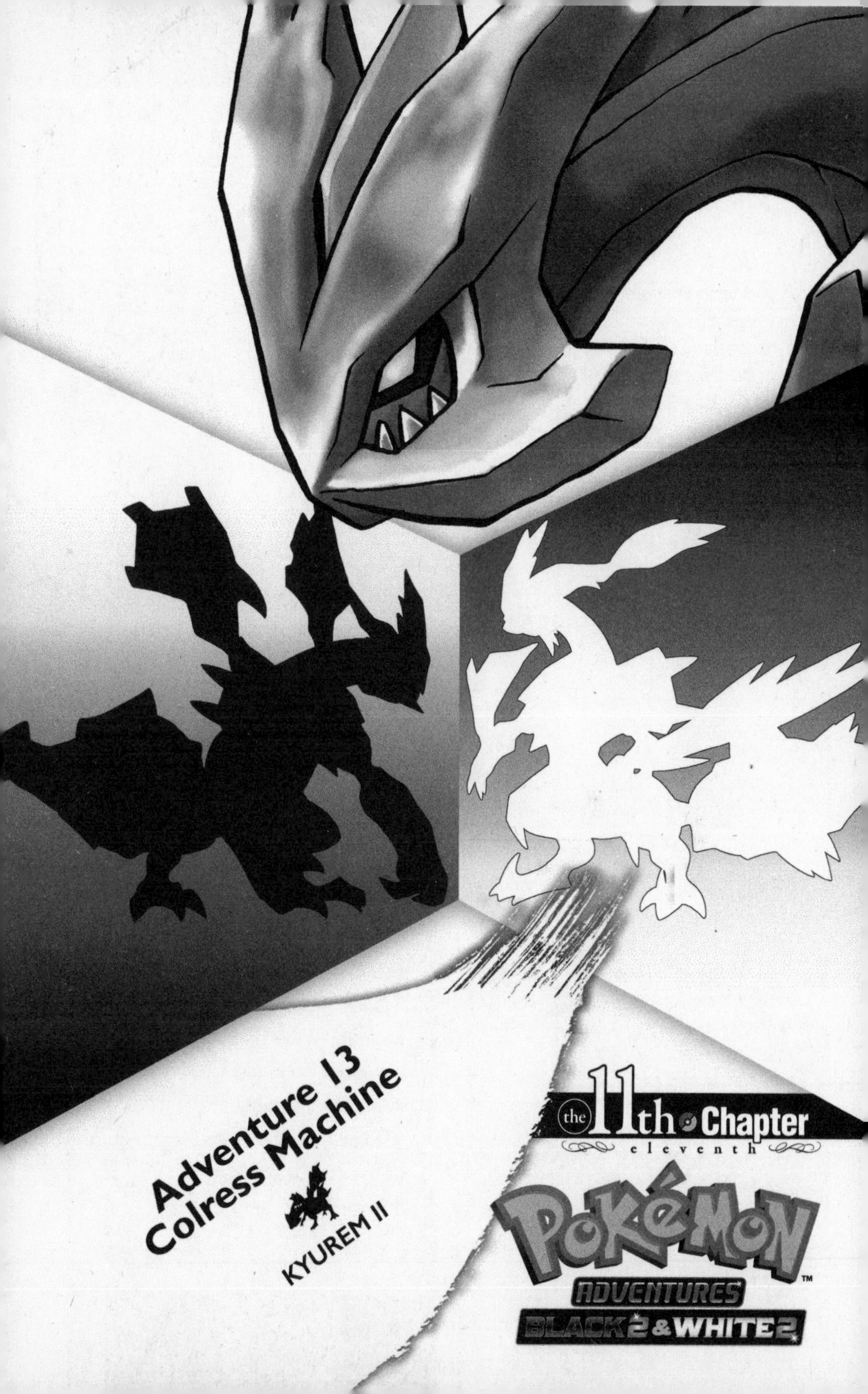
Adventure 13
Colress Machine
KYUREM II
the 11th Chapter
eleventh
POKÉMON™
ADVENTURES
BLACK 2 & WHITE 2

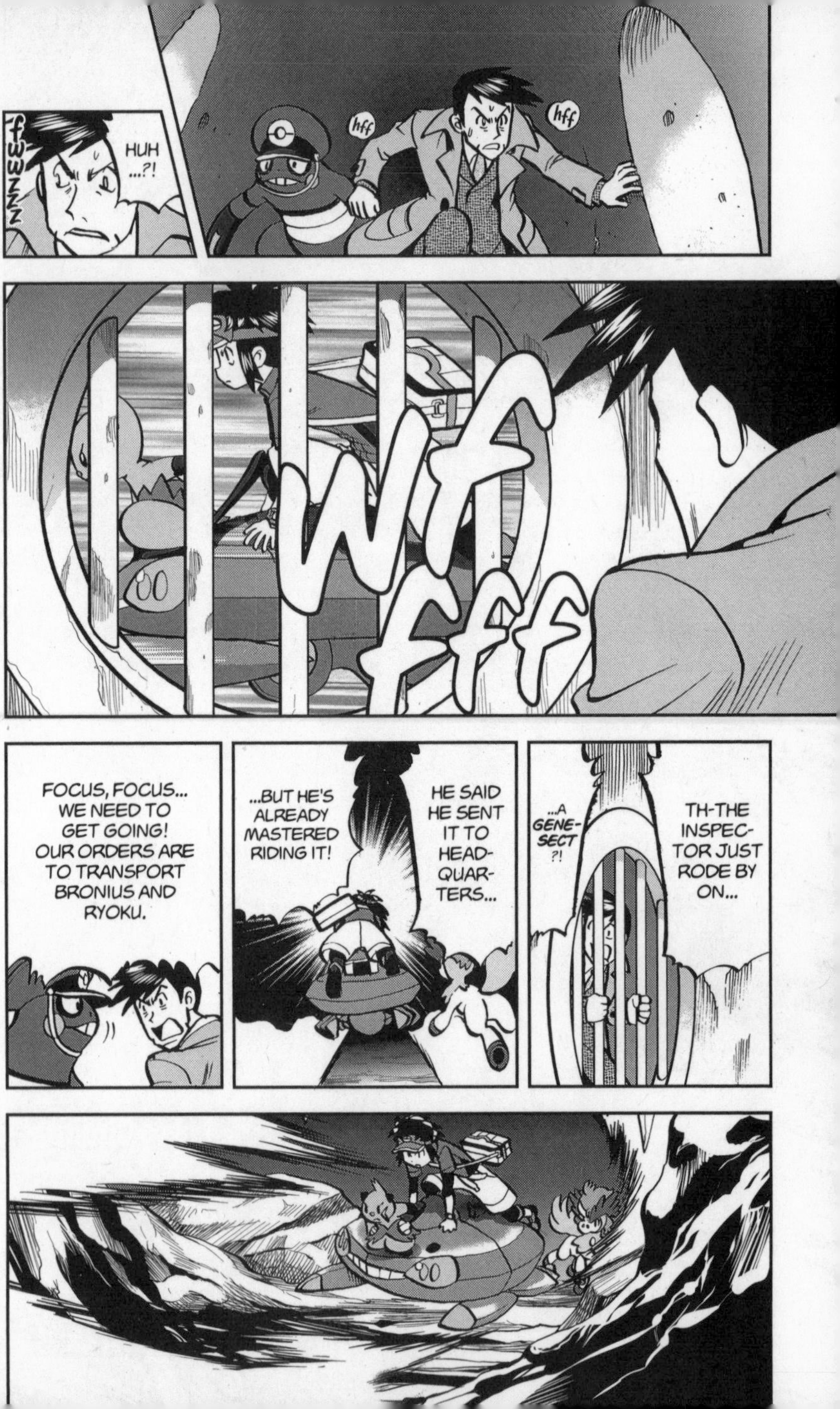
hff
hff
HUH ...?!
fwwzzz
wf
fff
TH-THE INSPECTOR JUST RODE BY ON...
...A GENESECT?!
HE SAID HE SENT IT TO HEADQUARTERS...
...BUT HE'S ALREADY MASTERED RIDING IT!
FOCUS, FOCUS... WE NEED TO GET GOING! OUR ORDERS ARE TO TRANSPORT BRONIUS AND RYOKU.

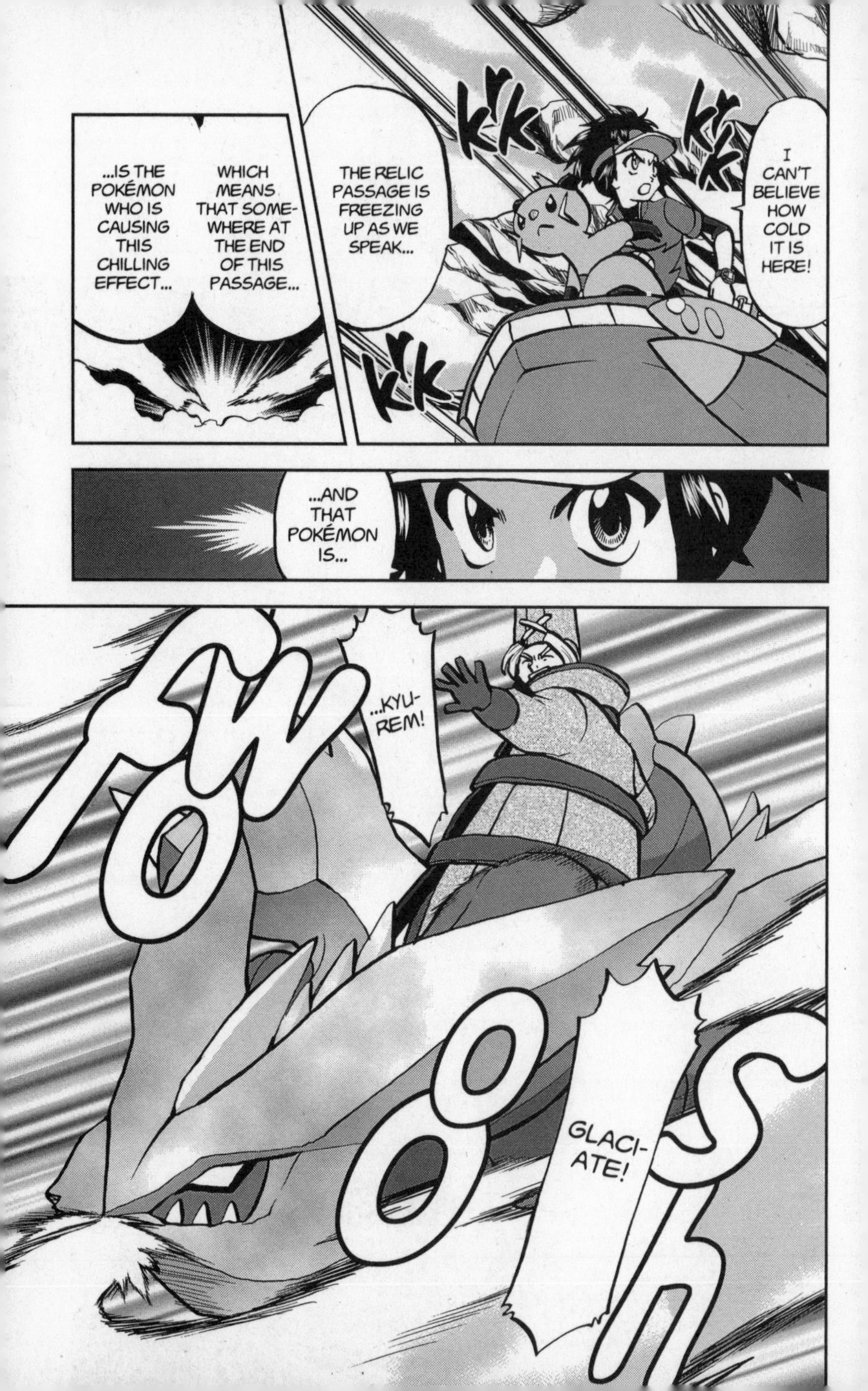
I CAN'T BELIEVE HOW COLD IT IS HERE!
THE RELIC PASSAGE IS FREEZING UP AS WE SPEAK...
WHICH MEANS THAT SOME-WHERE AT THE END OF THIS PASSAGE...
...IS THE POKÉMON WHO IS CAUSING THIS CHILLING EFFECT...
...AND THAT POKÉMON IS...
...KYU-REM!
GLACI-ATE!

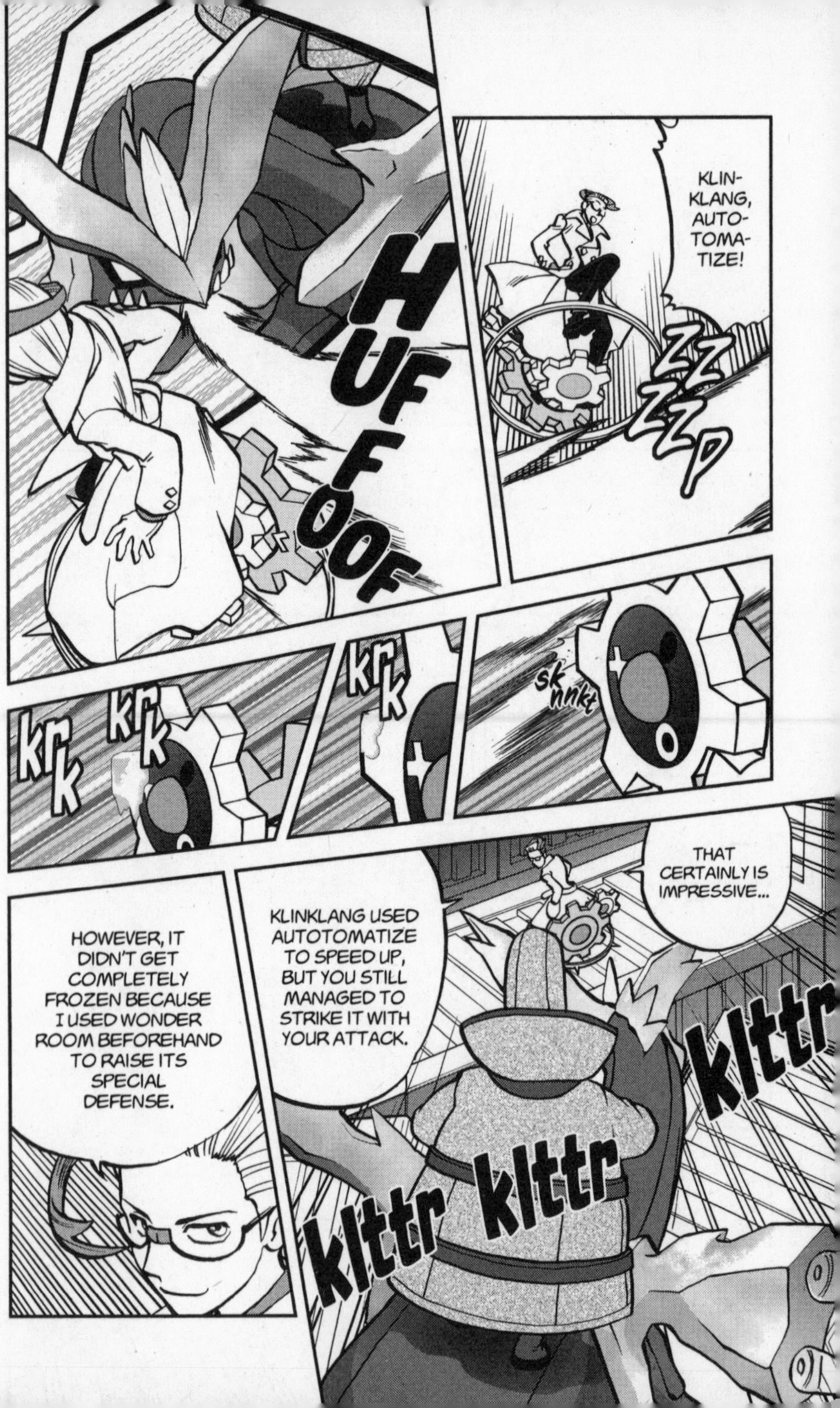
KLIN-KLANG, AUTO-TOMA-TIZE!
ZZZZP
HUFFOOF
sk nnkt
krk
krk krk
THAT CERTAINLY IS IMPRESSIVE...
KLINKLANG USED AUTOTOMATIZE TO SPEED UP, BUT YOU STILL MANAGED TO STRIKE IT WITH YOUR ATTACK.
kltter
kltter kltter
HOWEVER, IT DIDN'T GET COMPLETELY FROZEN BECAUSE I USED WONDER ROOM BEFOREHAND TO RAISE ITS SPECIAL DEFENSE.

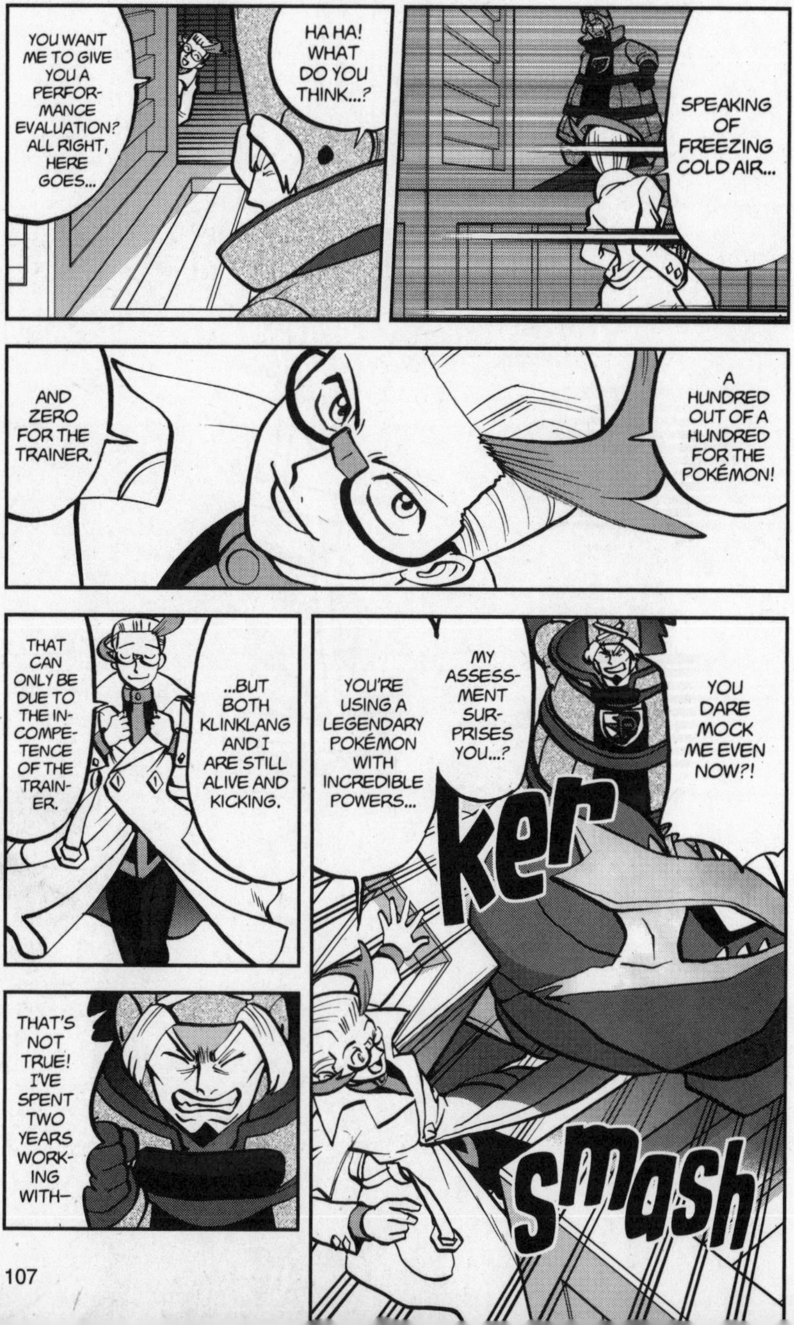
SPEAKING OF FREEZING COLD AIR...
HA HA! WHAT DO YOU THINK...?
YOU WANT ME TO GIVE YOU A PERFORMANCE EVALUATION? ALL RIGHT, HERE GOES...
A HUNDRED OUT OF A HUNDRED FOR THE POKÉMON!
AND ZERO FOR THE TRAINER.
YOU DARE MOCK ME EVEN NOW?!
MY ASSESSMENT SURPRISES YOU...?
YOU'RE USING A LEGENDARY POKÉMON WITH INCREDIBLE POWERS...
ker
smash
...BUT BOTH KLINKLANG AND I ARE STILL ALIVE AND KICKING.
THAT CAN ONLY BE DUE TO THE INCOMPETENCE OF THE TRAINER.
THAT'S NOT TRUE! I'VE SPENT TWO YEARS WORKING WITH—

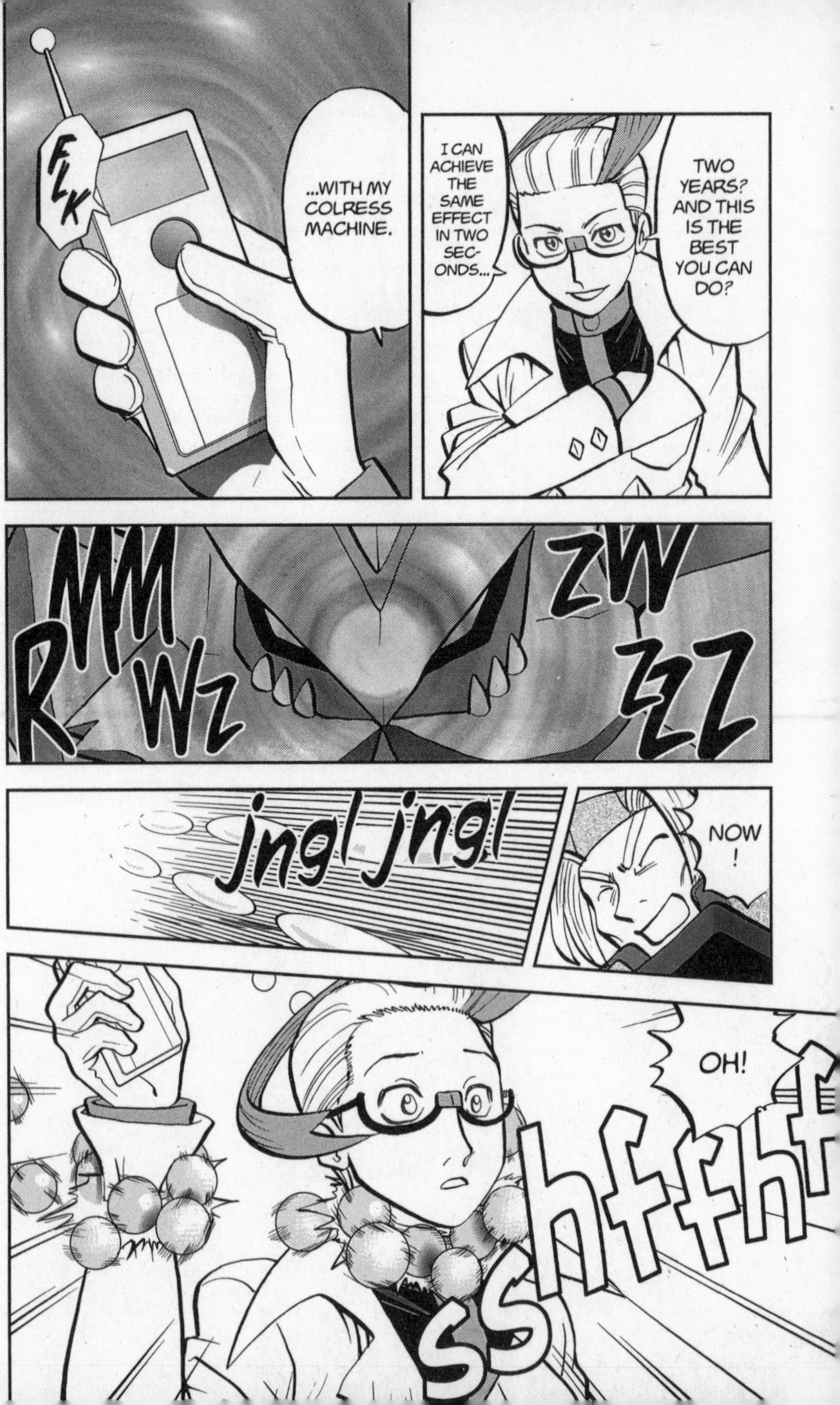
TWO YEARS? AND THIS IS THE BEST YOU CAN DO?
I CAN ACHIEVE THE SAME EFFECT IN TWO SECONDS...
...WITH MY COLRESS MACHINE.
FLK
ZWZZZ
RMMMWZ
NOW!
jngl jngl
OH!
sshffhf

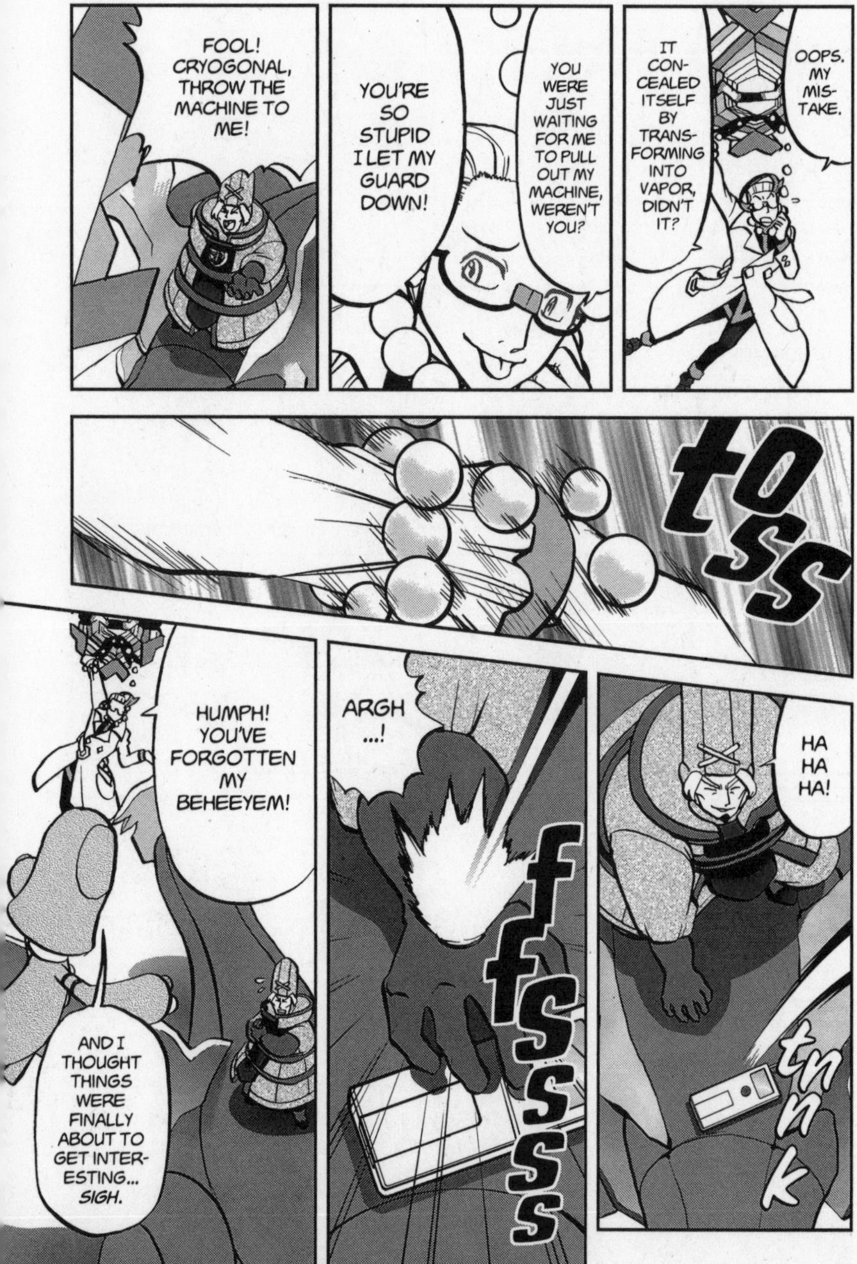
OOPS. MY MISTAKE.
IT CONCEALED ITSELF BY TRANSFORMING INTO VAPOR, DIDN'T IT?
YOU WERE JUST WAITING FOR ME TO PULL OUT MY MACHINE, WEREN'T YOU?
YOU'RE SO STUPID I LET MY GUARD DOWN!
FOOL! CRYOGONAL, THROW THE MACHINE TO ME!
toss
HA HA HA!
tnnk
ARGH ...!
ffssss
HUMPH! YOU'VE FORGOTTEN MY BEHEEYEM!
AND I THOUGHT THINGS WERE FINALLY ABOUT TO GET INTERESTING... SIGH.

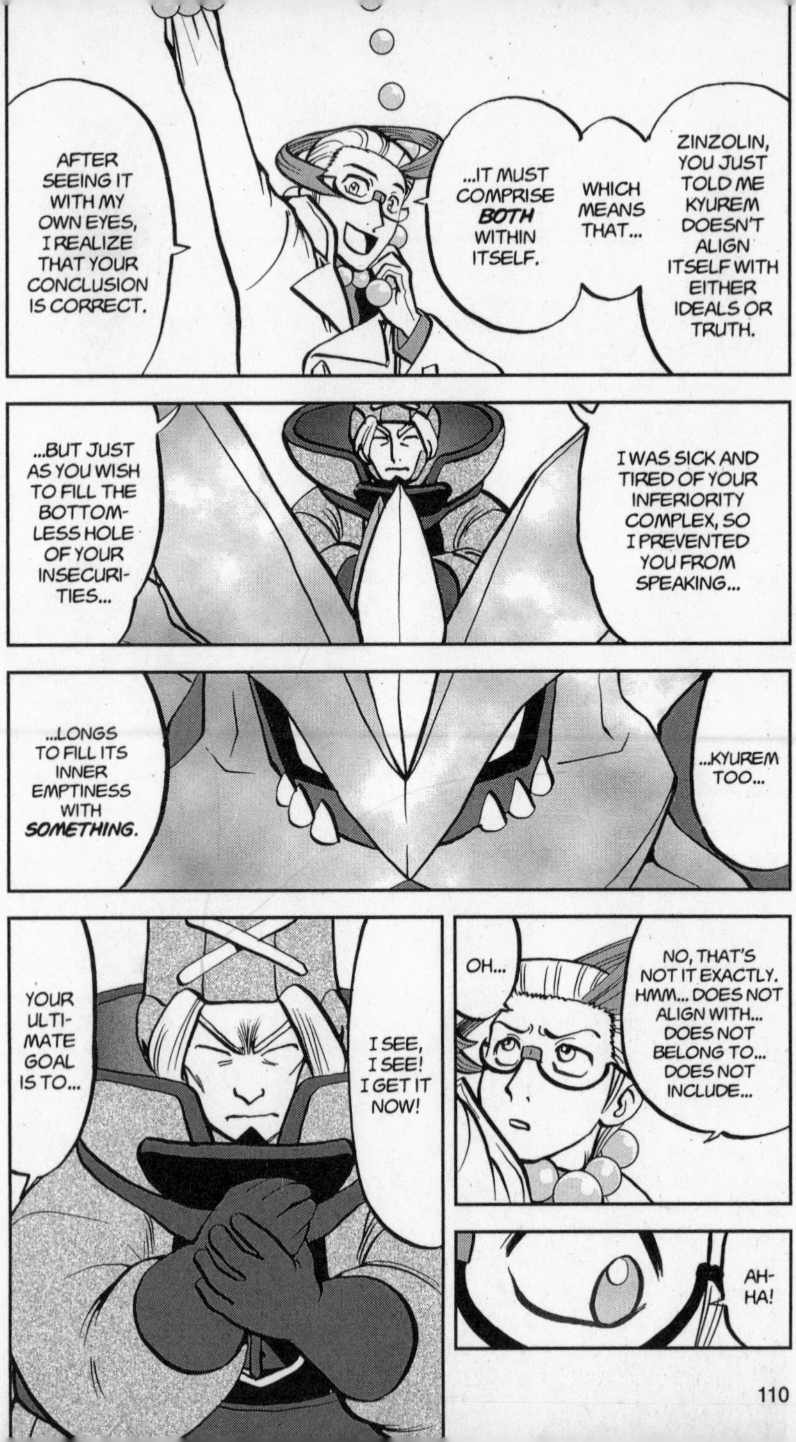
ZINZOLIN, YOU JUST TOLD ME KYUREM DOESN'T ALIGN ITSELF WITH EITHER IDEALS OR TRUTH.
WHICH MEANS THAT...
...IT MUST COMPRISE **BOTH** WITHIN ITSELF.
AFTER SEEING IT WITH MY OWN EYES, I REALIZE THAT YOUR CONCLUSION IS CORRECT.
I WAS SICK AND TIRED OF YOUR INFERIORITY COMPLEX, SO I PREVENTED YOU FROM SPEAKING...
...BUT JUST AS YOU WISH TO FILL THE BOTTOMLESS HOLE OF YOUR INSECURITIES...
...KYUREM TOO...
...LONGS TO FILL ITS INNER EMPTINESS WITH ***SOMETHING***.
NO, THAT'S NOT IT EXACTLY. HMM... DOES NOT ALIGN WITH... DOES NOT BELONG TO... DOES NOT INCLUDE...
OH...
AH-HA!
I SEE, I SEE! I GET IT NOW!
YOUR ULTIMATE GOAL IS TO...

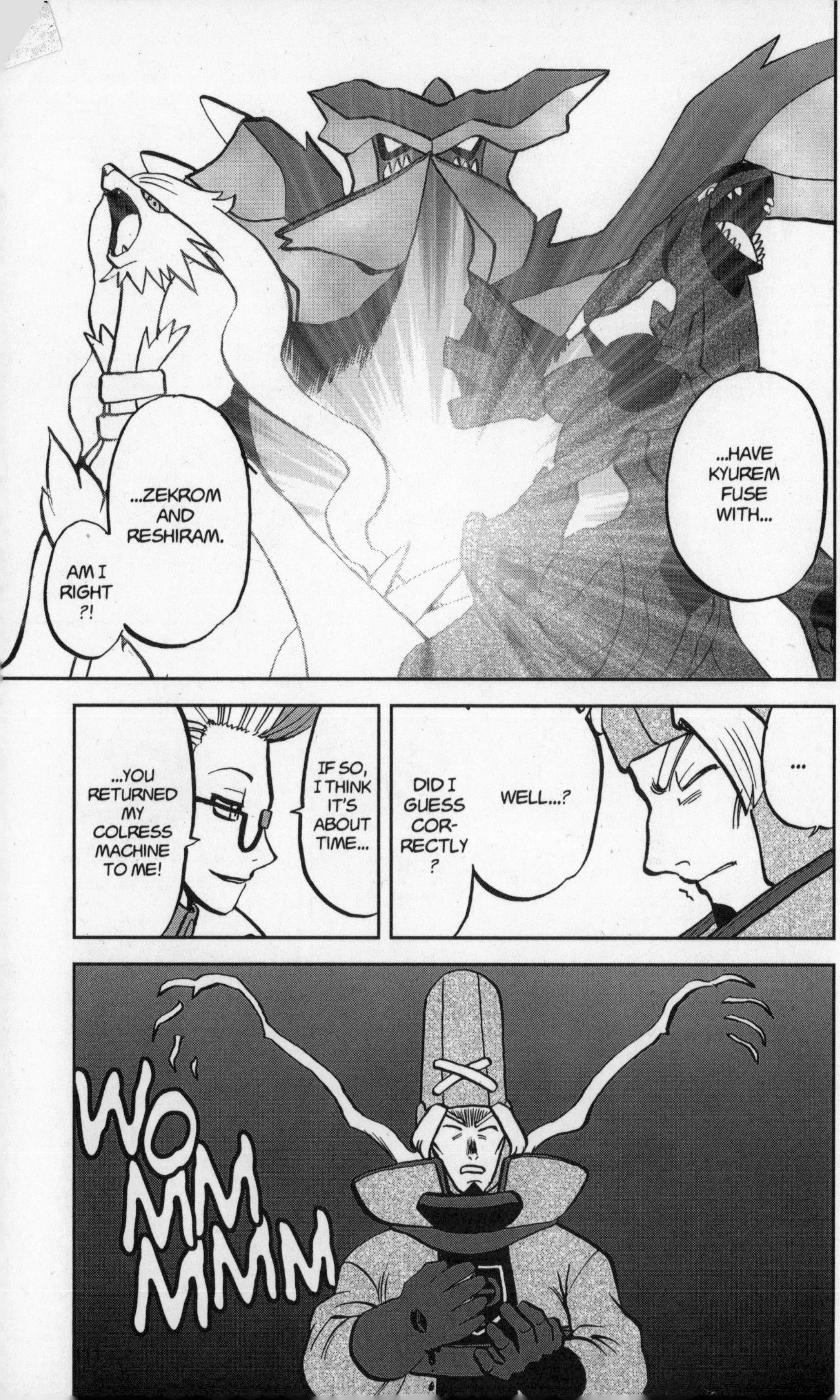
...HAVE KYUREM FUSE WITH...
...ZEKROM AND RESHIRAM.
AM I RIGHT ?!
...
WELL...?
DID I GUESS COR- RECTLY ?
IF SO, I THINK IT'S ABOUT TIME...
...YOU RETURNED MY COLRESS MACHINE TO ME!
WOMMMMMMM

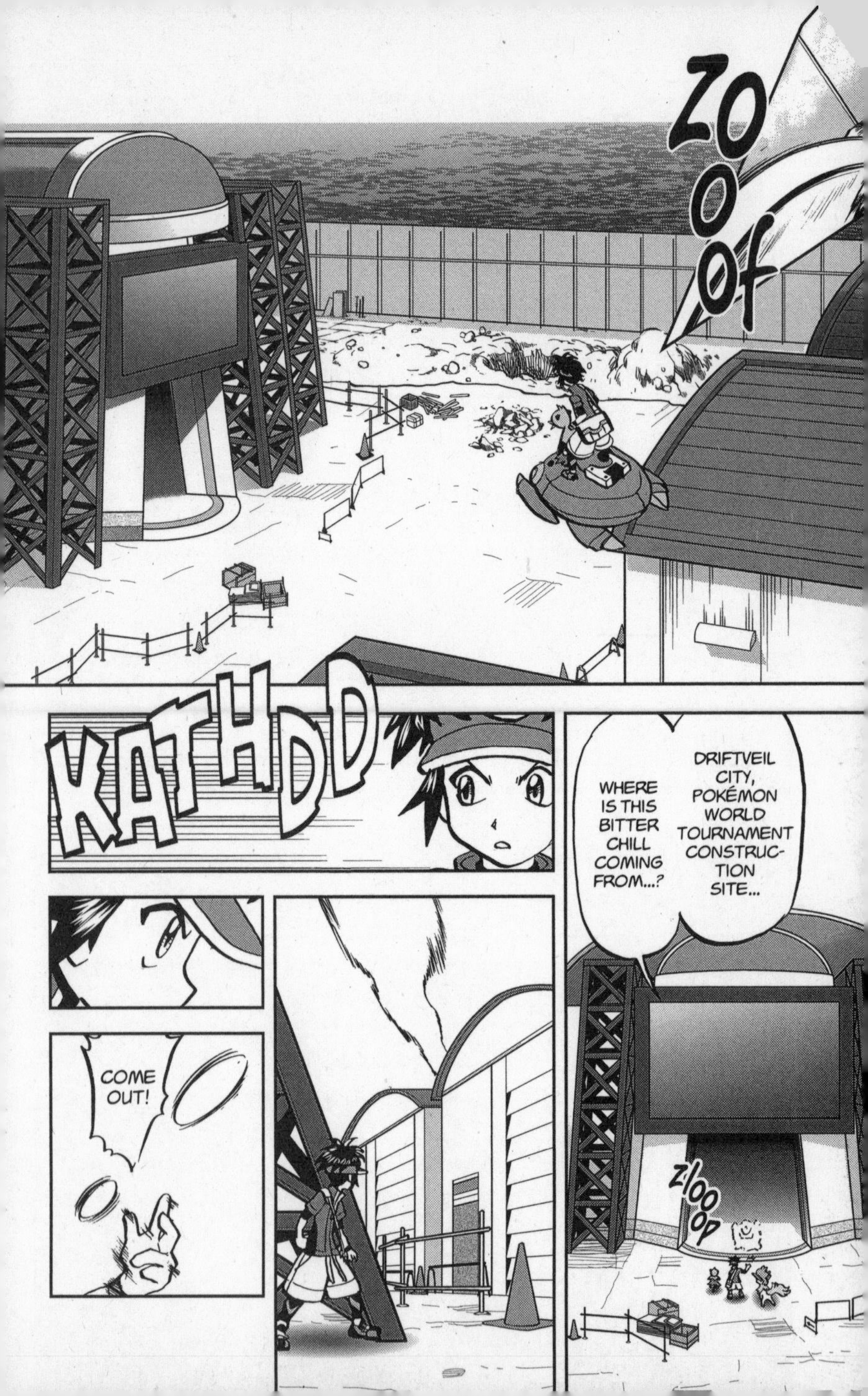
ZOOOF
DRIFTVEIL CITY, POKÉMON WORLD TOURNAMENT CONSTRUCTION SITE...
WHERE IS THIS BITTER CHILL COMING FROM...?
ZLOOOP
KATHDD
COME OUT!

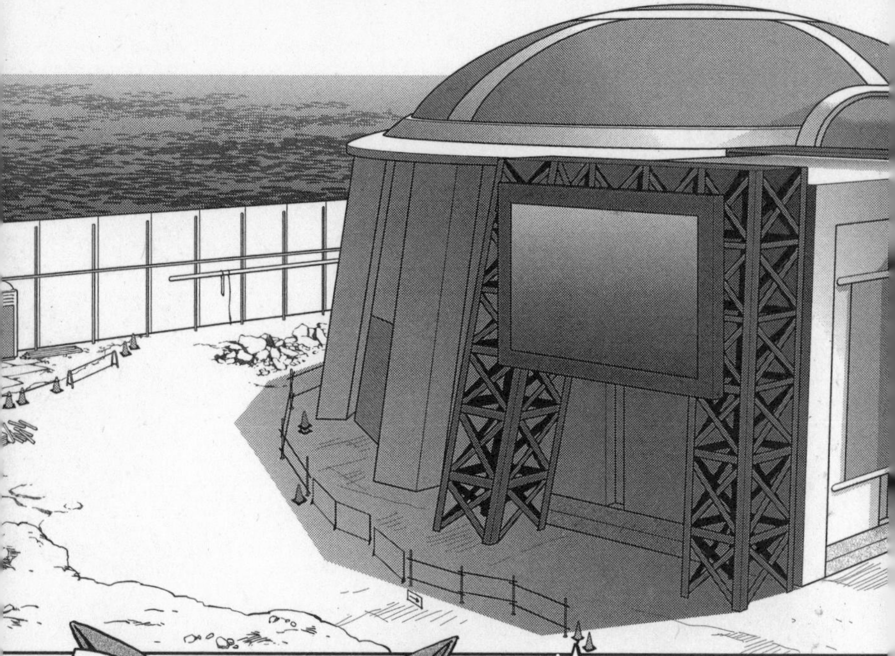

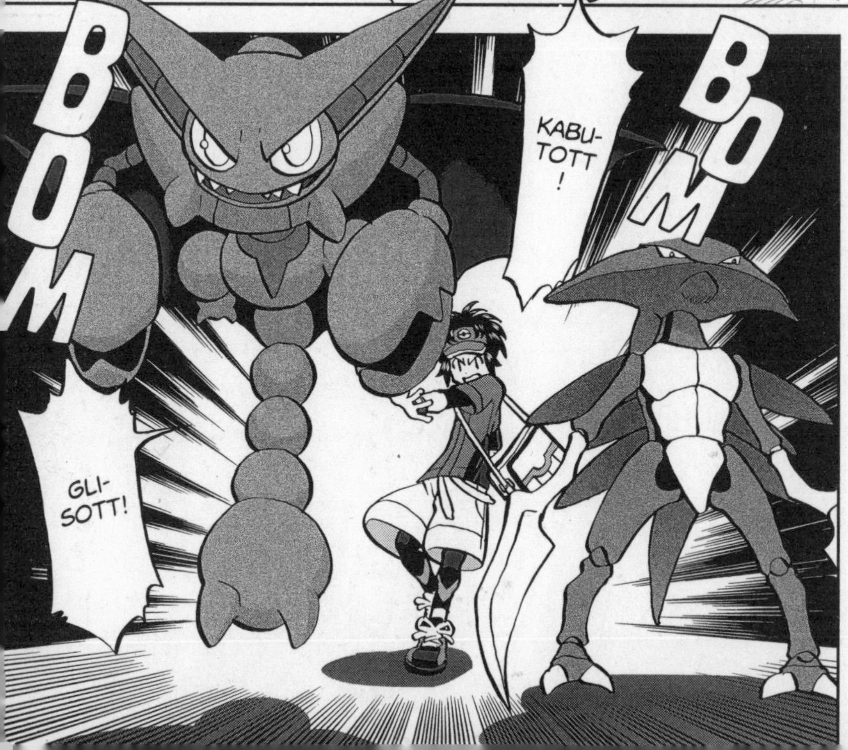
BOM
KABU-
TOTT
!
BOOM
GLI-
SOTT!

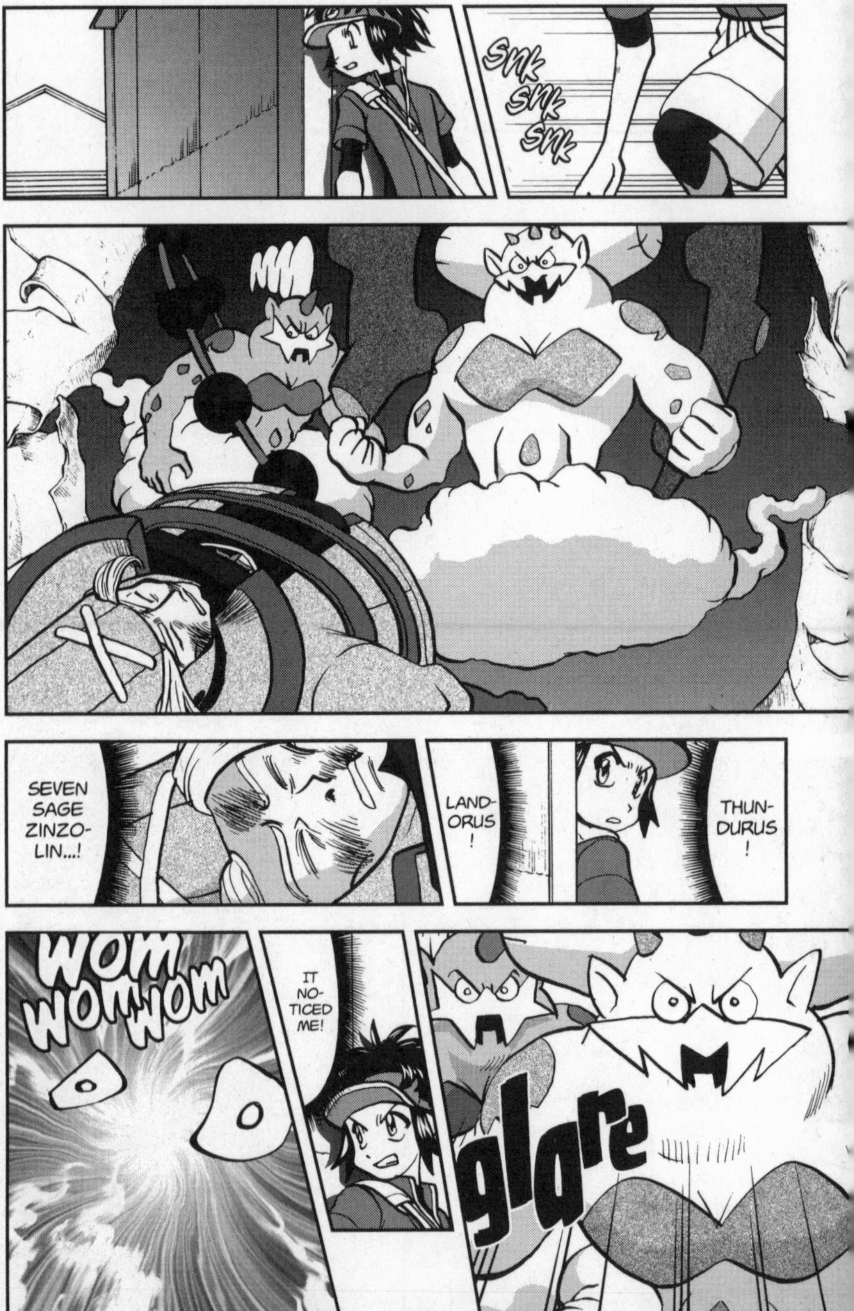
SNK
SNK
SNK
THUN-DURUS!
LAND-ORUS!
SEVEN SAGE ZINZOLIN...!
GLARE
IT NOTICED ME!
WOM
WOM WOM

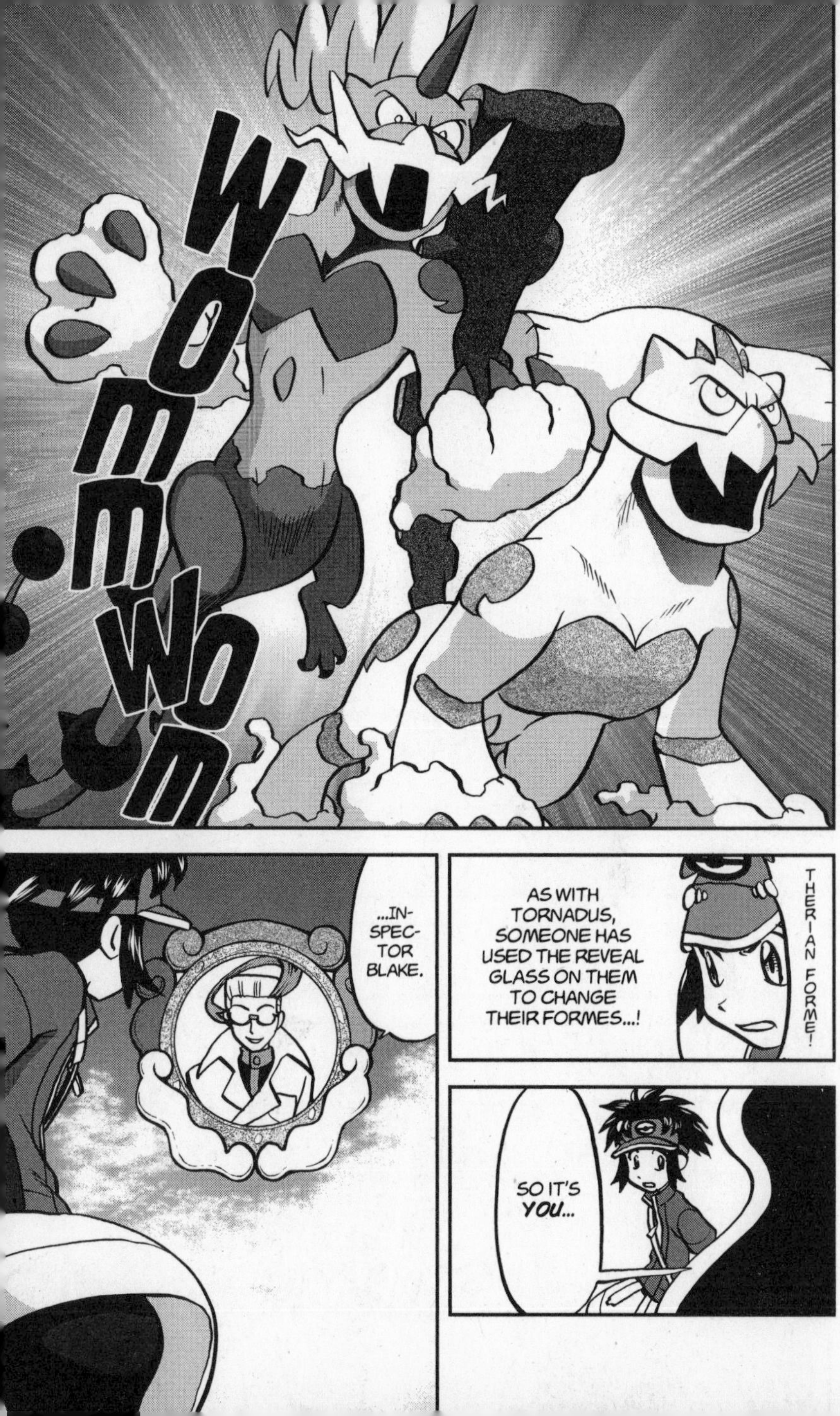
WOMMMWOM
THERIAN FORME!
AS WITH TORNADUS, SOMEONE HAS USED THE REVEAL GLASS ON THEM TO CHANGE THEIR FORMES...!
SO IT'S *YOU*...
...IN-SPEC-TOR BLAKE.

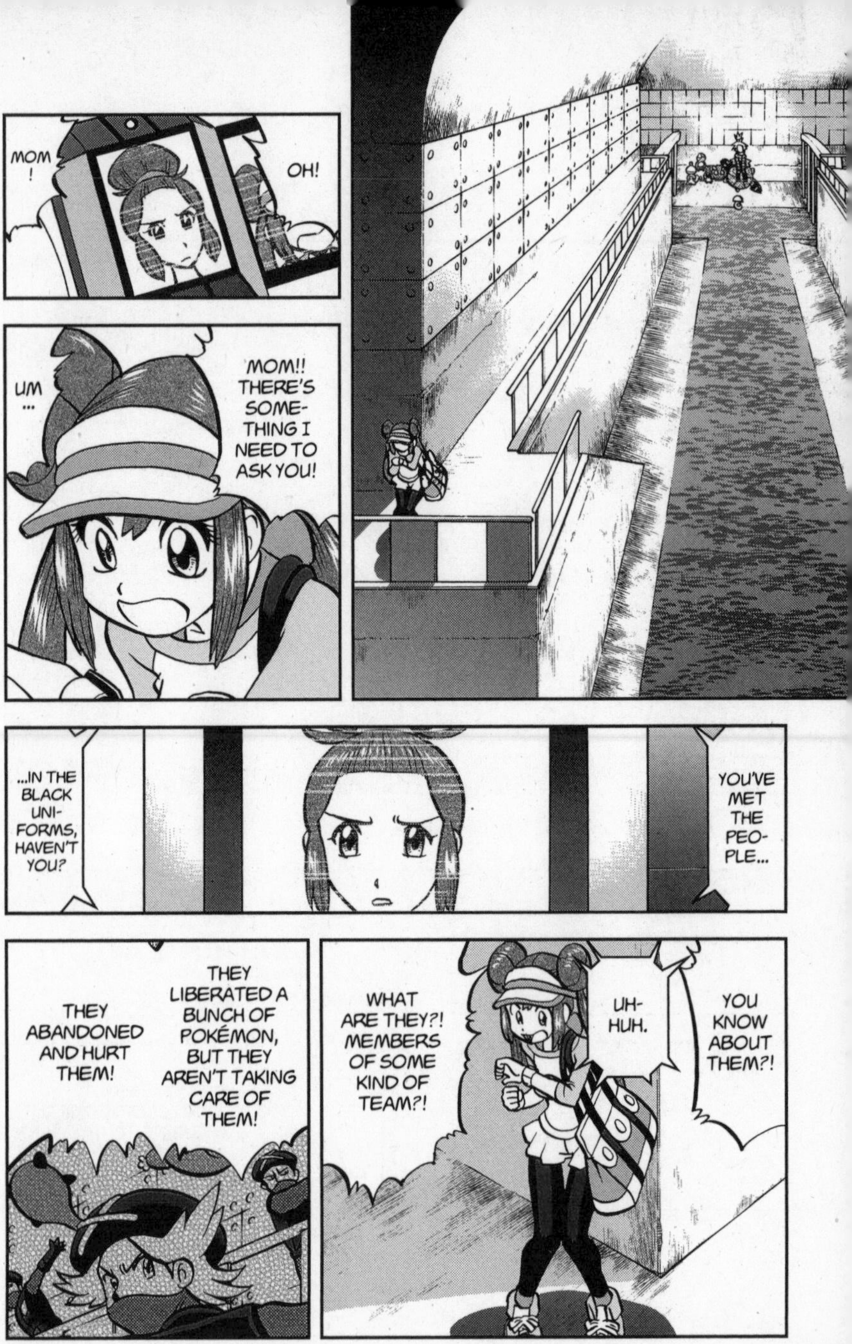
OH!
MOM !
MOM!! THERE'S SOME-THING I NEED TO ASK YOU!
UM ...
YOU'VE MET THE PEO-PLE...
...IN THE BLACK UNI-FORMS, HAVEN'T YOU?
YOU KNOW ABOUT THEM?!
UH-HUH.
WHAT ARE THEY?! MEMBERS OF SOME KIND OF TEAM?!
THEY LIBERATED A BUNCH OF POKÉMON, BUT THEY AREN'T TAKING CARE OF THEM!
THEY ABANDONED AND HURT THEM!

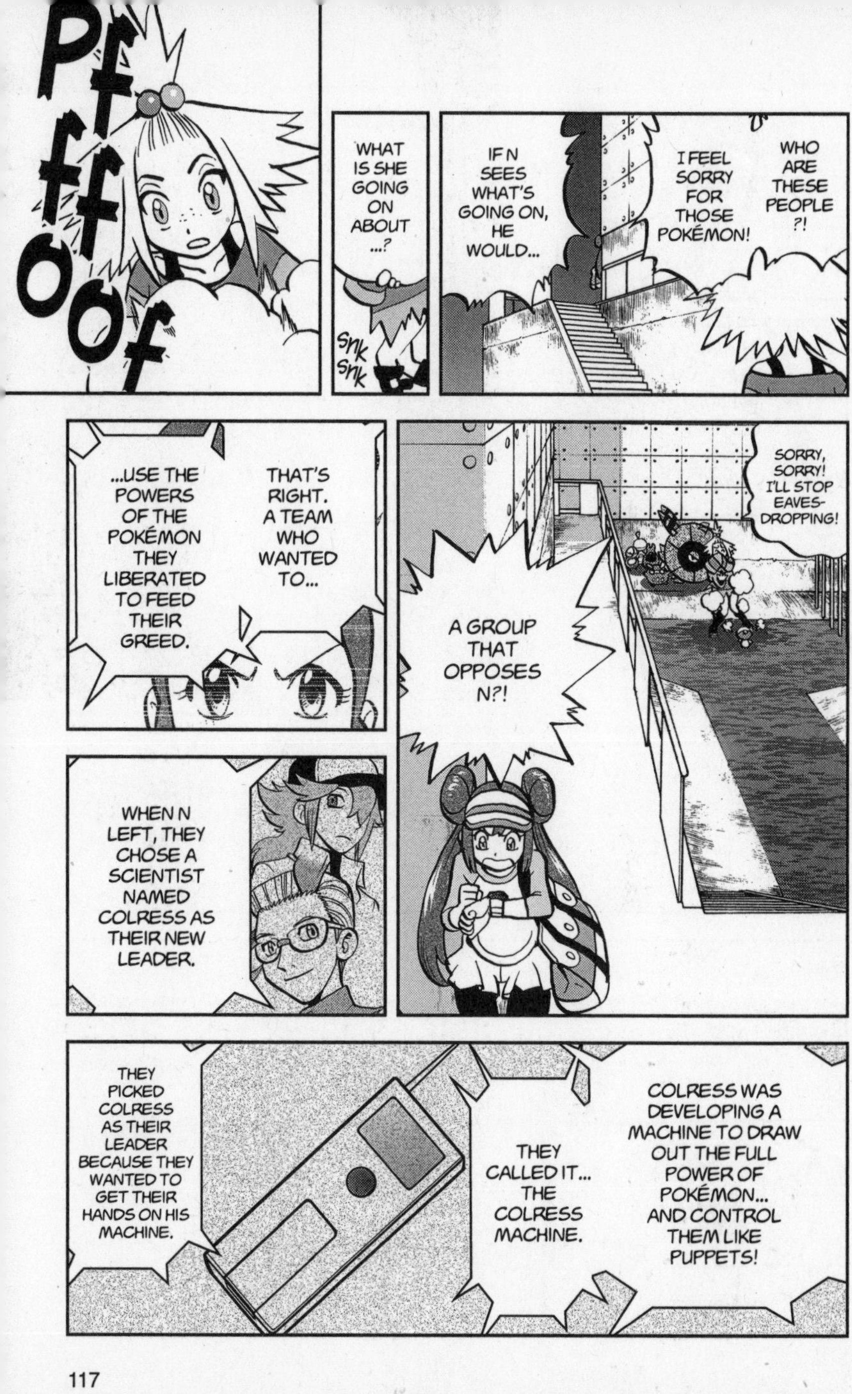
WHO ARE THESE PEOPLE ?!
I FEEL SORRY FOR THOSE POKÉMON!
IF N SEES WHAT'S GOING ON, HE WOULD...
WHAT IS SHE GOING ON ABOUT ...?
SNK SNK
PFFFOOF
SORRY, SORRY! I'LL STOP EAVES-DROPPING!
A GROUP THAT OPPOSES N?!
THAT'S RIGHT. A TEAM WHO WANTED TO...
...USE THE POWERS OF THE POKÉMON THEY LIBERATED TO FEED THEIR GREED.
WHEN N LEFT, THEY CHOSE A SCIENTIST NAMED COLRESS AS THEIR NEW LEADER.
COLRESS WAS DEVELOPING A MACHINE TO DRAW OUT THE FULL POWER OF POKÉMON... AND CONTROL THEM LIKE PUPPETS!
THEY CALLED IT... THE COLRESS MACHINE.
THEY PICKED COLRESS AS THEIR LEADER BECAUSE THEY WANTED TO GET THEIR HANDS ON HIS MACHINE.

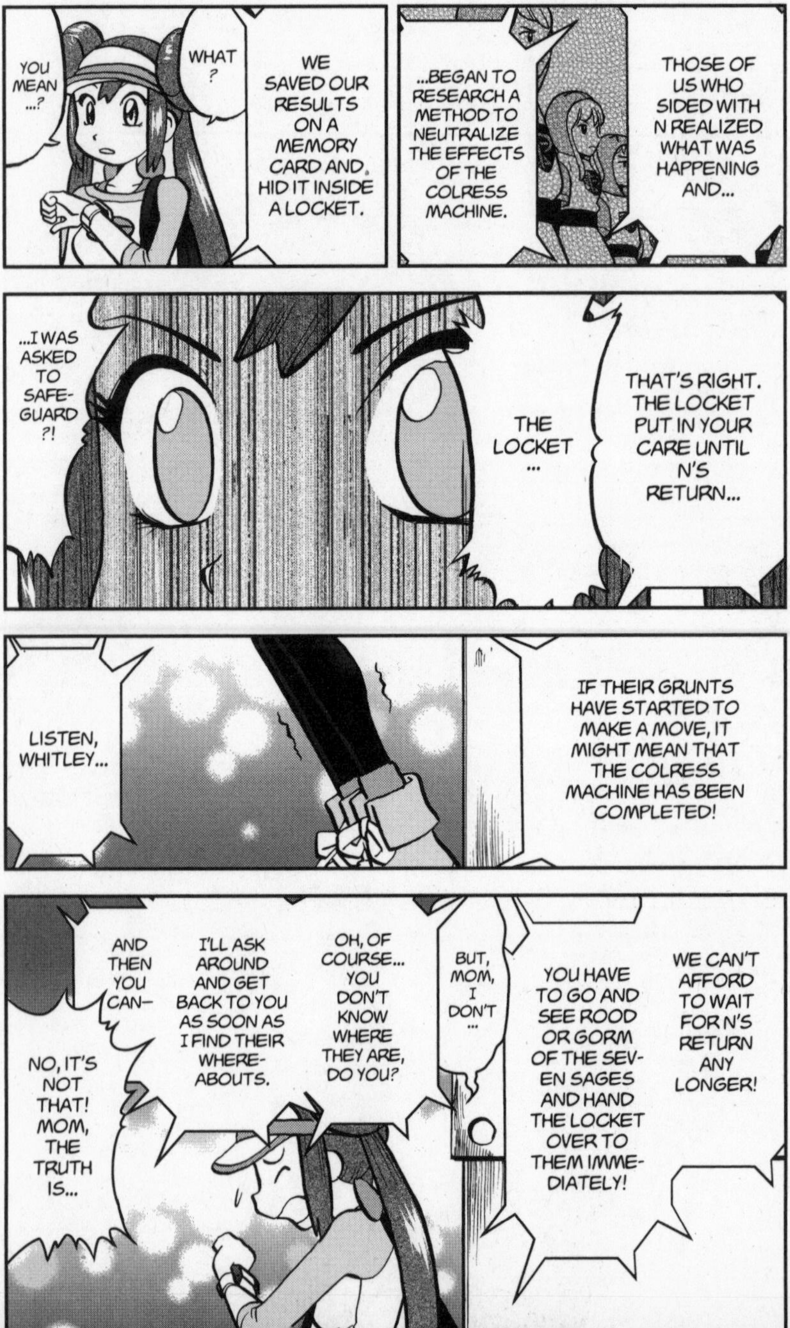
THOSE OF US WHO SIDED WITH N REALIZED WHAT WAS HAPPENING AND...
...BEGAN TO RESEARCH A METHOD TO NEUTRALIZE THE EFFECTS OF THE COLRESS MACHINE.
WE SAVED OUR RESULTS ON A MEMORY CARD AND HID IT INSIDE A LOCKET.
WHAT?
YOU MEAN...?
THAT'S RIGHT. THE LOCKET PUT IN YOUR CARE UNTIL N'S RETURN...
THE LOCKET...
...I WAS ASKED TO SAFE-GUARD?!
IF THEIR GRUNTS HAVE STARTED TO MAKE A MOVE, IT MIGHT MEAN THAT THE COLRESS MACHINE HAS BEEN COMPLETED!
LISTEN, WHITLEY...
WE CAN'T AFFORD TO WAIT FOR N'S RETURN ANY LONGER!
YOU HAVE TO GO AND SEE ROOD OR GORM OF THE SEV-EN SAGES AND HAND THE LOCKET OVER TO THEM IMME-DIATELY!
BUT, MOM, I DON'T...
OH, OF COURSE... YOU DON'T KNOW WHERE THEY ARE, DO YOU?
I'LL ASK AROUND AND GET BACK TO YOU AS SOON AS I FIND THEIR WHERE-ABOUTS.
AND THEN YOU CAN—
NO, IT'S NOT THAT! MOM, THE TRUTH IS...

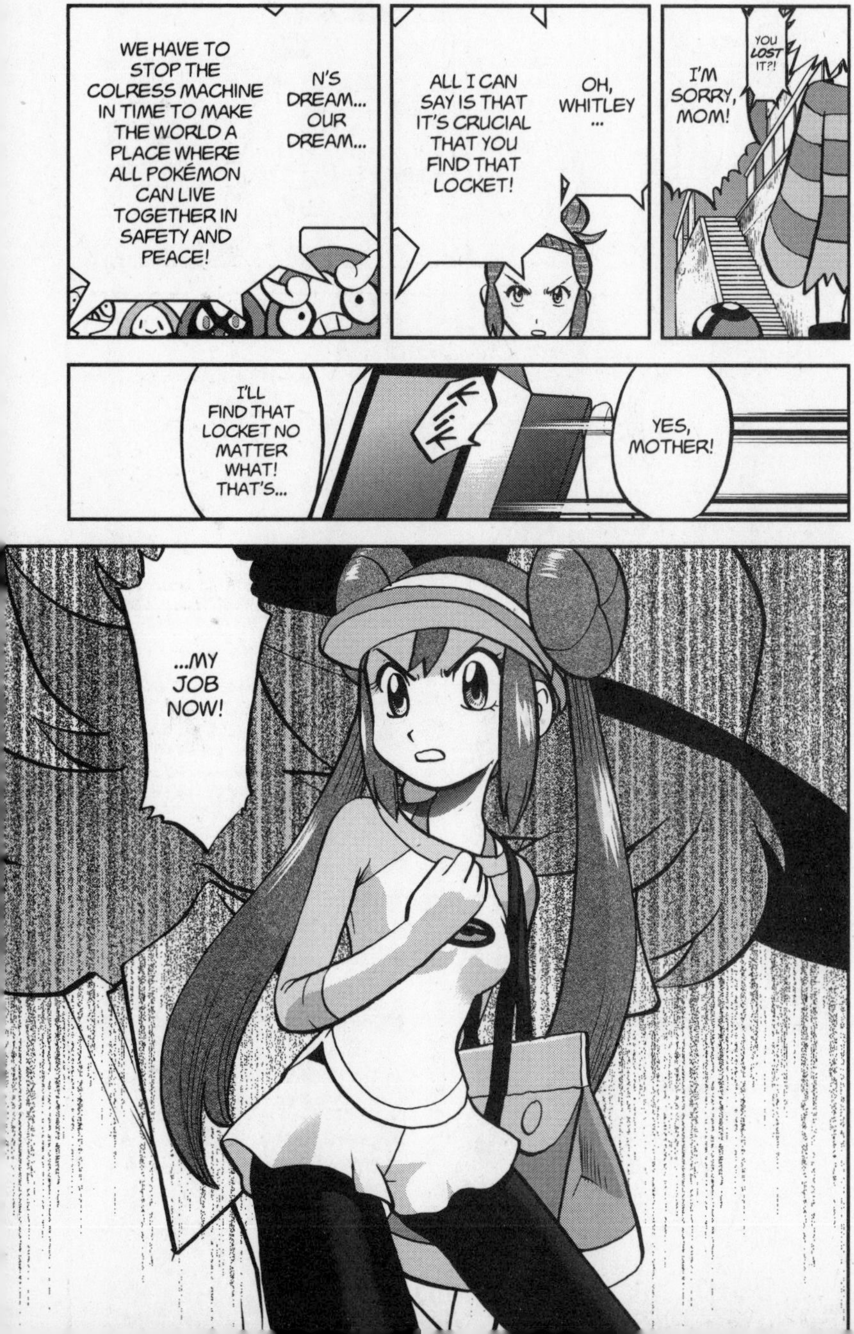
YOU LOST IT?!
I'M SORRY, MOM!
OH, WHITLEY...
ALL I CAN SAY IS THAT IT'S CRUCIAL THAT YOU FIND THAT LOCKET!
N'S DREAM... OUR DREAM...
WE HAVE TO STOP THE COLRESS MACHINE IN TIME TO MAKE THE WORLD A PLACE WHERE ALL POKÉMON CAN LIVE TOGETHER IN SAFETY AND PEACE!
YES, MOTHER!
Klik
I'LL FIND THAT LOCKET NO MATTER WHAT! THAT'S...
...MY JOB NOW!

CHARACTER PROFILE

LEO

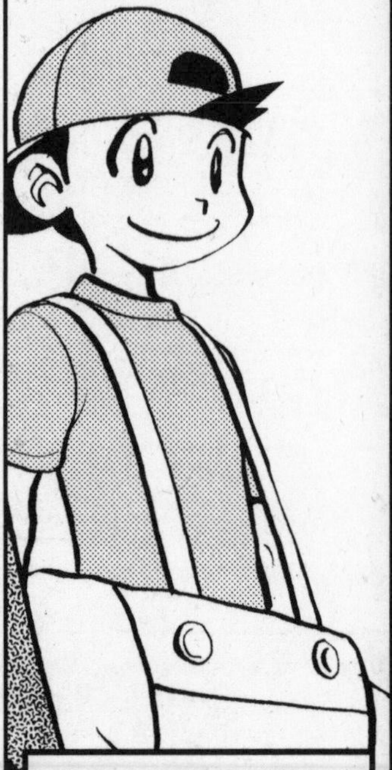

- Affiliated with: Trainers' School 75th Graduating Class, Class E (boarding student)
- Age: 11 years old (as of Adventure 13)
- Place of Birth: Lentimas Town
- Birthday: February
- Zodiac: Simipour
- Favorite Subject: Type Studies
- Grade Rank (First Semester) 75th Graduating Class, 8th out of 150 Students
- Awards: Unova Pokémon League Final Eight Contestant

LEO

A Trainers' School classmate of Blake, Whitley and Hugh. Leo is a skilled Deino Trainer who entered the Pokémon League two years ago. He was defeated by Cheren in the quarter finals but still managed to make it into the Final Eight. He was reunited with Cheren two years later when Cheren arrived at the school as a new teacher. Leo is reserved and not too physically active, but when push comes to shove one can rely upon him and his Pokémon battle skills. He lives in the dorms and shares a room with Hugh. Hugh has asked him to watch over his little sister after she followed him onto the ferry...

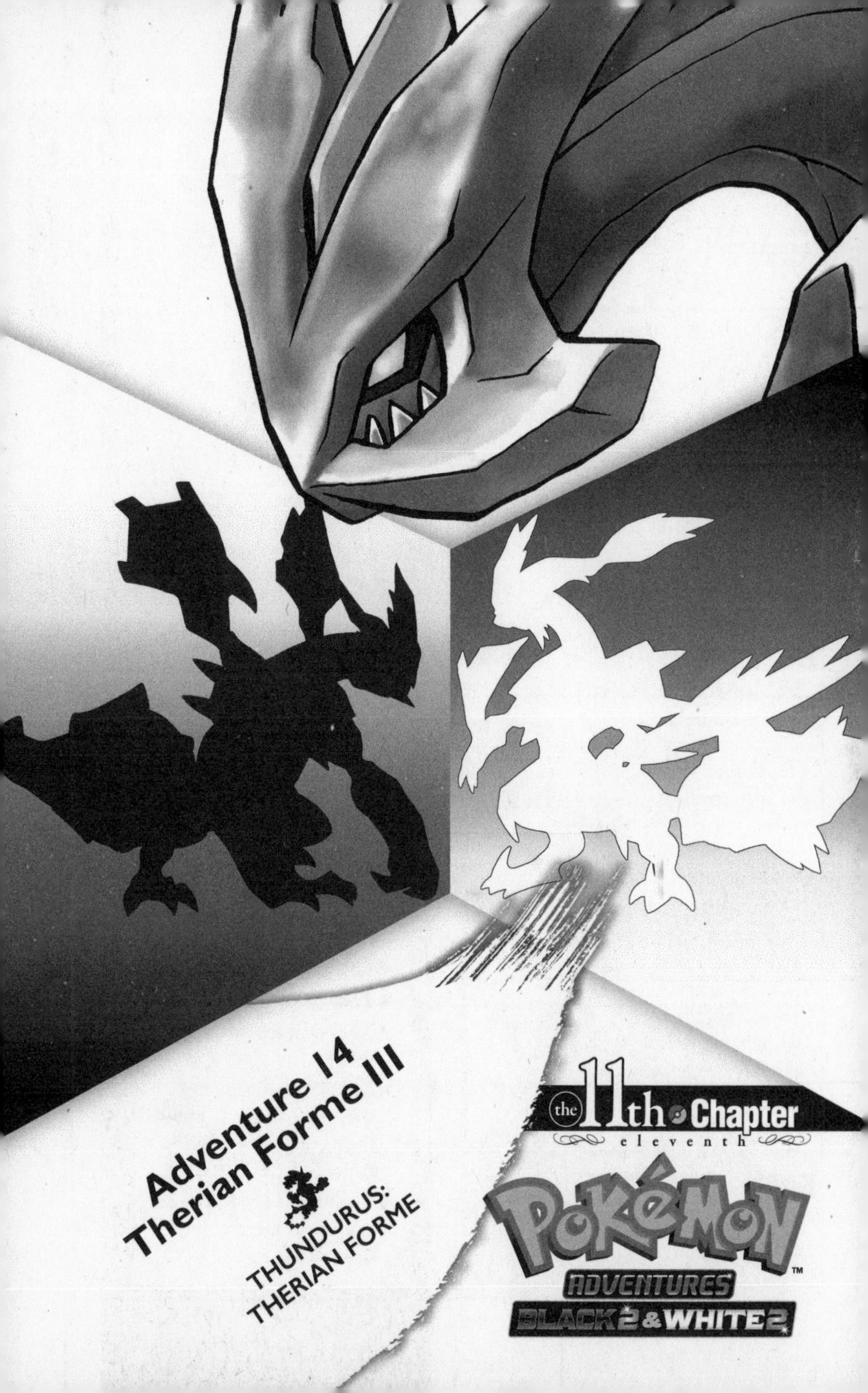
Adventure 14
Therian Forme III
THUNDURUS:
THERIAN FORME
the 11th Chapter
eleventh
POKéMON
ADVENTURES
BLACK 2 & WHITE 2

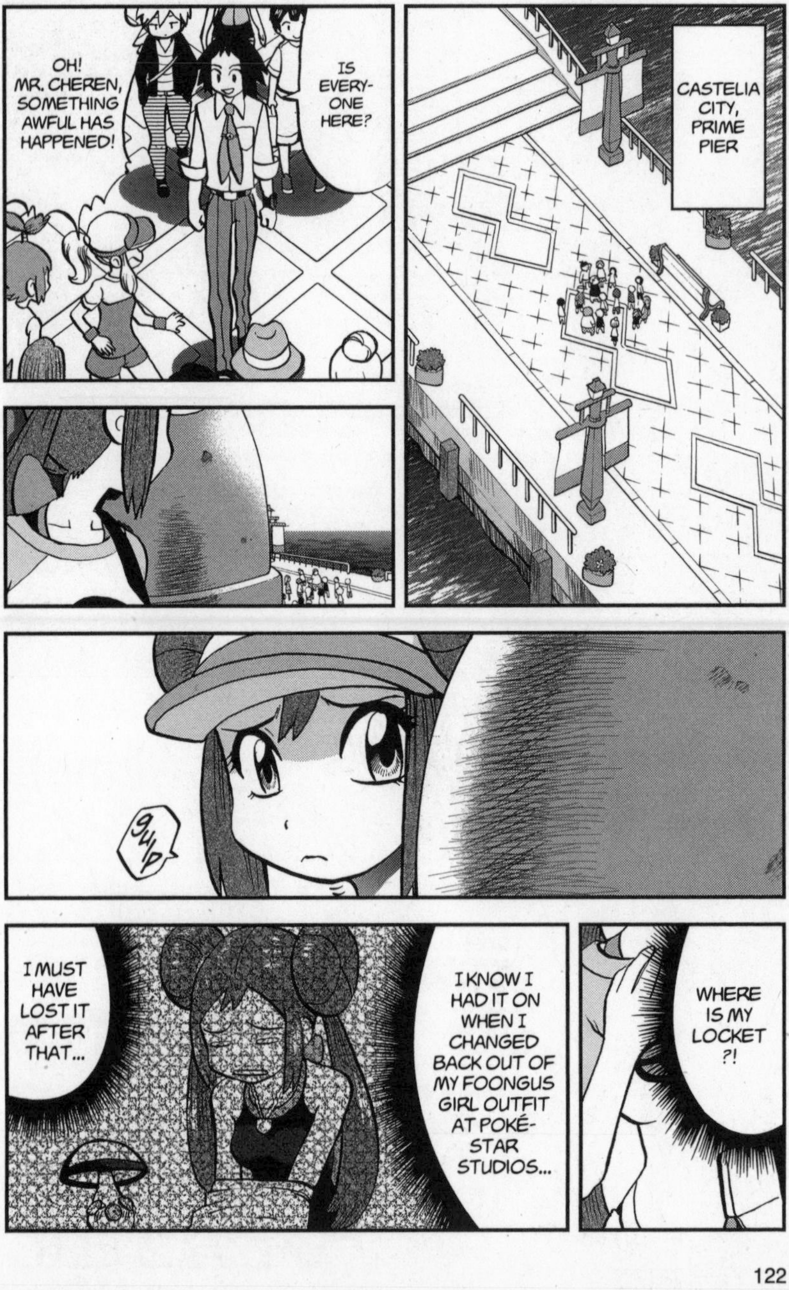
CASTELIA CITY, PRIME PIER
IS EVERYONE HERE?
OH! MR. CHEREN, SOMETHING AWFUL HAS HAPPENED!
gulp
WHERE IS MY LOCKET?!
I KNOW I HAD IT ON WHEN I CHANGED BACK OUT OF MY FOONGUS GIRL OUTFIT AT POKÉSTAR STUDIOS...
I MUST HAVE LOST IT AFTER THAT...

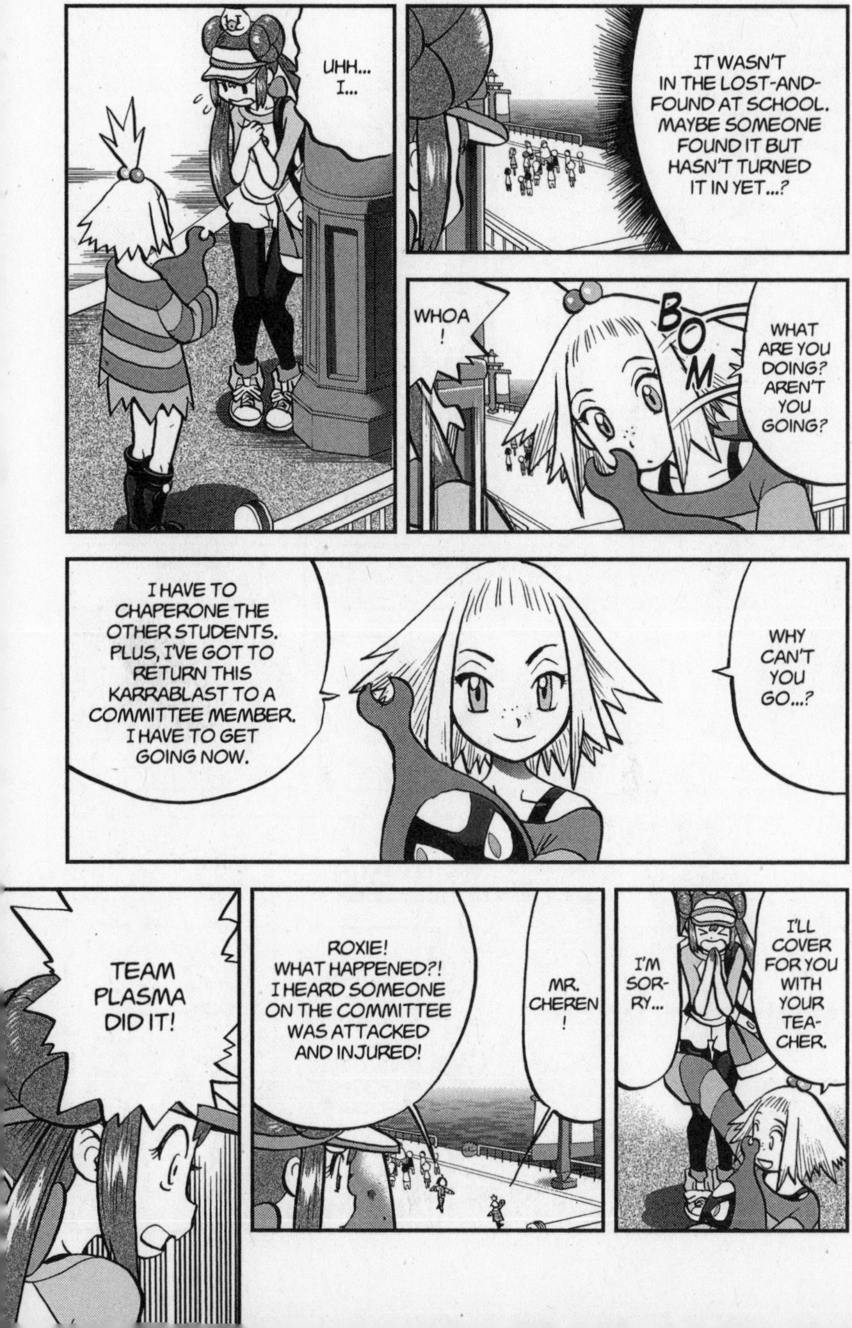
IT WASN'T IN THE LOST-AND-FOUND AT SCHOOL. MAYBE SOMEONE FOUND IT BUT HASN'T TURNED IT IN YET...?
WHAT ARE YOU DOING? AREN'T YOU GOING?
BOM
WHOA!
UHH... I...
WHY CAN'T YOU GO...?
I HAVE TO CHAPERONE THE OTHER STUDENTS. PLUS, I'VE GOT TO RETURN THIS KARRABLAST TO A COMMITTEE MEMBER. I HAVE TO GET GOING NOW.
I'LL COVER FOR YOU WITH YOUR TEA-CHER.
I'M SOR-RY...
MR. CHEREN!
ROXIE! WHAT HAPPENED?! I HEARD SOMEONE ON THE COMMITTEE WAS ATTACKED AND INJURED!
TEAM PLASMA DID IT!

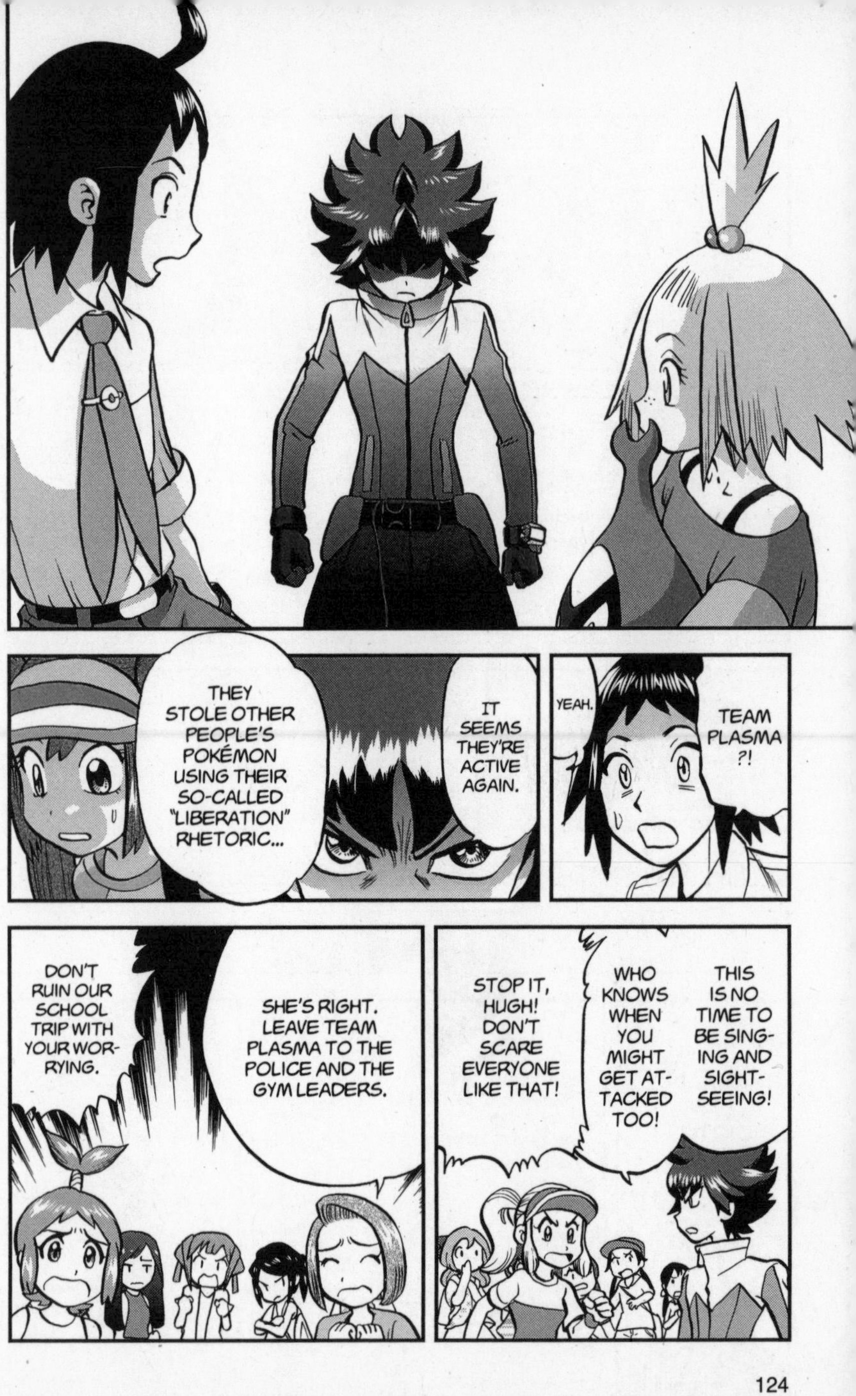
TEAM PLASMA?!
YEAH.
IT SEEMS THEY'RE ACTIVE AGAIN.
THEY STOLE OTHER PEOPLE'S POKÉMON USING THEIR SO-CALLED "LIBERATION" RHETORIC...
THIS IS NO TIME TO BE SINGING AND SIGHTSEEING!
WHO KNOWS WHEN YOU MIGHT GET ATTACKED TOO!
STOP IT, HUGH! DON'T SCARE EVERYONE LIKE THAT!
SHE'S RIGHT. LEAVE TEAM PLASMA TO THE POLICE AND THE GYM LEADERS.
DON'T RUIN OUR SCHOOL TRIP WITH YOUR WORRYING.

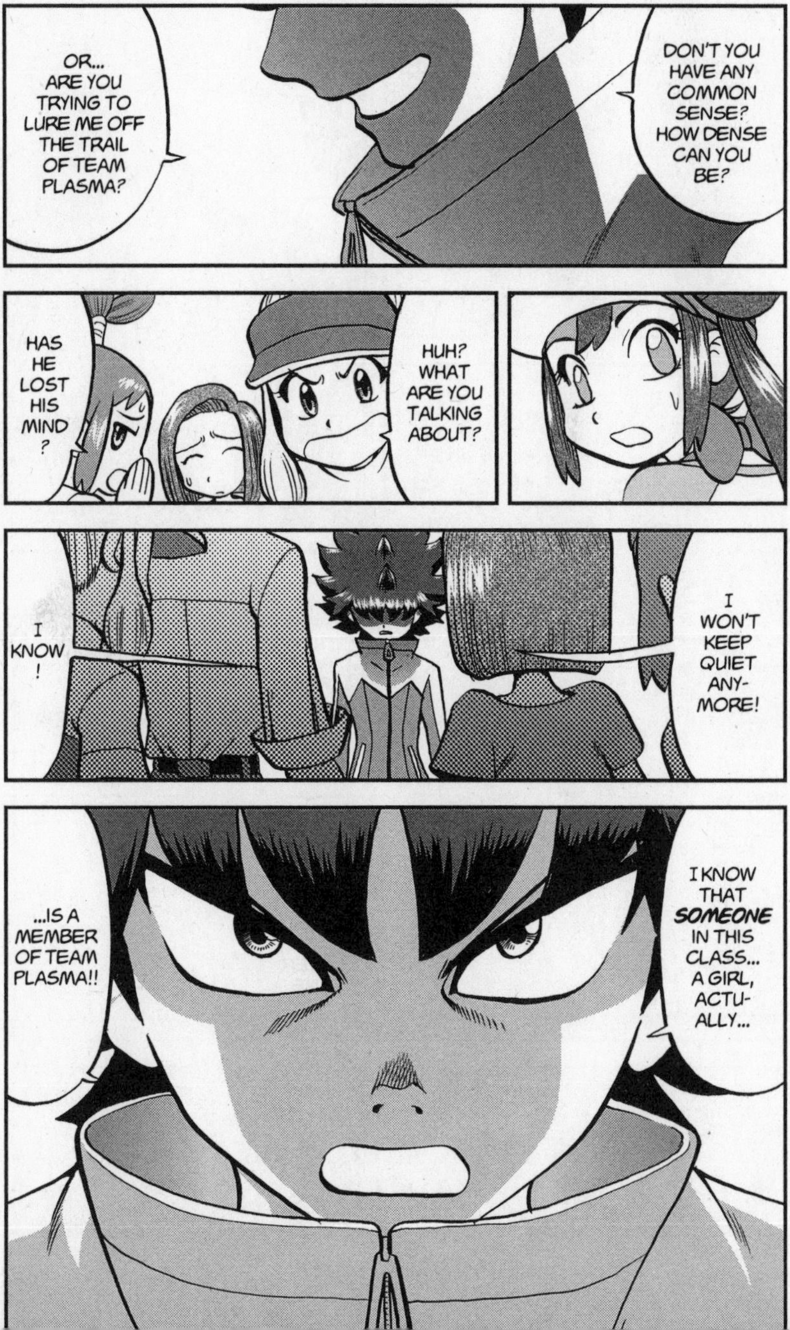
DON'T YOU HAVE ANY COMMON SENSE? HOW DENSE CAN YOU BE?
OR... ARE YOU TRYING TO LURE ME OFF THE TRAIL OF TEAM PLASMA?
HUH? WHAT ARE YOU TALKING ABOUT?
HAS HE LOST HIS MIND?
I WON'T KEEP QUIET ANY-MORE!
I KNOW!
I KNOW THAT **SOMEONE** IN THIS CLASS... A GIRL, ACTU-ALLY...
...IS A MEMBER OF TEAM PLASMA!!

IT'S TRUE, MR. CHEREN! ONE OF US IS A TEAM PLASMA MEMBER!

W-WHAT ARE YOU TALKING ABOUT, HUGH?!

GET OUT OF THIS CLASS— NO, THIS *SCHOOL*!

WE'RE SICK OF YOUR WILD THEORIES!

I CAN'T BELIEVE YOU, HUGH!

YOU DON'T NEED TO TELL ME TWICE, BECAUSE I'M LEAVING ANYWAY.

FINE!

I'M SORRY, MR. CHER-EN...

HUGH...

WHAT...?

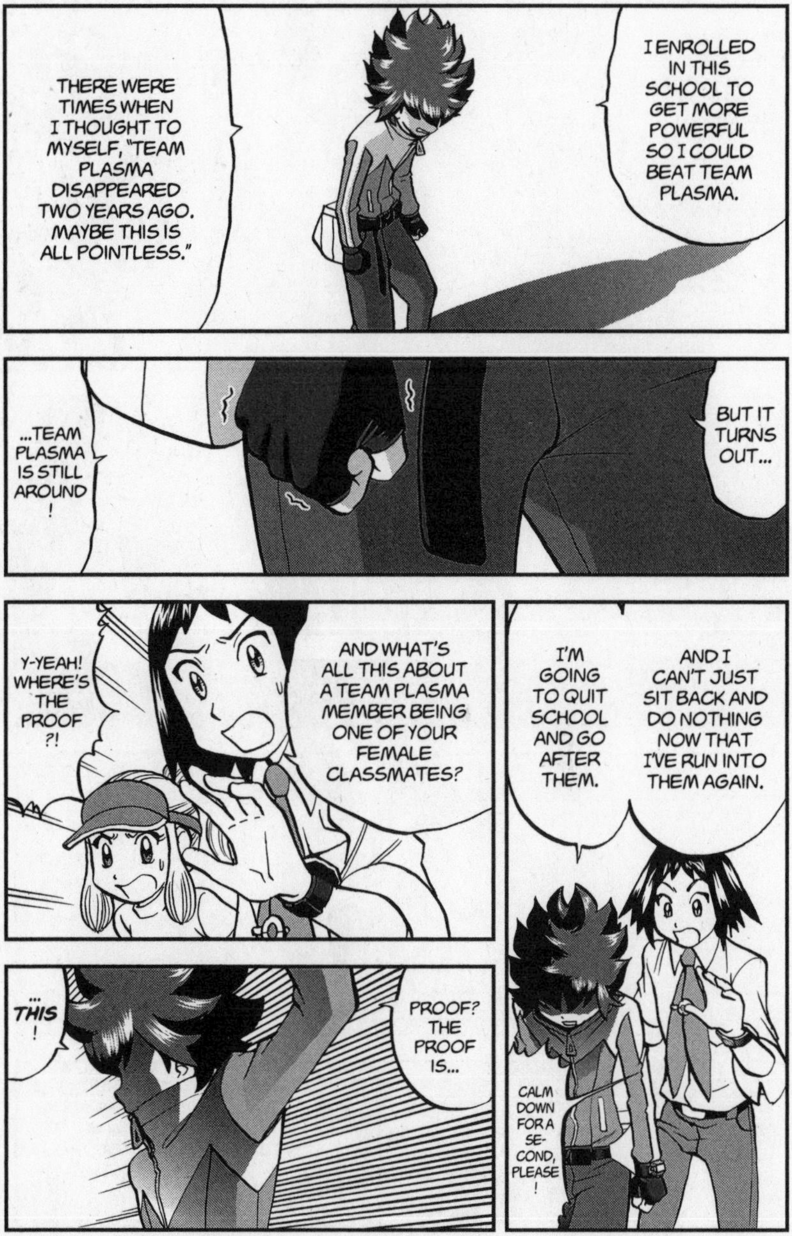
I ENROLLED IN THIS SCHOOL TO GET MORE POWERFUL SO I COULD BEAT TEAM PLASMA.
THERE WERE TIMES WHEN I THOUGHT TO MYSELF, "TEAM PLASMA DISAPPEARED TWO YEARS AGO. MAYBE THIS IS ALL POINTLESS."
BUT IT TURNS OUT...
...TEAM PLASMA IS STILL AROUND!
AND I CAN'T JUST SIT BACK AND DO NOTHING NOW THAT I'VE RUN INTO THEM AGAIN.
I'M GOING TO QUIT SCHOOL AND GO AFTER THEM.
CALM DOWN FOR A SE-COND, PLEASE!
AND WHAT'S ALL THIS ABOUT A TEAM PLASMA MEMBER BEING ONE OF YOUR FEMALE CLASSMATES?
Y-YEAH! WHERE'S THE PROOF?!
PROOF? THE PROOF IS...
...THIS!

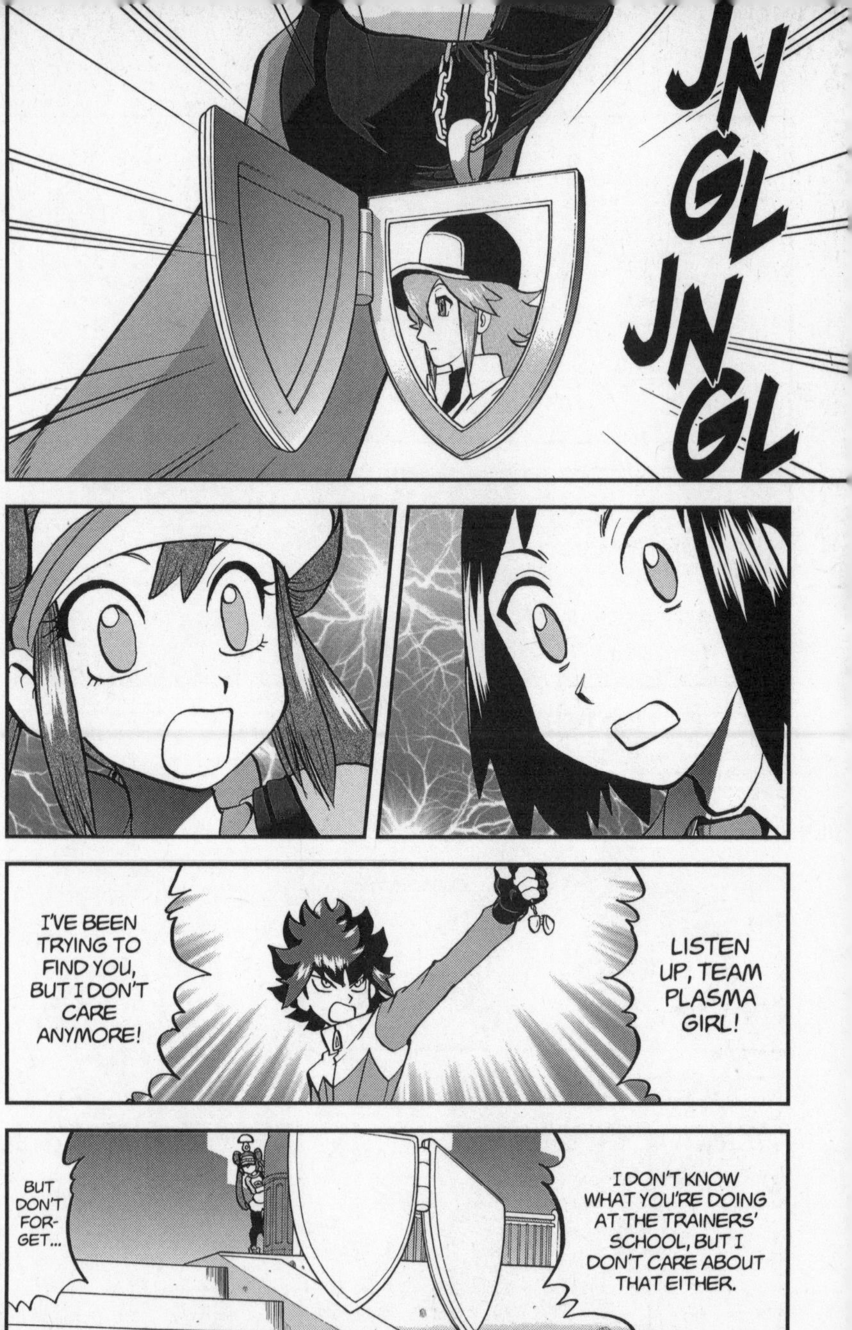
JNGL JNGL
LISTEN UP, TEAM PLASMA GIRL!
I'VE BEEN TRYING TO FIND YOU, BUT I DON'T CARE ANYMORE!
I DON'T KNOW WHAT YOU'RE DOING AT THE TRAINERS' SCHOOL, BUT I DON'T CARE ABOUT THAT EITHER.
BUT DON'T FOR-GET...

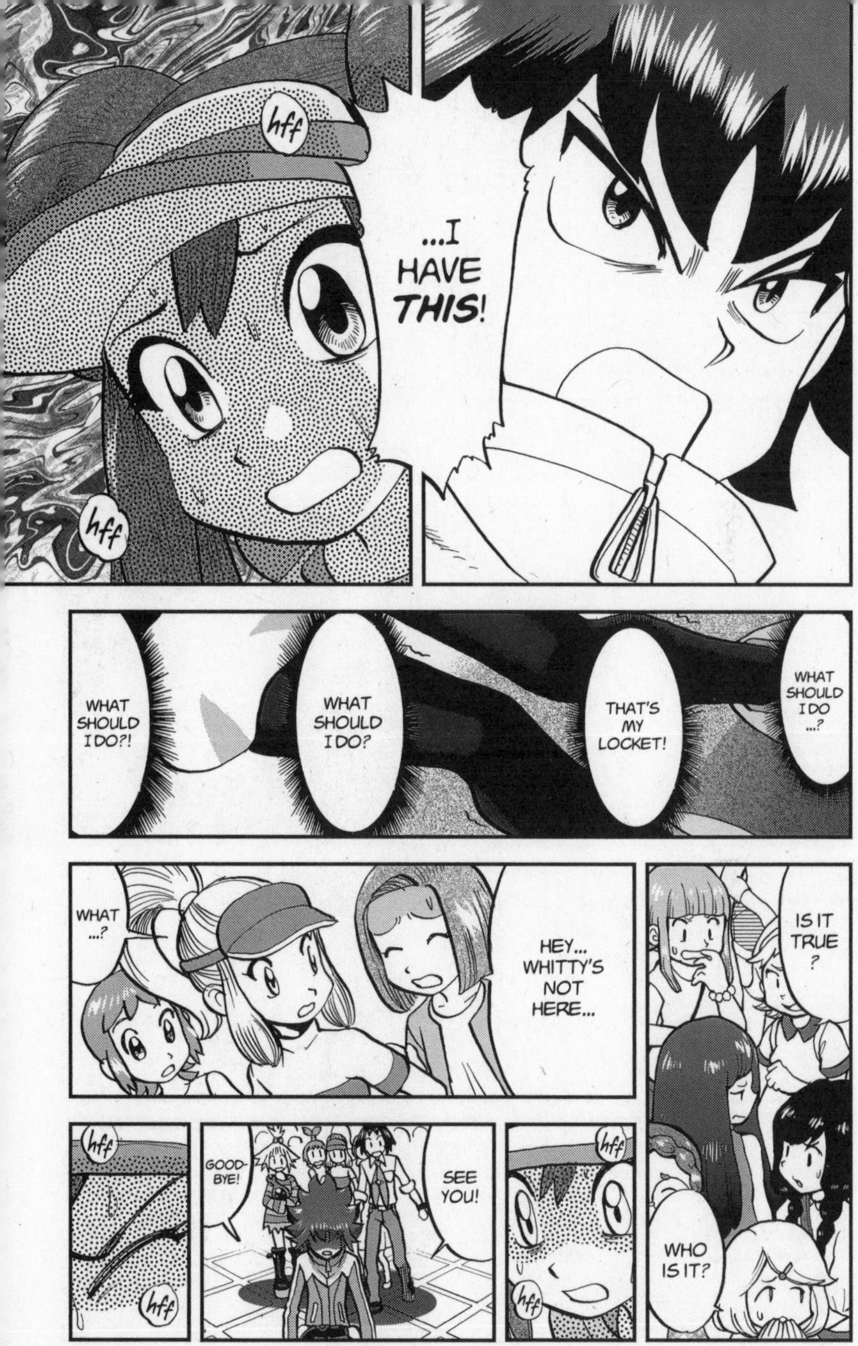
...I HAVE **THIS**!
hff
hff
WHAT SHOULD I DO ...?
THAT'S MY LOCKET!
WHAT SHOULD I DO?
WHAT SHOULD I DO?!
IS IT TRUE ?
WHO IS IT?
HEY... WHITTY'S NOT HERE...
WHAT ...?
hff
hff
SEE YOU!
GOOD-BYE!
hff
hff

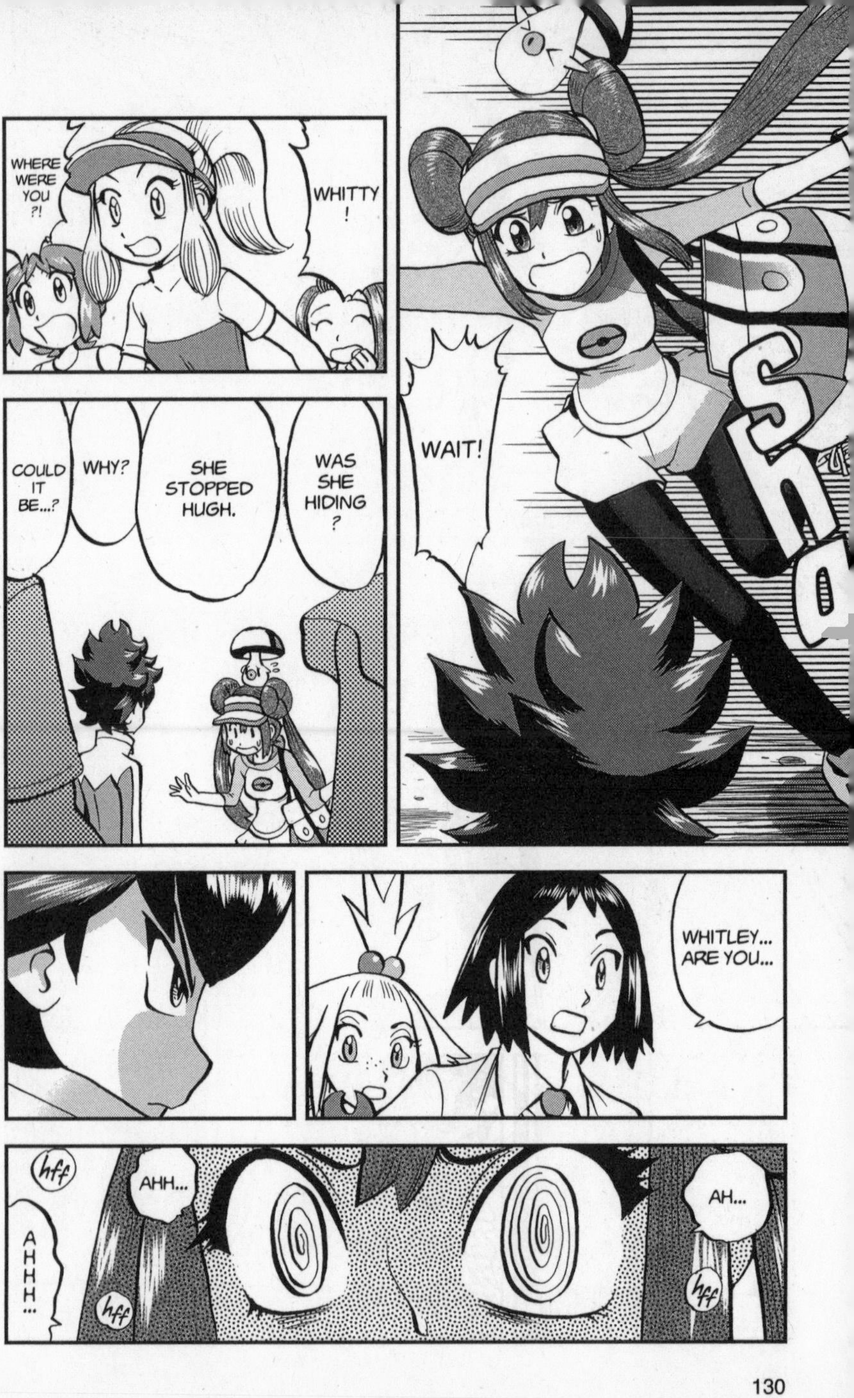
WAIT!
WHITTY!
WHERE WERE YOU?!
WAS SHE HIDING?
SHE STOPPED HUGH.
WHY?
COULD IT BE...?
WHITLEY... ARE YOU...
AH...
hff
AHH...
hff
AHHH...
hff

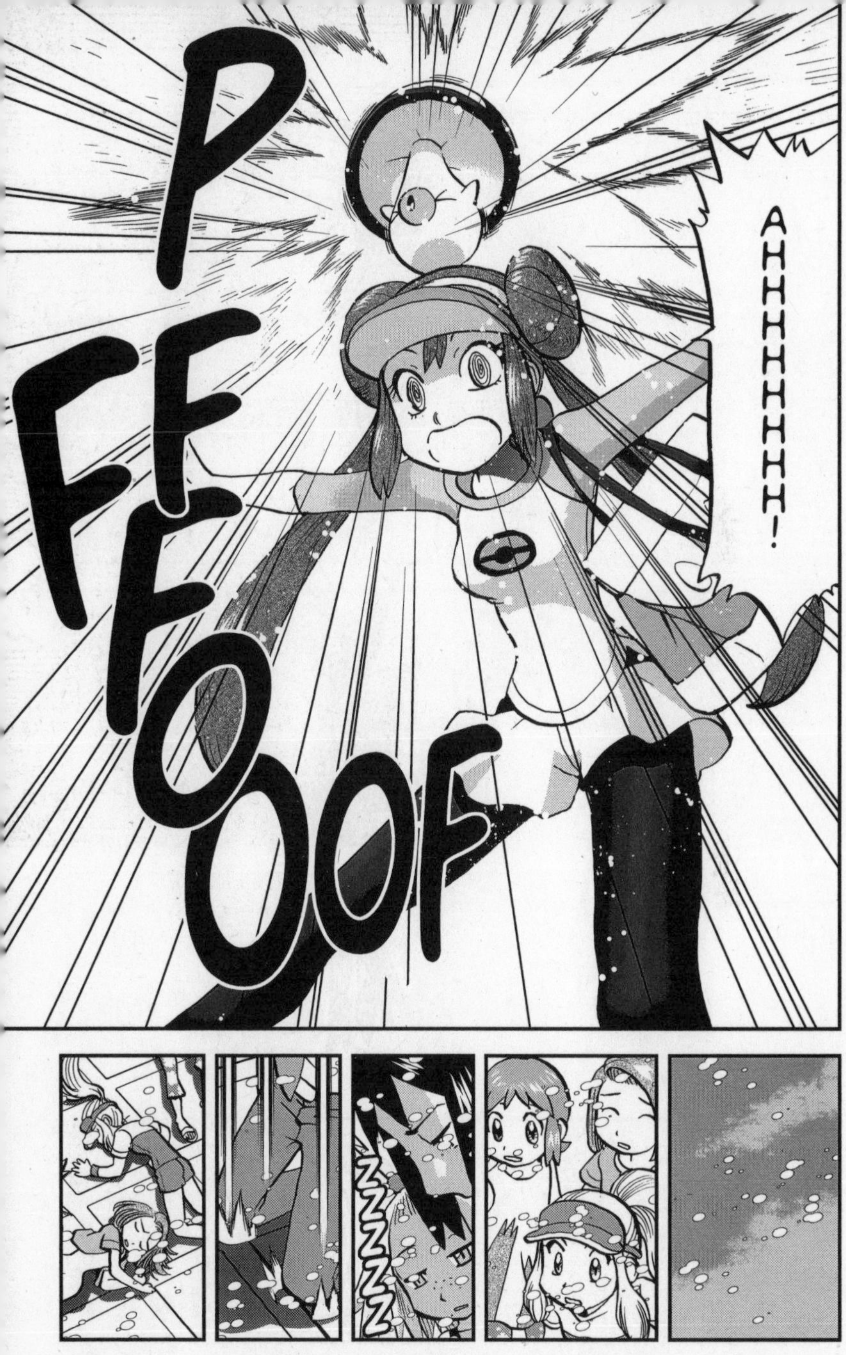
AHHHHHHHH!
PFFFOOOF
ZZZZZ

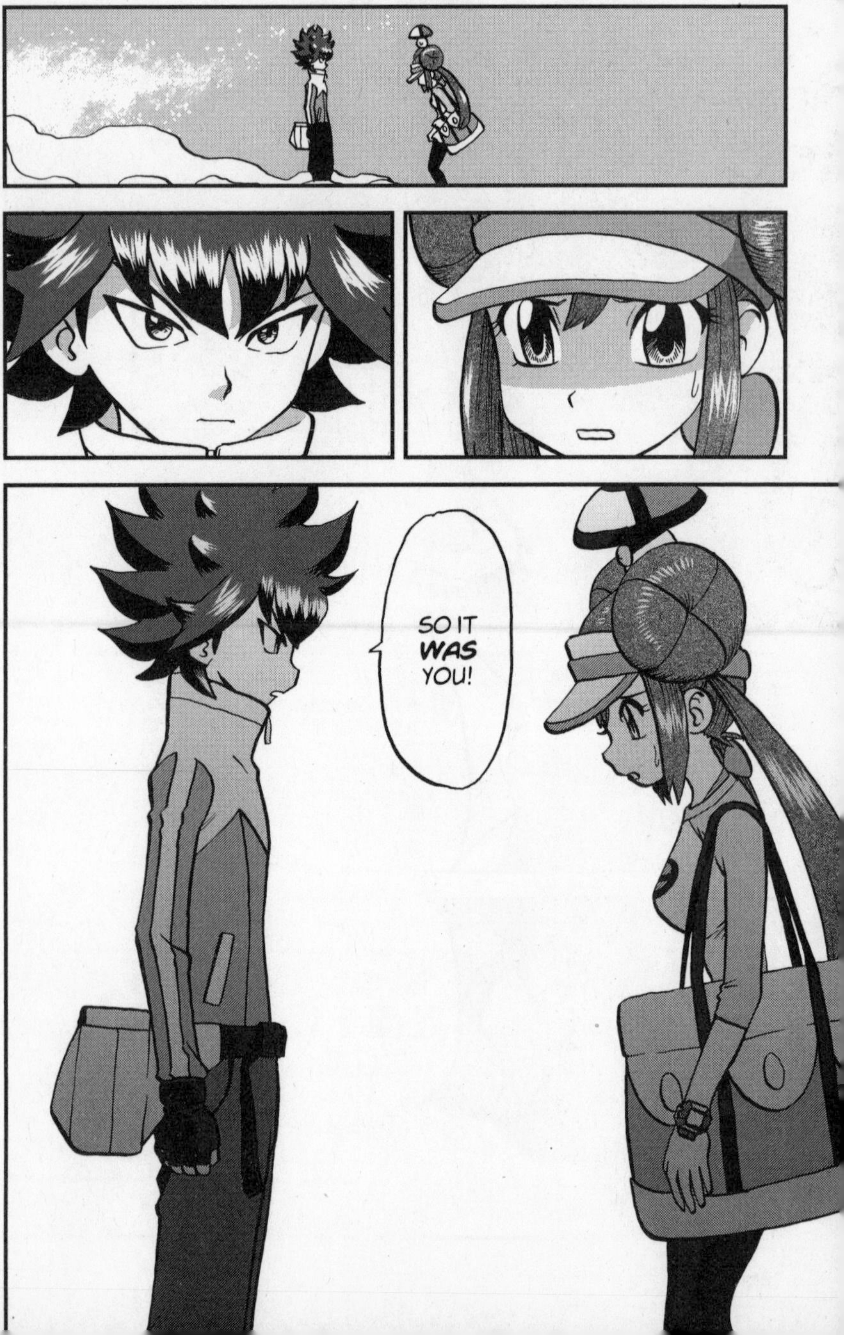
SO IT WAS YOU!

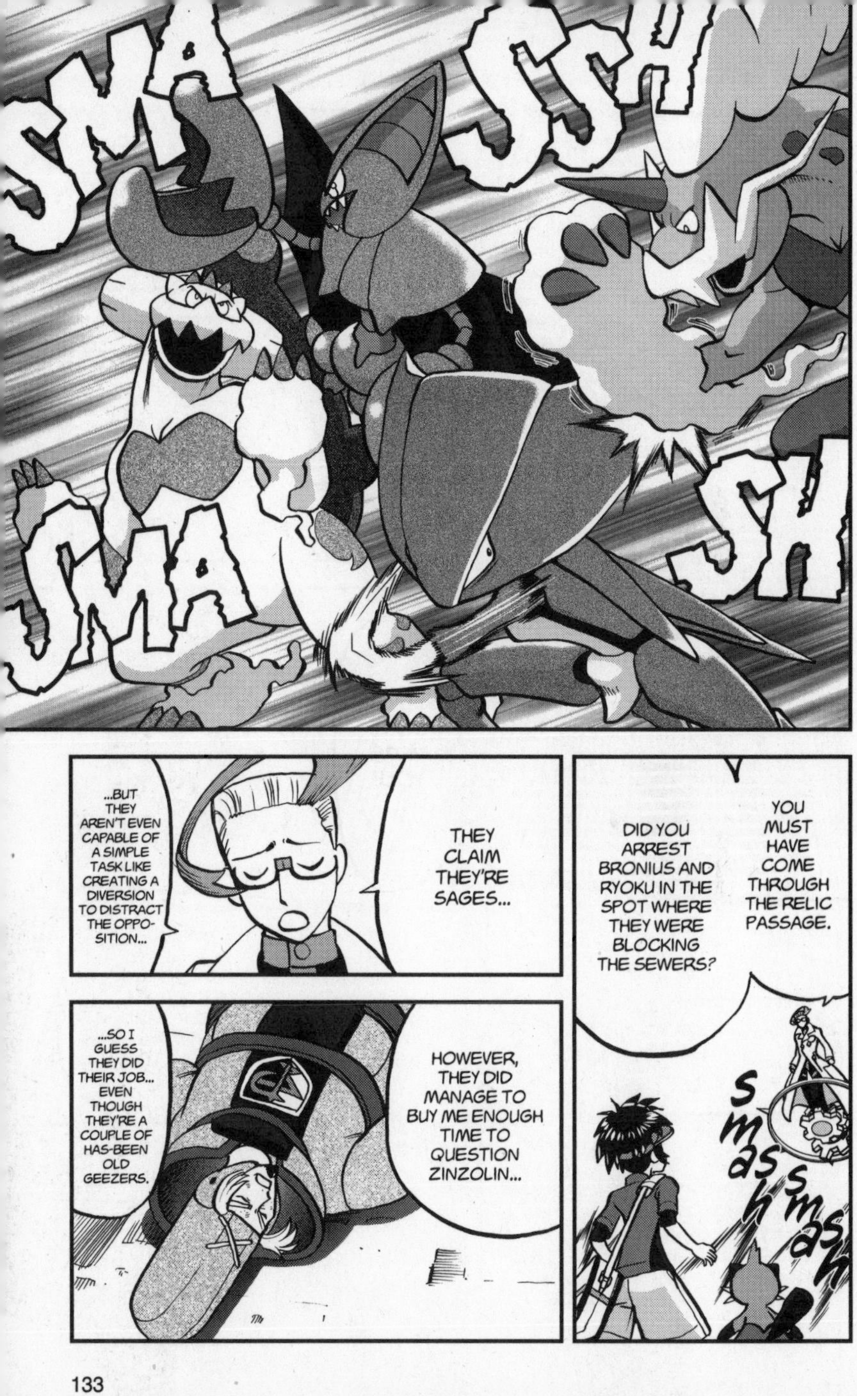
SMASH
SMASH
YOU MUST HAVE COME THROUGH THE RELIC PASSAGE.
DID YOU ARREST BRONIUS AND RYOKU IN THE SPOT WHERE THEY WERE BLOCKING THE SEWERS?
smash smash
THEY CLAIM THEY'RE SAGES...
...BUT THEY AREN'T EVEN CAPABLE OF A SIMPLE TASK LIKE CREATING A DIVERSION TO DISTRACT THE OPPO-SITION...
HOWEVER, THEY DID MANAGE TO BUY ME ENOUGH TIME TO QUESTION ZINZOLIN...
...SO I GUESS THEY DID THEIR JOB... EVEN THOUGH THEY'RE A COUPLE OF HAS-BEEN OLD GEEZERS.

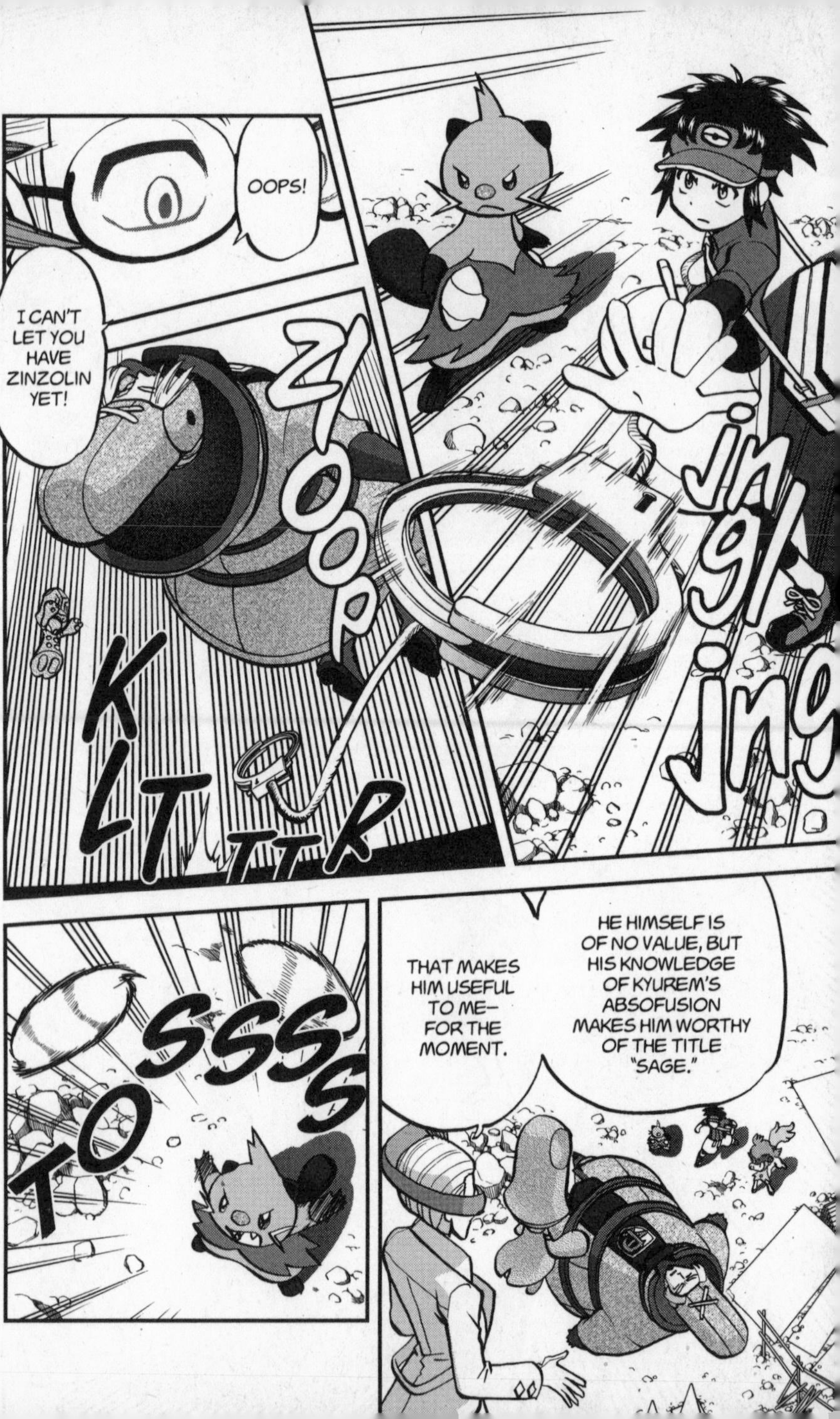
jngl jng
OOPS!
I CAN'T LET YOU HAVE ZINZOLIN YET!
ZOOOP
KLTTTTR
HE HIMSELF IS OF NO VALUE, BUT HIS KNOWLEDGE OF KYUREM'S ABSOFUSION MAKES HIM WORTHY OF THE TITLE "SAGE."
THAT MAKES HIM USEFUL TO ME— FOR THE MOMENT.
TOSSSS

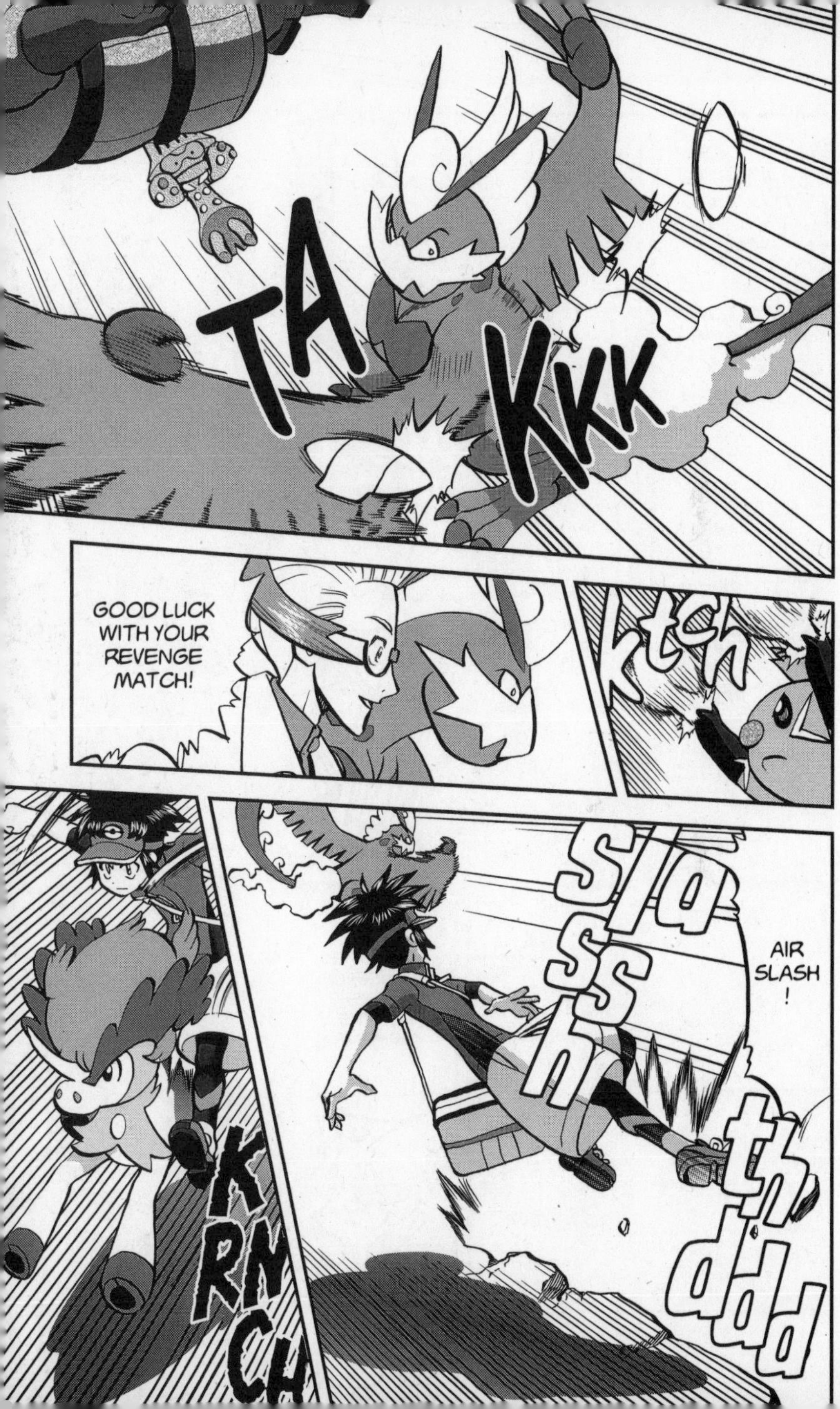
TA
KKK
ktch
GOOD LUCK WITH YOUR REVENGE MATCH!
AIR SLASH!
slassh
thddd
KRNCH

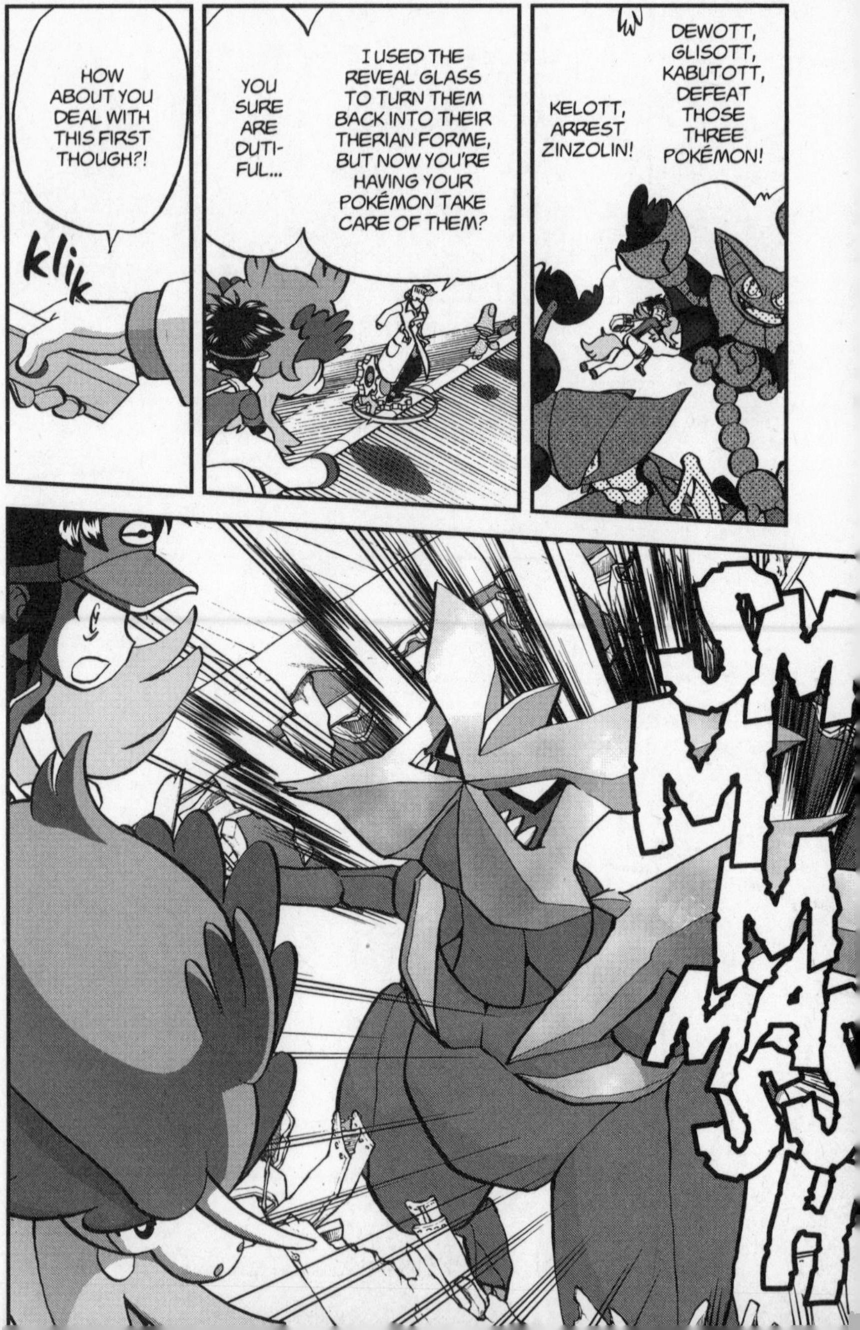
DEWOTT, GLISOTT, KABUTOTT, DEFEAT THOSE THREE POKÉMON!
KELOTT, ARREST ZINZOLIN!
YOU SURE ARE DUTI-FUL...
I USED THE REVEAL GLASS TO TURN THEM BACK INTO THEIR THERIAN FORME, BUT NOW YOU'RE HAVING YOUR POKÉMON TAKE CARE OF THEM?
HOW ABOUT YOU DEAL WITH THIS FIRST THOUGH?!
klik

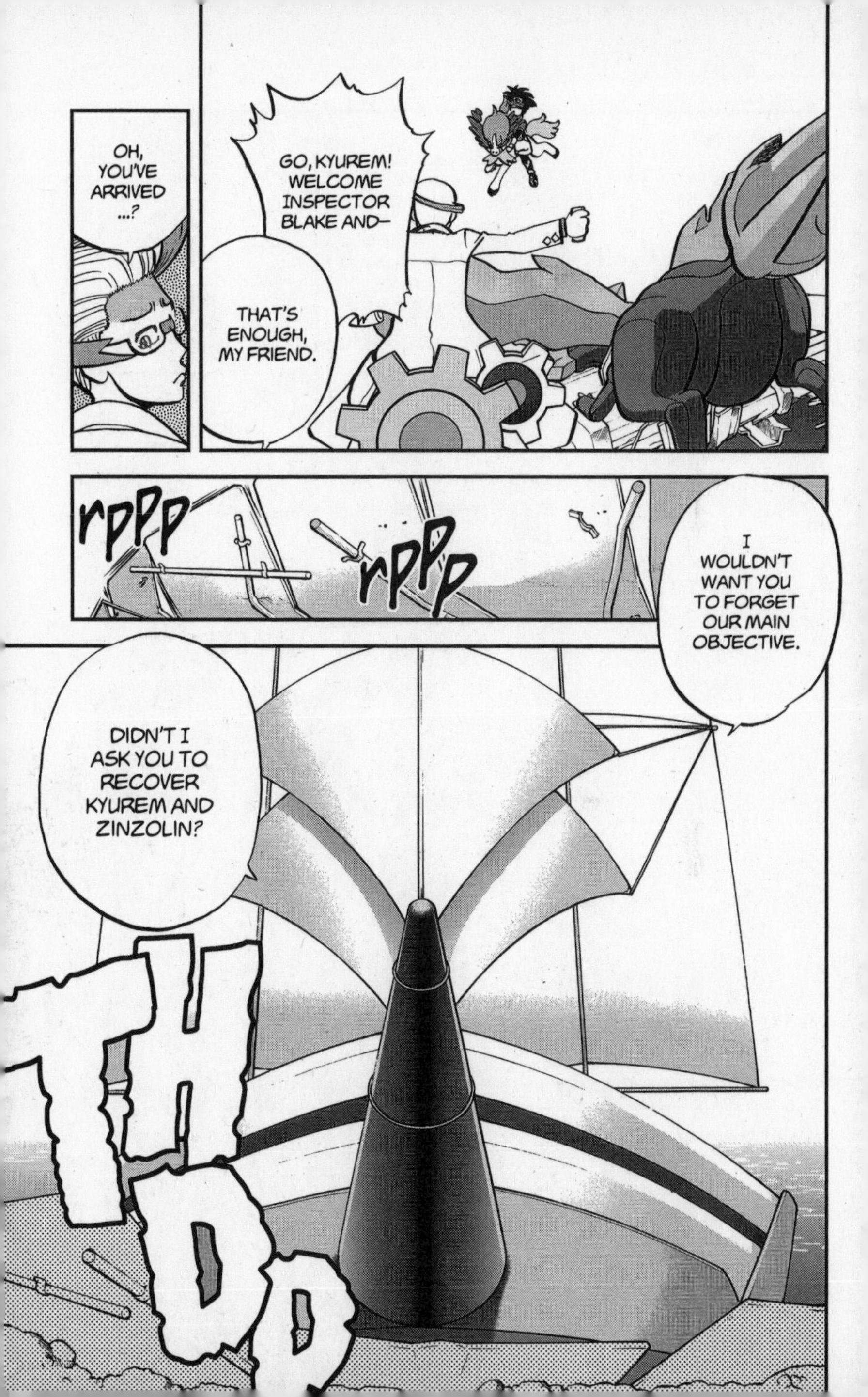
GO, KYUREM! WELCOME INSPECTOR BLAKE AND—
THAT'S ENOUGH, MY FRIEND.
OH, YOU'VE ARRIVED ...?
I WOULDN'T WANT YOU TO FORGET OUR MAIN OBJECTIVE.
rPPP
rPPP
DIDN'T I ASK YOU TO RECOVER KYUREM AND ZINZOLIN?
THD

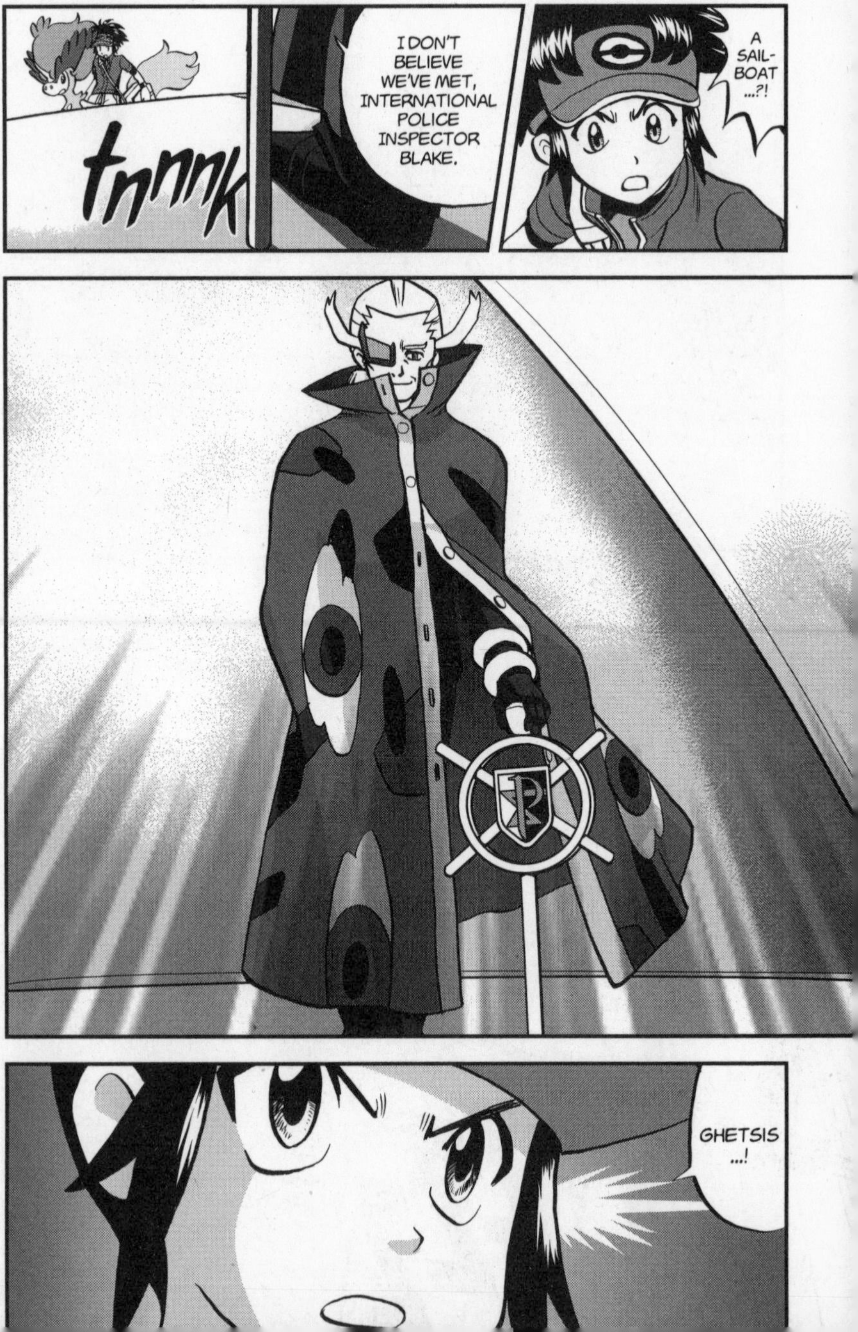
A SAIL-BOAT ...?!
I DON'T BELIEVE WE'VE MET, INTERNATIONAL POLICE INSPECTOR BLAKE.
tnnnk
GHETSIS ...!

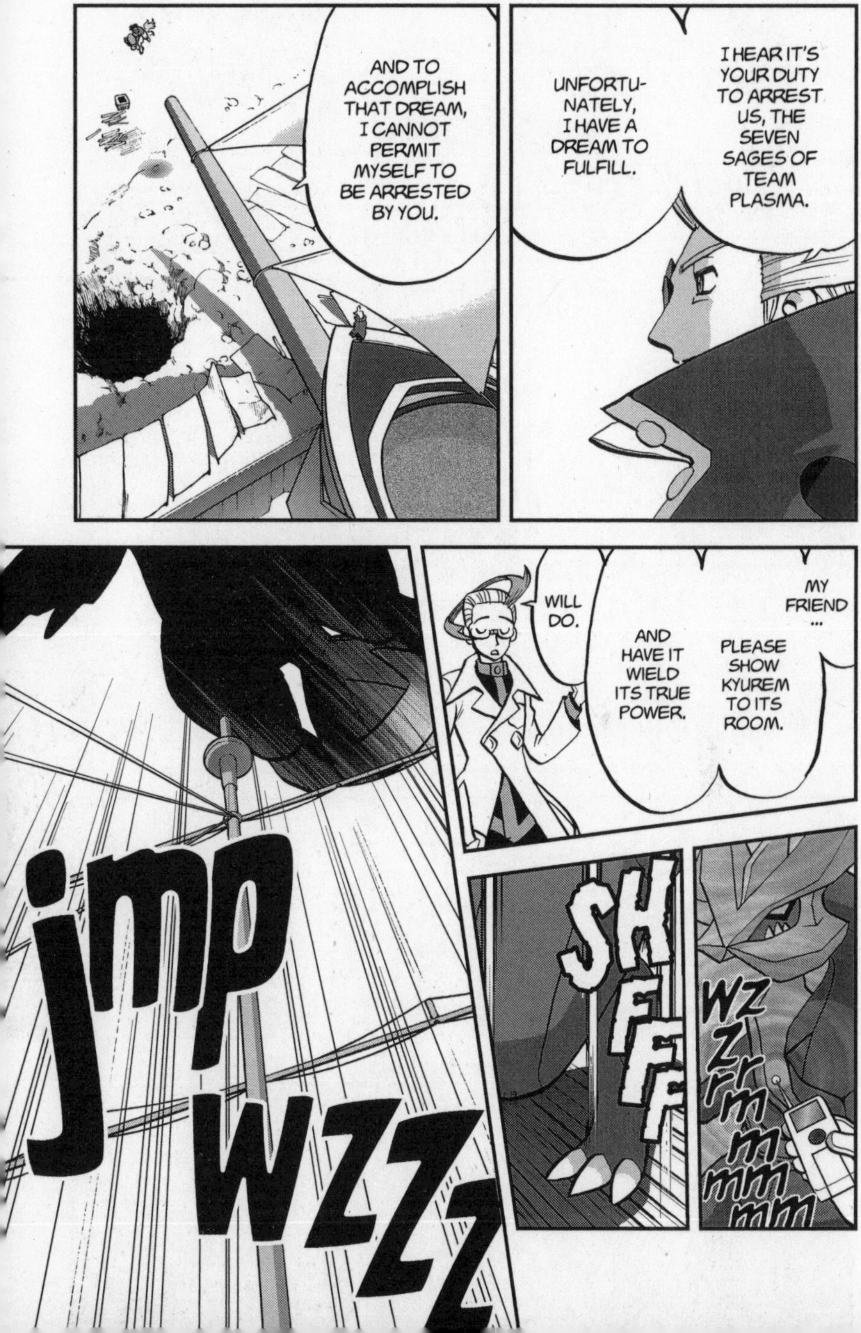
I HEAR IT'S YOUR DUTY TO ARREST US, THE SEVEN SAGES OF TEAM PLASMA.
UNFORTU-NATELY, I HAVE A DREAM TO FULFILL.
AND TO ACCOMPLISH THAT DREAM, I CANNOT PERMIT MYSELF TO BE ARRESTED BY YOU.
MY FRIEND...
PLEASE SHOW KYUREM TO ITS ROOM.
AND HAVE IT WIELD ITS TRUE POWER.
WILL DO.
WZ ZRRMMMMMMM
SHFFF
JMP
WZZZ

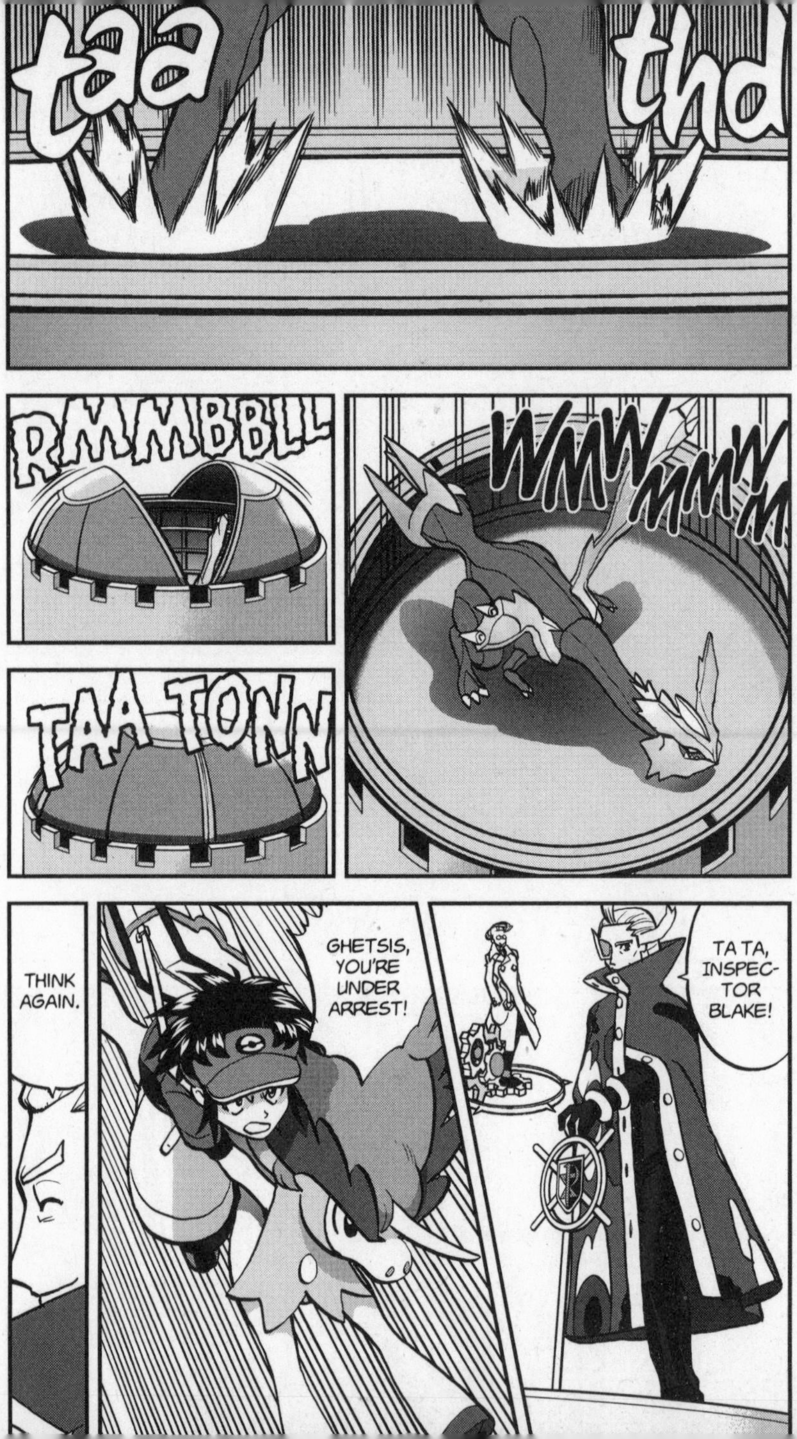
thd
taa
RMMBBLL
TAA TONN
TA TA, INSPECTOR BLAKE!
GHETSIS, YOU'RE UNDER ARREST!
THINK AGAIN.

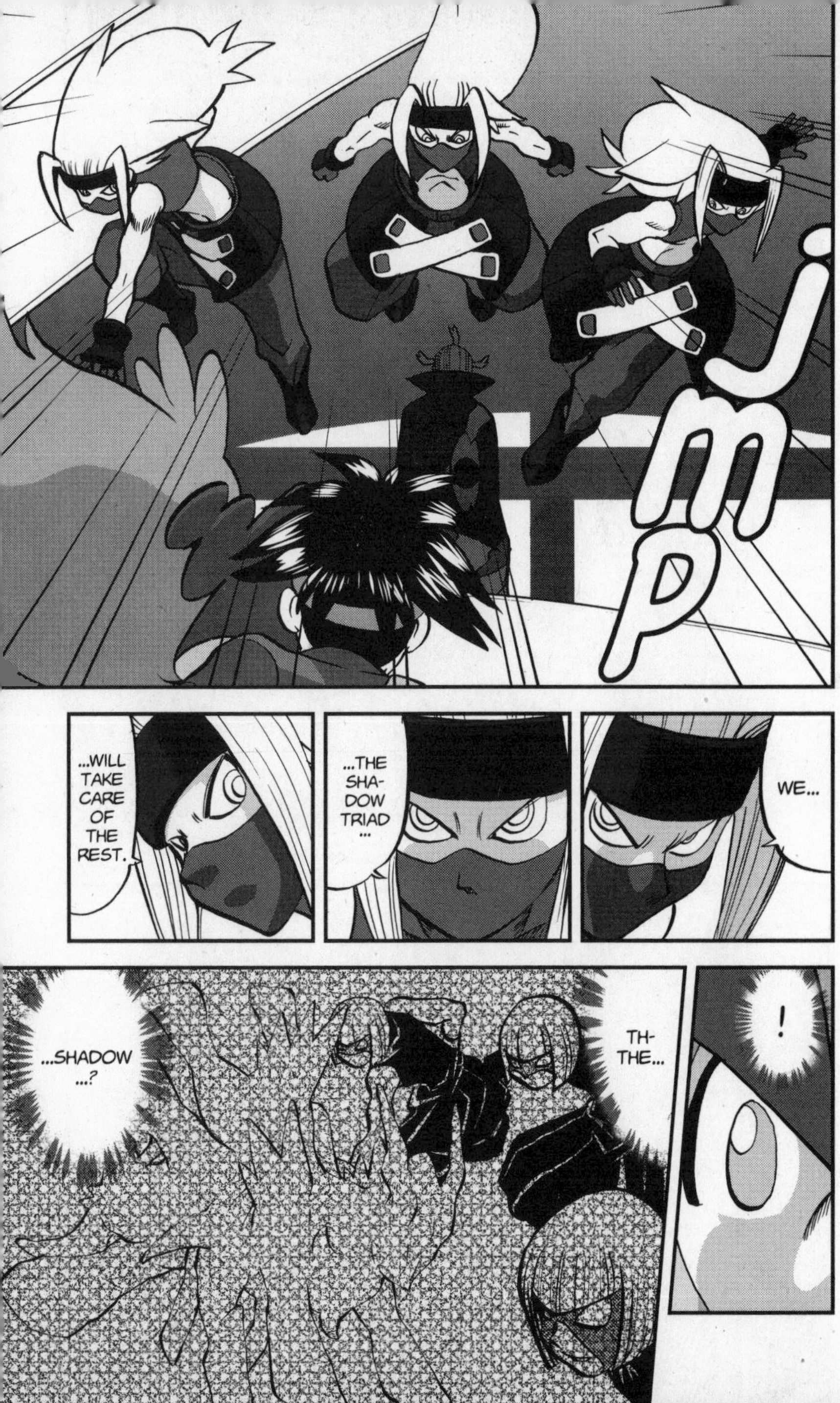
JMP
WE...
...THE SHADOW TRIAD...
...WILL TAKE CARE OF THE REST.
!
TH-THE...
...SHADOW...?

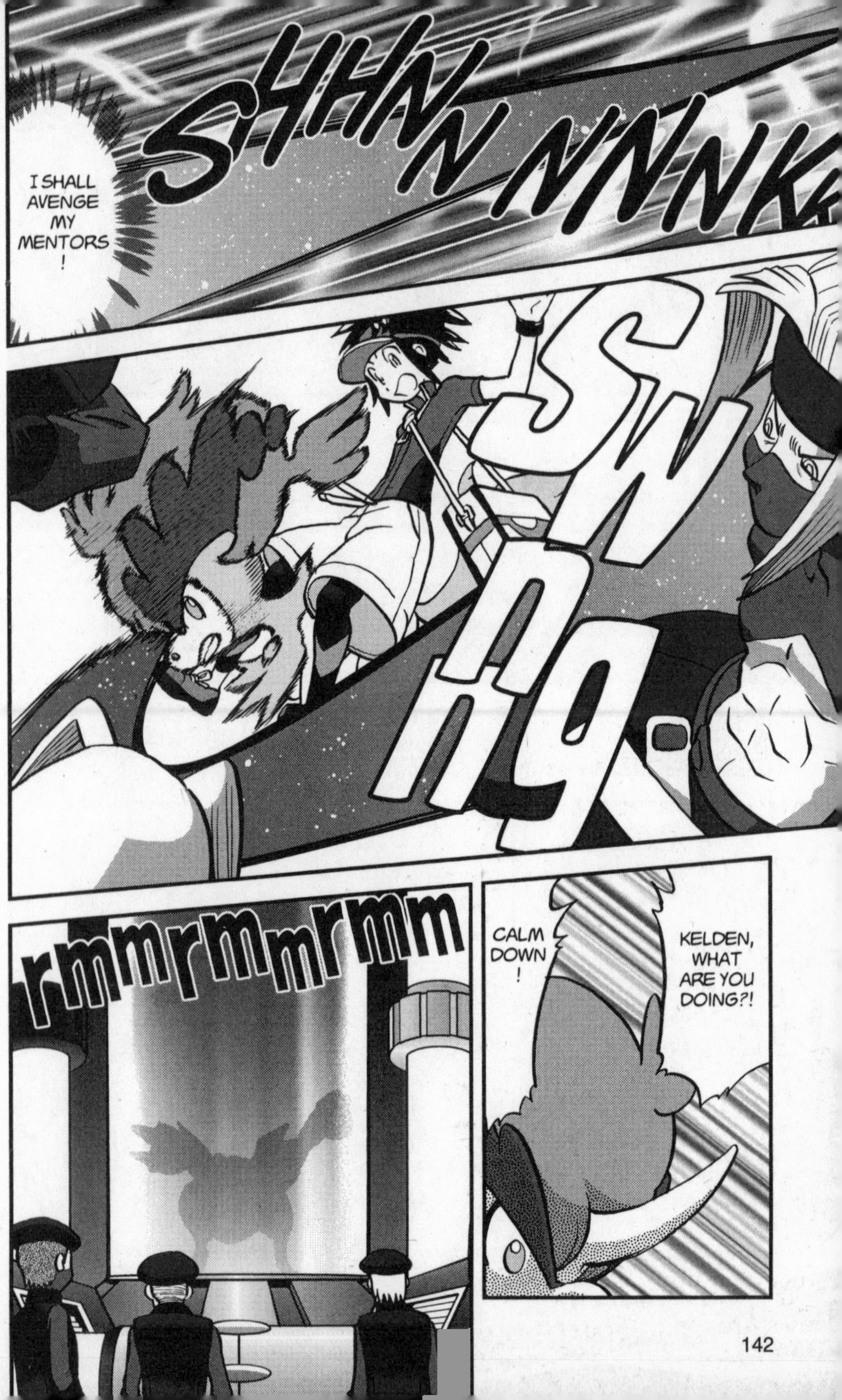
SHHNNNNNK
I SHALL AVENGE MY MENTORS!
SWNNG
KELDEN, WHAT ARE YOU DOING?!
CALM DOWN!
rmmrmmmrmm

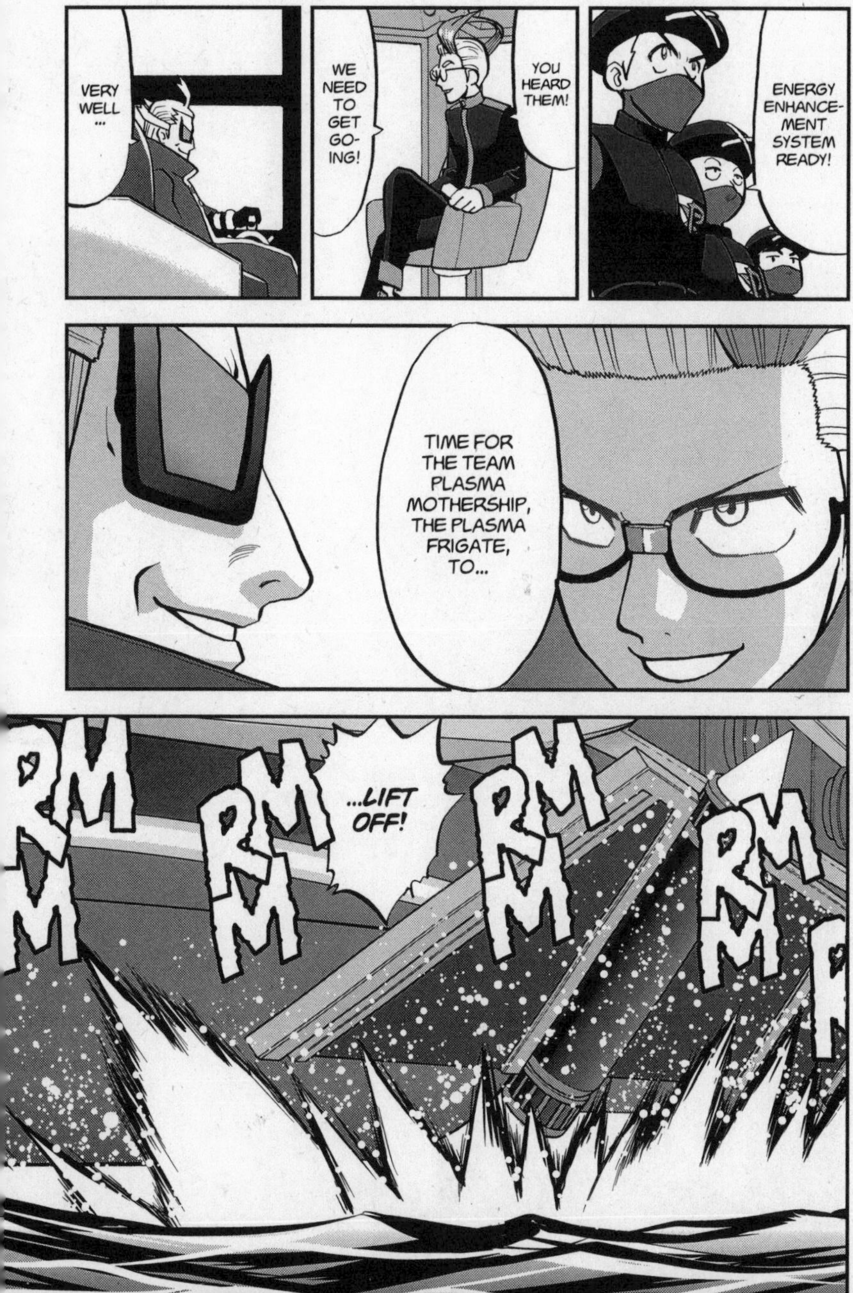
ENERGY ENHANCEMENT SYSTEM READY!
YOU HEARD THEM!
WE NEED TO GET GOING!
VERY WELL...
TIME FOR THE TEAM PLASMA MOTHERSHIP, THE PLASMA FRIGATE, TO...
RMM
RMM
...LIFT OFF!
RMM
RMM

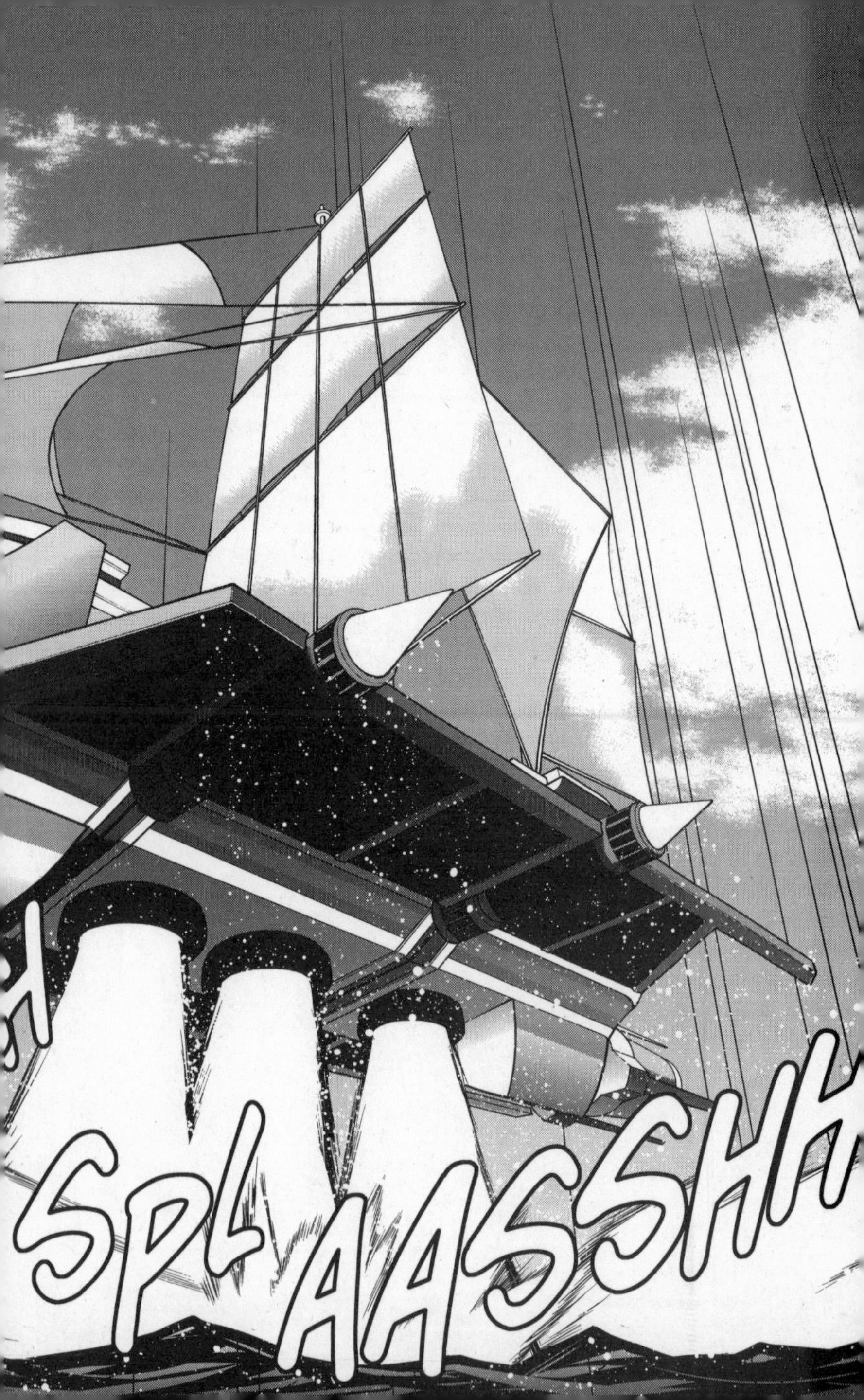
SPLAASSHH

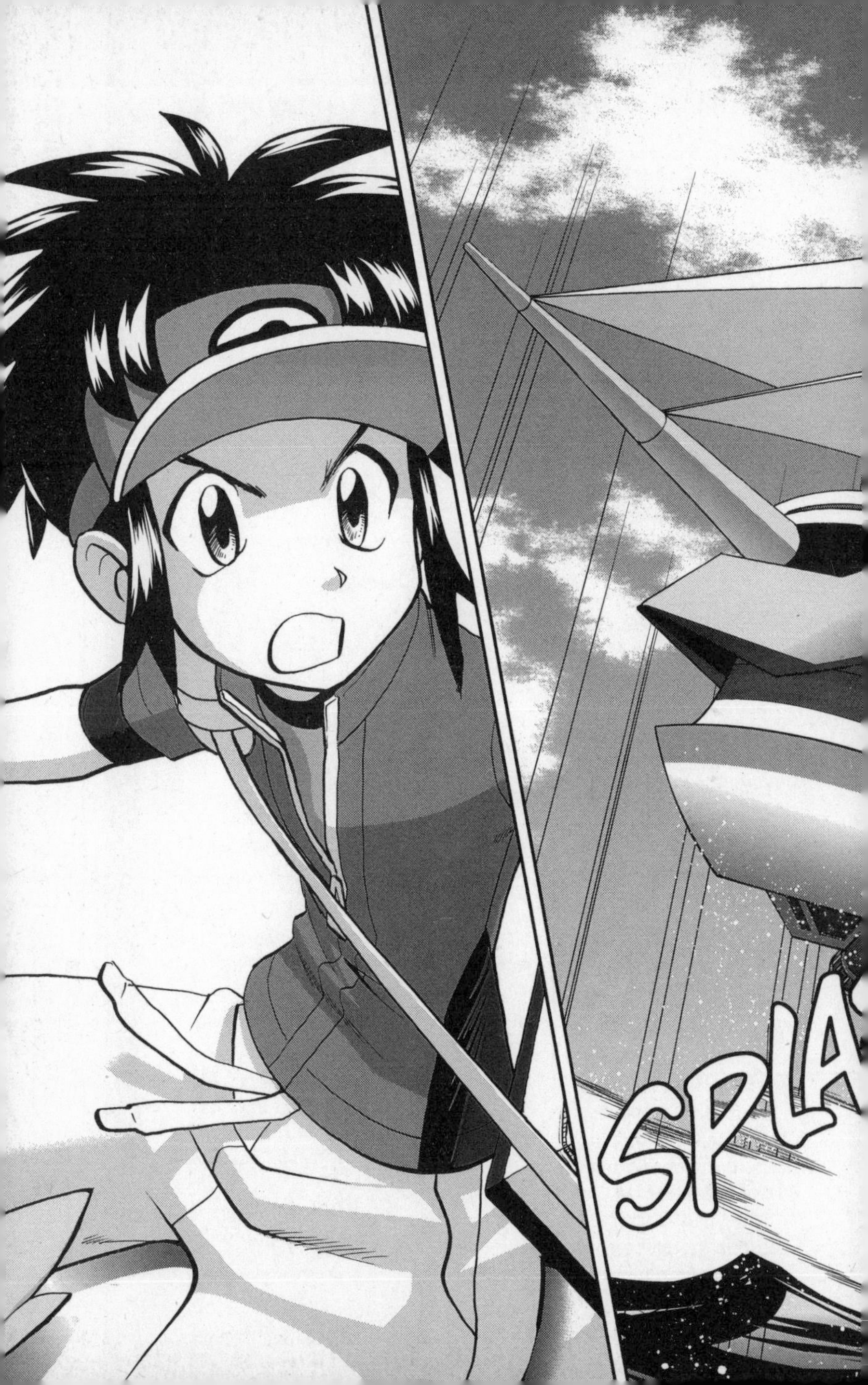
SPLA

A fellow student at the Trainers' School. He is a passionate Trainer who always strives to improve and grow stronger. Unfortunately, his single-minded focus makes it hard for other students to get along with him. When he was seven, Hugh gave his little sister a Purrloin for her birthday. But when he then pressured her to take part in a Pokémon battle, they were targeted by Team Plasma and the Purrloin was kidnapped. This event became the driving force behind Hugh's desire to grow more powerful so that he might face Team Plasma again and retrieve his sister's Purrloin. He happened to find Whitley's locket during a quarrel with some of the girls in his class, and on the locket's hidden memory card he discovered Team Plasma's list of Pokémon whom they had kidnapped under the pretext of "liberating" them.

HUGH

CHARACTER PROFILE

HUGH

- ● Affiliated with: Trainers' School 75th Graduating Class, Class E (boarding student)
- ● Age: 12 years old (as of Adventure 14)
- ● Place of Birth: Aspertia City
- ● Family Member: Little Sister, Grandfather
- ● Favorite Subject: Ability Studies, Practical Battle
- ● Grade Rank (First Semester) 75th Graduating Class, 5th out of 150 Students

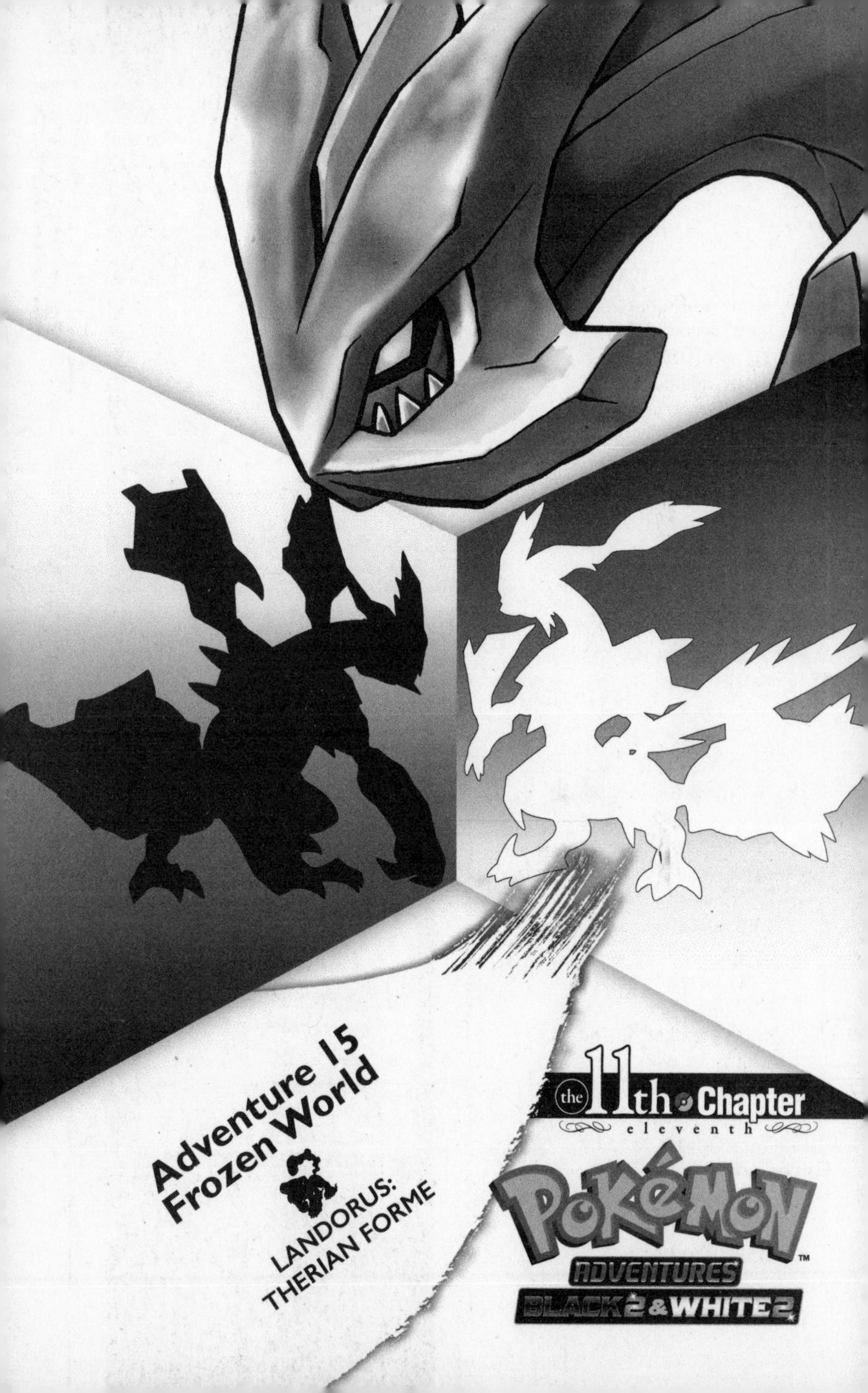
Adventure 15
Frozen World
LANDORUS:
THERIAN FORME
the 11th Chapter
eleventh
POKÉMON™
ADVENTURES
BLACK 2 & WHITE 2

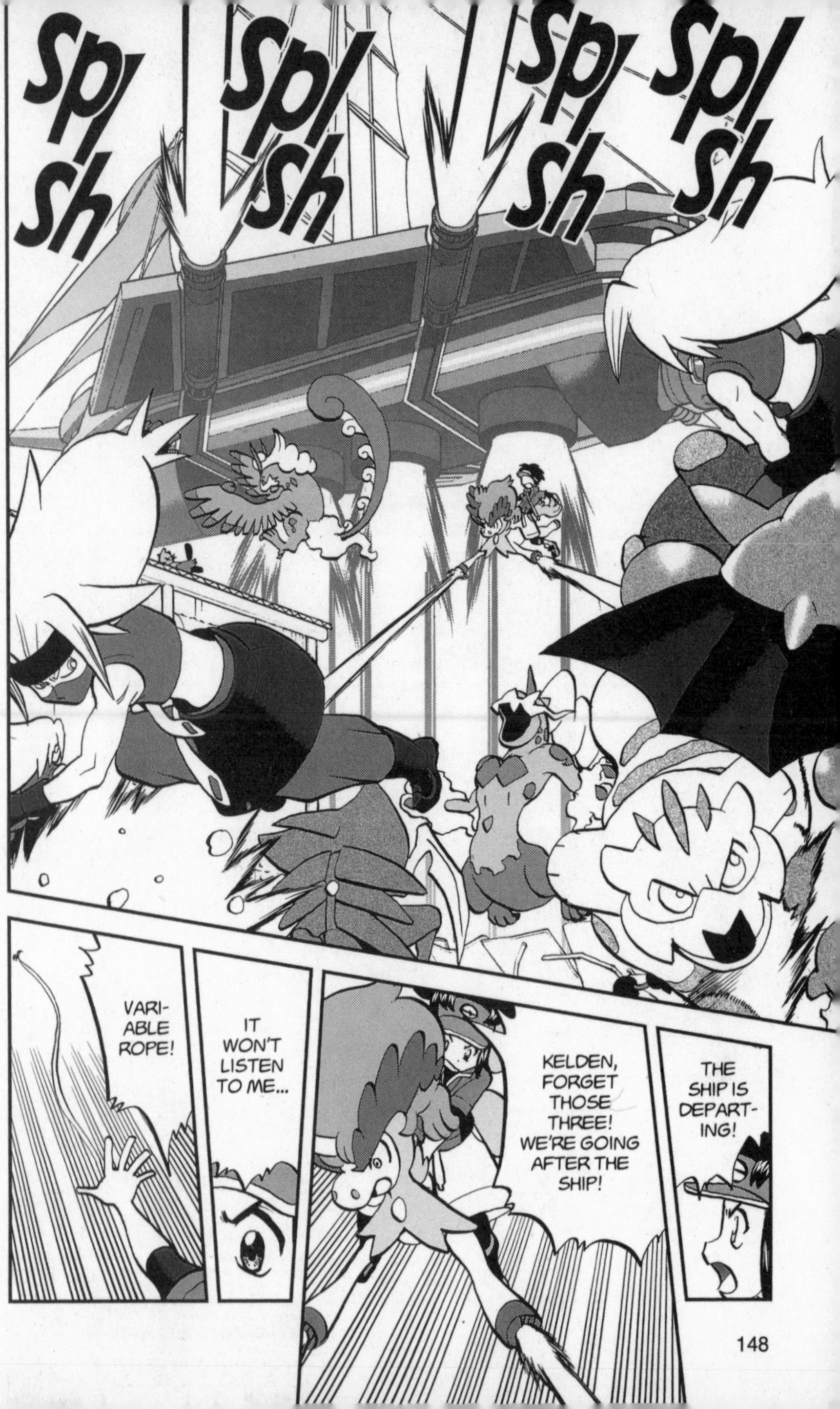
Spl Sh
Spl Sh
Spl Sh
Spl Sh
THE SHIP IS DEPART-ING!
KELDEN, FORGET THOSE THREE! WE'RE GOING AFTER THE SHIP!
IT WON'T LISTEN TO ME...
VARI-ABLE ROPE!

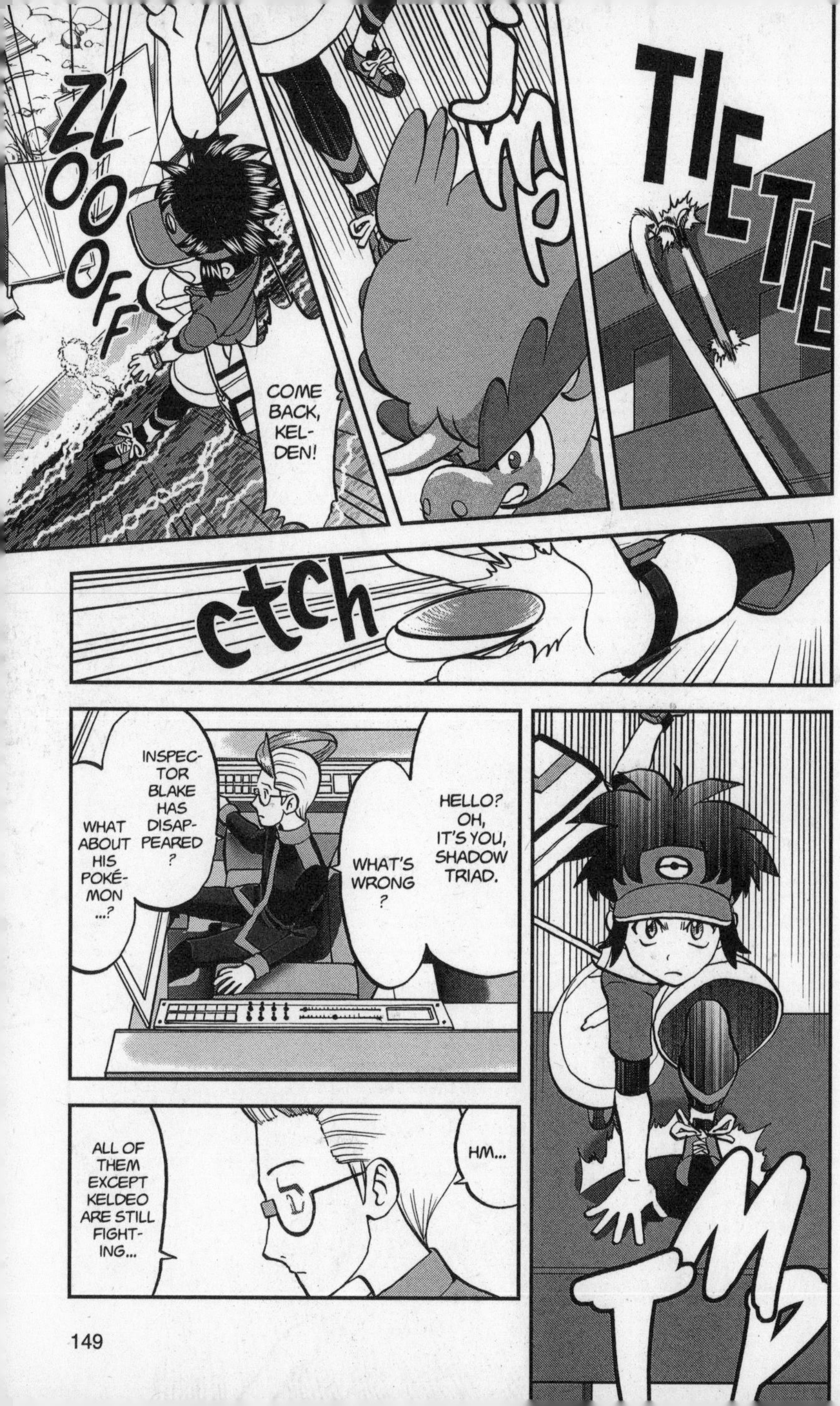
TIE TIE TIE
jmp
ZOOOOFF
COME BACK, KEL-DEN!
ctch
HELLO? OH, IT'S YOU, SHADOW TRIAD.
WHAT'S WRONG?
INSPECTOR BLAKE HAS DISAPPEARED?
WHAT ABOUT HIS POKÉMON...?
HM...
ALL OF THEM EXCEPT KELDEO ARE STILL FIGHTING...

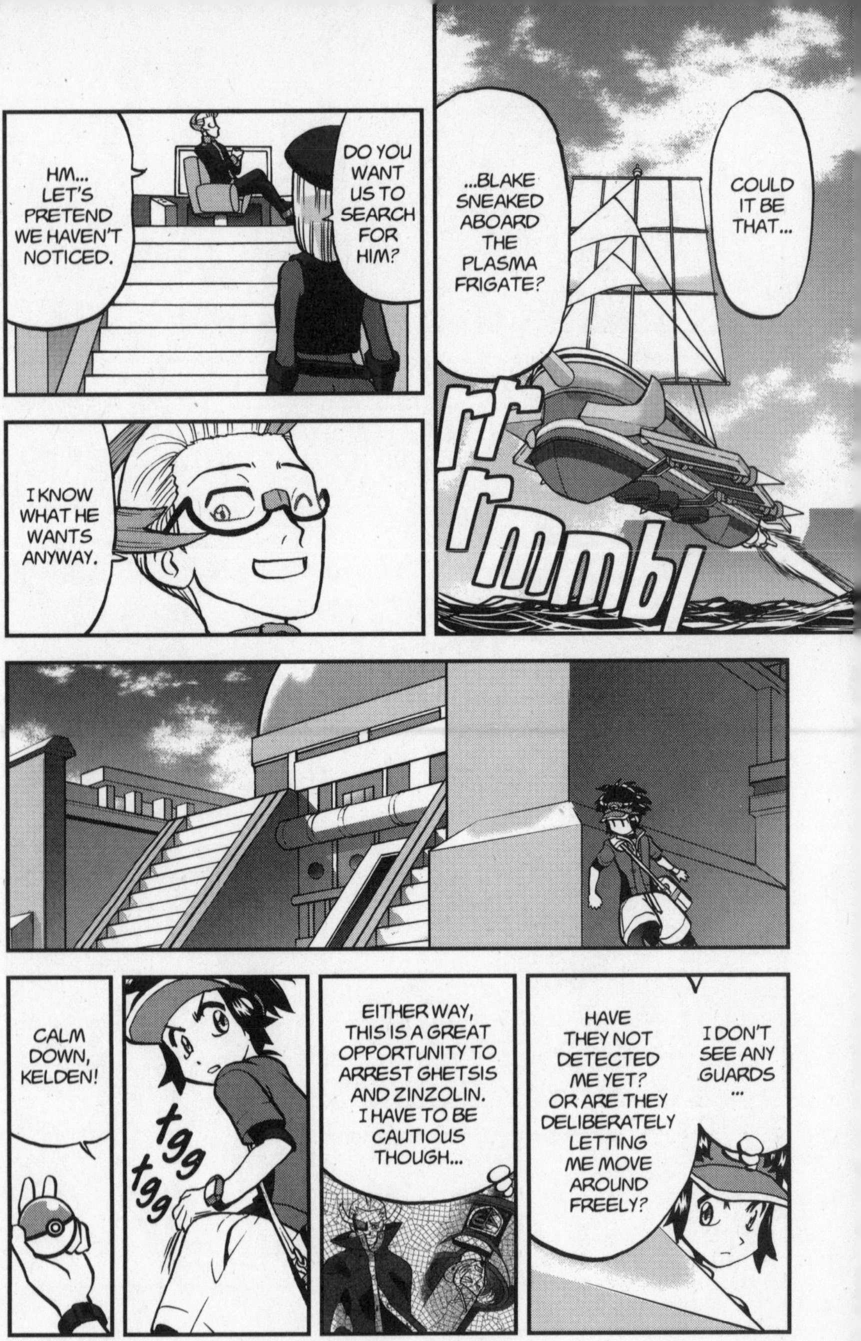
COULD IT BE THAT...
...BLAKE SNEAKED ABOARD THE PLASMA FRIGATE?
rr rrmmbl
DO YOU WANT US TO SEARCH FOR HIM?
HM... LET'S PRETEND WE HAVEN'T NOTICED.
I KNOW WHAT HE WANTS ANYWAY.
I DON'T SEE ANY GUARDS ...
HAVE THEY NOT DETECTED ME YET? OR ARE THEY DELIBERATELY LETTING ME MOVE AROUND FREELY?
EITHER WAY, THIS IS A GREAT OPPORTUNITY TO ARREST GHETSIS AND ZINZOLIN. I HAVE TO BE CAUTIOUS THOUGH...
tgg tgg
CALM DOWN, KELDEN!

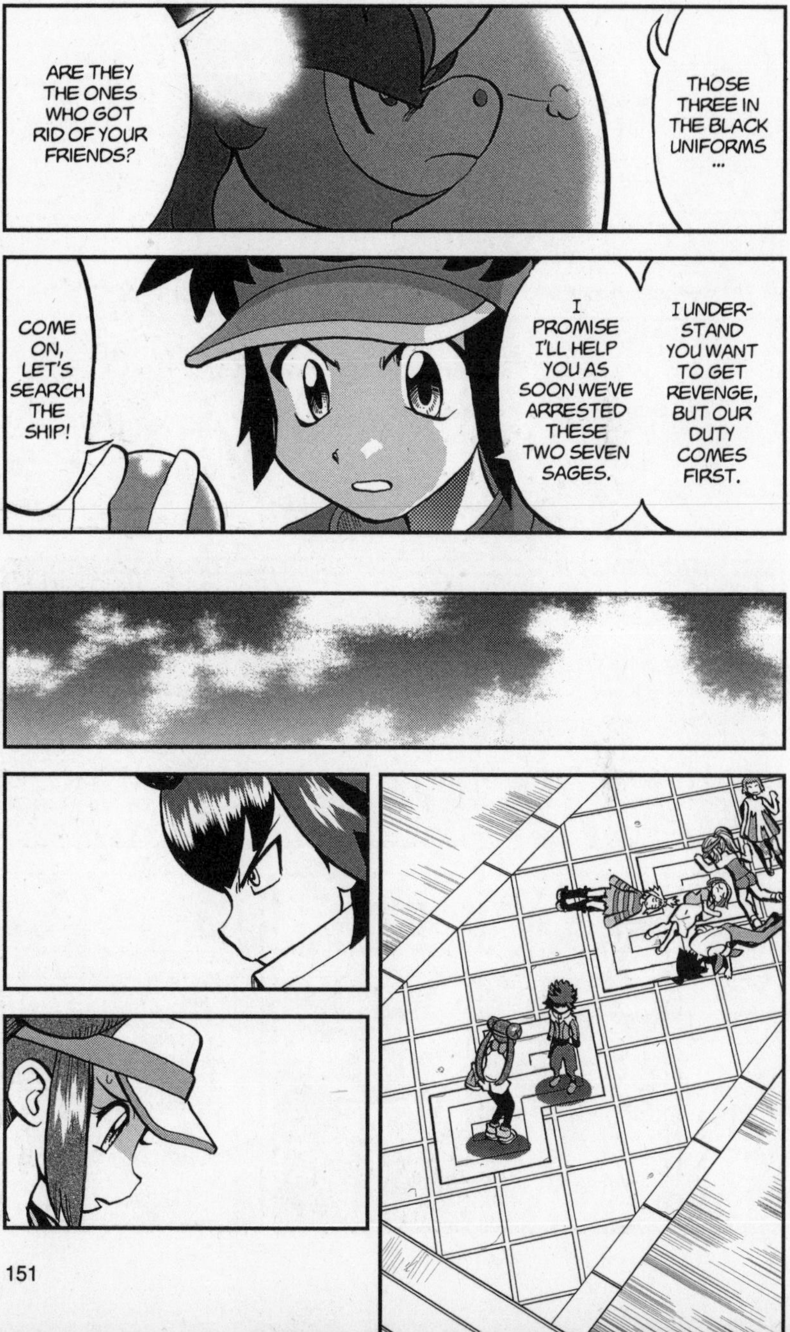
THOSE THREE IN THE BLACK UNIFORMS ...
ARE THEY THE ONES WHO GOT RID OF YOUR FRIENDS?
I UNDER-STAND YOU WANT TO GET REVENGE, BUT OUR DUTY COMES FIRST.
I PROMISE I'LL HELP YOU AS SOON WE'VE ARRESTED THESE TWO SEVEN SAGES.
COME ON, LET'S SEARCH THE SHIP!

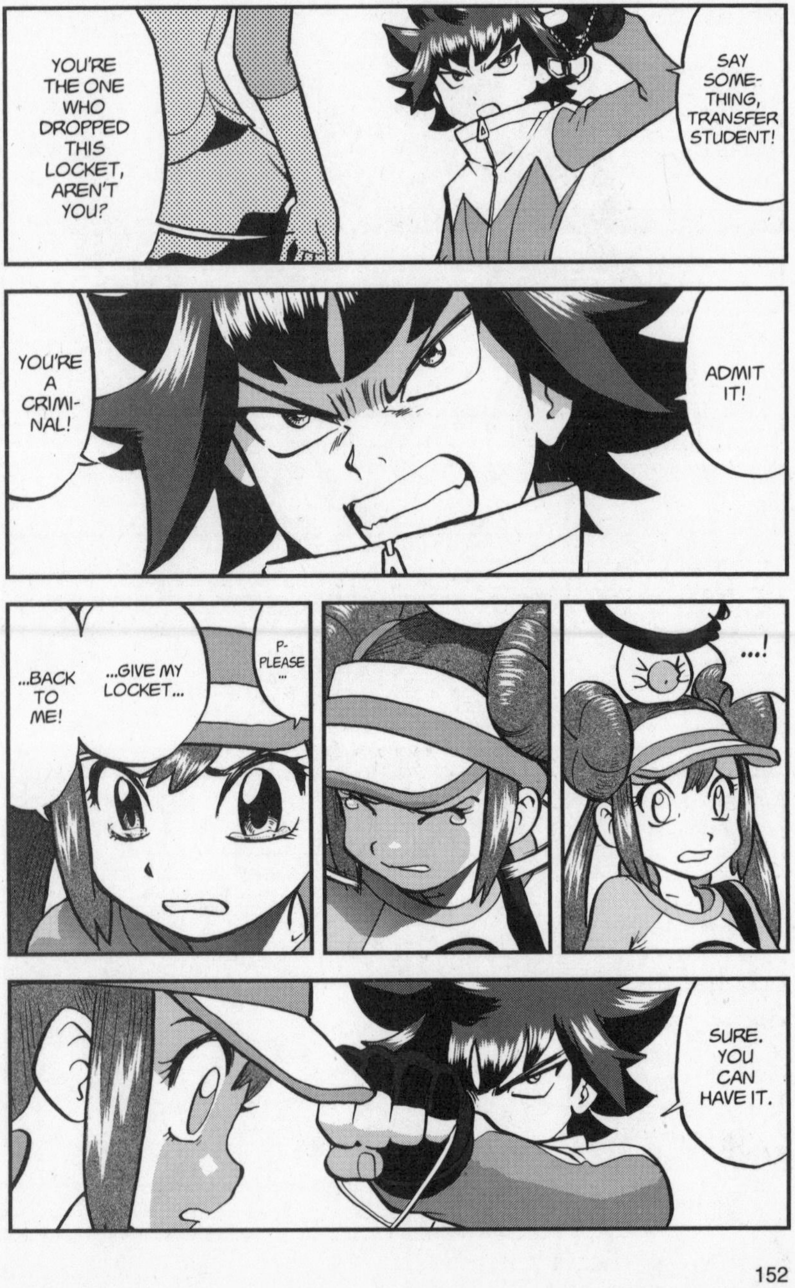
SAY SOMETHING, TRANSFER STUDENT!
YOU'RE THE ONE WHO DROPPED THIS LOCKET, AREN'T YOU?
ADMIT IT!
YOU'RE A CRIMINAL!
...!
P-PLEASE ...
...GIVE MY LOCKET...
...BACK TO ME!
SURE. YOU CAN HAVE IT.

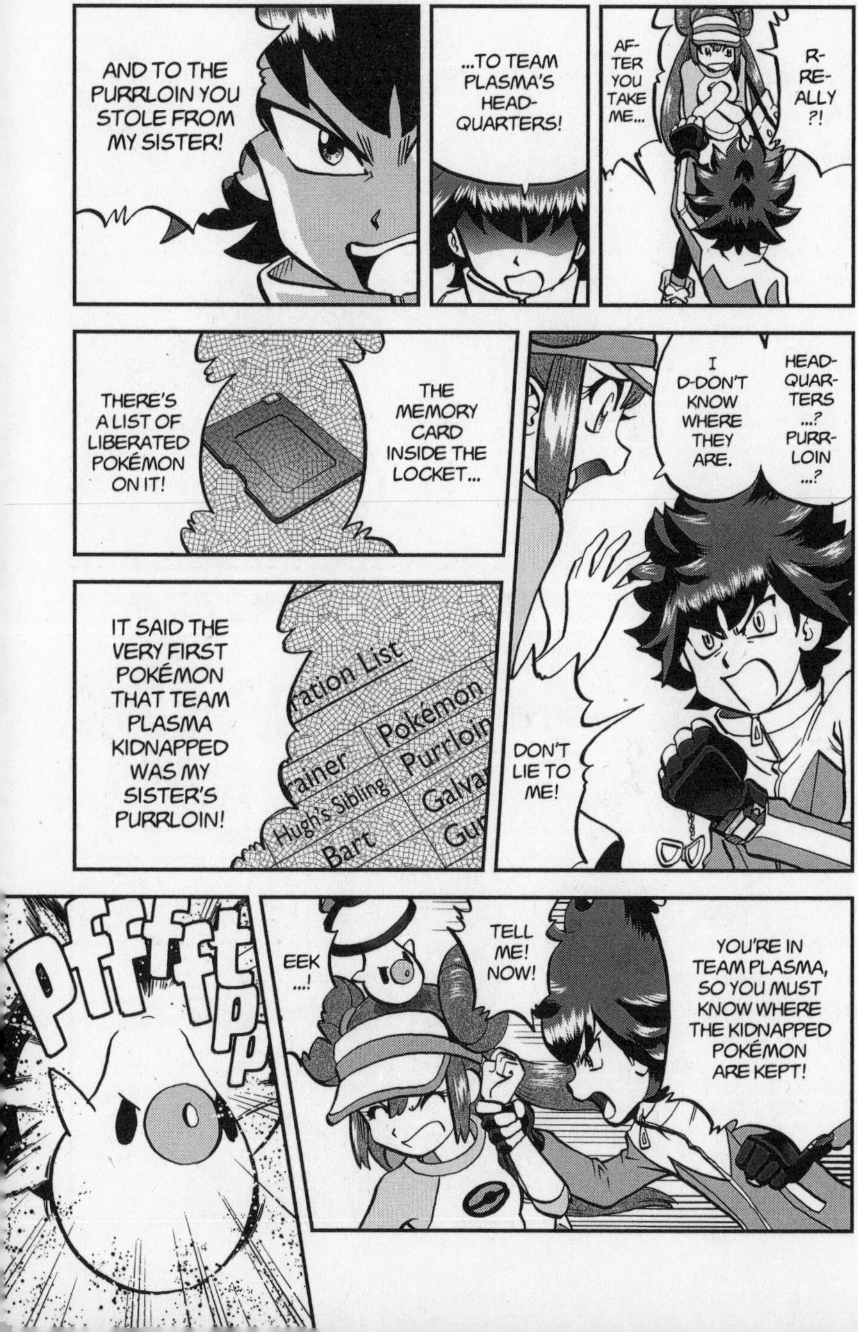
R-RE-ALLY?!
AF-TER YOU TAKE ME...
...TO TEAM PLASMA'S HEAD-QUARTERS!
AND TO THE PURRLOIN YOU STOLE FROM MY SISTER!
HEAD-QUAR-TERS ...? PURR-LOIN ...?
I D-DON'T KNOW WHERE THEY ARE.
DON'T LIE TO ME!
THE MEMORY CARD INSIDE THE LOCKET...
THERE'S A LIST OF LIBERATED POKÉMON ON IT!
IT SAID THE VERY FIRST POKÉMON THAT TEAM PLASMA KIDNAPPED WAS MY SISTER'S PURRLOIN!
ration List
rainer
Pokémon
Hugh's Sibling
Purrloin
Bart
Galva
Gu
YOU'RE IN TEAM PLASMA, SO YOU MUST KNOW WHERE THE KIDNAPPED POKÉMON ARE KEPT!
TELL ME! NOW!
EEK ...!
pffffftpp

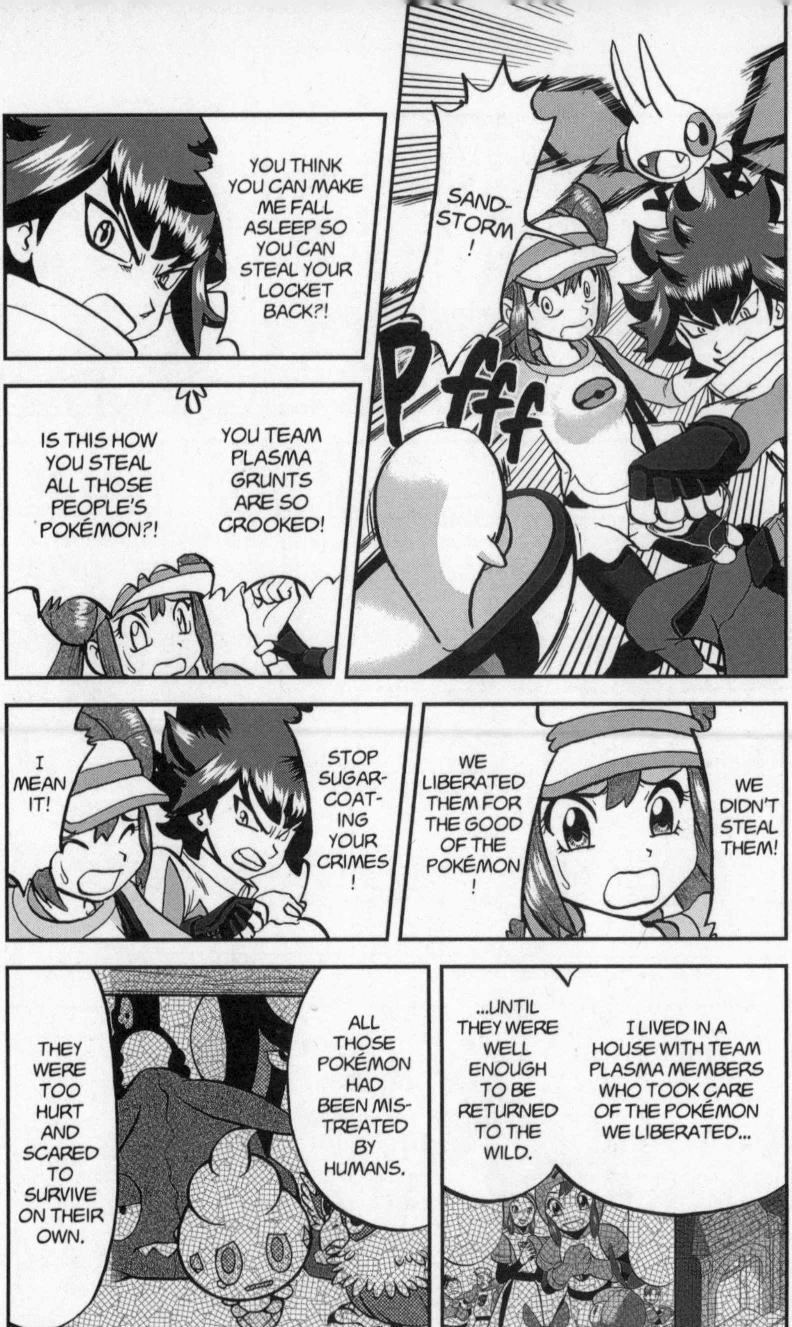
SANDSTORM!
Pfff
YOU THINK YOU CAN MAKE ME FALL ASLEEP SO YOU CAN STEAL YOUR LOCKET BACK?!
YOU TEAM PLASMA GRUNTS ARE SO CROOKED!
IS THIS HOW YOU STEAL ALL THOSE PEOPLE'S POKÉMON?!
WE DIDN'T STEAL THEM!
WE LIBERATED THEM FOR THE GOOD OF THE POKÉMON!
STOP SUGARCOATING YOUR CRIMES!
I MEAN IT!
I LIVED IN A HOUSE WITH TEAM PLASMA MEMBERS WHO TOOK CARE OF THE POKÉMON WE LIBERATED...
...UNTIL THEY WERE WELL ENOUGH TO BE RETURNED TO THE WILD.
ALL THOSE POKÉMON HAD BEEN MISTREATED BY HUMANS.
THEY WERE TOO HURT AND SCARED TO SURVIVE ON THEIR OWN.

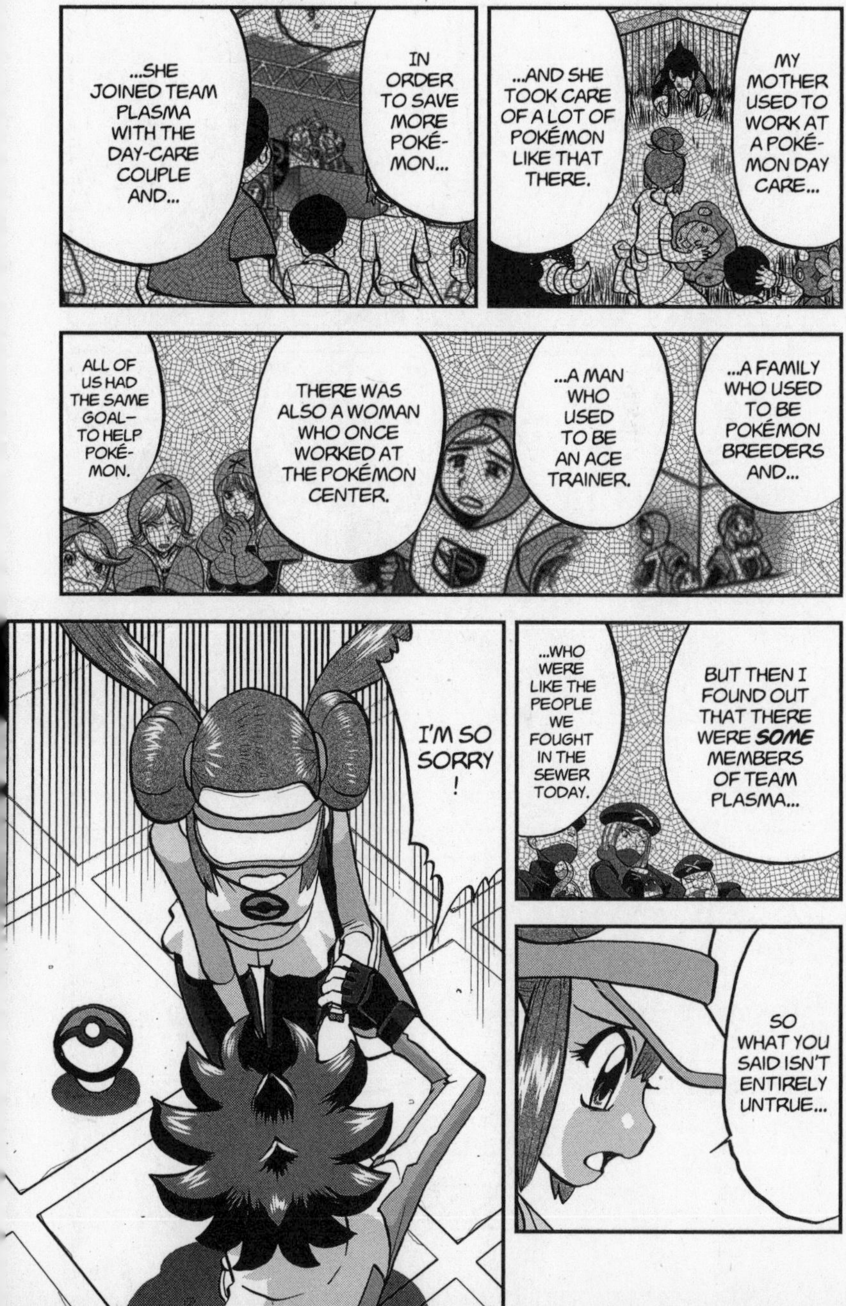
MY MOTHER USED TO WORK AT A POKÉ-MON DAY CARE...
...AND SHE TOOK CARE OF A LOT OF POKÉMON LIKE THAT THERE.
IN ORDER TO SAVE MORE POKÉ-MON...
...SHE JOINED TEAM PLASMA WITH THE DAY-CARE COUPLE AND...
...A FAMILY WHO USED TO BE POKÉMON BREEDERS AND...
...A MAN WHO USED TO BE AN ACE TRAINER.
THERE WAS ALSO A WOMAN WHO ONCE WORKED AT THE POKÉMON CENTER.
ALL OF US HAD THE SAME GOAL— TO HELP POKÉ-MON.
BUT THEN I FOUND OUT THAT THERE WERE ***SOME*** MEMBERS OF TEAM PLASMA...
...WHO WERE LIKE THE PEOPLE WE FOUGHT IN THE SEWER TODAY.
SO WHAT YOU SAID ISN'T ENTIRELY UNTRUE...
I'M SO SORRY!

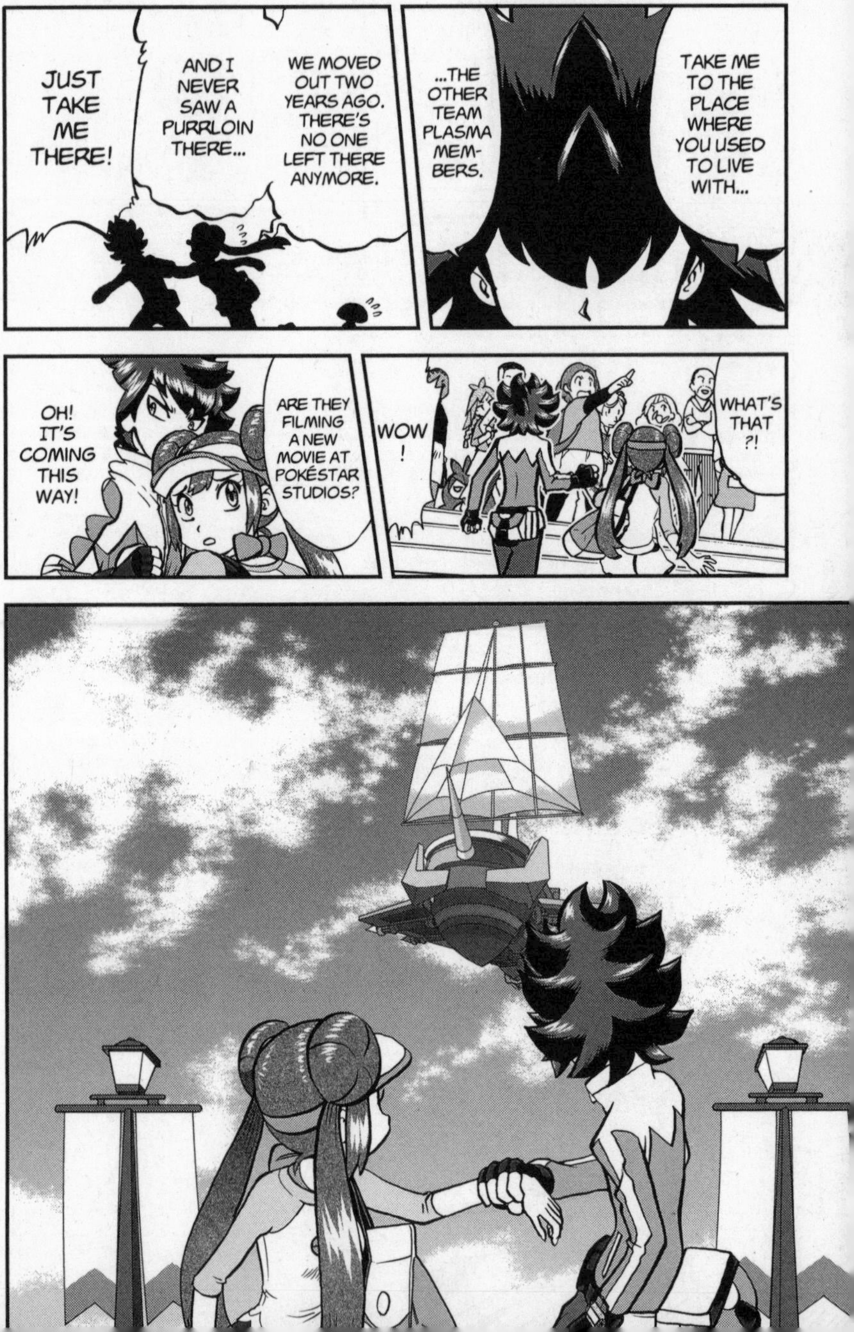
TAKE ME TO THE PLACE WHERE YOU USED TO LIVE WITH...
...THE OTHER TEAM PLASMA MEM-BERS.
WE MOVED OUT TWO YEARS AGO. THERE'S NO ONE LEFT THERE ANYMORE.
AND I NEVER SAW A PURRLOIN THERE...
JUST TAKE ME THERE!
WHAT'S THAT ?!
WOW !
ARE THEY FILMING A NEW MOVIE AT POKÉSTAR STUDIOS?
OH! IT'S COMING THIS WAY!

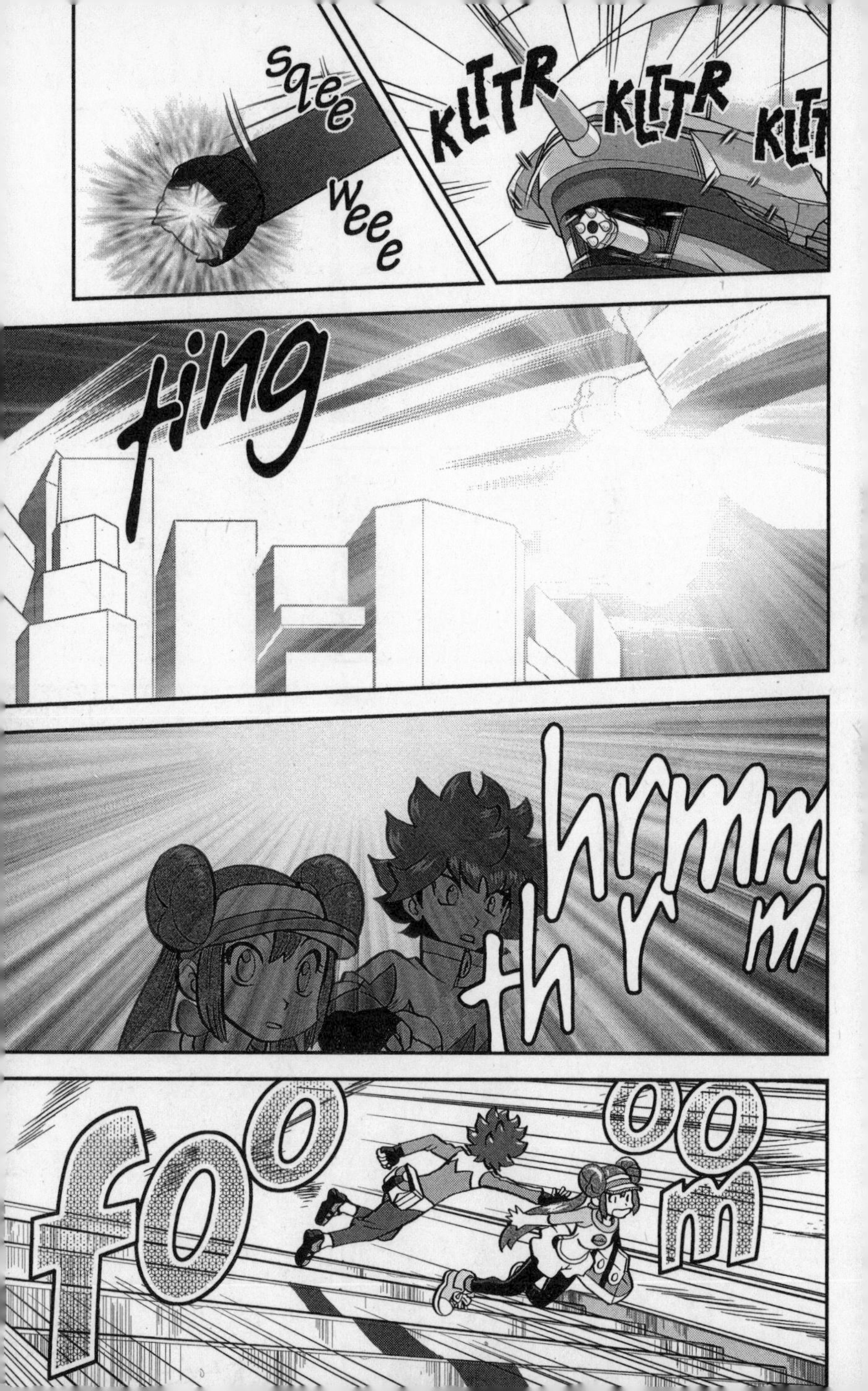
KLTTR KLTTR KLTT
sqee
weee
ting
hrmm
thrm
foooom

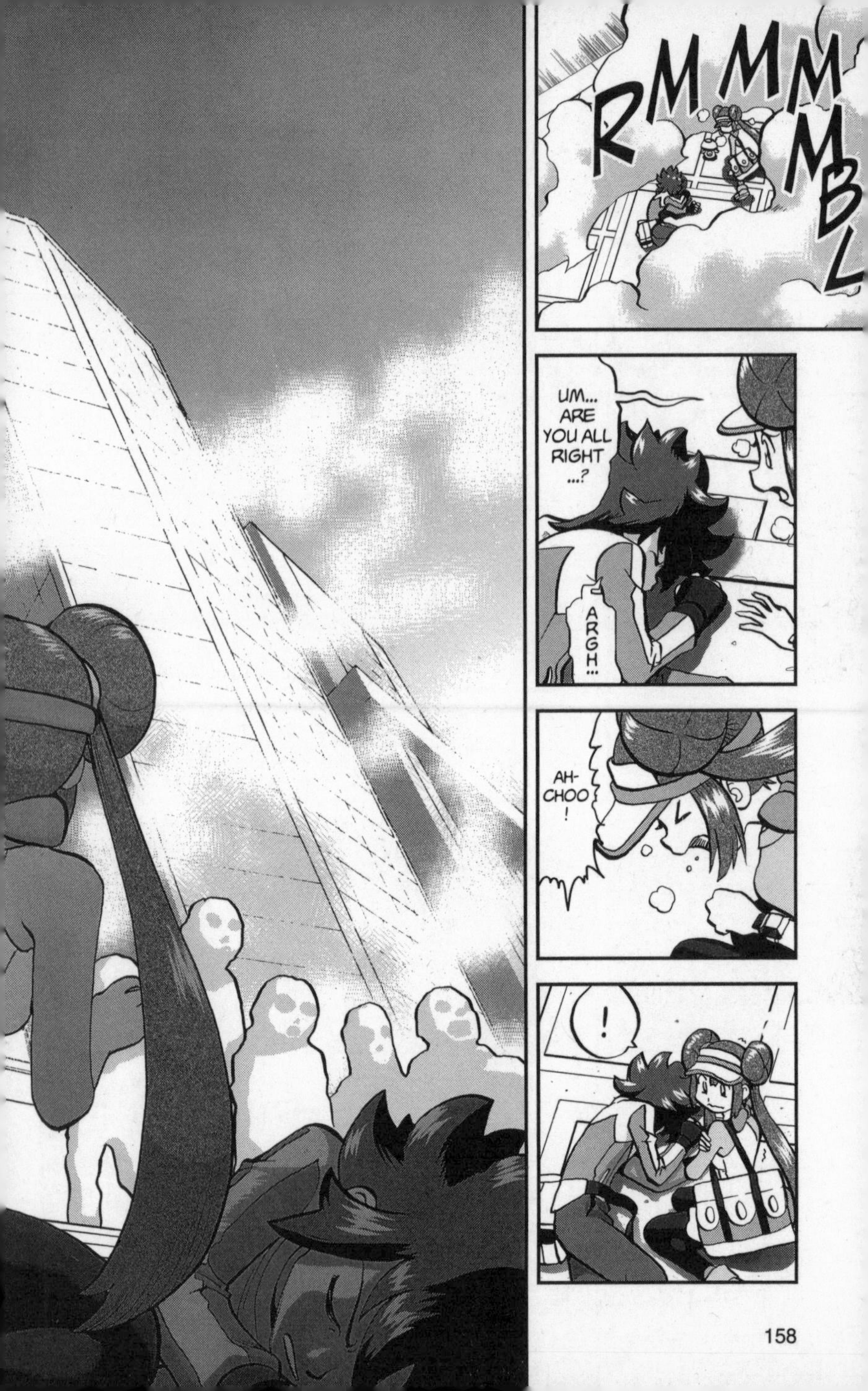
RMMMMMBL
UM... ARE YOU ALL RIGHT ...?
ARGH...
AH-CHOO!
!

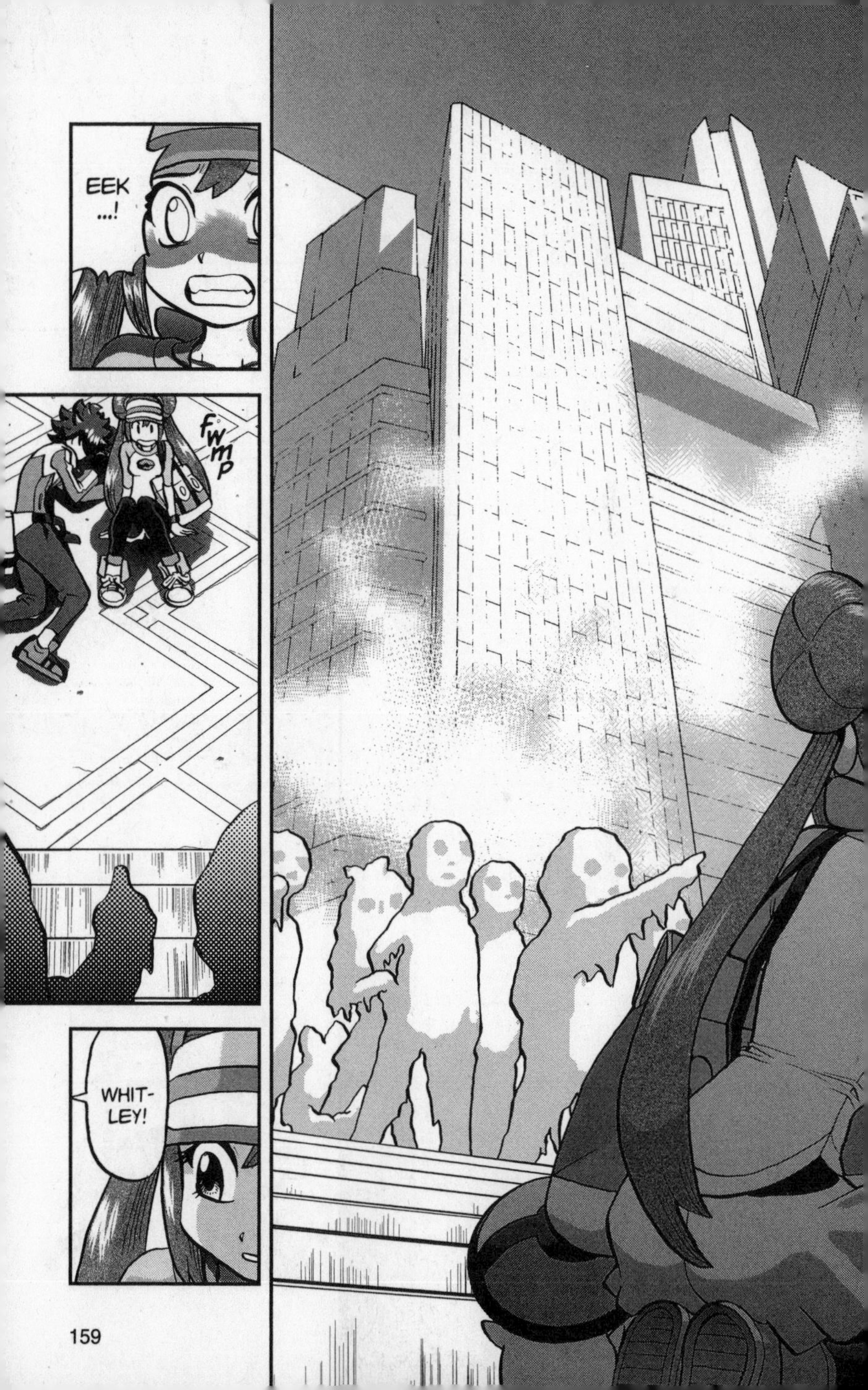
EEK ...!
fwmp
WHIT-LEY!

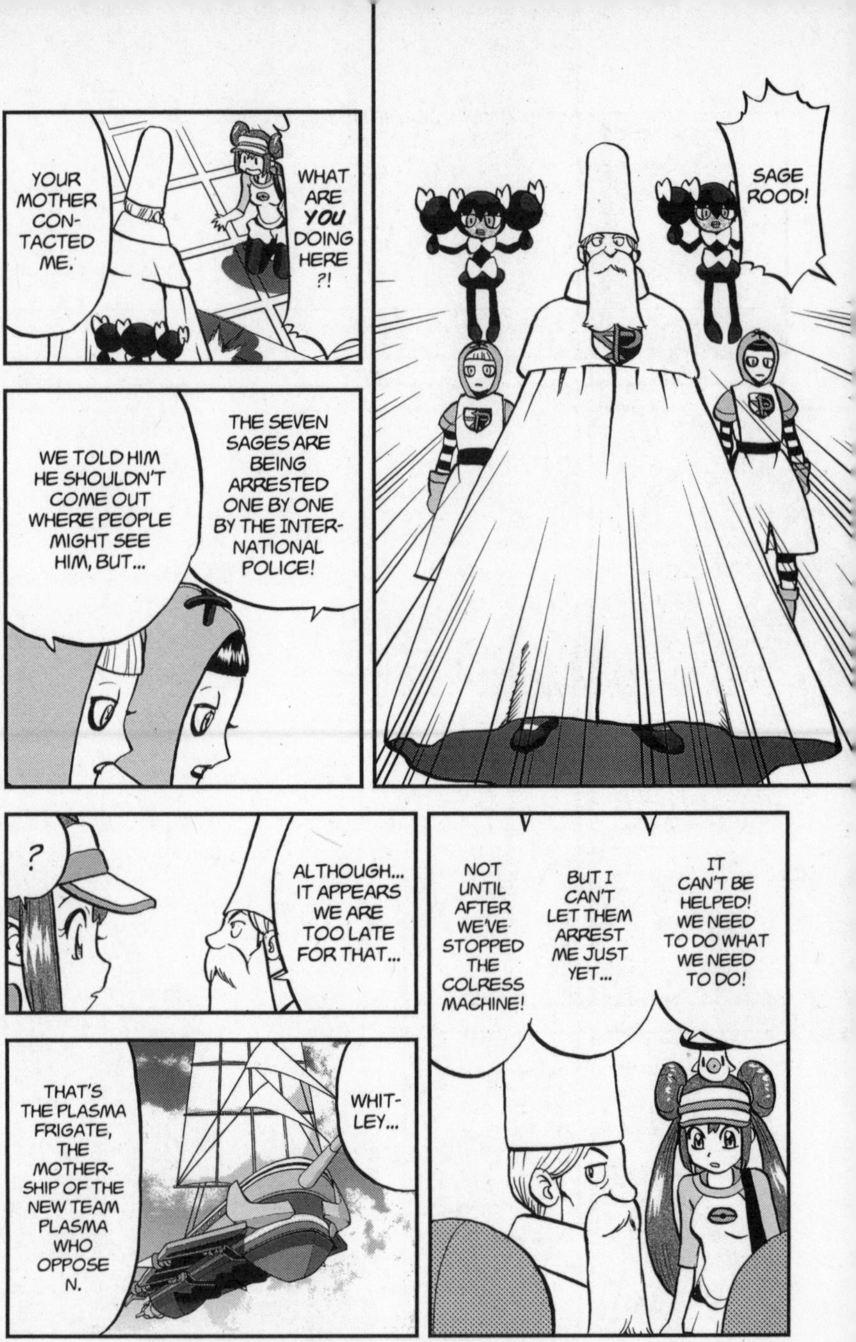
SAGE ROOD!
WHAT ARE YOU DOING HERE?!
YOUR MOTHER CONTACTED ME.
THE SEVEN SAGES ARE BEING ARRESTED ONE BY ONE BY THE INTERNATIONAL POLICE!
WE TOLD HIM HE SHOULDN'T COME OUT WHERE PEOPLE MIGHT SEE HIM, BUT...
IT CAN'T BE HELPED! WE NEED TO DO WHAT WE NEED TO DO!
BUT I CAN'T LET THEM ARREST ME JUST YET...
NOT UNTIL AFTER WE'VE STOPPED THE COLRESS MACHINE!
ALTHOUGH... IT APPEARS WE ARE TOO LATE FOR THAT...
?
WHITLEY...
THAT'S THE PLASMA FRIGATE, THE MOTHERSHIP OF THE NEW TEAM PLASMA WHO OPPOSE N.

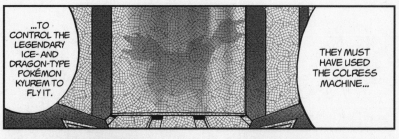

THEY MUST HAVE USED THE COLRESS MACHINE...
...TO CONTROL THE LEGENDARY ICE- AND DRAGON-TYPE POKÉMON KYUREM TO FLY IT.
WHITLEY, I HEAR YOU'VE LOST THE LOCKET...
Y-YES. BUT... THIS BOY FOUND IT...
I SEE.
WE HAD BETTER HURRY UP AND RETRIEVE THE MEMORY CARD.
SAGE ROOD! IT ISN'T IN HERE!
WHAT?
THE LOCKET IS *EMPTY*... IT'S NOT IN HIS POCKET OR HIS BAG EITHER.
HE SAID HE SAW THE LIST RECORDED ON THE MEMORY CARD...
MAYBE HE LEFT IT SOMEWHERE AT SCHOOL? OR IN HIS DORM ROOM?
THE TRAINERS' SCHOOL...
VERY WELL, WE HAD BETTER HEAD FOR ASPERTIA RIGHT AWAY.
W-WAIT A MINUTE, SAGE ROOD!

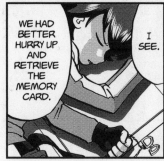

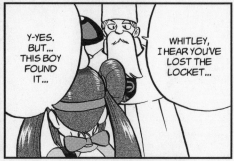

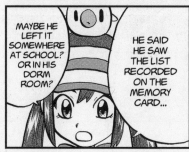

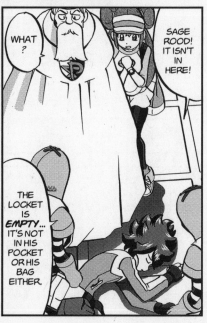

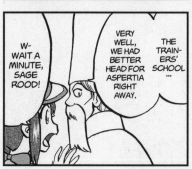

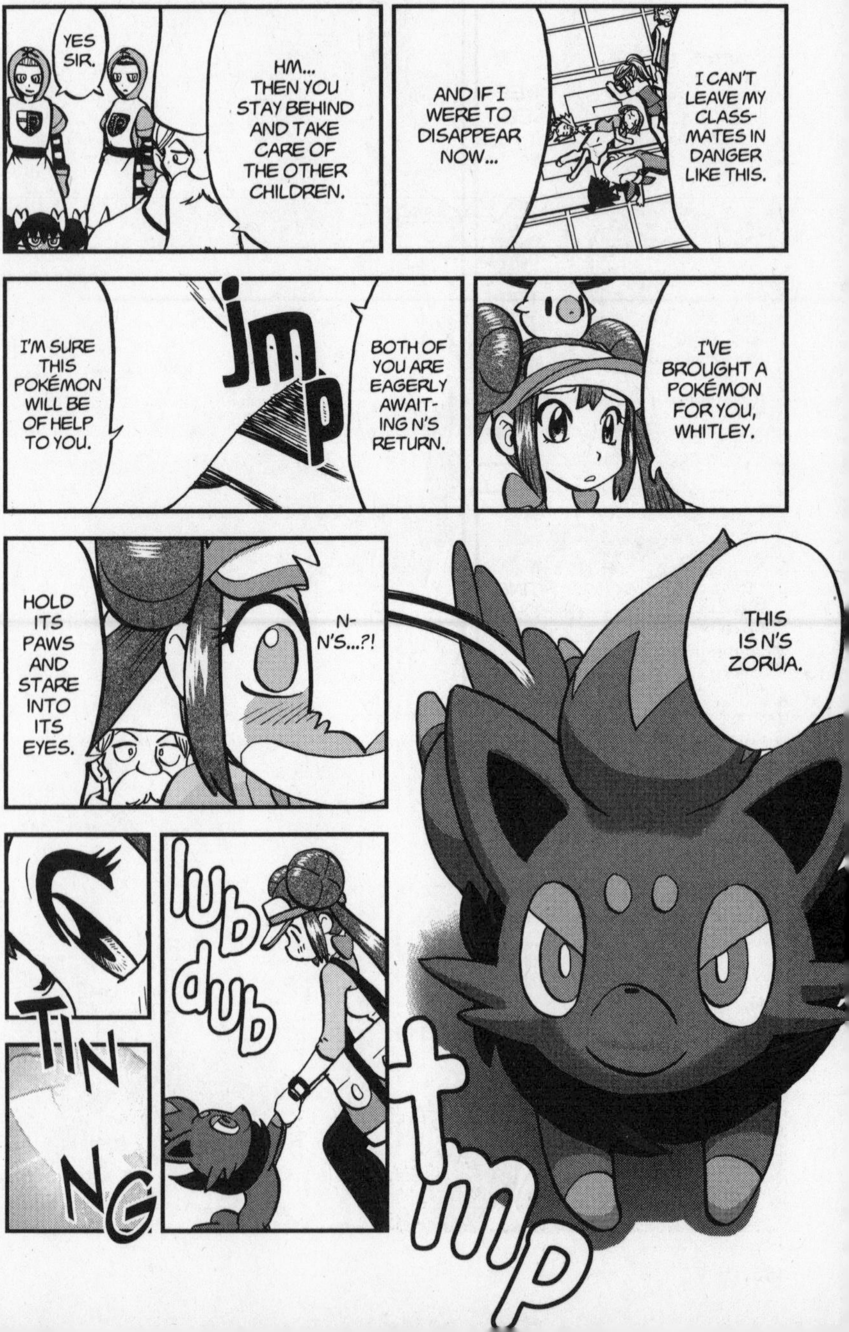
I CAN'T LEAVE MY CLASS-MATES IN DANGER LIKE THIS.
AND IF I WERE TO DISAPPEAR NOW...
HM... THEN YOU STAY BEHIND AND TAKE CARE OF THE OTHER CHILDREN.
YES SIR.
I'VE BROUGHT A POKÉMON FOR YOU, WHITLEY.
BOTH OF YOU ARE EAGERLY AWAIT-ING N'S RETURN.
jmp
I'M SURE THIS POKÉMON WILL BE OF HELP TO YOU.
THIS IS N'S ZORUA.
tmp
N- N'S...?!
HOLD ITS PAWS AND STARE INTO ITS EYES.
lub dub
TINNG

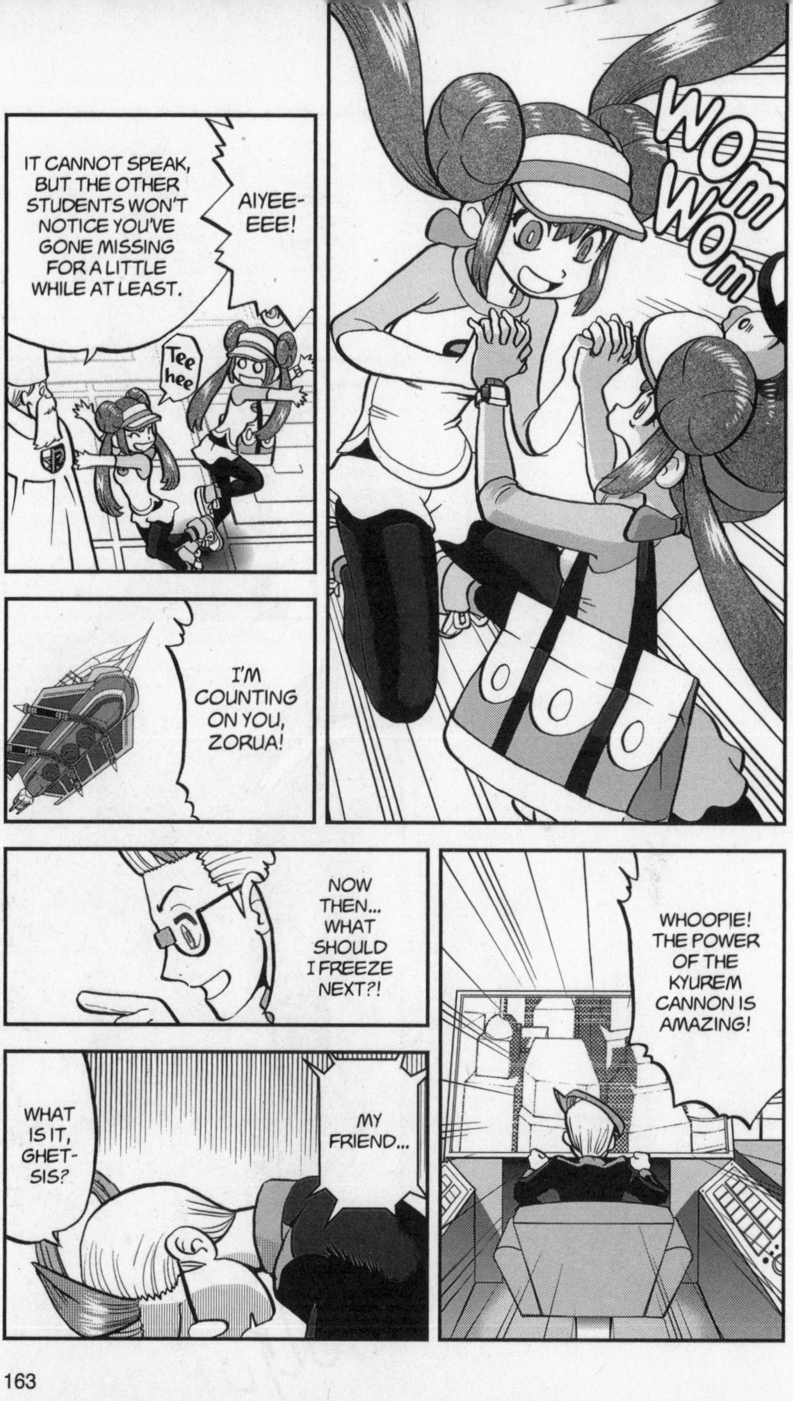
WOM WOM WOM
AIYEE-EEE!
IT CANNOT SPEAK, BUT THE OTHER STUDENTS WON'T NOTICE YOU'VE GONE MISSING FOR A LITTLE WHILE AT LEAST.
Tee hee
I'M COUNTING ON YOU, ZORUA!
WHOOPIE! THE POWER OF THE KYUREM CANNON IS AMAZING!
NOW THEN... WHAT SHOULD I FREEZE NEXT?!
MY FRIEND...
WHAT IS IT, GHET-SIS?

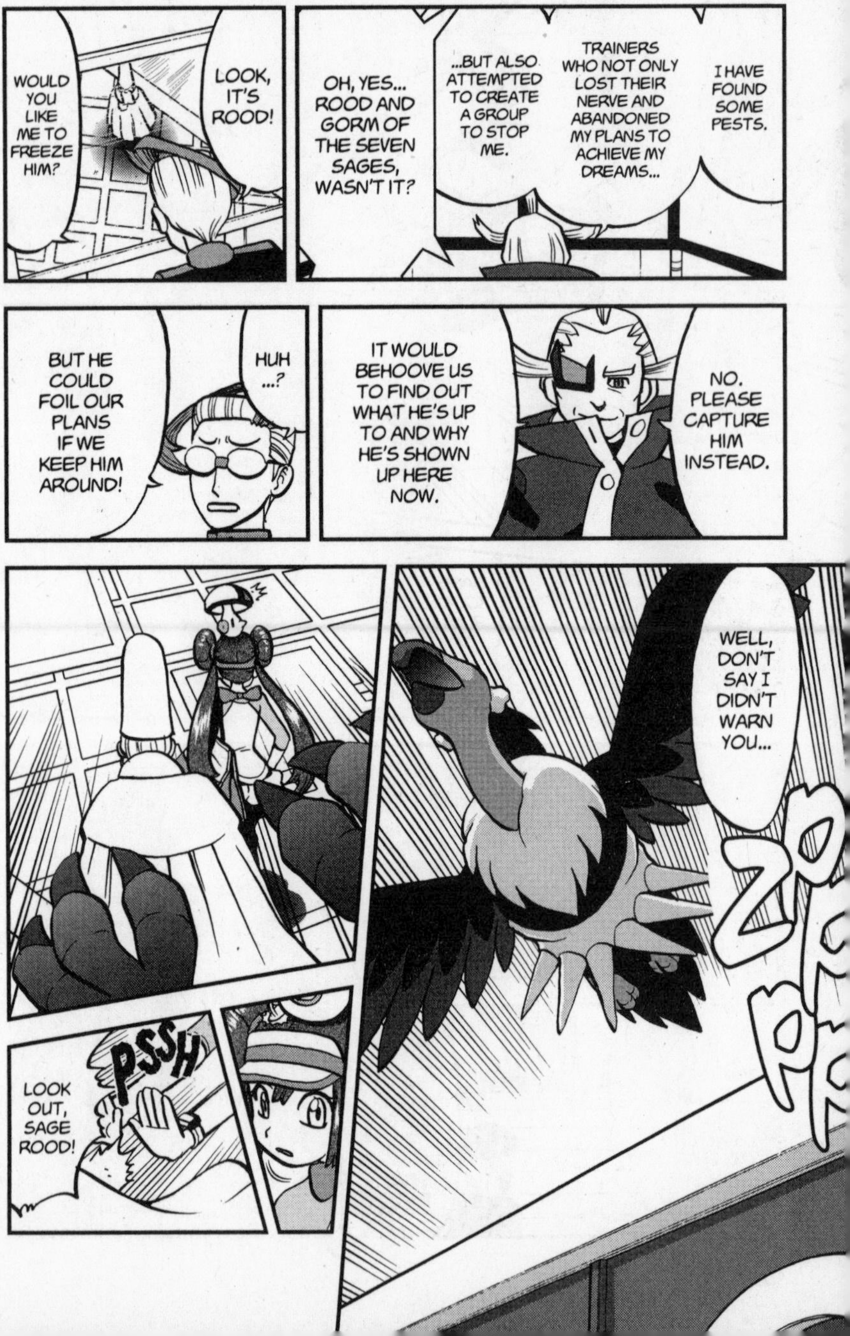
I HAVE FOUND SOME PESTS.
TRAINERS WHO NOT ONLY LOST THEIR NERVE AND ABANDONED MY PLANS TO ACHIEVE MY DREAMS...
...BUT ALSO ATTEMPTED TO CREATE A GROUP TO STOP ME.
OH, YES... ROOD AND GORM OF THE SEVEN SAGES, WASN'T IT?
LOOK, IT'S ROOD!
WOULD YOU LIKE ME TO FREEZE HIM?
NO. PLEASE CAPTURE HIM INSTEAD.
IT WOULD BEHOOVE US TO FIND OUT WHAT HE'S UP TO AND WHY HE'S SHOWN UP HERE NOW.
HUH ...?
BUT HE COULD FOIL OUR PLANS IF WE KEEP HIM AROUND!
WELL, DON'T SAY I DIDN'T WARN YOU...
PSSH
LOOK OUT, SAGE ROOD!

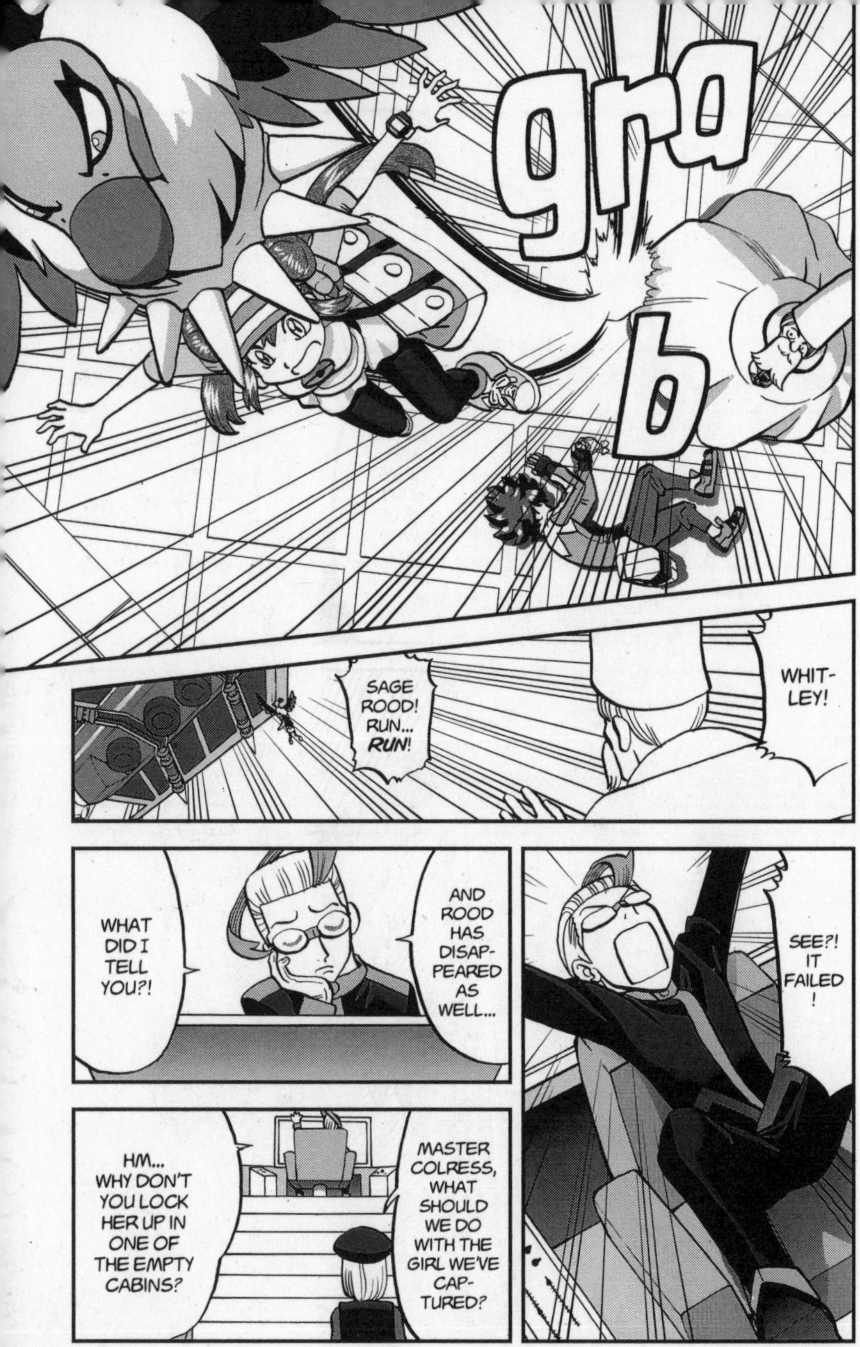
grab
WHIT-LEY!
SAGE ROOD! RUN... RUN!
SEE?! IT FAILED!
AND ROOD HAS DISAP-PEARED AS WELL...
WHAT DID I TELL YOU?!
MASTER COLRESS, WHAT SHOULD WE DO WITH THE GIRL WE'VE CAP-TURED?
HM... WHY DON'T YOU LOCK HER UP IN ONE OF THE EMPTY CABINS?

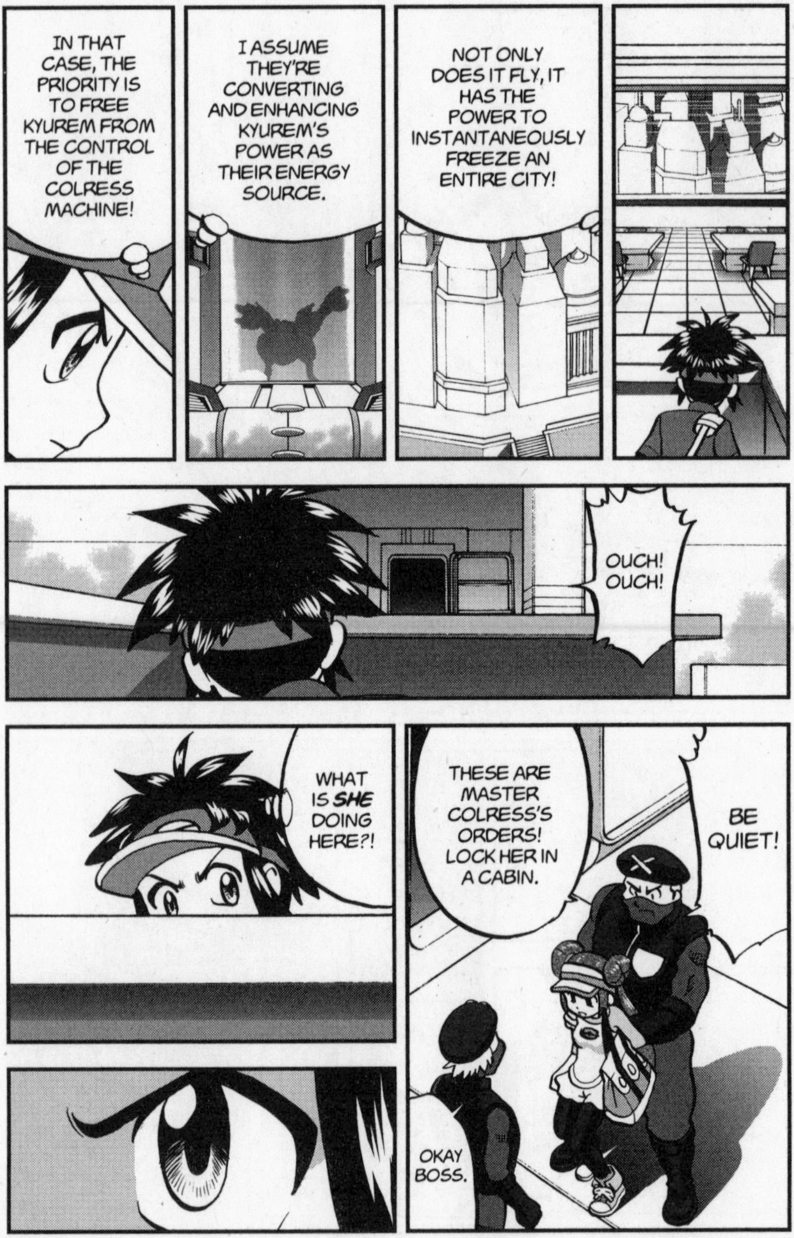
NOT ONLY DOES IT FLY, IT HAS THE POWER TO INSTANTANEOUSLY FREEZE AN ENTIRE CITY!
I ASSUME THEY'RE CONVERTING AND ENHANCING KYUREM'S POWER AS THEIR ENERGY SOURCE.
IN THAT CASE, THE PRIORITY IS TO FREE KYUREM FROM THE CONTROL OF THE COLRESS MACHINE!
OUCH! OUCH!
BE QUIET!
THESE ARE MASTER COLRESS'S ORDERS! LOCK HER IN A CABIN.
OKAY BOSS.
WHAT IS SHE DOING HERE?!

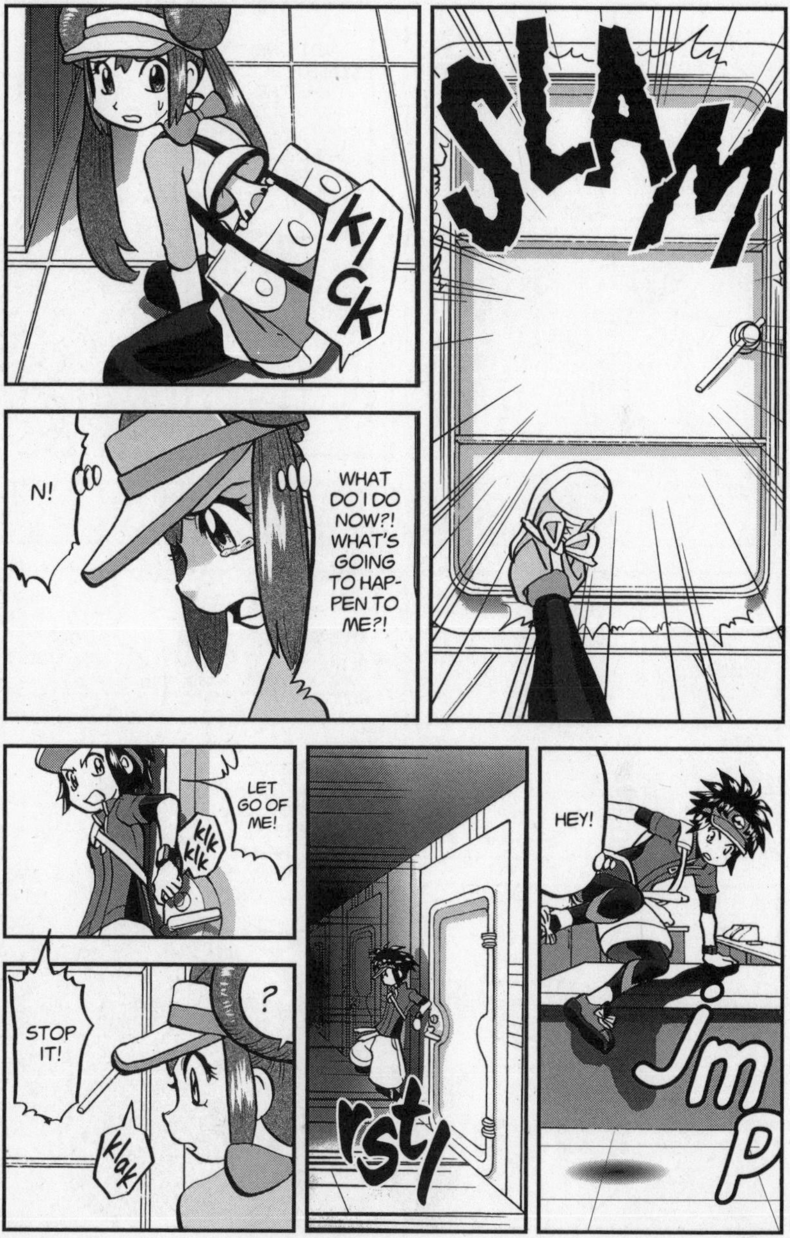
SLAM
KICK
WHAT DO I DO NOW?! WHAT'S GOING TO HAP-PEN TO ME?!
N!
HEY!
jmp
rstl
LET GO OF ME!
klk klk
?
STOP IT!
klak

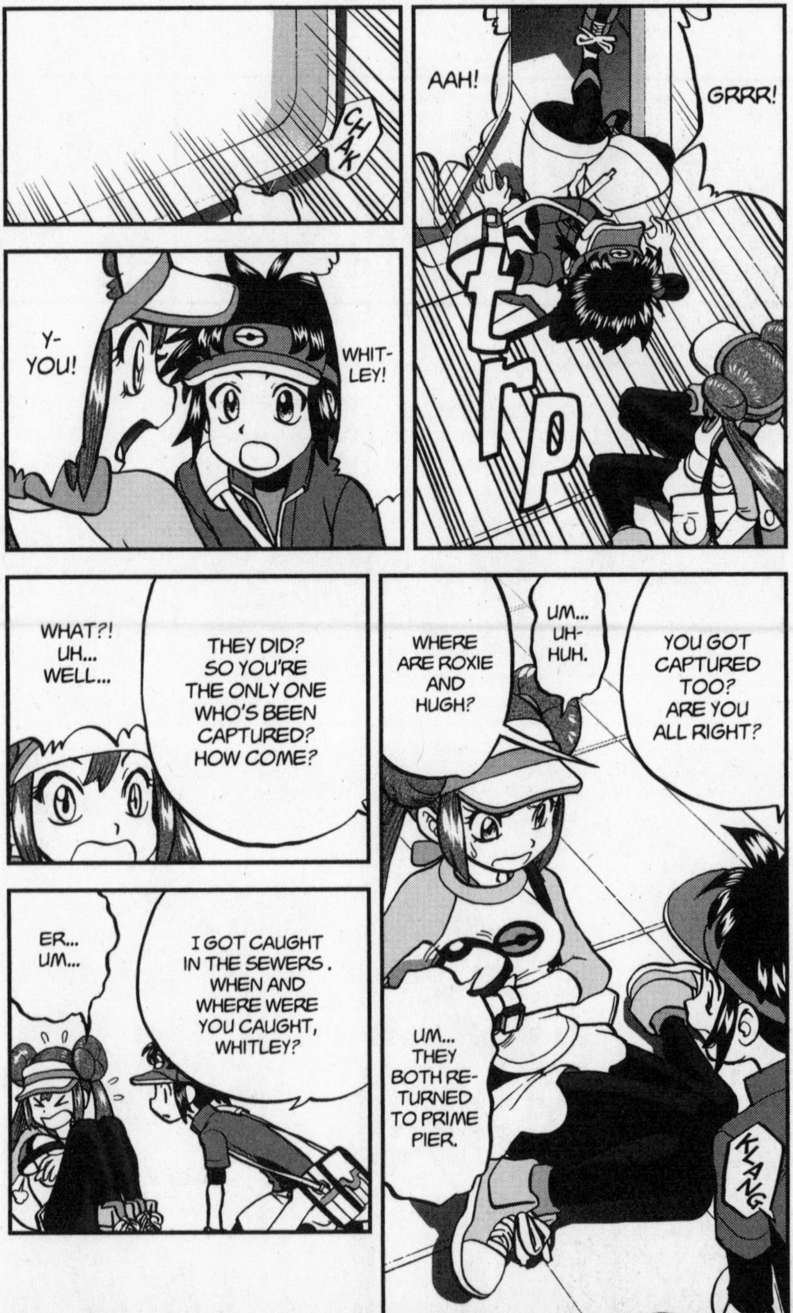
GRRR!
AAH!
trp
CHAK
WHIT-LEY!
Y-YOU!
YOU GOT CAPTURED TOO? ARE YOU ALL RIGHT?
UM... UH-HUH.
WHERE ARE ROXIE AND HUGH?
UM... THEY BOTH RE-TURNED TO PRIME PIER.
KLANG
THEY DID? SO YOU'RE THE ONLY ONE WHO'S BEEN CAPTURED? HOW COME?
WHAT?! UH... WELL...
I GOT CAUGHT IN THE SEWERS. WHEN AND WHERE WERE YOU CAUGHT, WHITLEY?
ER... UM...

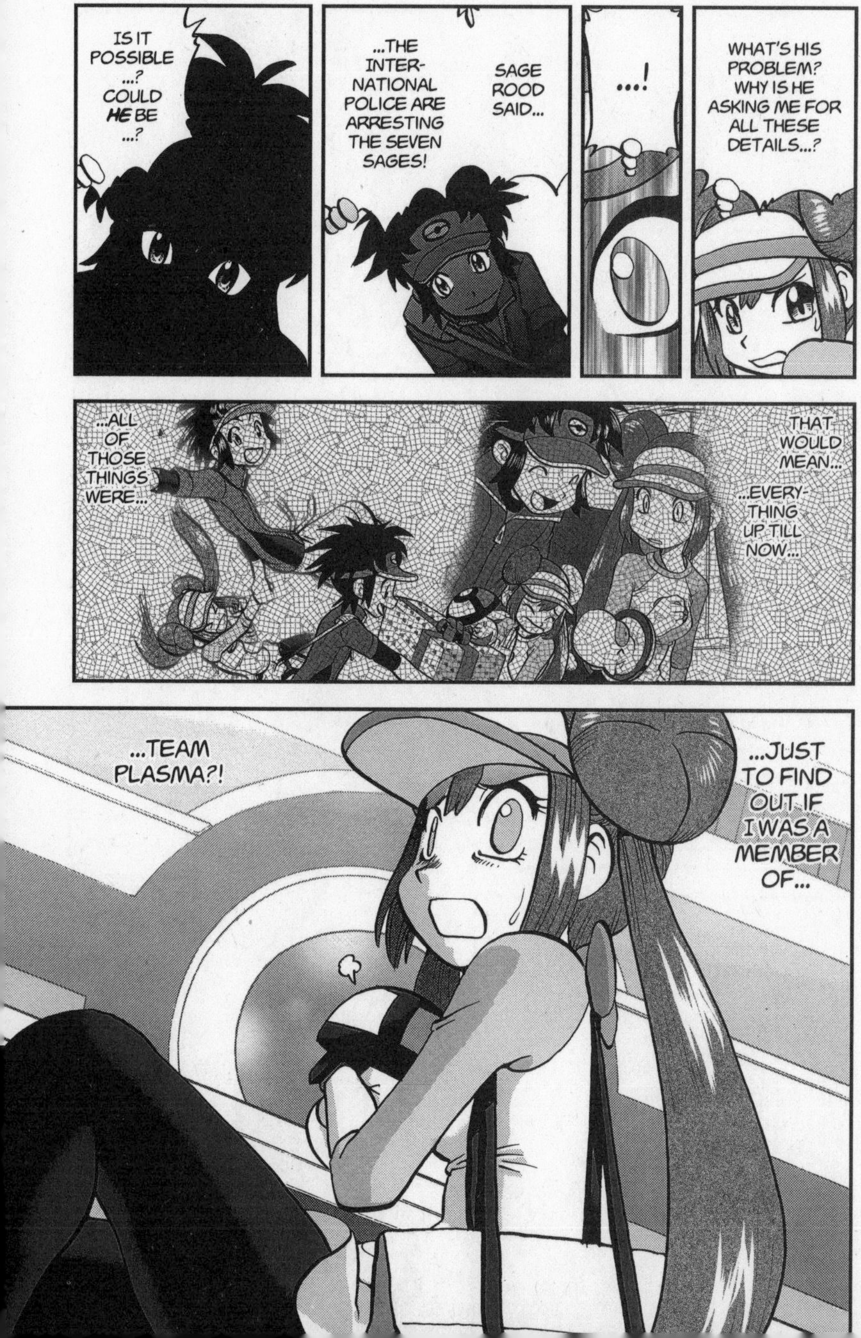
WHAT'S HIS PROBLEM? WHY IS HE ASKING ME FOR ALL THESE DETAILS...?
...!
SAGE ROOD SAID...
...THE INTER-NATIONAL POLICE ARE ARRESTING THE SEVEN SAGES!
IS IT POSSIBLE ...? COULD HE BE ...?
THAT WOULD MEAN...
...EVERY-THING UP TILL NOW...
...ALL OF THOSE THINGS WERE...
...JUST TO FIND OUT IF I WAS A MEMBER OF...
...TEAM PLASMA?!

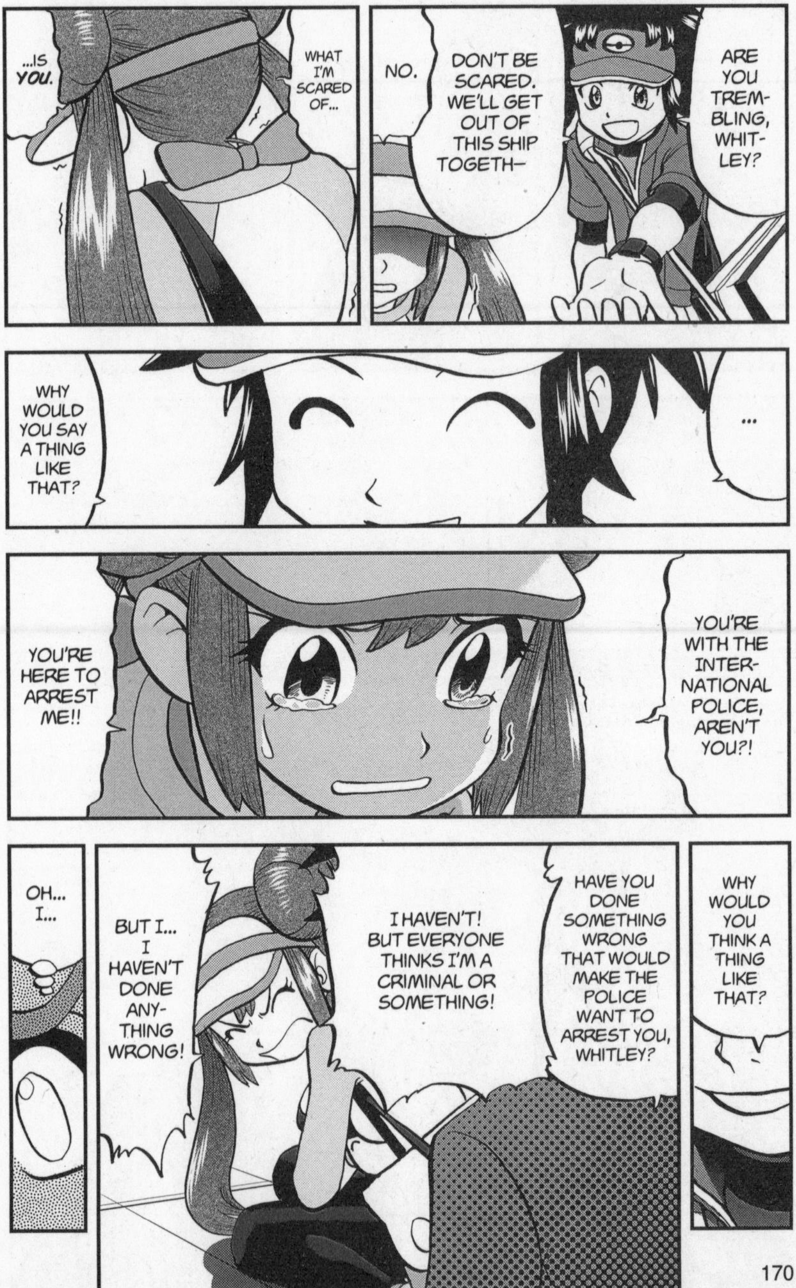
ARE YOU TREMBLING, WHITLEY?
DON'T BE SCARED. WE'LL GET OUT OF THIS SHIP TOGETH—
NO.
WHAT I'M SCARED OF...
...IS *YOU.*
...
WHY WOULD YOU SAY A THING LIKE THAT?
YOU'RE WITH THE INTERNATIONAL POLICE, AREN'T YOU?!
YOU'RE HERE TO ARREST ME!!
WHY WOULD YOU THINK A THING LIKE THAT?
HAVE YOU DONE SOMETHING WRONG THAT WOULD MAKE THE POLICE WANT TO ARREST YOU, WHITLEY?
I HAVEN'T! BUT EVERYONE THINKS I'M A CRIMINAL OR SOMETHING!
BUT I... I HAVEN'T DONE ANYTHING WRONG!
OH... I...

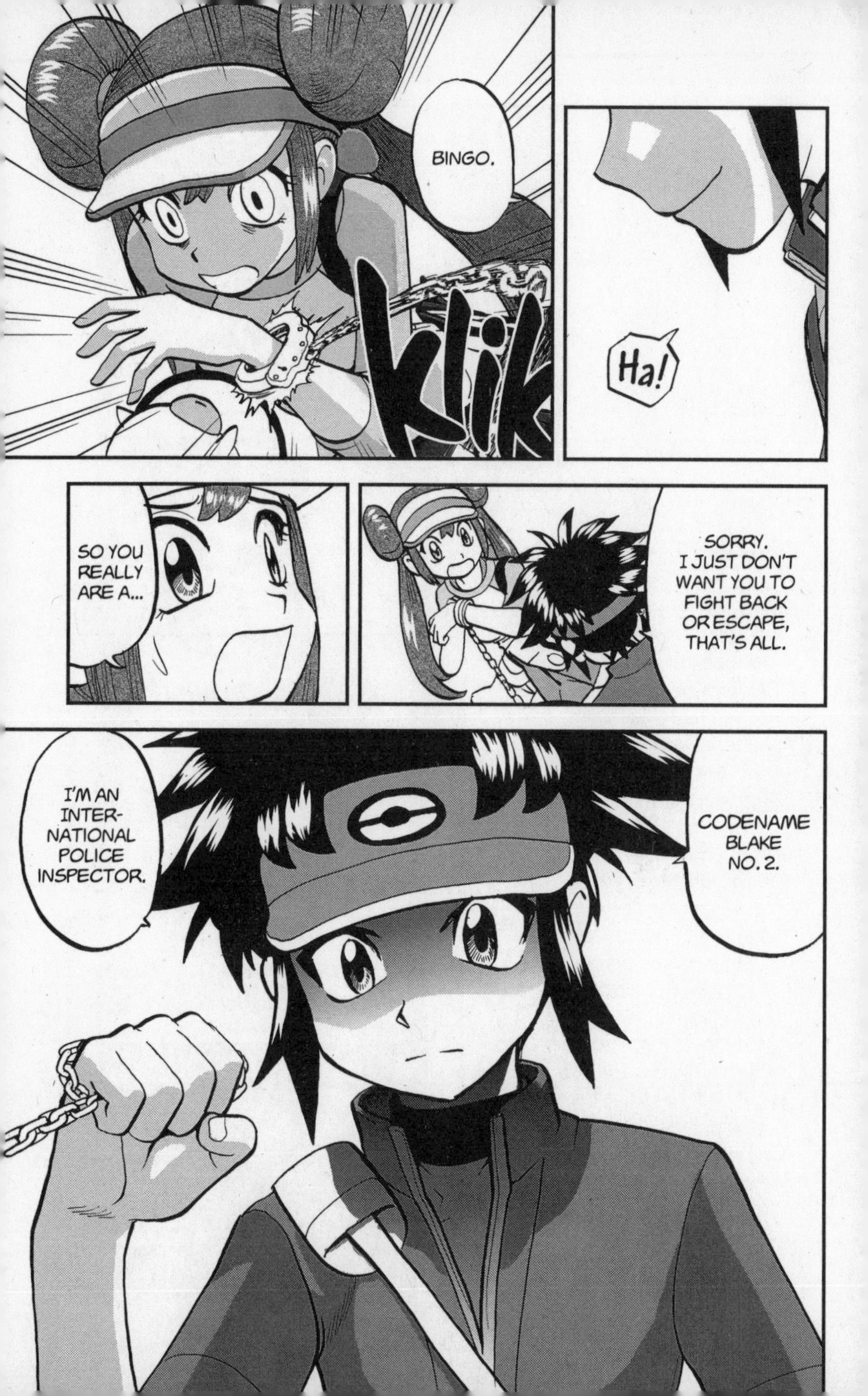
Ha!
BINGO.
klik
SORRY. I JUST DON'T WANT YOU TO FIGHT BACK OR ESCAPE, THAT'S ALL.
SO YOU REALLY ARE A...
CODENAME BLAKE NO. 2.
I'M AN INTER-NATIONAL POLICE INSPECTOR.

LOOKER

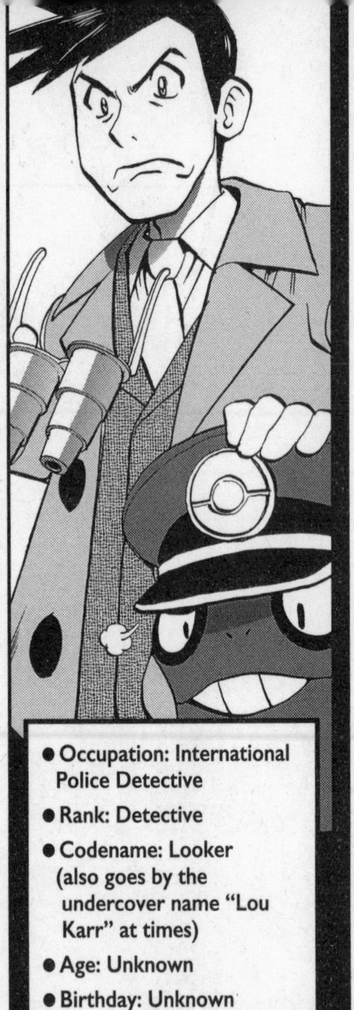

- Occupation: International Police Detective
- Rank: Detective
- Codename: Looker (also goes by the undercover name "Lou Karr" at times)
- Age: Unknown
- Birthday: Unknown
- Place of Birth: Unknown

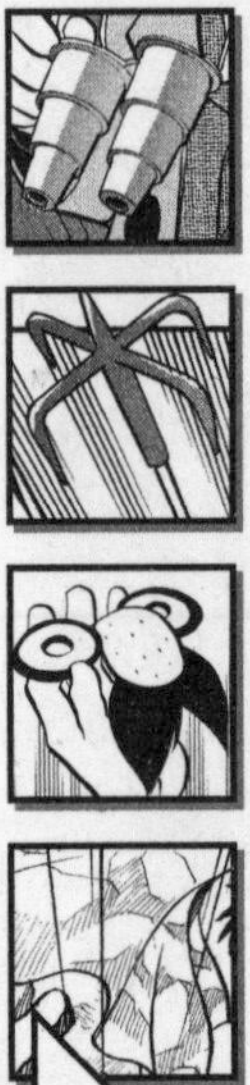

LOOKER

A veteran detective of the International Police Force. He was involved in a large investigation in the Sinnoh region, where he helped to solve the "Team Galactic: Distortion World Case," which revolved around Giratina. He was then dispatched to the Unova region to deal with Team Plasma incidents, going so far as to enter the Pokémon League as an undercover officer. He has been pursuing Team Plasma for more than two years now. Although a bit clumsy, he is passionate about his job and trustworthy. Headquarters holds him in high regard because he never gives up on a case. Looker is currently the officer assisting and supporting Blake.

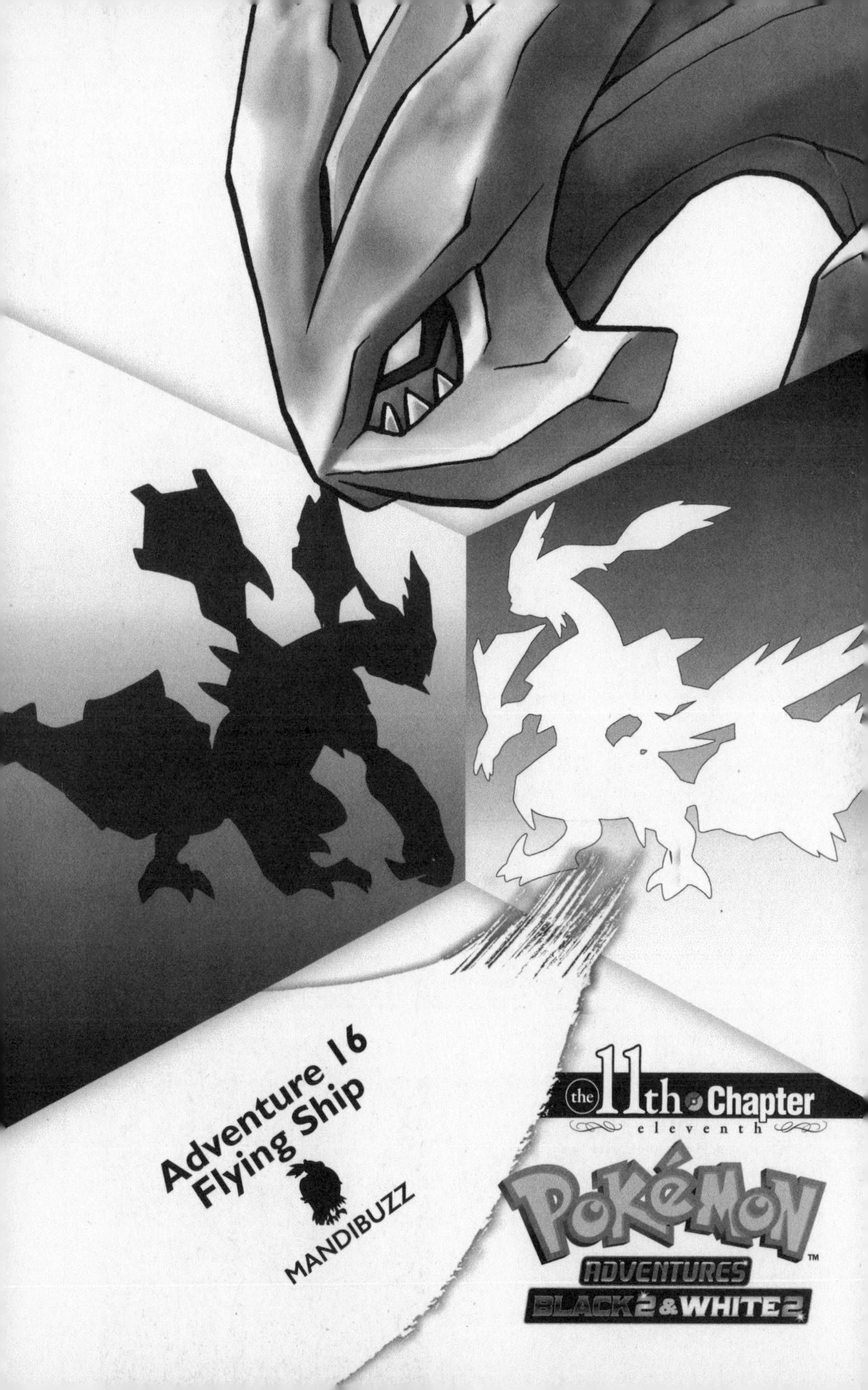
Adventure 16
Flying Ship
MANDIBUZZ
the 11th Chapter
eleventh
POKÉMON
ADVENTURES
BLACK 2 & WHITE 2

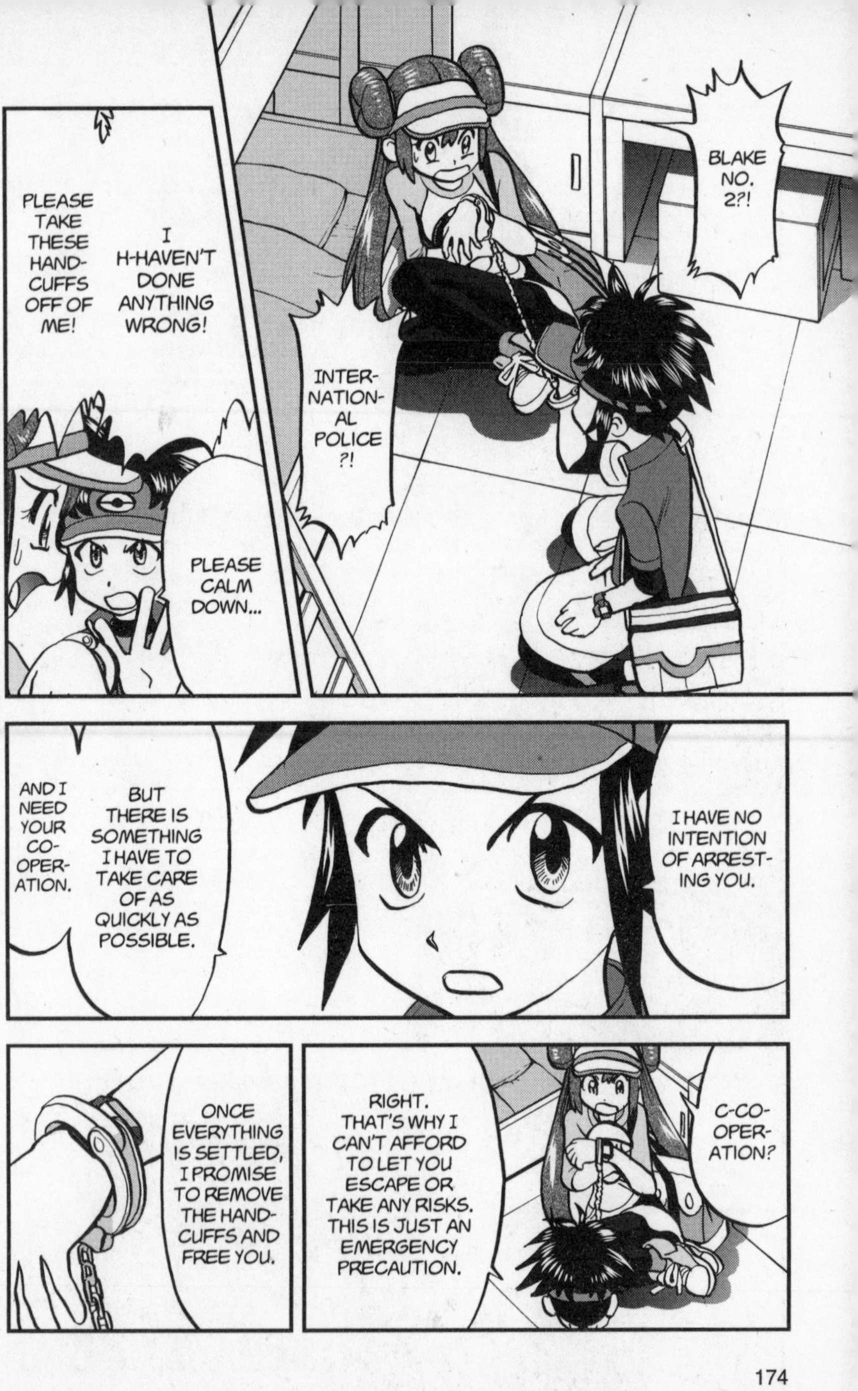
BLAKE NO. 2?!
INTERNATIONAL POLICE?!
I H-HAVEN'T DONE ANYTHING WRONG!
PLEASE TAKE THESE HANDCUFFS OFF OF ME!
PLEASE CALM DOWN...
I HAVE NO INTENTION OF ARRESTING YOU.
BUT THERE IS SOMETHING I HAVE TO TAKE CARE OF AS QUICKLY AS POSSIBLE.
AND I NEED YOUR COOPERATION.
C-COOPERATION?
RIGHT. THAT'S WHY I CAN'T AFFORD TO LET YOU ESCAPE OR TAKE ANY RISKS. THIS IS JUST AN EMERGENCY PRECAUTION.
ONCE EVERYTHING IS SETTLED, I PROMISE TO REMOVE THE HANDCUFFS AND FREE YOU.

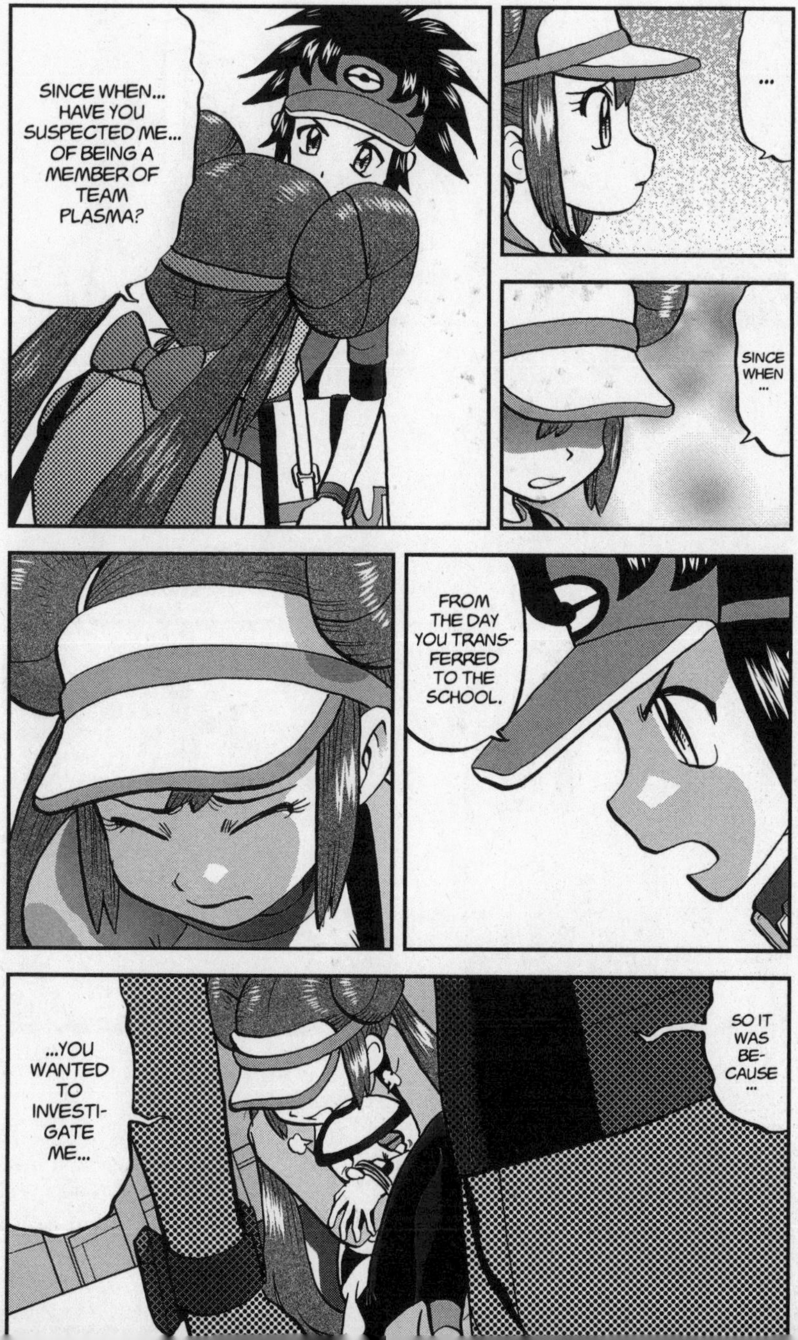
...
SINCE WHEN...
SINCE WHEN... HAVE YOU SUSPECTED ME... OF BEING A MEMBER OF TEAM PLASMA?
FROM THE DAY YOU TRANS-FERRED TO THE SCHOOL.
SO IT WAS BE-CAUSE...
...YOU WANTED TO INVESTI-GATE ME...

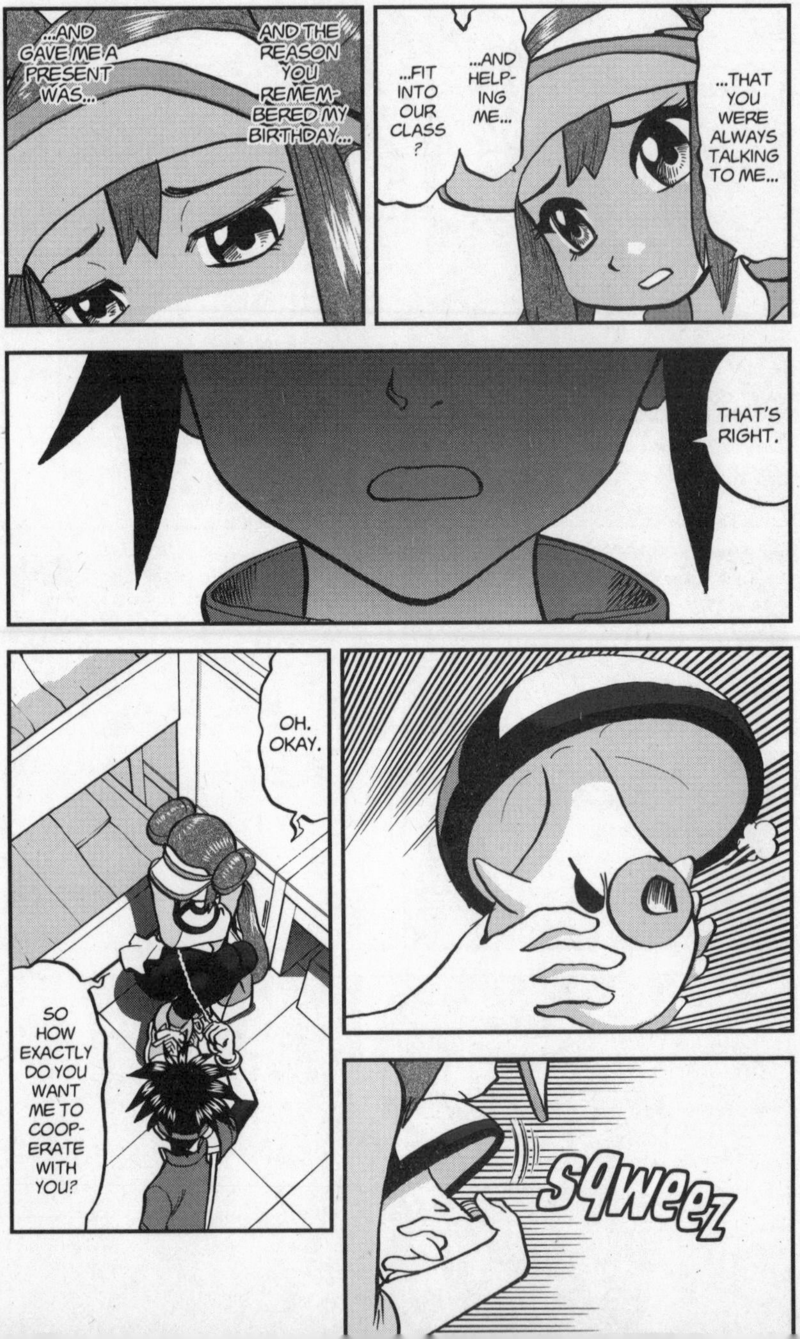
...THAT YOU WERE ALWAYS TALKING TO ME...
...AND HELPING ME...
...FIT INTO OUR CLASS?
AND THE REASON YOU REMEMBERED MY BIRTHDAY...
...AND GAVE ME A PRESENT WAS...
THAT'S RIGHT.
SQWEEZ
OH. OKAY.
SO HOW EXACTLY DO YOU WANT ME TO COOPERATE WITH YOU?

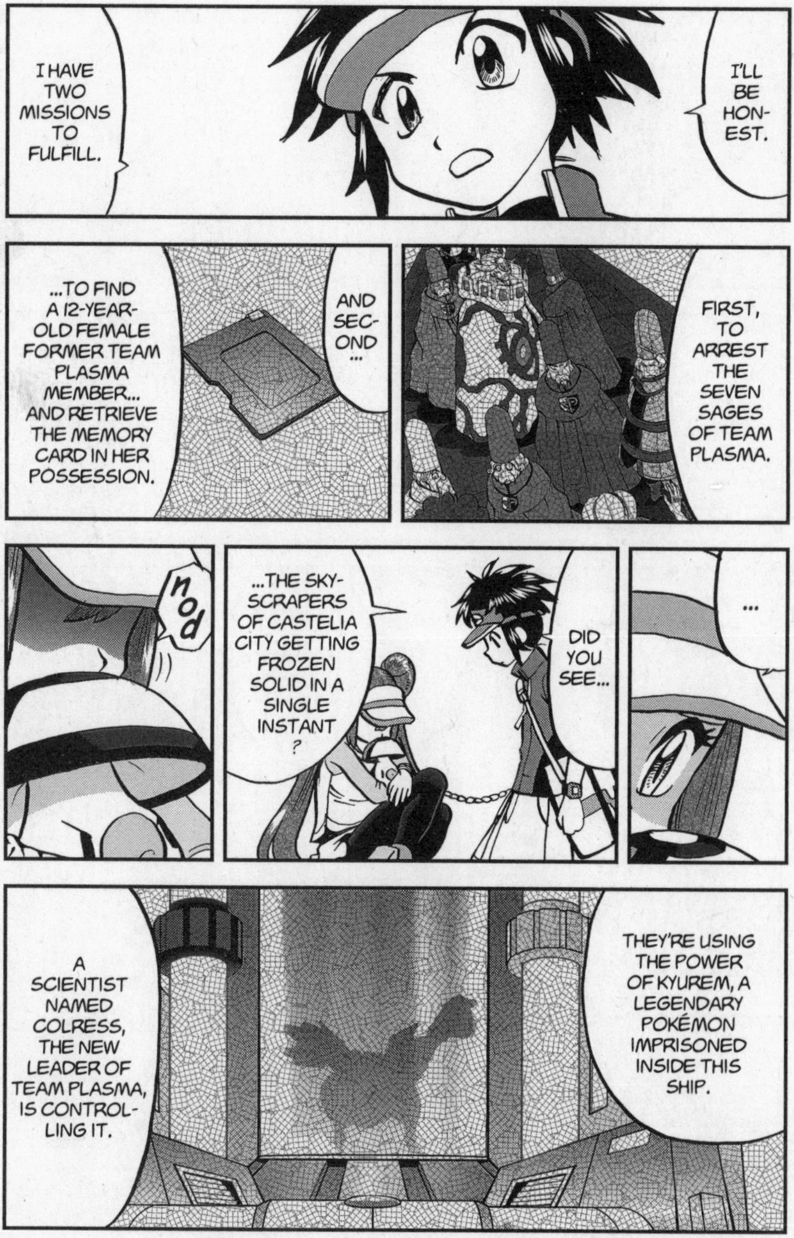
I'LL BE HON-EST.
I HAVE TWO MISSIONS TO FULFILL.
FIRST, TO ARREST THE SEVEN SAGES OF TEAM PLASMA.
AND SEC-OND...
...TO FIND A 12-YEAR-OLD FEMALE FORMER TEAM PLASMA MEMBER... AND RETRIEVE THE MEMORY CARD IN HER POSSESSION.
...
DID YOU SEE...
...THE SKY-SCRAPERS OF CASTELIA CITY GETTING FROZEN SOLID IN A SINGLE INSTANT?
nod
THEY'RE USING THE POWER OF KYUREM, A LEGENDARY POKÉMON IMPRISONED INSIDE THIS SHIP.
A SCIENTIST NAMED COLRESS, THE NEW LEADER OF TEAM PLASMA, IS CONTROL-LING IT.

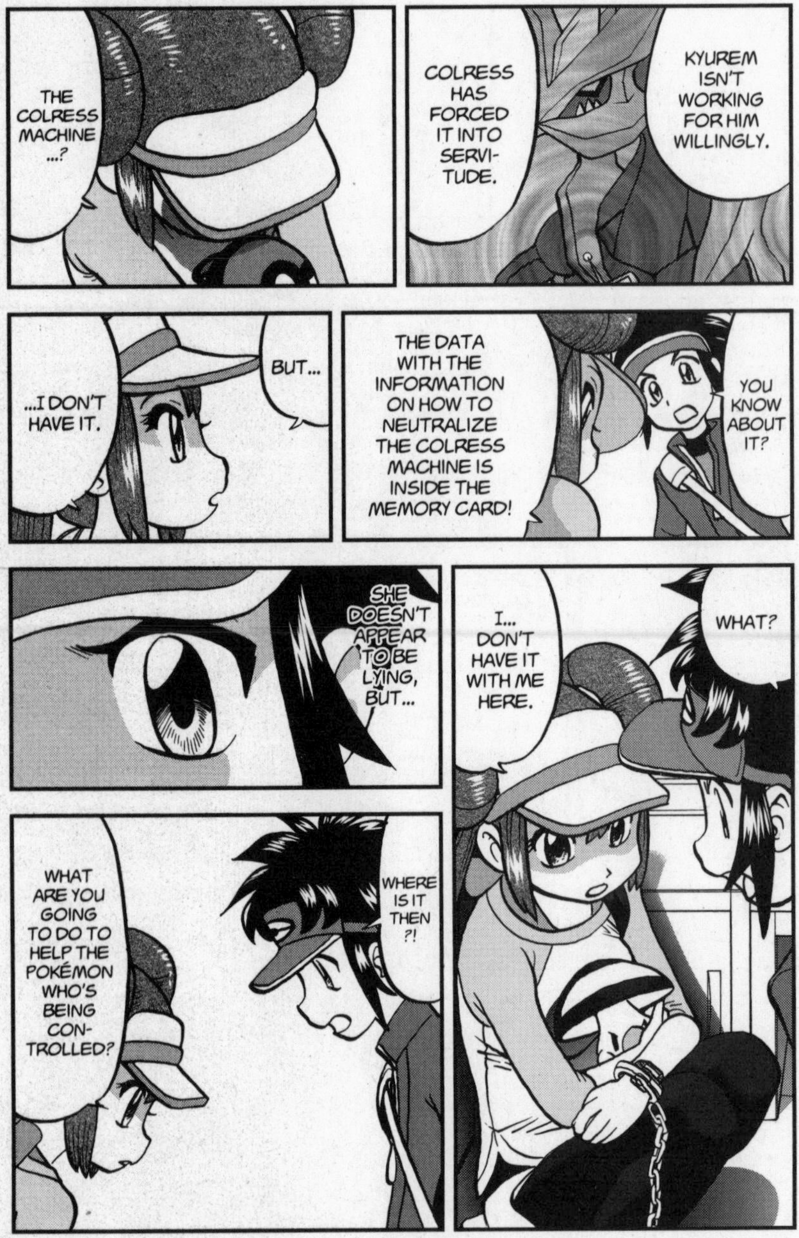
KYUREM ISN'T WORKING FOR HIM WILLINGLY.
COLRESS HAS FORCED IT INTO SERVI-TUDE.
THE COLRESS MACHINE ...?
YOU KNOW ABOUT IT?
THE DATA WITH THE INFORMATION ON HOW TO NEUTRALIZE THE COLRESS MACHINE IS INSIDE THE MEMORY CARD!
BUT...
...I DON'T HAVE IT.
WHAT?
I... DON'T HAVE IT WITH ME HERE.
SHE DOESN'T APPEAR TO BE LYING, BUT...
WHERE IS IT THEN ?!
WHAT ARE YOU GOING TO DO TO HELP THE POKÉMON WHO'S BEING CON-TROLLED?

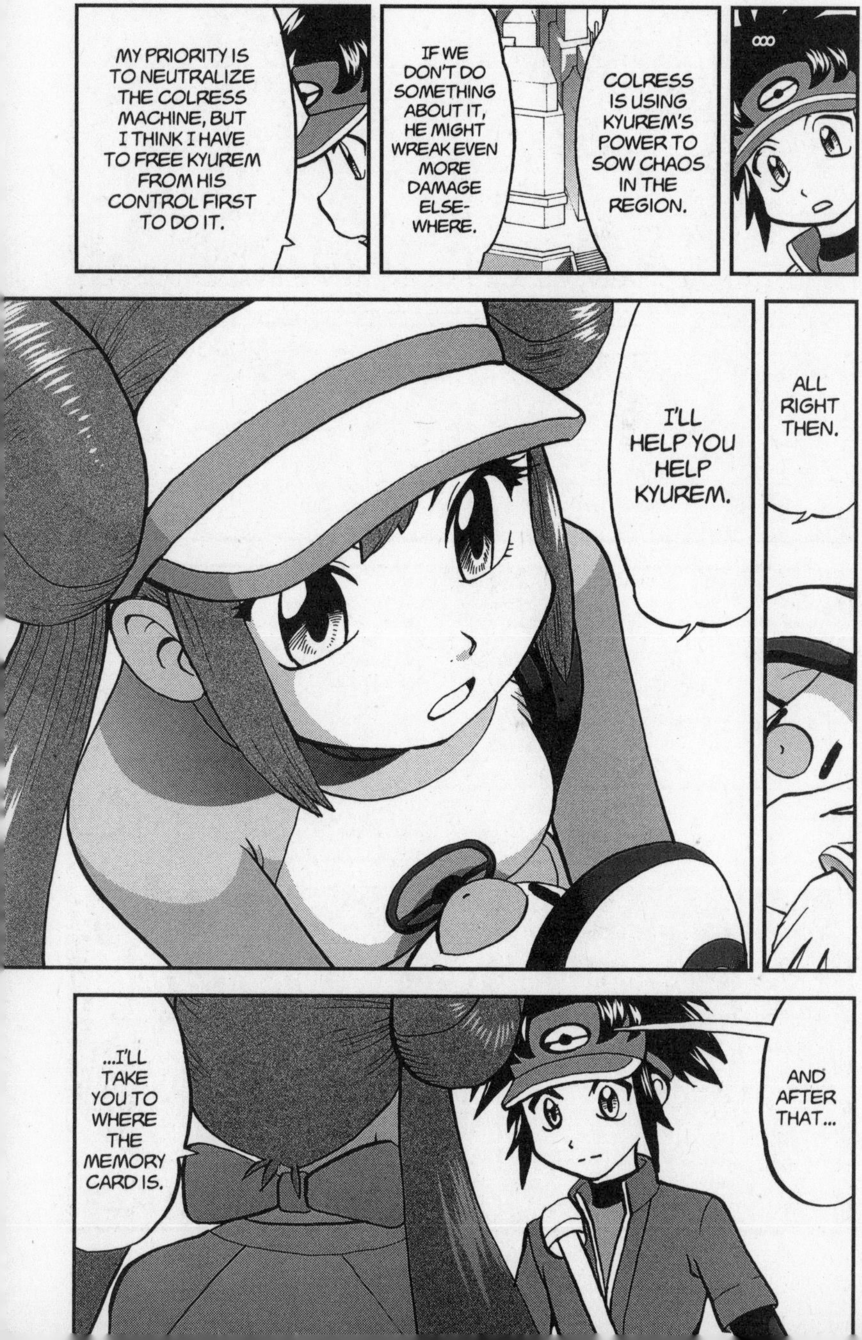
COLRESS IS USING KYUREM'S POWER TO SOW CHAOS IN THE REGION.
IF WE DON'T DO SOMETHING ABOUT IT, HE MIGHT WREAK EVEN MORE DAMAGE ELSE-WHERE.
MY PRIORITY IS TO NEUTRALIZE THE COLRESS MACHINE, BUT I THINK I HAVE TO FREE KYUREM FROM HIS CONTROL FIRST TO DO IT.
ALL RIGHT THEN.
I'LL HELP YOU HELP KYUREM.
AND AFTER THAT...
...I'LL TAKE YOU TO WHERE THE MEMORY CARD IS.

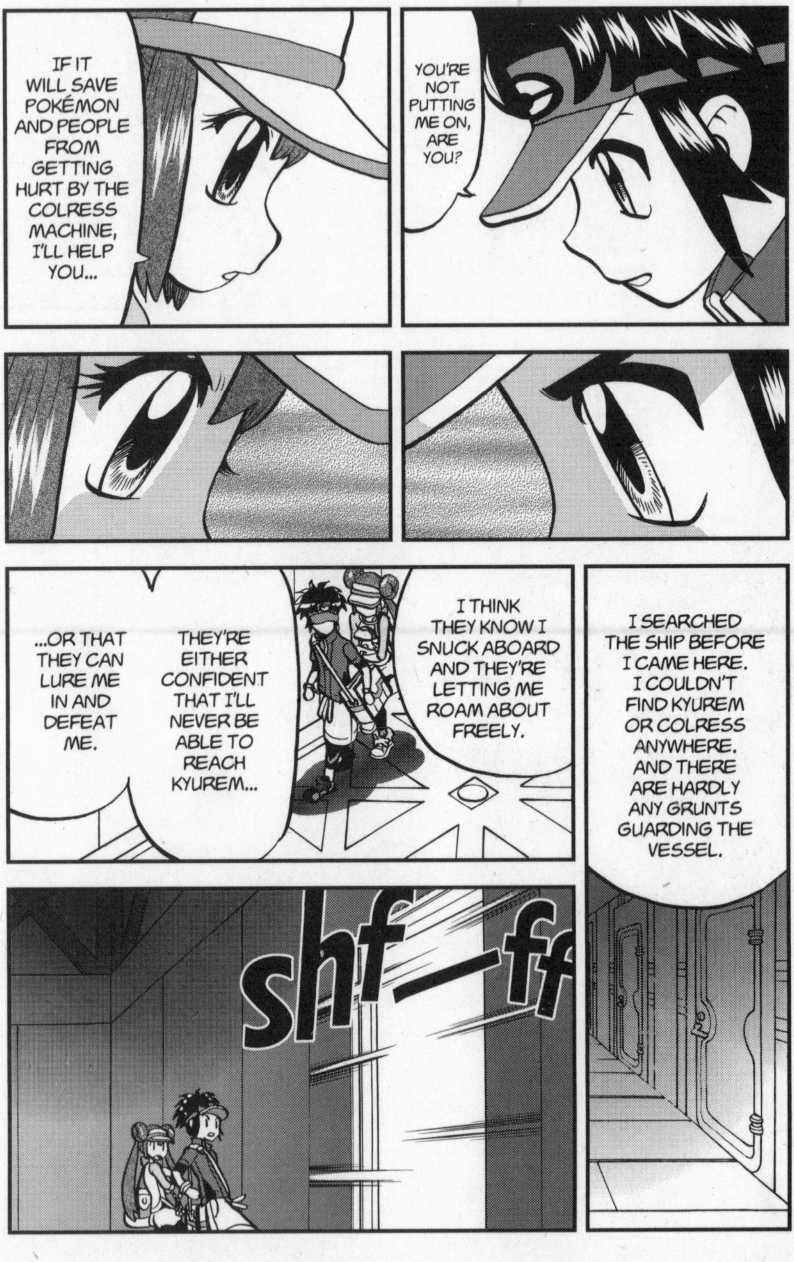
YOU'RE NOT PUTTING ME ON, ARE YOU?
IF IT WILL SAVE POKÉMON AND PEOPLE FROM GETTING HURT BY THE COLRESS MACHINE, I'LL HELP YOU...
I SEARCHED THE SHIP BEFORE I CAME HERE. I COULDN'T FIND KYUREM OR COLRESS ANYWHERE. AND THERE ARE HARDLY ANY GRUNTS GUARDING THE VESSEL.
I THINK THEY KNOW I SNUCK ABOARD AND THEY'RE LETTING ME ROAM ABOUT FREELY.
THEY'RE EITHER CONFIDENT THAT I'LL NEVER BE ABLE TO REACH KYUREM...
...OR THAT THEY CAN LURE ME IN AND DEFEAT ME.
shf—ff

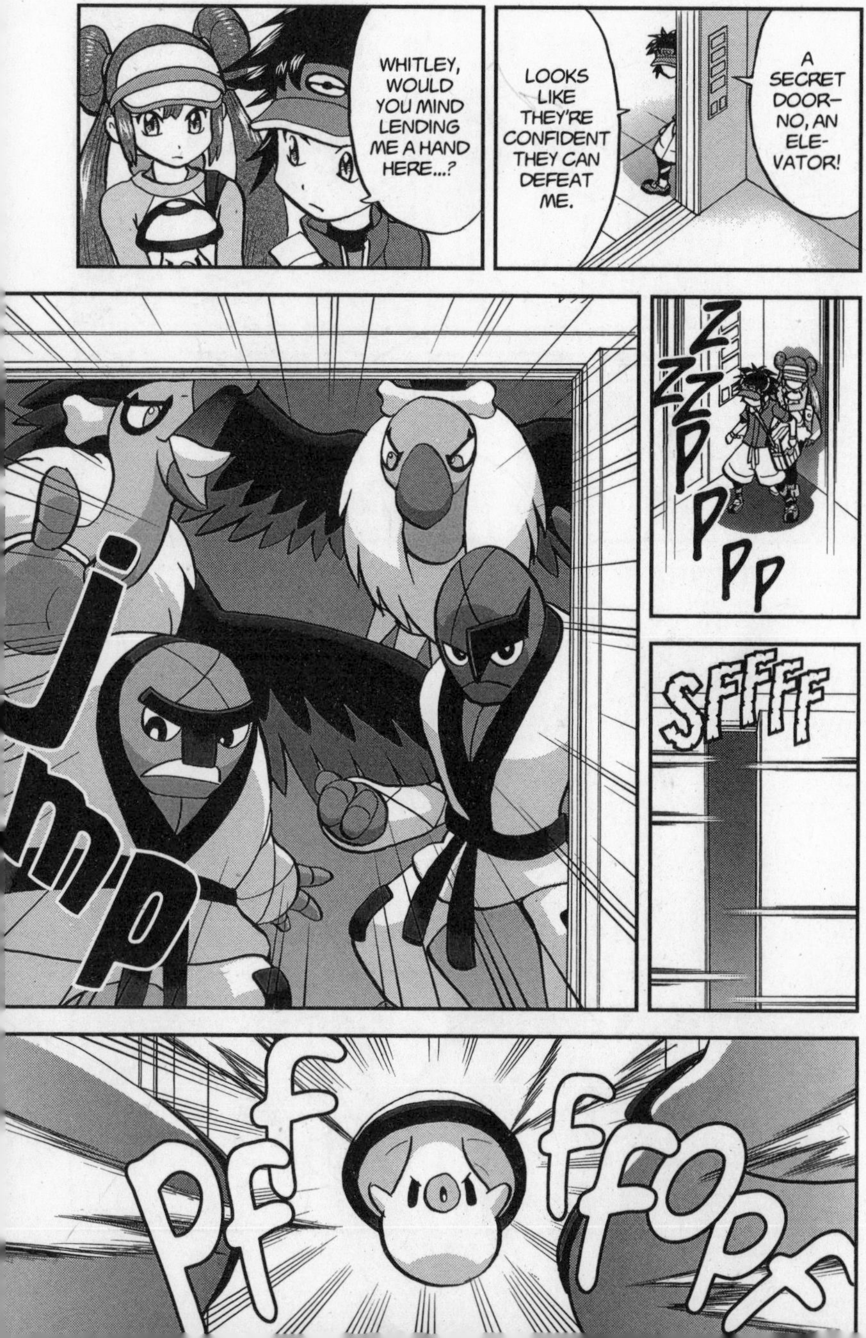
A SECRET DOOR—NO, AN ELEVATOR!
LOOKS LIKE THEY'RE CONFIDENT THEY CAN DEFEAT ME.
WHITLEY, WOULD YOU MIND LENDING ME A HAND HERE...?
ZZZPPPP
SFFFF
PFF
FFOPF

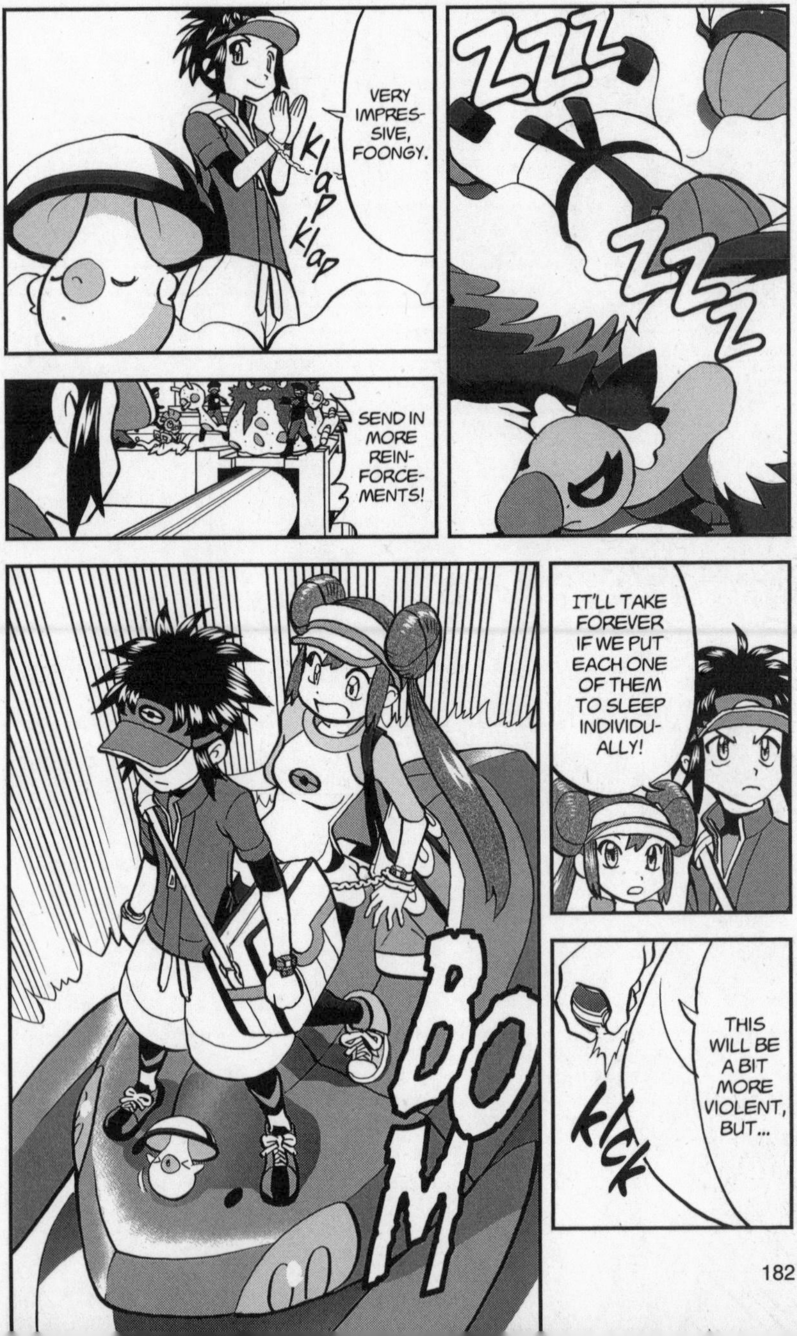
ZZZ
ZZZ
VERY IMPRES-SIVE, FOONGY.
klap klap klap
SEND IN MORE REIN-FORCE-MENTS!
IT'LL TAKE FOREVER IF WE PUT EACH ONE OF THEM TO SLEEP INDIVIDU-ALLY!
THIS WILL BE A BIT MORE VIOLENT, BUT...
kick
BOOM

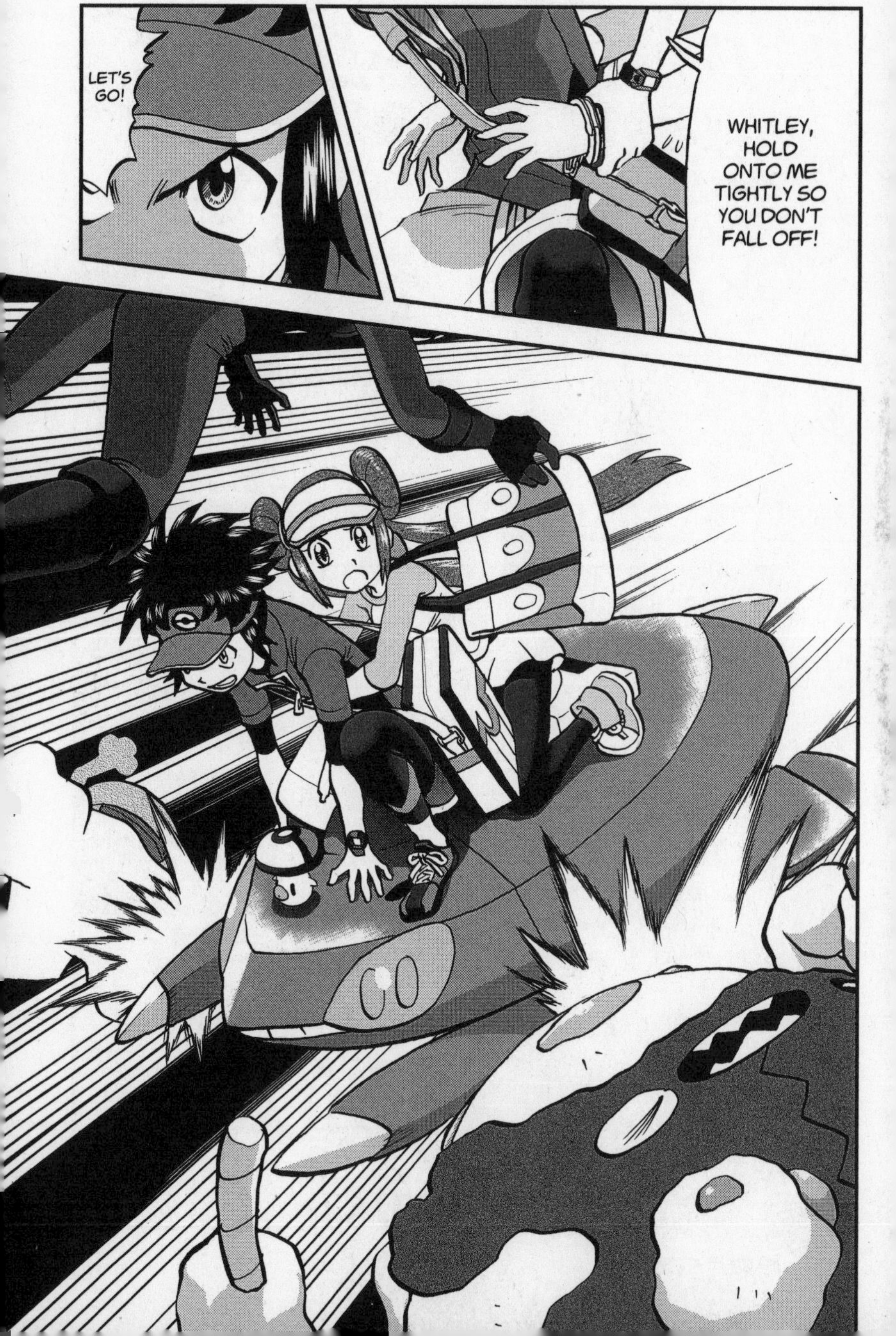
WHITLEY, HOLD ONTO ME TIGHTLY SO YOU DON'T FALL OFF!
LET'S GO!

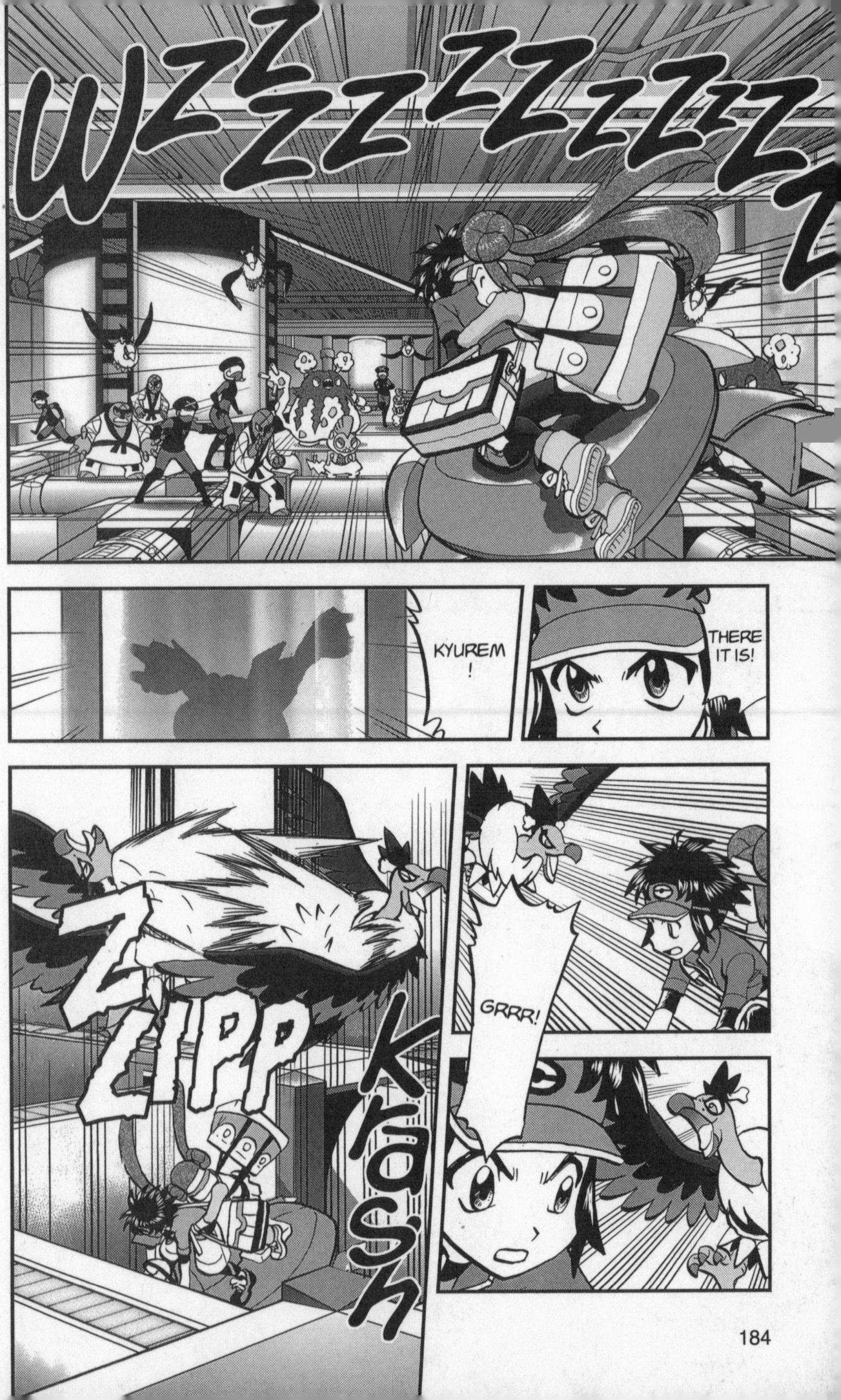
WZZZZZZZZZZZZZ
THERE IT IS!
KYUREM!
GRRR!
ZIPP
krash

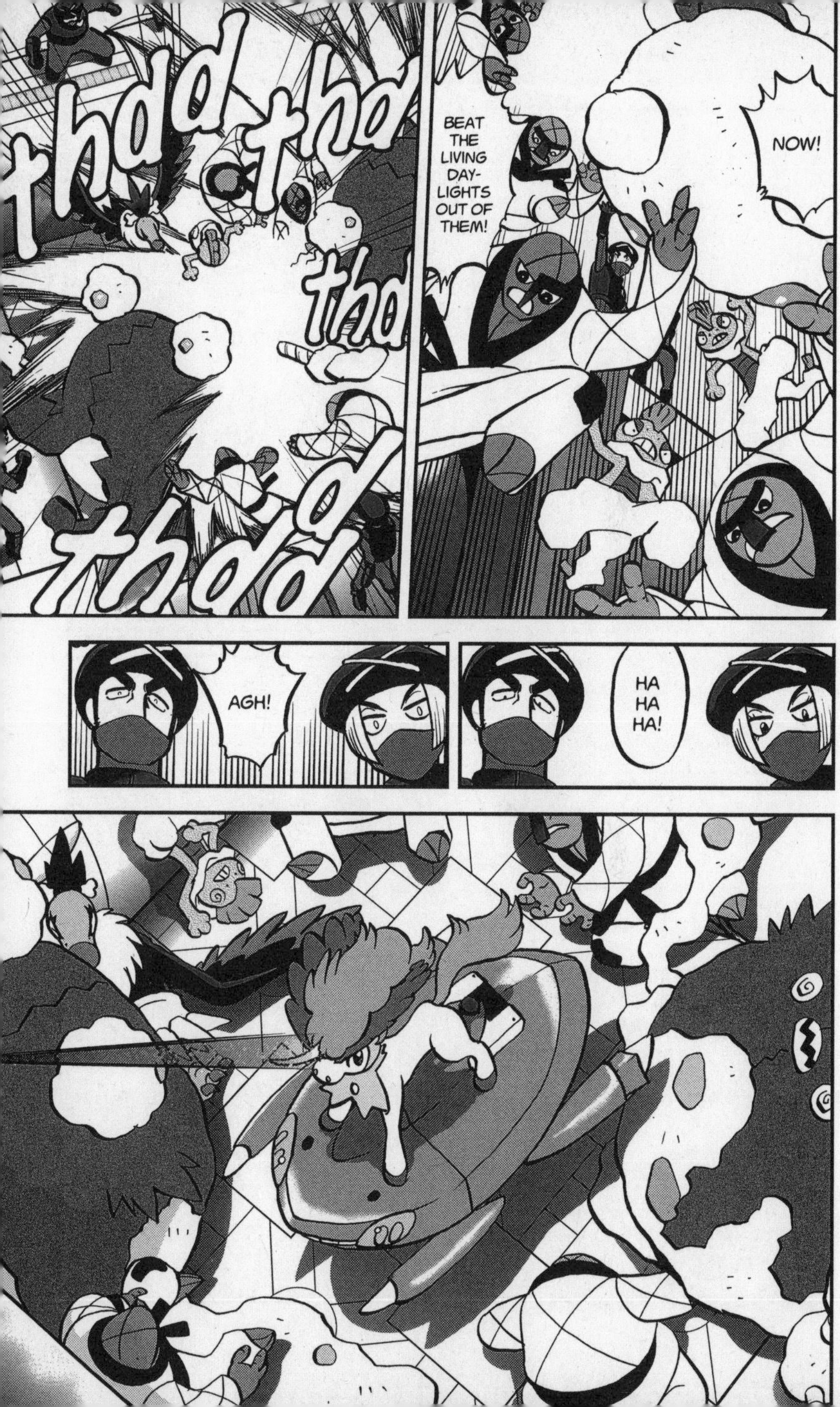
NOW!
BEAT THE LIVING DAY-LIGHTS OUT OF THEM!
thdd thd
thd
thdd
HA HA HA!
AGH!

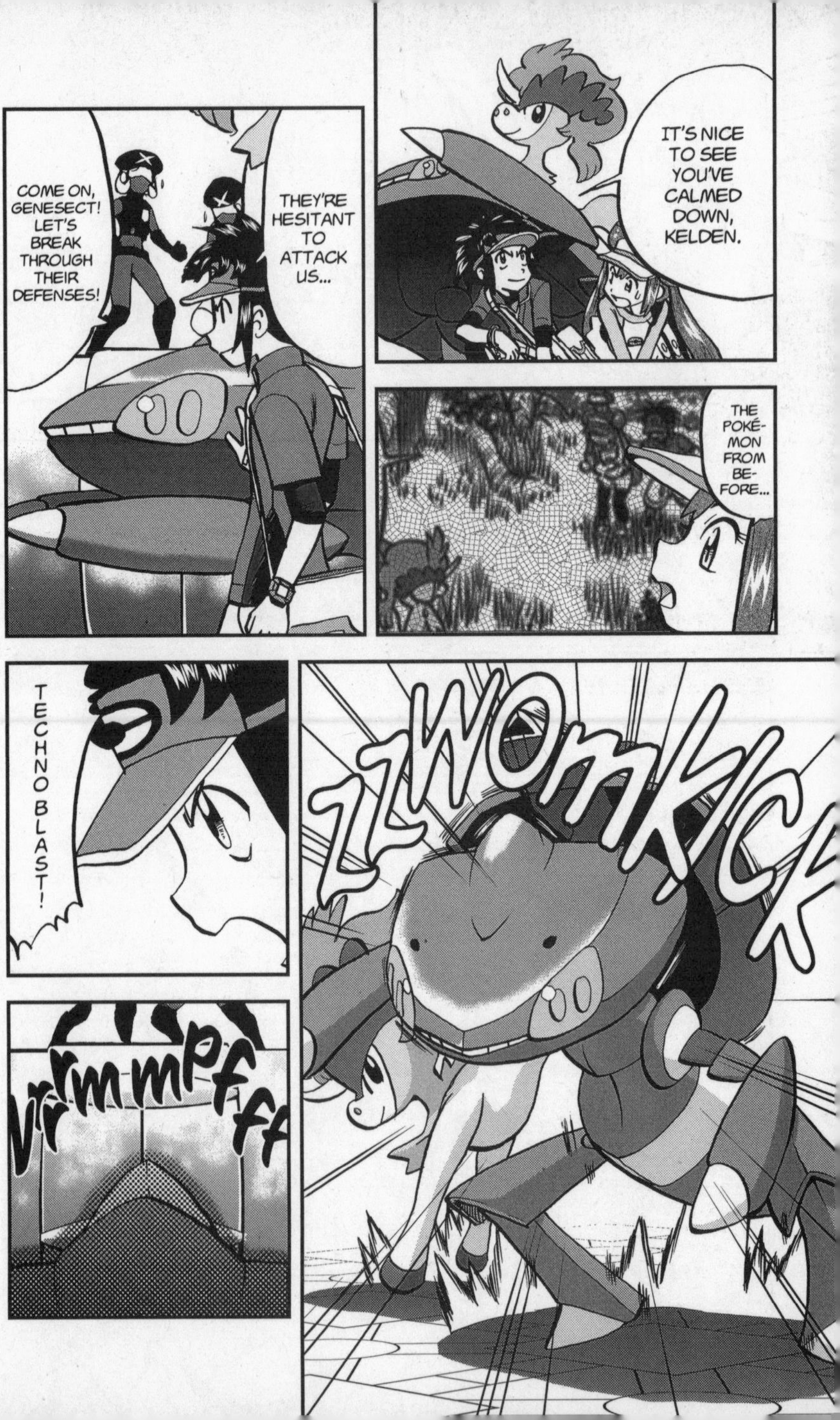
IT'S NICE TO SEE YOU'VE CALMED DOWN, KELDEN.
THE POKÉ-MON FROM BE-FORE...
THEY'RE HESITANT TO ATTACK US...
COME ON, GENESECT! LET'S BREAK THROUGH THEIR DEFENSES!
ZZWOMKICK
TECHNO BLAST!
VRRMMPFFF

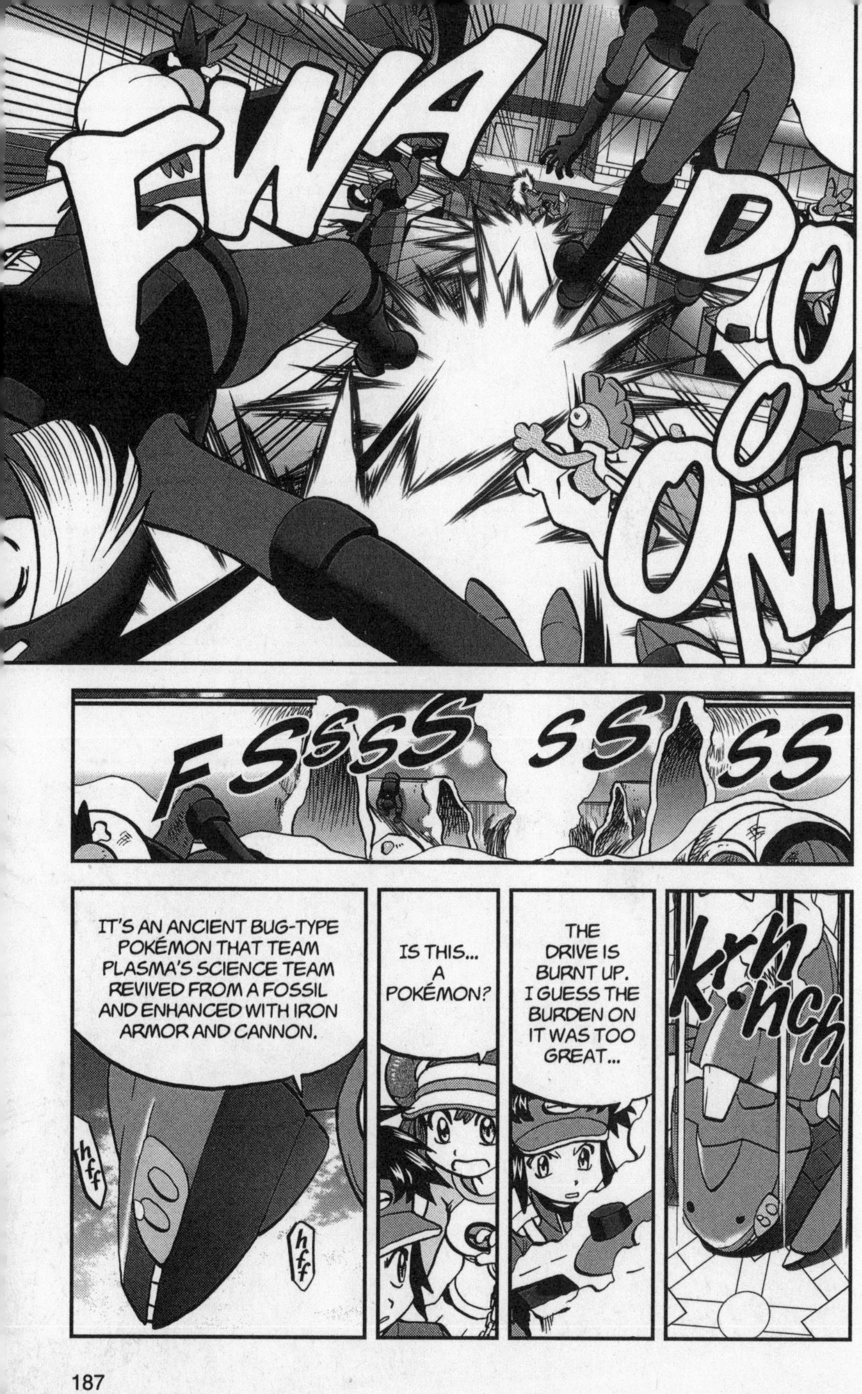

FWA
DOOOOM
FSSSS SS SS
krh nch
THE DRIVE IS BURNT UP. I GUESS THE BURDEN ON IT WAS TOO GREAT...
IS THIS... A POKÉMON?
IT'S AN ANCIENT BUG-TYPE POKÉMON THAT TEAM PLASMA'S SCIENCE TEAM REVIVED FROM A FOSSIL AND ENHANCED WITH IRON ARMOR AND CANNON.
hff
hff

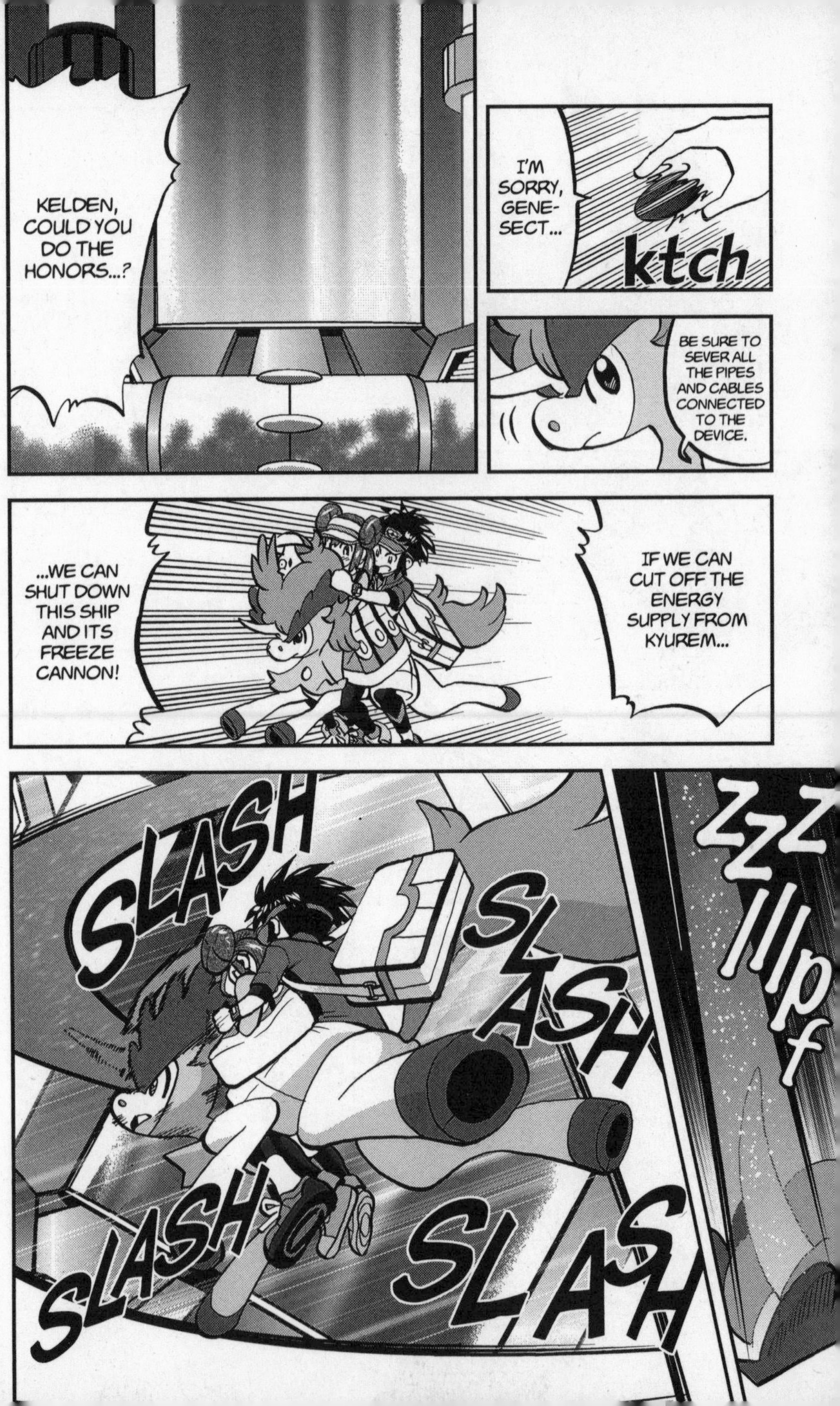
ktch
I'M SORRY, GENE-SECT...
BE SURE TO SEVER ALL THE PIPES AND CABLES CONNECTED TO THE DEVICE.
KELDEN, COULD YOU DO THE HONORS...?
IF WE CAN CUT OFF THE ENERGY SUPPLY FROM KYUREM...
...WE CAN SHUT DOWN THIS SHIP AND ITS FREEZE CANNON!
ZZZ
llpf
SLASH
SLASH
SLASH
SLASH

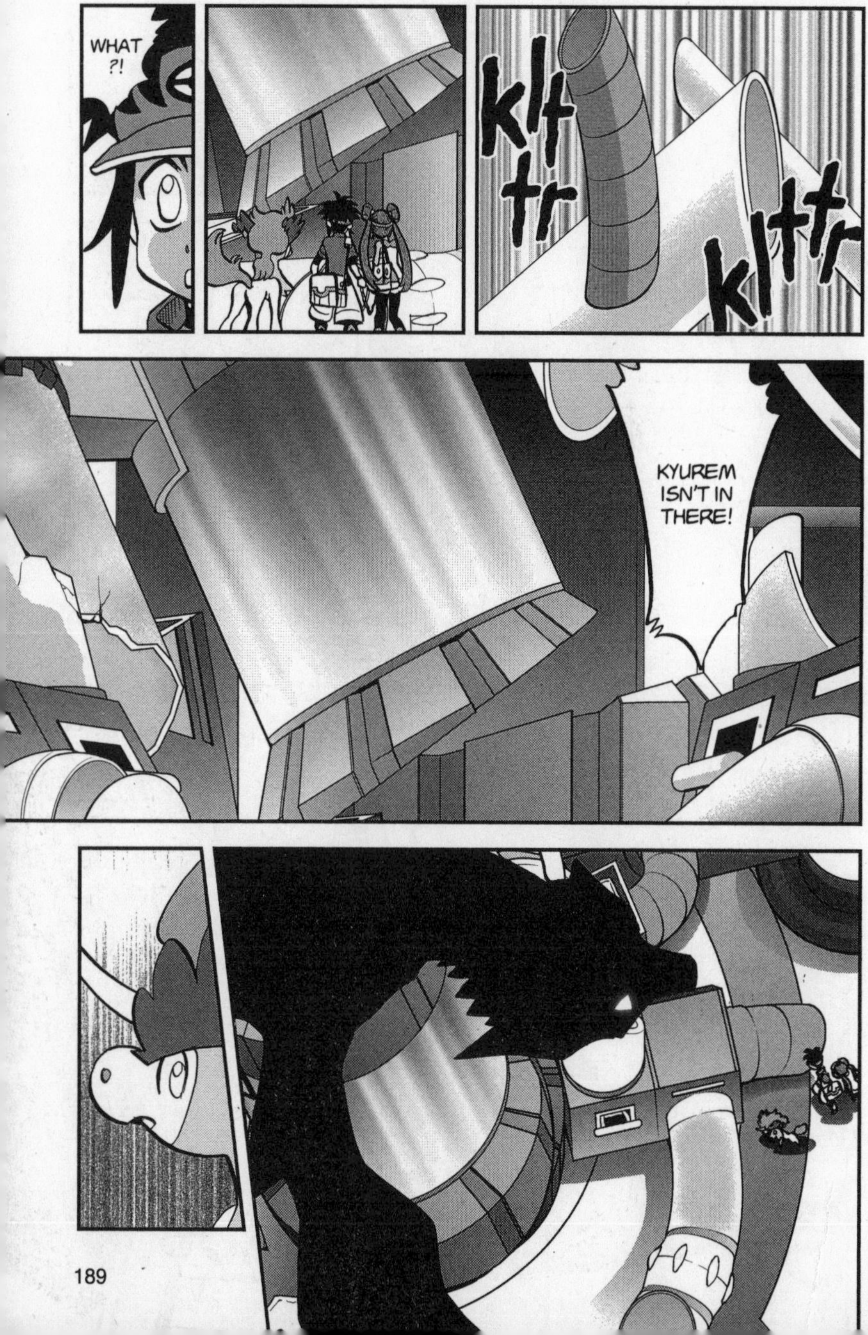
KLTTR
KLTTR
WHAT ?!
KYUREM ISN'T IN THERE!

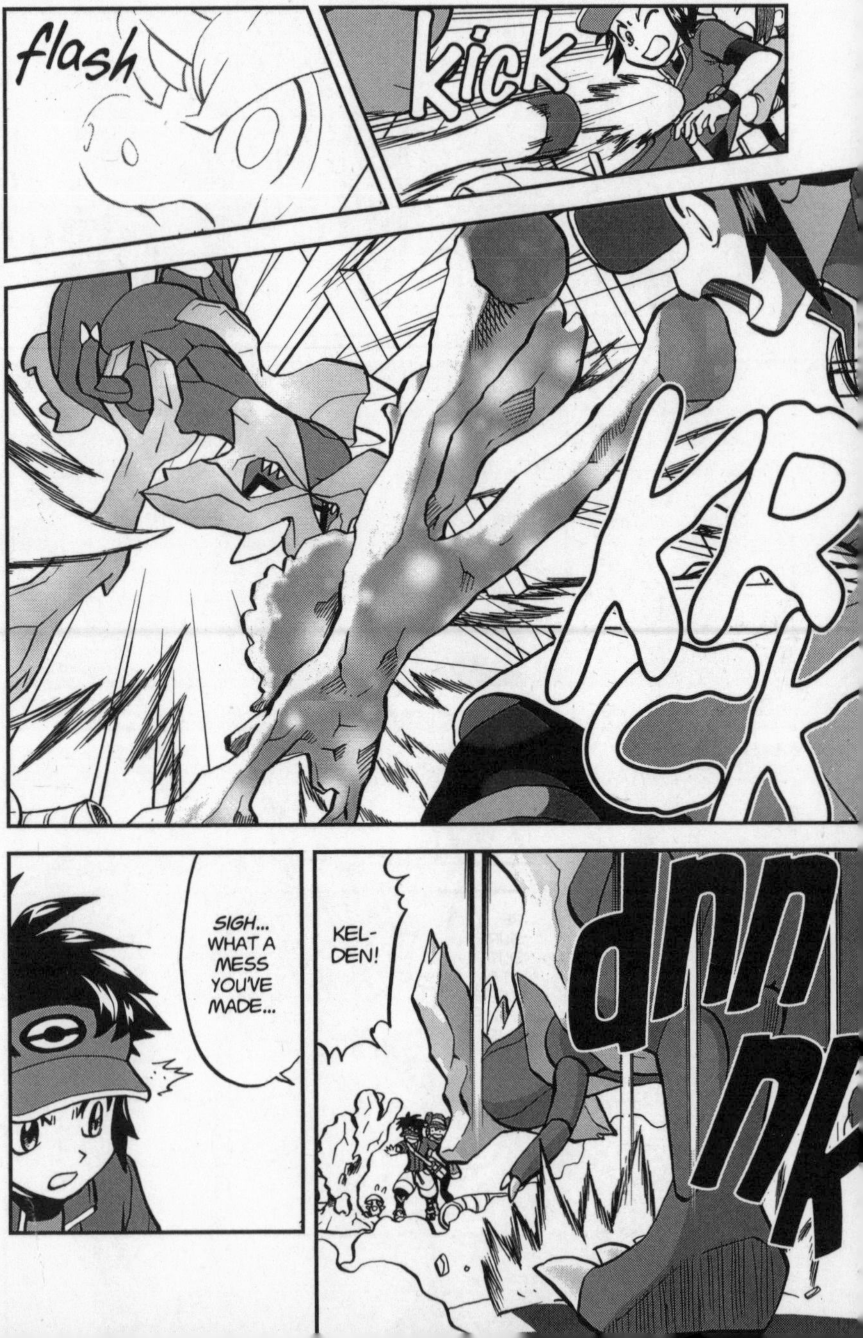
kick
flash
KEL-DEN!
SIGH... WHAT A MESS YOU'VE MADE...

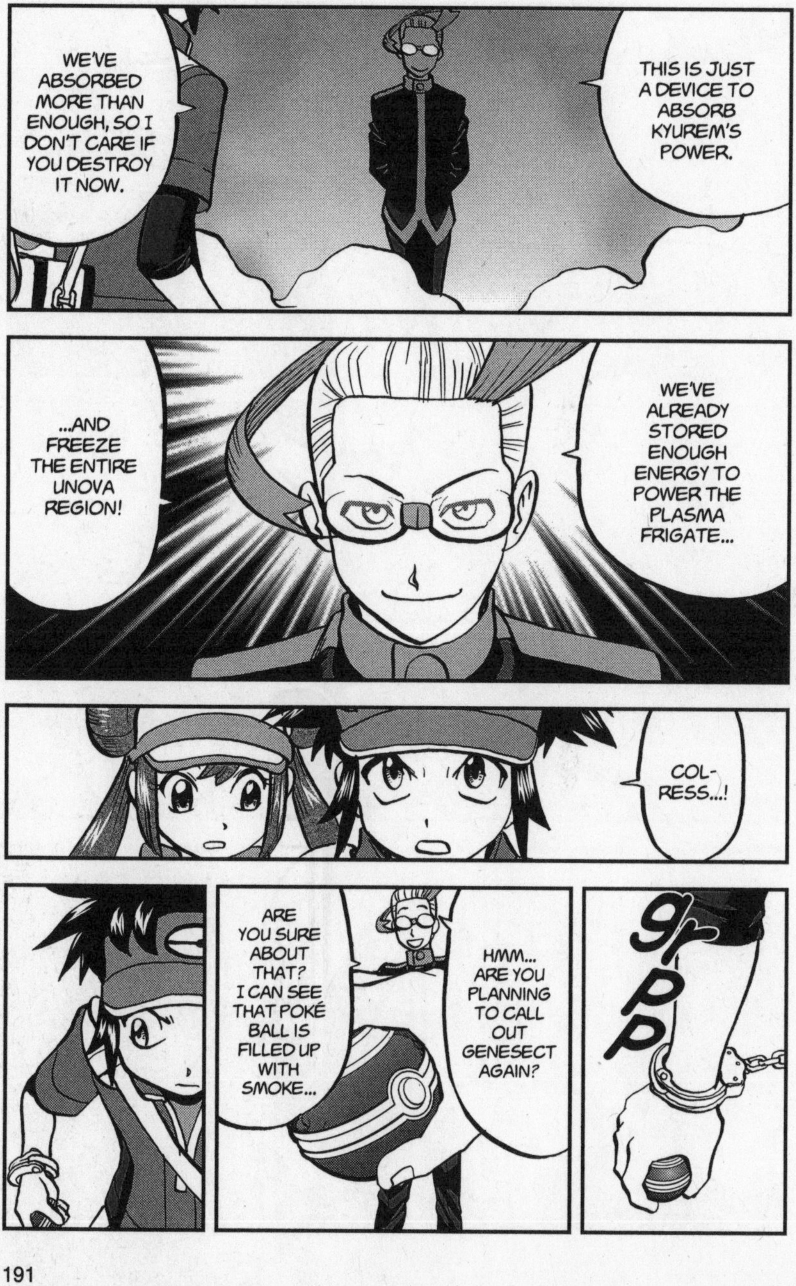
THIS IS JUST A DEVICE TO ABSORB KYUREM'S POWER.
WE'VE ABSORBED MORE THAN ENOUGH, SO I DON'T CARE IF YOU DESTROY IT NOW.
WE'VE ALREADY STORED ENOUGH ENERGY TO POWER THE PLASMA FRIGATE...
...AND FREEZE THE ENTIRE UNOVA REGION!
COL-RESS...!
grpp
HMM... ARE YOU PLANNING TO CALL OUT GENESECT AGAIN?
ARE YOU SURE ABOUT THAT? I CAN SEE THAT POKÉ BALL IS FILLED UP WITH SMOKE...

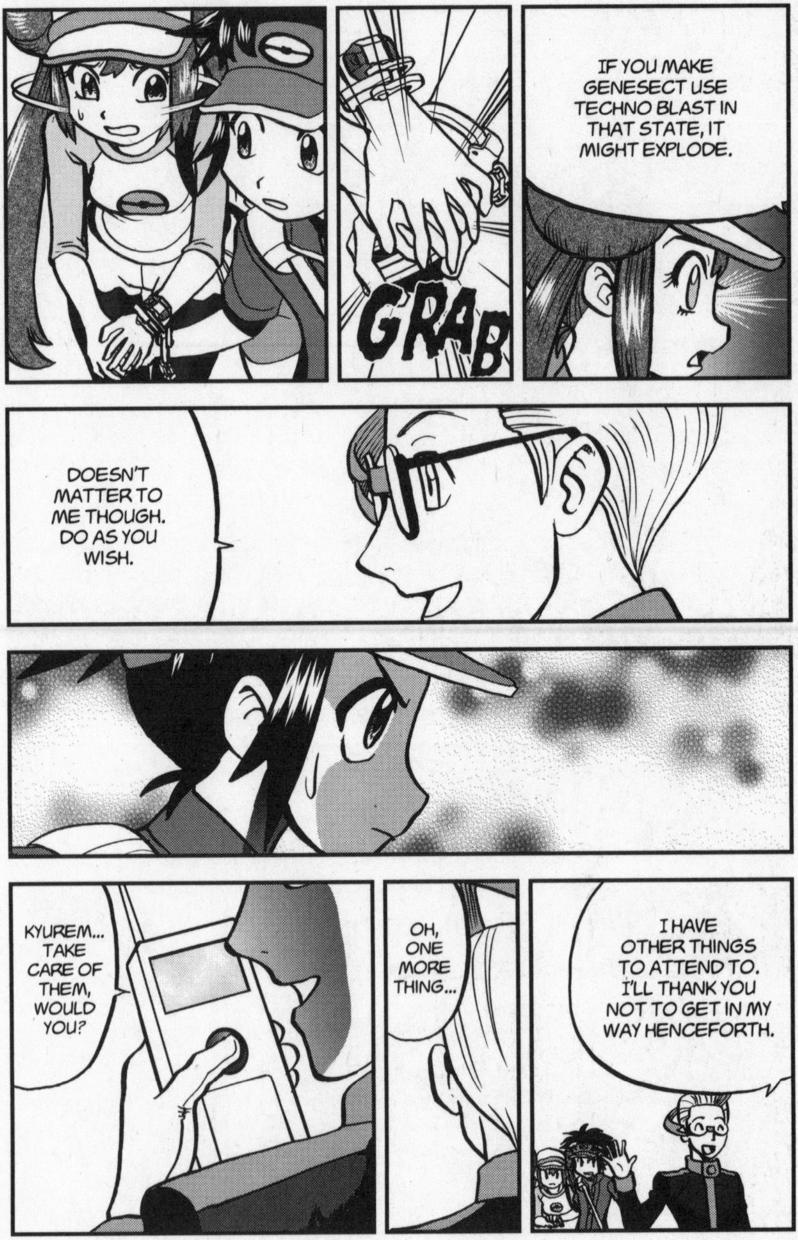
IF YOU MAKE GENESECT USE TECHNO BLAST IN THAT STATE, IT MIGHT EXPLODE.
GRAB
DOESN'T MATTER TO ME THOUGH. DO AS YOU WISH.
I HAVE OTHER THINGS TO ATTEND TO. I'LL THANK YOU NOT TO GET IN MY WAY HENCEFORTH.
OH, ONE MORE THING...
KYUREM... TAKE CARE OF THEM, WOULD YOU?

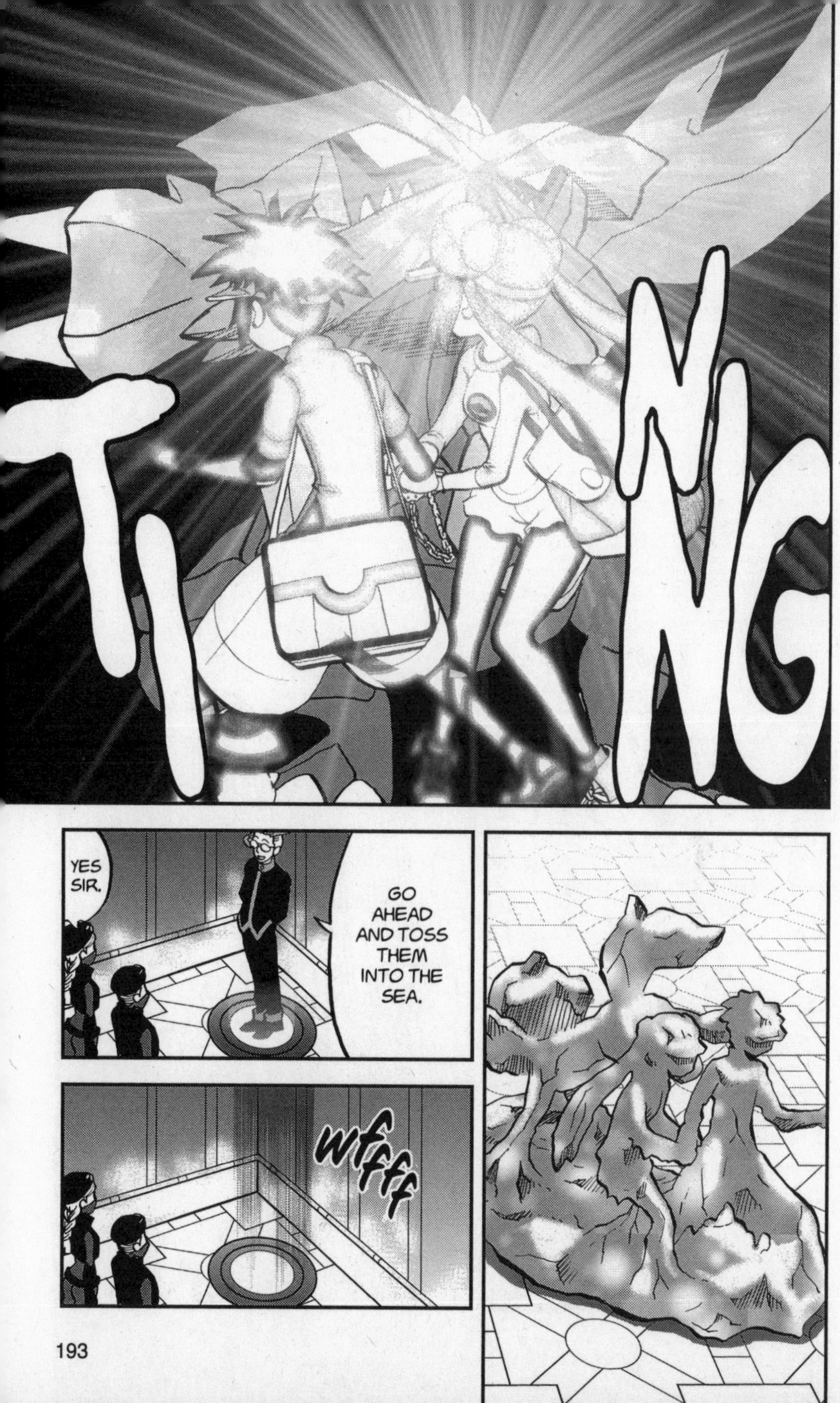
TINNG
GO AHEAD AND TOSS THEM INTO THE SEA.
YES SIR.
wffff

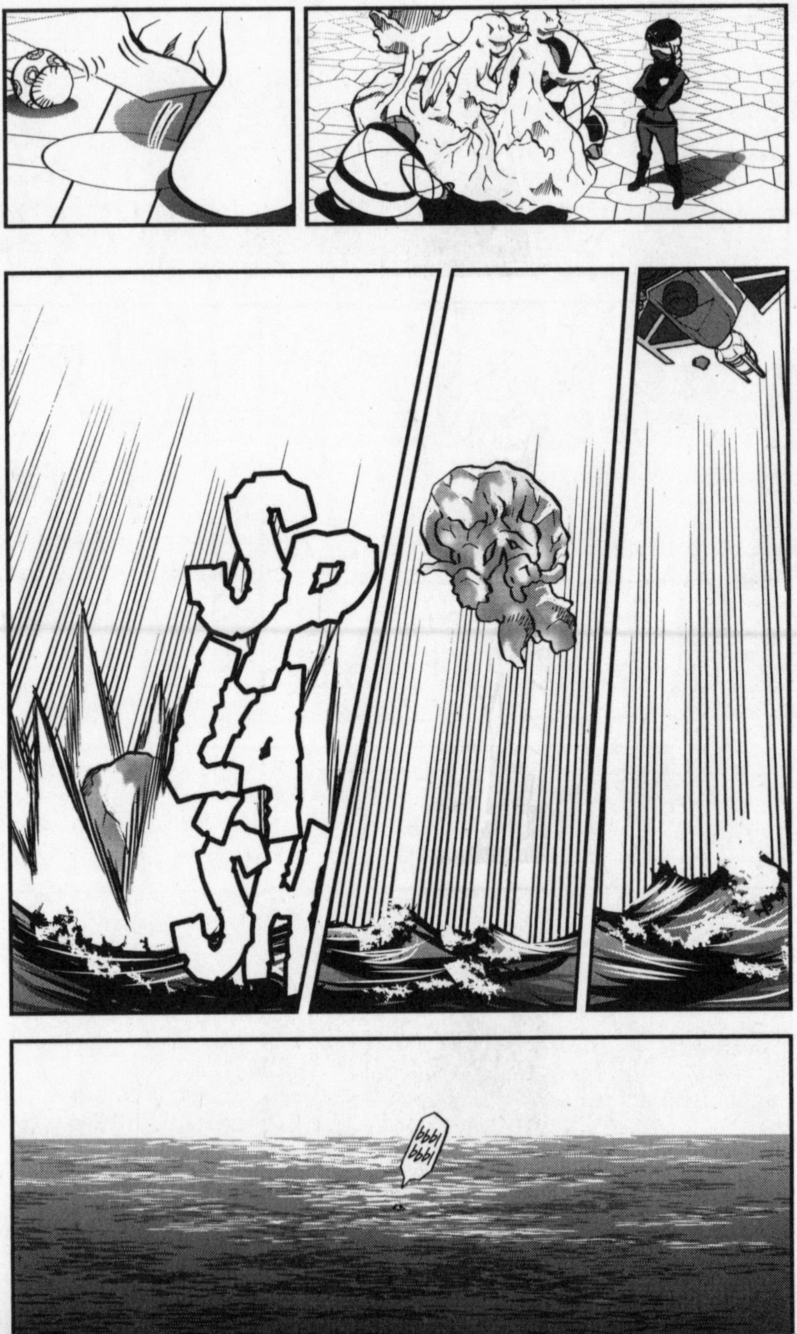
SPLASH
bbbl
bbbl

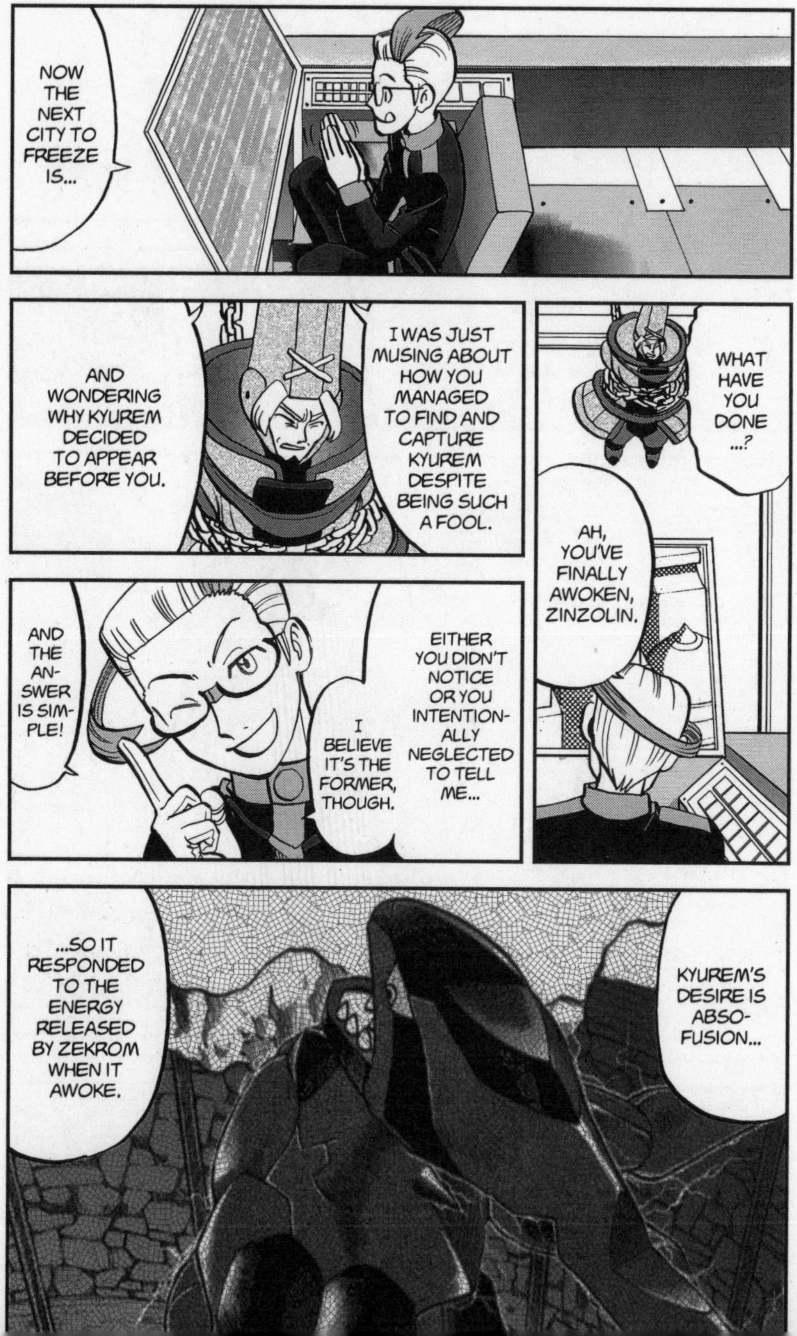
NOW THE NEXT CITY TO FREEZE IS...
WHAT HAVE YOU DONE ...?
AH, YOU'VE FINALLY AWOKEN, ZINZOLIN.
I WAS JUST MUSING ABOUT HOW YOU MANAGED TO FIND AND CAPTURE KYUREM DESPITE BEING SUCH A FOOL.
AND WONDERING WHY KYUREM DECIDED TO APPEAR BEFORE YOU.
EITHER YOU DIDN'T NOTICE OR YOU INTENTION-ALLY NEGLECTED TO TELL ME...
I BELIEVE IT'S THE FORMER, THOUGH.
AND THE AN-SWER IS SIM-PLE!
KYUREM'S DESIRE IS ABSO-FUSION...
...SO IT RESPONDED TO THE ENERGY RELEASED BY ZEKROM WHEN IT AWOKE.

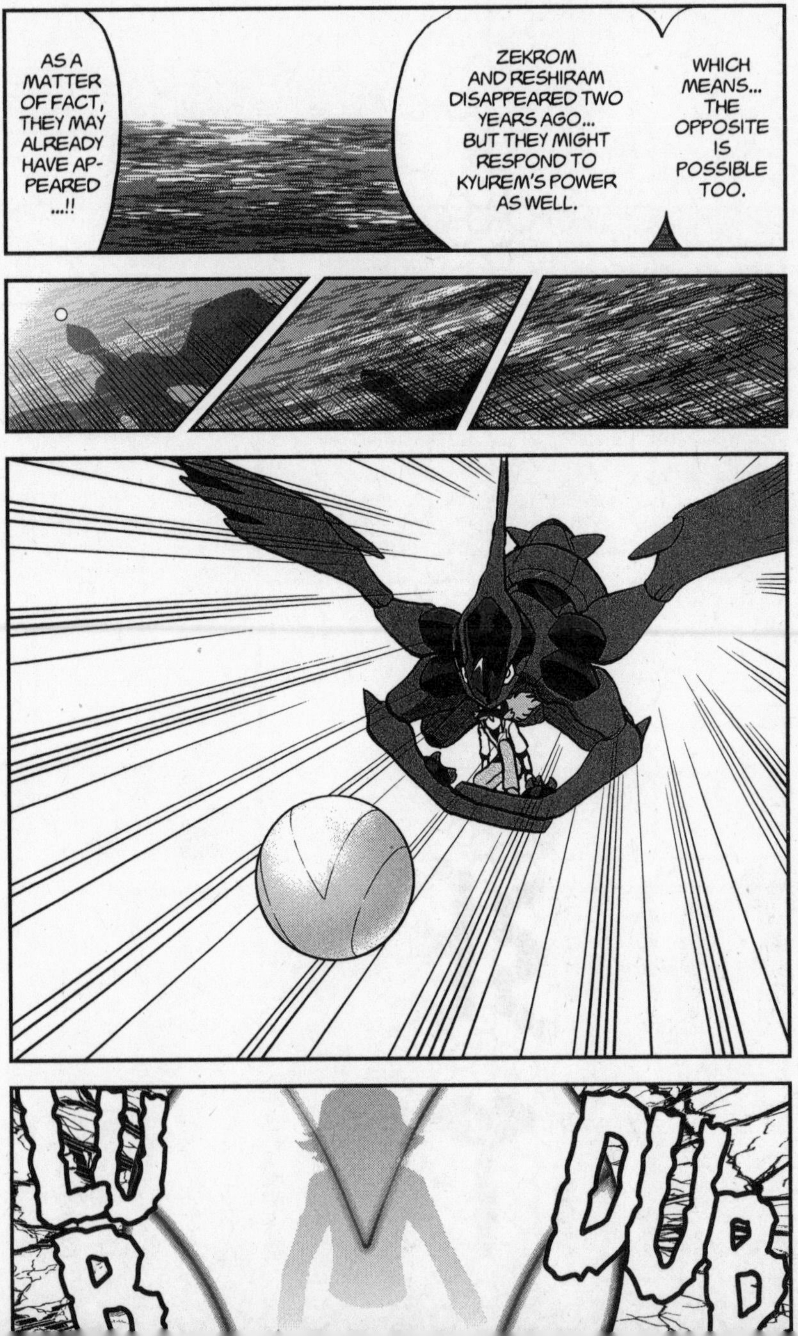
WHICH MEANS... THE OPPOSITE IS POSSIBLE TOO.
ZEKROM AND RESHIRAM DISAPPEARED TWO YEARS AGO... BUT THEY MIGHT RESPOND TO KYUREM'S POWER AS WELL.
AS A MATTER OF FACT, THEY MAY ALREADY HAVE AP-PEARED ...!!
DUB
LUB

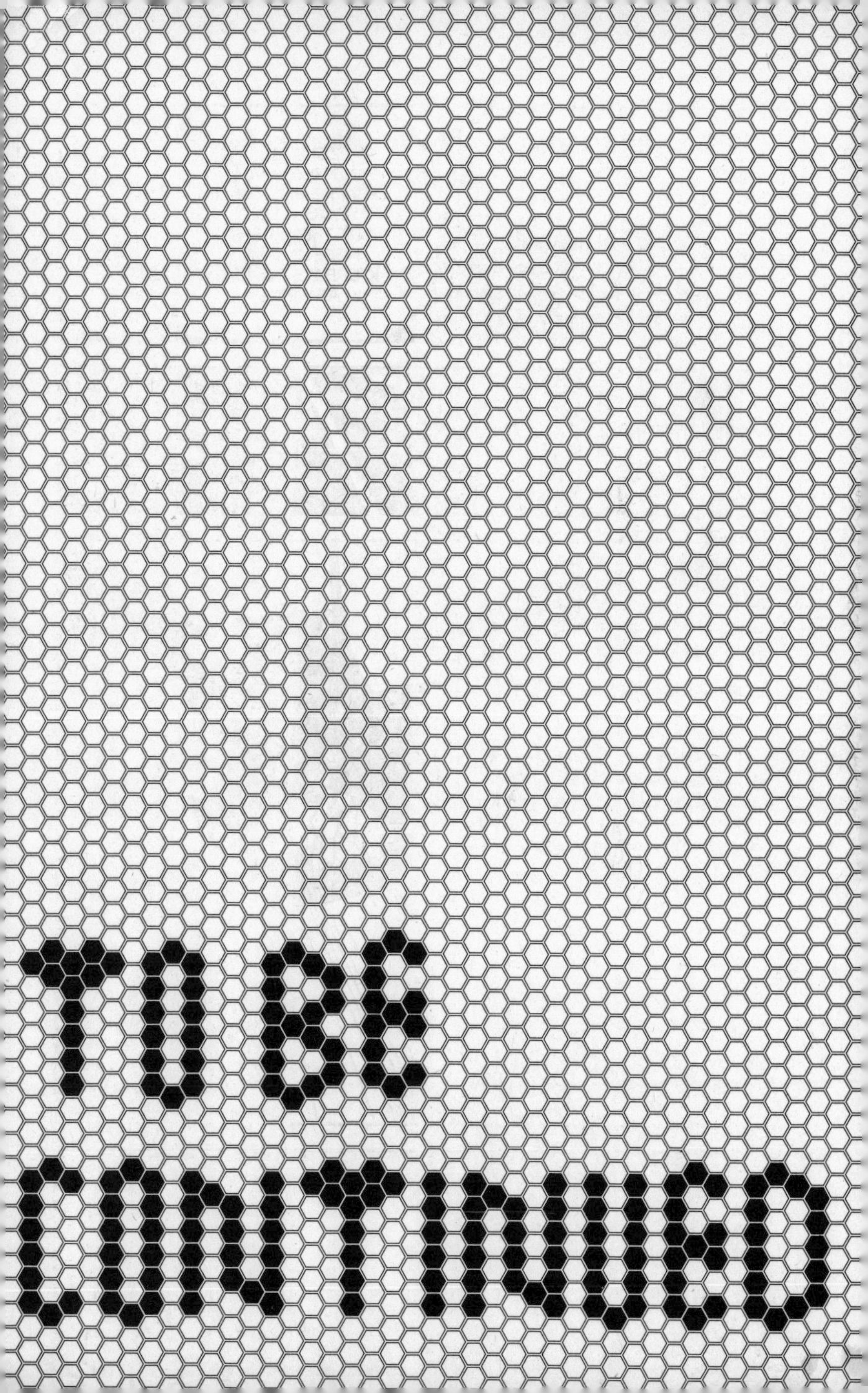
TO BE
CONTINUED

International Police Investigation File (Report)

Unova Region
The Legendary Ice Pokémon, Kyurem

TOP SECRET

Blake No. 2 hailing headquarters! After going undercover, I researched the rare Pokémon of this region and discovered that Kyurem is at the center of Team Plasma's plot. Here are the details.

Blake No. 2

[Empty Shell]

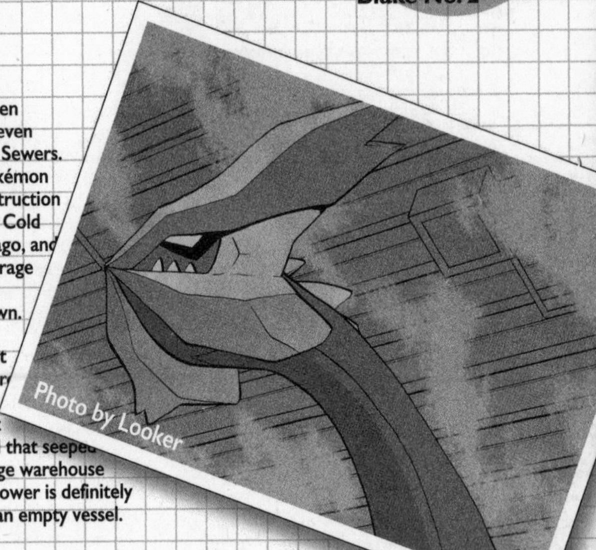
Photo by Looker

By pure coincidence, I encountered Kyurem when I was searching for the Seven Sages inside the Castelia Sewers. The location was the Pokémon World Tournament construction site. It was known as the Cold Storage until two years ago, and there are still several storage warehouses in the area remaining to be torn down.

Kyurem appeared out of one of them. Accor to the Unova legend is an empty shell, but judging from the chill that seeped out of the cold storage warehouse into the sewers, its power is definitely greater than that of an empty vessel.

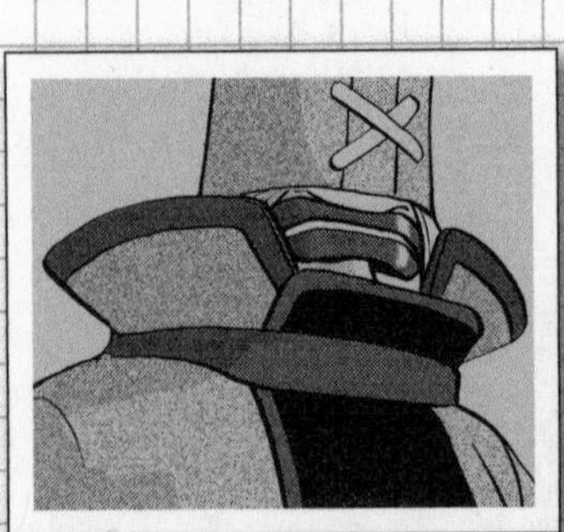

[Zinzolin]

I discovered the Seven Sage Zinzolin and Colress, the leader of New Team Plasma, at the scene with Kyurem. There were signs that they had fought each other, so there is a possibility that power struggles exist even inside the New Team Plasma. I would like to review the data on Gray at the Pokémon League two years ago that is stored in our headquarters' archives. Please send.

[Energy Source]

The most surprising discovery is the appearance of a flying frigate. In the previous incident, Team Plasma built the Castle—a moving underground fortress—that rose to the surface during the Pokémon League finals. I fear that the damage this time may be even greater. I have also discovered that Kyurem is the energy source behind the frigate's flight and ice cannon.

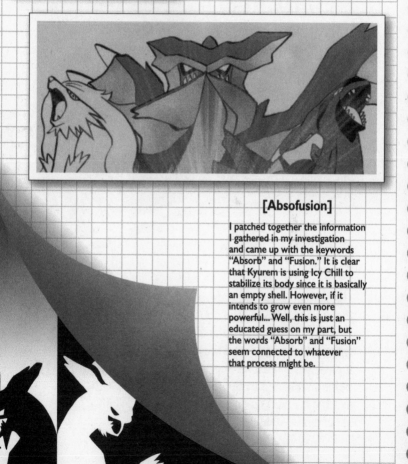

[Absofusion]

I patched together the information I gathered in my investigation and came up with the keywords "Absorb" and "Fusion." It is clear that Kyurem is using Icy Chill to stabilize its body since it is basically an empty shell. However, if it intends to grow even more powerful... Well, this is just an educated guess on my part, but the words "Absorb" and "Fusion" seem connected to whatever that process might be.

Message from
Hidenori Kusaka

Students, teachers, classmates, classes, special events, romance... School is a place filled with all sorts of excitement. That's why TV dramas and manga set in schools have become a classic genre and are always popular. And so, I decided to challenge myself by trying my hand at creating *Pokémon Adventures'* first school-based arc. I apologize for keeping you waiting so long, but finally a new semester at the Pokémon Trainers' School has begun!!

Message from
Satoshi Yamamoto

The first time I played *Pokémon White*, I noticed that when I talked to the nonplayer townsfolk, they often said things like, "I think I'm doing very well with my Pokémon," as if they were trying to convince themselves. I felt a bit of peer pressure, which made me more intimidated by the ordinary townspeople than the evil Team Plasma members. When I draw Whitley, I try to remember that.

Pokémon ADVENTURES
BLACK 2 & WHITE 2
Volume 2
VIZ Media Edition

Story by **HIDENORI KUSAKA**
Art by **SATOSHI YAMAMOTO**

©2018 The Pokémon Company International.
©1995–2017 Nintendo / Creatures Inc. / GAME FREAK inc.
TM, ®, and character names are trademarks of Nintendo.
POCKET MONSTERS SPECIAL Vol. 53
by Hidenori KUSAKA, Satoshi YAMAMOTO
© 1997 Hidenori KUSAKA, Satoshi YAMAMOTO
All rights reserved.
Original Japanese edition published by SHOGAKUKAN.
English translation rights in the United States of America, Canada,
the United Kingdom, Ireland, Australia, New Zealand
and India arranged with SHOGAKUKAN.

Translation/Tetsuichiro Miyaki
English Adaptation/Annette Roman
Touch-up & Lettering/Susan Daigle-Leach
Design/Shawn Carrico
Editor/Annette Roman

Printed in the U.S.A.

Published by VIZ Media, LLC
P.O. Box 77010
San Francisco, CA 94107

10 9 8 7 6 5 4 3 2 1
First printing, July 2018

www.viz.com

POCKET COMICS

STORY & ART BY SANTA HARUKAZE

BLACK & WHITE

LEGENDARY POKÉMON

X•Y

A Pokémon pocket-sized book chock-full of
four-panel gags, Pokémon trivia and fun quizzes
based on the characters you know and love!

viz media

www.viz.com

Begin your Pokémon Adventure here in the Kanto region!

POKÉMON ADVENTURES

RED & BLUE BOX SET

Story by **HIDENORI KUSAKA**   Art by **MATO**

Includes **POKÉMON ADVENTURES** Vols. 1-7 and a collectible poster!

All your favorite Pokémon game characters jump out of the screen into the pages of this action-packed manga!

Red doesn't just want to train Pokémon, he wants to be their friend too. Bulbasaur and Poliwhirl seem game. But independent Pikachu won't be so easy to win over!

And watch out for Team Rocket, Red... They only want to be your enemy!

Start the adventure today!

POKéMON™

ADVENTURES

HeartGold & SoulSilver

Story by HIDENORI KUSAKA
Art by SATOSHI YAMAMOTO

The adventure continues in the Johto region!

POKÉMON™ ADVENTURES

GOLD & SILVER BOX SET

Includes POKÉMON ADVENTURES Vols. 8-14 and a collectible poster!

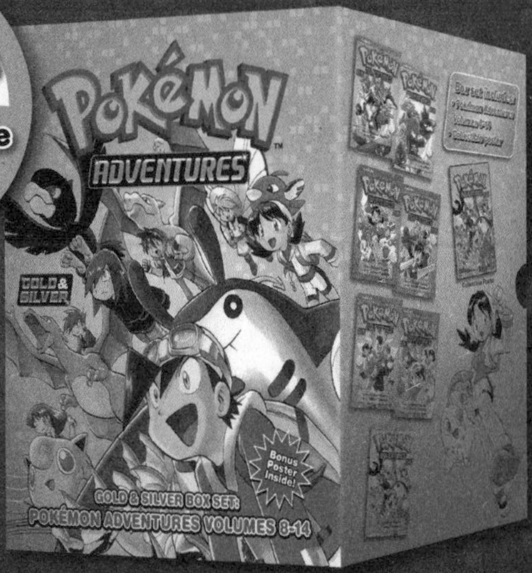

POKÉMON
ADVENTURES
GOLD & SILVER
Bonus Poster Inside!
GOLD & SILVER BOX SET:
POKÉMON ADVENTURES VOLUMES 8-14

Story by
HIDENORI KUSAKA

Art by
MATO, SATOSHI YAMAMOTO

More exciting Pokémon adventures starring Gold and his rival Silver! First someone steals Gold's backpack full of Poké Balls (and Pokémon!). Then someone steals Prof. Elm's Totodile. Can Gold catch the thief—or thieves?!

Keep an eye on Team Rocket, Gold... Could they be behind this crime wave?

VIZ media
www.viz.com
PERFECT SQUARE
RATED A FOR ALL AGES
ratings.viz.com

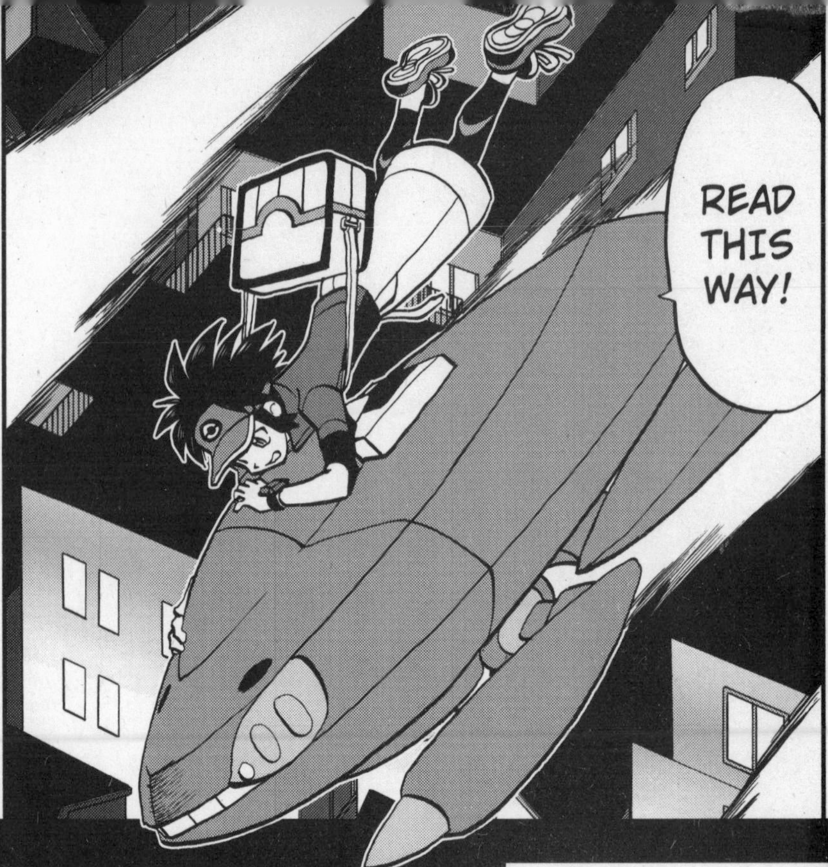
READ THIS WAY!

THIS IS THE END OF THIS GRAPHIC NOVEL!

To properly enjoy this VIZ Media graphic novel, please turn it around and begin reading from right to left.

This book has been printed in the original Japanese format in order to preserve the orientation of the original artwork.

Have fun with it!

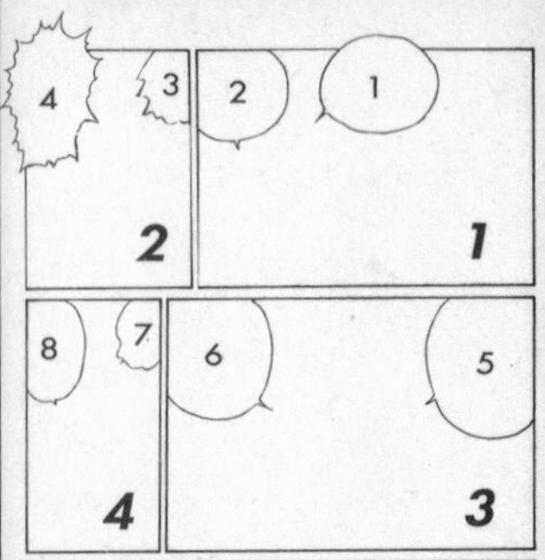

FOLLOW THE ACTION THIS WAY.

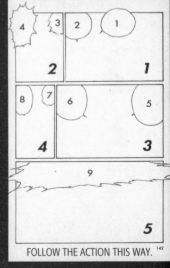